The Demon Rift

A novel by

<u>Marjorie Kaye Noble</u>

For Carol, my guide, and Alex, my fellow traveler and writer

ACKNOWLEDGEMENTS

A Thank you to Jude Roth, filmmaker, and screenwriter, for her counsel and encouragement. *The Floating Mall* is partially based on *The Mall from Hell*, a screenplay Jude and I co-wrote. Thanks to director and writer, the late Paul Almond when I began this novel. Thankyou to my sister, Carol Arnold, who provided patient feedback and invaluable suggestions. And to Daniel Oldis, author, dream researcher and my biggest fan. Lastly, thanks to my son, Alexander Noble, writer and inspiration.

CONTENTS

Patty

I'm a kid. I know you're a grownup, but I'm still your big sister. Sometimes I wish I coulda become a grownup. Mostly I don't care.

What happened after they took me, Patty? Where did you go?

It wasn't a bad place. I made friends. We were doin' fine until the rat spoiled it. The rat will get his. I'm waitin' for the day.

Who's the rat, anyway?

He's what Ma would call a scoundrel.

Ma was the biggest one. Is she here?

They don't let people like Ma stay here.

How will you know when the rat gets it?

I made somethin', Emily. There's this thing called a Time Ribbon. I found some stuff on it. Remember that time we snuck into the nickelodeon? It's like that.

You mean like moving pictures?

I don't know. The Time Ribbon will help me explain.

Relationships

1900 Redhill, Ohio

Stella Tobin Caulkins. Becka Tobin (sister)
Robert Tobin (brother)

1906 Cuyahoga County Orphanage

Patty: *charity kid* Emily (sister, adopted)
Hugo: *charity kid.* Hildy, (sister)
Lonnie: *orphan* Michael: *orphan*

1960 Redhill, Ohio

Nora Tobin. grandniece of Stella Tobin Caulkins,
John Arnold: son of Emily (Patty's nephew)
Emma Arnold Bedonne. Nora and John's daughter

1960 Redhill Correctional Facility

John Arnold: *prisoner*
Luke Michaels: prisoner (orphan Lonnie's son)
Ray Gibbs: *prisoner*

2004 The Redhill Mall

Madonna Bedonne: Emma Arnold Bedonne's daughter
Gordon Bedonne: Emma's son
Caleb Michaels: Amos Michaels' son (prisoner Luke's

grandson)

    Alec Gibbs, prisoner Ray Gibbs' grandson

"68% of the Universe is dark energy. It is a complete mystery what it is." National Aeronautics and Space Administration (NASA)

ONE

Rabbit Stew

New London, Connecticut

November 1895

"Well, luv, what do you think? Shall we tell him tomorrow?" Crispin enjoyed the rabbit stew. Sucking the delicate bones of the dead rabbit, he watched the woman as she finished cleaning the bar top. It was late, past midnight on a Monday. The "Dancing Stag" was empty, save for the barmaid, her new suitor and Bernie, the suitor's small son, who was sleeping peacefully under a corner table. Several carvings of Crispin's, including an impressive Stag's head, hung above a shelf behind the bar. The sales had afforded him and Bernie a room in a nearby boarding house. He regretted the fact that they would soon be leaving. He had enjoyed the bed and the occasional baths. Bernie said it must be tomorrow.

Crispin glanced at the corner where Bernie slept. Was he really sleeping? Doubtful. Willie said the boy made her uncomfortable. Crispin had reassured her. "He needs the love of a mother; it's been hard on the boy." She folded her apron, creasing the folds. Her brown eyes had the look of a dying fawn. He reached up and stroked her hair. Good to feel a woman again, he thought. He'd been too long without. Not a girl, though. She was older than the thirty-two she professed. More like forty-two and a bit too large for his taste, but still . . . overripe for the plucking.

"Let's go in the back," he whispered, "just for a while . . ."

She took a quick look in the corner. The boy seemed asleep. Crispin saw her shudder.

"Such a little boy, I don't know why I . . ."

"What, luv?" he asked, knowing exactly what.

She shrugged. "Okay Crispin, but just for a few minutes."

"That's my girl." He nuzzled her neck, then reached around and cupped her breast.

"A few minutes is all, then we must stop."

"Of course, dear girl, after the wedding there will be time."

Much later, when he thought about it, he was glad she came. It startled him. He was just finishing himself when she let out a stream of moaning. Like a cow wanting milking, he laughed to himself. They had but a few minutes in the crowded closet. "He might wake." She was nervous.

"Don't worry dear heart, he'll be fine." In a rare spirit of generosity, (he admitted it was rare) he saw it was fitting that she had a small bit of pleasure, considering what happened and all.

He puzzled over what happened that night for weeks, trying to make sense of it. Did they open a door? Is that what happened? "They'll know it was us," he worried. He had no objections to anything; however, he didn't like the thought of hanging.

"Do what I tell you and you'll be rewarded." The child's eyes threatened.

Crispin nodded enthusiastically. Hanging was preferable to what Bernie might inflict. "Of course, lad, whatever you say, I'm completely on board."

Tuesday night, her house smelled of onions and bread. Crispin sat on the settee, its velvet freshly brushed and crimson in the shadow of an ornate lamp. A few eventful moments in their brief courtship told him that there was nothing of value in the tidy white house. Still, he approved of her excellent housekeeping. Aunt Meg could have learned a thing or two. He was surprised to see Bernie eat everything, including the tapioca pudding. Unusual. He knew the boy was selective, despite their periods of hunger. Candles— how many were there? He had hidden them in the pull wagon near the house. Bernie had been collecting candles, taking them while Crispin distracted their owners with his wooden carvings. *Won't they see you?* Bernie assured him they would not. He wondered what purpose they served. That night he saw what happened when the candles burned.

He struck her with a wooden club he had carved the day before. Crispin made a show of announcing their "engagement" to his "son." Willie sat at his right; her eyes downcast, unable to look at the boy. "Not too hard," Bernie had warned, "she must wake before we finish." Bernie spilled a glass of milk. As she reached to retrieve it, Crispin struck an expert blow. She was unconscious for an hour. When she woke, the satisfaction in Bernie's yellow eyes made Crispin proud.

The star drawn in blood, whose blood, was it? They were all naked. In the candlelight, pools of blood were like puddles after a cloudburst. Bernie's hands dripped, adding to the puddles. Smears and streaks covered most of his frail child's body. Did Bernie draw the star using his own blood? Bits of that night were a blank. He remembered the awful smell, wondering if he had soiled himself and fearing the consequences. Bernie seemed indifferent to it.

Bernie cut his palm, smearing the blood on the woman before she woke. He was afraid Bernie would want to cut him too, but Bernie turned his attention to the barmaid. When she woke, Willie screamed, and the boy grabbed her tongue, slicing it off. The screams soon became moans. Not as loud now, Crispin thought approvingly.

The moaning reminded him of when she came. Interesting, how similar the cries were, one of pleasure and the other . . . She was tied down (securely, Crispin was careful) and the candles were all around . . . and eyes, he saw eyes coming through a tunnel, watching. Why did he think of a door? He remembered a ripping sound, like fabric being torn and then a boom like a cannon that rattled the house. Crispen would have ducked for cover if he hadn't been startled by the sight of black wings and the clicking sound from wings slapping or breaking through, what?

Bernie knelt near the woman . . . his little body rocking back and forth. Willie's fawn eyes followed the sway. The child was whispering, while she kept trying to say (plead?), "Kill me." She had no tongue, but he was sure that's what she meant to say. He held her tethered hands to keep her steady as Bernie continued to slice her. Tears ran down the barmaid's cheek and fell into the thick red puddles.

As he pressed his palms firmly down on her wrists, Crispin allowed himself to wonder what came next. He decided it was best to keep quiet, do as you're told. Bernie's hands, clots of the barmaid's blood clinging to his fingers, rose abruptly as the light from the candles floated free, the flames dancing and spinning.

Fear clutched at Crispin's throat. What if those flames, what if they mean to . . .? Then there was a sudden sensation, indescribable, oh the pleasure! His "reward," he thought with delight and wonder. It poured into him as if he were a wine glass, filling him to the brim.

The Demon Rift

Overwhelmed, he gazed at Willie. She looked back with supreme indifference.

As if she found it all incredibly tiresome, her eyes turned away from him, her face relaxed and tilting her head slowly to her shoulder, she died. The boy cooed as he stroked her hand, his strange face content. The candles dimmed. The floating eyes were gone. "We leave now," the boy commanded. They cleaned the blood from their bodies and took the ropes from the dead woman. Crispin carried her to her bed. After dressing, they set fire to Willie, her bed, and her small, neat house.

"Won't they know it was us?" He was afraid.

"Stupid Crispin, I told you not to worry. They'll think she killed herself because you left her. I suggested it already when the bar was full of people." Bernie was losing patience with him. Crispin decided to keep his doubts to himself. They were on the road a few hours before the pleasure began to fade. He was depressed. He hated the cold.

Patty

That Willie person wasn't wise to Bernie. Bernie looked like a little kid, but he was a giant rat. I've been looking at the Time Ribbon for more parts about Bernie. If it glows on the Ribbon, it hasn't happened yet. Gram told me to be careful and not butt in. If I do, I won't tell Gram.

I won't tell. Who is Bernie?

A giant rat who has only one story, but he's tricky. His story has different pieces. It started with a monster sticking its big fat claw where it don't belong. Bernie was creepy in his first life, and a bigger creep when he became a high-toned senator.

A senator? When did that happen?

I don't know. He pretended to someone else. It don't matter now.

If you want, we can talk about it some other time.

We can do whatever we want. There are no clocks to tell us what to do. I mean I'm eleven and that's it unless I change my mind. I kinda miss birthdays. I'll be eleven forever, I guess. There are no bullies to fight. Everyone is nice and it's pretty. I like the parks and the snow in the winter places. There's lots of cake.

That sounds nice. Let's go eat some.

Yeah, cake is good.

Can I see the Time Ribbon?

I'll show you some of it and then we can play hoops. I met some other kids. I can introduce you. Gram put some messages in the Ribbon. I don't know what they mean. Maybe you can explain them to me after I get rid of the rat.

I'll try.

Okay.

TWO

PATTY

This is from the last Bernie day, after Bernie stole the life from some guy he double-crossed in prison.

What happens here?

Bernie is a rich old man and he's planning to do steal another life. The planet monster wants him to kill a lot of people on Christmas. The Ribbon won't tell me what happens, except he's still a louse with rat teeth.

How awful!

The End and the Beginning
Residence of Senator John Arnold
Redhill, Ohio, December 24, 2004,

Bernie stood naked before the floor length mirror. Soon, its usefulness at an end, this body would be gone. He would miss its appetites, but not the discomforts of age. The wood floor beneath his feet was cold, aggravating the throbbing pain in both knees that had swelled from the hours required for the next Great Offering. The Others applied compresses to lessen the swelling, but they would have to re-administer them within the hour.

All was ready. His white shirt and Armani suit hung waiting; his expensive black shoes were carefully polished. He wrapped himself in his plush robe and stepped into warm slippers. Moving to the Moroccan table, he began to eat his last meal as John Arnold. Arnold would die a hero, saving his beloved granddaughter, Madonna, who would emerge tearfully from the tragedy of the terrible mall fire where many hundreds would perish.

The Senator smiled, remembering the screams from the phantom building that gave such pleasure and just as fondly, the delicious agony of the prison. Mourning the death of her brother and subsequent suicide of her alcoholic mother, the story of Madonna's plight will move the hearts of the wealthy and influential. Ah, little Emma. How he looked forward to seeing her bewildered and heartbroken over the loss of her son then savoring her terror as the one whom she thought was her little girl inflicts prolonged suffering and painful death.

He looked forward to collecting debts. Cabrizzi, for example, he had plans for him. The loose ends, Gordon, the girl's brother, the boy Alec, and the security guard, he would give to the Others as toys. Bernie wondered what it was going to be like—being a woman. The Others appeared to the world as beautiful young women, but they were much more, objects of desire and instruments of death. He had probed for signs of what would follow in the aftermath of the coming sacrifice, but nothing was revealed or even implied.

Whatever happens, it will be wonderful. No hint came forth of where the next vessel might be found. The clairvoyance of Madonna will be helpful in divining such important information. Perhaps the next vessel, yet to be born, will have access to even greater power than the Senator's influence and the girl's psychic gifts. The girl's gifts were marvelous, but sadly underdeveloped. Wasted for now, but soon—oh—soon—a magnificent reward. As Bernie contemplated his years of sacrifices and rewards, he ate dessert—hokey pokey with blue sprinkles.

THREE

PATTY

This is what happened to Bernie's ma before he was born. I wanted to know how he got to be so mean. His ma was stupid too and his pa also. There was some stupid rich people and they let the bad thing come in.

Rich people do that a lot.

"His Office is to discover the Virtues of the Birds and precious stones" (The Book of the Goetia of Solomon the King)

The Moroccan Table
London, England, 1885

"He's a lecherous old one, mind you. What we done; he'd do to you if he could." Matthew's handsome face was full of concern. His caring was a lie, but she enjoyed the pretense.

"You sound just like Mum," she sighed. She stroked the wisps of blond whiskers on his face. He was nineteen but could pass for younger and he was not much taller than she, Linda, who was fourteen. "I'll be careful, as careful as can be." Linda gave him a lingering kiss.

"So, what do you think they do?" He was getting excited.

"Sex orgies," she whispered, her eyes wide with feigned horror, "with them running about all naked . . ."

"What a sight," he said, and he did a dance, miming a lot of flopping skin, "some of them old ones, bouncing about!"

Her auburn hair in disarray, the girl threw her head back and laughed. The sound of her shrill giggle carried throughout the stable and a horse began to kick its stall. Matthew sat up and looked to see if anyone heard. They were alone. She collapsed into the fresh hay. Matthew put his finger to his lips. "Careful; we don't want anyone to hear, do we?" He fell beside her and slipped his hand under her starched white apron.

Linda removed his hand and buttoned her blouse. She stood up, straightened her apron and frowning, she looked for telltale straw. The boy reached up and pulled her skirt. He was not ready for her to leave, just yet.

"That's enough," she said, "got work to do and so do you."

"Tomorrow," he demanded, tugging on her skirt, "you'll tell me, spill all of it. Promise!"

"I'll let you know tomorrow." Mischief filled her brown eyes. "Or not!" His curiosity was her hold on him. His place being in the stables, he rarely came to the house. *Something else, Matthew Oldman, something else will soon hold you.* Looking down at his pleading face, she enjoyed the moment, before freeing her skirt from his grasp.

Walking briskly across the grounds, she smiled and slipped through the back entrance, pausing behind a closed door to hear her mother Rebecca complaining to Cook, ". . . and I don't know what to do. The girl won't listen. If only her dad hadn't died . . . "

Adjusting her cap, she checked the clock. Almost two. Good. She'd spent less than half an hour in the stables. Opening a closet, she slid out the stack of embroidered robes and hurried into the laundry room. Seeing Mrs. Hamilton, she gave her a bright smile.

"All finished, Mrs. H., shall I put them in the library?" Linda glanced at her mother. Rebecca gave her a suspicious look.

I don't care, thought Linda, whose exotic name came from her mother's own dreams of a holiday in Spain. *She's almost thirty-one,* Linda decided, *and past it all. She has no idea of what it is to be young.*

Mrs. Hamilton's clipped speech showed her low opinion of her young subordinate. "What do you think, girl? Use your brain. Of course, the library."

Lord Towning's annual gathering of selected members of "The Hermetic Order of the Golden Dawn" (Cook called it the Heretic Order of the Golden Dawn) always put Mrs. Hamilton in a sour mood. Tending to over twenty weekend guests, their varied whims and special requirements taxed her limited patience.

Linda carried the ceremonial robes up the narrow stairs and onto the ground floor. She had spent the early morning ironing the flowing gowns, taking care not to snag the intricate embroidery. Down the marbled hallway, she could see that the tall doors of the library were ajar. Inside, several men were moving a massive table, recently delivered, especially for the coming event. "From Morocco, found it last year," Linda heard Lord Towning boast. Linda wished he'd lost it after he found it. It was an eyesore and with all the curves, carvings, and crevices (Matthew laughed when she described it), a nightmare to dust and polish.

The library itself was an inviting place where many windows let in the afternoon light. The graceful Oriental drapes pulled back, allowing light to fill the room. While perched on a ladder, swiping her duster across the innumerable books that lined the walls, or carefully rubbing the endless pieces of exotic art and treasure gathered from Lord Towning's trips, Linda would often lay her duster down and descend the ladder. After checking both sides of the long hall and listening for footsteps, she'd close the door. Selecting a book from a lower shelf, the maid crawled into one of the plush chairs. She could barely read but felt it only proper to have an open book in her lap.

Nestled in the soft cushions, she pretended she was a lady. Only for a minute or two, she'd tell herself. She imagined the family portraits hanging throughout the room glaring with disapproval at her liberties.

Bugger off, she answered, glaring back at the generations of wealth and privilege. She was better off than any of them. They were all dead. While she polished the Moroccan table, an idea had come to her. She would hide and find out just what went on during the "special event."

The Demon's Dance

"May I see it?" Voices startled her awake. A sliver of light reminded her of where she was. Linda huddled within the lower shelf of one of his lordship's acquisitions, an ornate monstrosity. It sat near the fireplace, and the lower half was large enough to contain a girl of fourteen years if she were willing to hug her knees to her chest. Linda's left foot was asleep, and her legs ached from being folded for over an hour.

Curious about what there was to see, she sincerely hoped that it wasn't the part of Sir Charles he decided to show her one late afternoon in the hallway, before the appearance of Mrs. Hamilton prevented whatever his Lordship had in mind. Matthew went breathless with laughter when she described Mrs. Hamilton's face. "Her bulging eyes popped out even more, and her mouth hung like it came loose from its hinges."

"In time, dear lady, in time," said Sir Charles. The master of the house was a corpulent man in his early sixties with thinning white hair. A bald man with a curled mustache chuckled when someone made light of "Crowley's obsession." Another claimed to be offended and suggested that the topic be changed. There were "ladies" to consider.

While one servant collected emptied champagne glasses, another served full ones. How many guests? Matthew would ask. Peering out as much as she dared, she counted. At least eighteen. She couldn't see the entire room unless she risked discovery. Unthinkable. There were several foreign accents. French, she decided, and Polish, or . . . not important.

Eighteen hours of ironing, dusting, folding, and cleaning weighed on her decision to hide. A woman ordered the servants to leave. Except for three beautiful women, the younger wives of wealthy men, the guests were impossibly old.

Exhausted, Linda wanted to leave with the other servants. Hiding in this cramped cabinet, for what? Why would she want to watch foolish old rich people prance around naked, the men with their wrinkled willies and the women with swaying, saggy breasts?

She would make up a story, perhaps devil worship with human sacrifice.

As they enjoyed refreshments and speculated on what Lord Towning had planned for the evening's secret event, the guests wore the robes Linda had spent hours ironing. Mrs. Hamilton had given her strict orders. "Lord Towning is very concerned that his instructions be followed. All of the embroidery, especially the images of trees and birds in flight must be free of any creases," said Mrs. H., looking quite the witch with her widow's peak. The housekeeper wore her light brown hair in a narrow roll at her nape, allowing no stray hair to escape. The hairline framed a high forehead. Linda, who followed current fashion, wondered why the older woman didn't try to soften it with a fringe of curls.

Threads in the embroidery glinted as the robes passed through the light. Candles placed throughout the room caused a trick of the eye. The images seemed to move, the birds' wings flapping. She was surprised to see the pattern on the creamy Oriental drapes matched that of the robes.

Drapes were drawn shut. Whatever happened in the candlelight would remain secret.

The brass on the tall doors clanked as they opened and shut. The locks slid. "Now," Sir Charles announced, pride heavy in his tremulous voice, "The Key of Solomon!" As if it were a newborn and he its proud mother, he held up a large book, laced with thick gold threads. An excited murmur arose.

"Silence!" He thundered. "We SUMMON Him. We CALL His dreaded army from Planes of Power. We summon—HE who grants new life! We summon—HE who devours the weak!" Chanting began as he moved through the room. "Place your offerings. Pledge your faith. Pay tribute," he droned.

A curious "ping" caused Linda to open the cabinet door another inch. Each participant placed a small stone in a silver dish that lay on the table. A woman presented a large sack and pulled out a black rooster that protested, flapping its wings. Wielding a ceremonial knife, Sir Charles decapitated it and plopped the severed head into the silver dish as the woman caught the spewing blood in a silver bucket, causing several women to turn away as the hissing gush struck the smooth surface.

The barrier undulated and shimmered as the blood flowed. Too small a death, the tribute was dismissed. They waited, hissing at the man and his droning praise. Praise, tribute and promise called it, but all was in order and there would be no rift.

Their eyes burning, demons clawed the thinning wall, a barrier that separated different universes. Like pearls on a string, each universe was unique. One was home to the darkest of energies and the endless chaos of destruction. The other was a teetering mass of creation, springing from a blend of order to chaos. Within the dark universe, life of a different sort had fashioned its own world. It was already old when, peering through the shifting folds of the barrier, it had glimpsed our world. For eons, it observed Earth's smoldering beginning, then its parade of life and the rise of Man. Then it entered our dreams, whispering, cajoling, hissing its promises of glory and power.

As the women whimpered, Sir Charles demanded those in the room be quiet. Men trembled, mopping their brows, hiding their fear under embroidered linen. Fear and terror spread, seeping into the barrier, which began to soften. Dots of light stippled the murky surface.

Soon, there is a tear.

A squeal of rage sounds as a talon fails to widen the rift, hoping to make it large enough for some to pass through. The rift fails to grow. Fleeting, it will soon disappear. Though rage burns through layers, the tear keeps mending and disappearing fast until . . .

THERE IS ANOTHER!!

A new rift appears, the result of the one hidden, uninvited. As Linda cowers behind a wooden door, her fear reveals her presence.

Wafting deliciously through the room is the girl's terror, its promise of a feast tearing through the wall. Eager tongues lap Linda's fear like mother's milk. Her fear explodes, ripping and widening the opening. Ah, the girl offers no tribute. Words offer no protection now, only the elixir of pain, sweetened by terror. Now, there is death. The legions howl.

In an instant, flames escape from the confining hearth. Some in the room laugh nervously and move away. There are sighs as the flames die until, without warning, the blaze detaches itself from the hearth. A woman whimpers as flames like glowing tongues, free themselves from their source and float through the room. Another woman cringes, moving to the doors. With shaking hands, she pulls on the bolt, trying to slide it. The lock refuses. She removes her rings. Perhaps they prevent her from getting an adequate grip. No difference. The woman begins to cry, and a man reaches over, grasping the knob firmly and pulls. No release.

A parade of flames dance, moving to a wall of books, illuminating their titles, crawling from volume to volume. A few leap to the portraits, moving up and down, licking the proud faces.

Satisfied with the success of his magic, Sir Charles cries: "We call you! Ehieh, Iod, TetragrammatonElohim, El, Elohim Gibor, Eloah Va-Daath, El Adonai Tzabaoth, ElohimTzabaoth, Shaddai. Ningiszida"! Again, he cried, "Ehieh, Iod, Tetragrammaton Elohim, El, ElohimGibor, Eloah Va-Daath, El Adonai Tzabaoth, ElohimTzabaoth, Shaddai. Ningiszida!"

The room is cold. Terrified guests shiver. Someone calls for an end to the ceremony. Many crowd the doors while others move to the windows. Seeming to come from the fireplace, a hiss becomes a low, steady groan, which gives way to a screaming laugh.

Then, a moment of silence. Terrified guests try to open the doors. Pounding on them, they demand they be opened. There's a nibbling, crunching sound. Angry squeals, as if an army of mice are gnawing on bits of crackers, then turning on each other in rage.

From the shadows, a crow appears. With a shrieking CAW, it drops down to the table. It perches on the edge of the silver dish and pecks at the stones. Its eyes glowing red, the bird waves its head back and forth as it regards the guests.

A man shouts, "Break the glass, damn you!" He struggles to open the windows. He pounds the glass with a brass candlestick, but the glass remains inviolate. Women are crying. The crow cocks its head to one side and letting out another CAW, it flies, circling the room.

The Moroccan table trembles, causing the pebbles to rattle in the silver dish. Someone is chuckling, someone with a deep rich voice, terribly amused. Pebbles float, rising from the bowl and striking foreheads, bouncing playfully, striking one and springing to another. Popping sounds like gunfire cause a man to duck. Seeping into the room is an odor, rich with decay.

Discovery is the least of Linda's fears. She feels an awful dread. Of what she wishes for, the most urgent is to run, to burst from her hiding place, cross the room, hurry out the tall doors and into the safety of her mother's arms. Trying to flee she discovers she is paralyzed, her muscles frozen. She stares at the horror before her.

The cabinet door flies off its hinges and strikes a woman, slamming her head down and blood spills on the polished floor.

Linda's eyes water, tears spilling down her cheeks. The guests, those who are still alive, scream. A man trips on the edge of his robe, knocking another man down and onto the edge of a table. She hears a loud snap as the second man's neck broke.

One of the young wives struggles to remove her robe. She's shrieking, "It's stuck, it's stuck; someone help me!" Tears continue down Linda's face as she sees the woman's graceful fingers claw her melting ceremonial robe. Before she is blinded, Linda sees flames bouncing throughout the room.

Eyes float . . . A mist appears and becomes a yawning mouth. Sir Charles is lifted, his fat white body exposed, as the robe hikes up and covers his face. He bellows like an old bull led to the slaughter before the fog-mouth swallows him whole.

Dark. She floats, not far. She can hear the faint cries of the guests. Something, something, a being within her, searching . . . for what? Yes, the baby, yes, of course. She considers her child, the thing that made her scheme, to punish Matthew, make him pay, as she would surely pay, and now . . . It doesn't matter.

Snaking through the rift they discover the treasure in the girl's womb. The umbilical cord shakes and invisible whiskers erupt along the placenta, which begins to undulate like a gentle tide. As if welcoming a guest, the baby nods and the tendrils of energy become colored threads. The threads

The Demon Rift

become like yarn around a kitten, but instead, it is the yarn that plays. It winds around the child and a stinger pierces the tiny heart and brain. Like a needle, it stitches and weaves in and out, binding the child to another world.

There is a port now; an outstation exists and now a spy. The port is secured; it lies snug within the child, a secret base in a foreign land. They revel in the pain and blood, but the carnage at hand is but a taste. As the feeding ended, questions buzzed along the healing breach. The next rift, when would it be? How many times would the rift disappear before it stayed? Much was revealed in the wall's timeline, but not the most important question. When would they feast forever? In the meantime, there is the child; there is a saboteur.

Linda follows the sinewy being, its long fingers outstretched and groping as it discovers the tiny human curled within her. Yellow flames in its eyes detach and clung to red claws as they trail wisps like maypole ribbons. The creature dances. The baby's eyes follow the swirl of ribbons. The creature whispers something in her child's unformed ear. The baby nods its head and waves its stubby arms and legs. She struggles to get closer. What is it saying that stirs her child? The baby wants to detach and leave her. Linda wishes it could leave; she would let it go.

But her baby stayed, for a while.

FOUR

Aberdare, Wales
November 6, 1885

The train lurched and hissed as Rebecca watched for the tavern. She would see it soon, the sign *Ram's Head*. Though it was early in the day, there would be comings and goings of men through the pub's door. Those without work, their shoulders rounded, and hands stuffed deep into pockets, crept in and later emerged unchanged hours later. Clouds of steam rising in the cold air obscured everything but the dark movement of scattered figures, people waiting to greet the train from London. She saw the shake of a horse's head before she saw the wagon.

Where was the *Ram's Head*? Her only memory from the day she left. Pints, singing, darts, an occasional fight, the *Ram's Head* was where her brothers spent so many hours, hours not in the mine. Not a place for a young girl, they said. Go home now or we'll tell. The mine took them when the cage fell, and she swore she'd never come back. Nowhere to go now but Aberdare.

Early in their journey, Linda's whispered pleas, "N-n-n-ooo . . ." resulted in the migration of fellow passengers to other cars. Mother and daughter rode alone, the rows of empty seats rattling as Rebecca traveled the path she vowed to leave behind. The train pulled in, Rebecca peered through the window and Linda lay stretched across her mother's lap.

Clouds threatened a storm as Rebecca searched for the "Ram's Head" and found her father instead. His cap was pulled down hiding his face, but she knew the faded coat; she had mended it countless times. She recognized two older men, acquaintances of her father's. Certainly not friends, her father tolerated little that would pass for friendship. The men nodded as they boarded the train and found the women alone. One carried Linda and the other, luggage to her father's wagon. Rebecca trembled as she followed them. It had been fifteen years. Her father, his tall frame bent from years of shoeing horses, stood quietly, his eyes distant. He loaded their belongings next to his limp granddaughter.

"Your hair, it's white," she said. His brows still showed red as they hung low over his brown eyes.

He climbed onto the wagon and in his graveled voice, a voice strangled with cold disappointment, he said, "Let's get her home while there's no rain."

Riding in the wagon to the house where she was born, Rebecca looked for familiar faces. A few appeared; a playmate she barely recognized waved shyly. Most avoided her glance or stared, hoping for a glimpse of Linda. The wagon swayed and bumped along the uneven road, but Linda remained unaware, caught deep in whatever dream held her. As the horse drew them near the small cottage, Rebecca's only thought was that it needed paint; the white peeling, the wood underneath revealed.

He never looked in her direction, nor did he glance at Linda. Her dead mother had been the only link between them. Rebecca and her blacksmith father were strangers, but she had no one else nor did Linda.

He carried the sleeping girl into the dingy bedroom of Rebecca's childhood. He placed his granddaughter on the narrow bed, the blankets thick with dust and neglect. "There's soup for the both of you. I expect you to earn your keep." With those words, he left.

Even in Aberdare, people had heard. Twenty people, including Lord Towning, died that night; all but Sir Charles had burned, their robes melted onto their charred bodies. Sir Charles bled to death, his body discovered on the Moroccan table, a silver bowl wedged between his legs. When the resistant doors suddenly opened for the bewildered servants, other than the charred corpses, they revealed no evidence of fire or intruders.

While her father sheltered his widowed daughter and her child, Rebecca earned their keep by taking in laundry. It wasn't long before Linda's pregnancy was obvious. Wincing at his scorn, she was relieved when her father didn't turn them out.

Months passed, uneventful but for the girl's changing body. At times, Rebecca thought Linda was coming back. The girl's dark eyes would dart back and forth, her expression frantic. It was the whispered word repeated—No—no-no-no-no-no-no . . . that frightened Rebecca.

As she awaited the birth of her grandchild, she bathed and fed Linda, who was helpless as a newborn. "Do you think she can hear me?" Rebecca was hopeful.

"I don't have any idea, perhaps," the midwife answered. She leaned over and studied her patient's placid face. "Linda, dear, Linda. Listen to me, the baby's coming. Do you hear me, girl? Your baby, it's coming soon." The midwife put her ear near the girl's slack mouth.

Linda lay unmoving, her eyes closed. The hair that grew between the scars on Linda's scalp was still a glorious auburn. It hung in thin patches. On Linda's face were few scars, but her complexion had a grayish cast. Rebecca comforted herself by thinking it was better than the charred black it had been.

"Oh dear, oh my dear . . ." The midwife frowned as she listened to Linda's heart. She tucked clean rags and towels under her patient, replacing those that were blood soaked. She sighed, "Your girl is dying."

Staring at the bloodstained rags, Rebecca felt nothing. *Is this how it is? Is this how you get through the loss of a child?*

The baby slipped out and into the midwife's gnarled hands. Linda's eyes sprang open and rolled back. The midwife wrapped the new baby boy in a blanket as Rebecca stroked her daughter's face. Holding her daughter's dead hand, she sang a lullaby.

The midwife tapped Rebecca's shoulder. "You have a grandson; hold him now."

Taking the small bundle, Rebecca slid her index finger between the soft folds of the blanket, uncovering the baby's face. Revulsion overwhelmed her as the infant's eyes, yellow and cold, stared back.

Three days later, Rebecca found an old woman willing to take her grandson, named Bernard after her father, to a London orphanage. She hoped he would die there, but she doubted he would. The child had a way of making his needs met. She wanted him far away while he was small and weak, and her mind still belonged to her.

Nine years passed. Linda rested in the ground next to the two uncles she never met. Rebecca lived in the cottage alone, her stern father dead from a cancer that took his dignity along with his life. The post had arrived the day before. She sat rocking, her body aching from scrubbing and ironing the laundry of single men and the well-to-do. She opened an envelope marked: St. Stephen's

Home for Orphans. *He's dead, she thought, hoped—please, I can't .
. .*

A newspaper clipping detailed the murder of Mrs. Rita Croft and the disappearance of Crispin Baker, known as Professor Theosopho, a self-proclaimed psychic. Police were questioning guests at a fundraiser held for the benefit of an orphanage, attended by Mrs. Croft and the Professor. Someone had circled a name. The charity event was at the same orphanage where her grandson had been taken.

The note enclosed with the clipping said, "He's missing. Say a prayer that he stays lost." That night, Rebecca prayed that her grandson stayed lost forever.

FIVE

PATTY

This happened the first time Bernie got caught. I feel sorry for Stella. She was chasing Bernie because she wanted to save her sister. It was before I knew Bernie so I couldn't help.

Sisters are important.

I'm sorry I couldn't save you from the red-nosed woman, Emily.

It wasn't your fault.

The Searching Heart

Stella Tobin Caulkins

Redhill, Ohio

December 24, 1900

Spiraling mists of new snow blinded her. *Am I lost?* Stella peered through a clot of leaves and knotted vines. The lolling branches signaling the narrow path beckoned but lay out of reach. Shaking her head, she chopped and hacked at a tangled mass piled high and thick, leaves and vines held tight by twigs and fallen branches. With each swing, the branches threatened to rebound and knock her off her feet. She dodged its blows and kept at it until . . . Was it giving way? Please, be quick. Wedging the handle, she straightened her arms, pulling it back and forth. A whine came from the dead leaves. *You can't be serious.*

The wind . . . keep going! She slid the handle under a thick branch, praying that it was all that kept the wall from collapsing. Her frozen hands were clumsy in the heavy gloves, her thumbs slipping before she let them slide and come to rest. She ignored the pain; the pain would have its due when Becka was home. She heard a thump as the wind caught heavy clumps of snow, pelting her coat, and knitted cap. *The leaves whispered, "What folly, Stella the fool. You think you can catch them now?"* She answered with her fist and the end of her ax.

The wall collapsed. Oh God, thank you. It leaned, swinging to the side. It was only waist high; maybe she could slide . . . Ah! Needles on sticks caught her coat, threatening to hold her. *Thought you'd get away; we'll see . . .* She lifted her boot and kicked, yanking at the restraints.

Oh God at last! It gave way just enough.

She inched back onto the path, and the wind resumed its torment. *Save your strength, keep up, find her before . . .* The men's voices were growing even fainter. "Too much for a woman your age," the sheriff had warned her. He was mistaken.

Under her glove, she wore the pearl ring. Earlier, as her shaking fingers struggled with her coat buttons, she spied Becka's gift, hidden behind a bowl of pinecones. "To Stella Bella from Becka," the card said.

The ring had been on Mrs. Collin's bureau for a dozen years. Although it was a gift from her son Davey, a merchant marine, Mrs. Collins never wore it. "Too fancy," was all she would say. Stella had long suspected that it was something else, something strange about the ring . . . Despite its clumsy setting, the prongs gripping like small fingers, the pearl's odd markings, Stella never missed a chance to . . . Becka knew . . .

Hope! The hounds were baying! Her heart, pounding in her ears, caught the sound of the pack, and their cries pulsed through her veins. No! The clearing disappeared; her path blocked again. She was gaining—Becka! Shifting sideways, she pushed on through the tangles of brush. A clearing and smoke in the distance was less than a mile. A branch caught her face with a smack. Pain welled as a thorn pierced her forehead, the blood trickling, freezing before it reached the scarf hiding her trembling jaw. They had been searching for seven hours, not stopping for food, or resting more than a minute.

Becka, where are you?

Sleeping Beauty? The forest of thorns . . . the most exciting part of the story. Mother's worn face, softened by the lamp as she read to Stella and her brother. Stella knew the Lord would take her mother within the year, like she'd known about her father's death long before the horse had thrown him.

The dogs kept howling. She stumbled in her haste to reach them, until someone caught her arm. Bobbo. He pulled her to her feet as she searched her brother's face. Was there hope? His eyes told nothing.

"Up ahead," he said, "shake a leg." Rifle in hand, he ran towards the hounds, his long legs covering twice the distance of hers as she scrambled, her frozen feet uncertain when they touched the ground. Branches waved above her head; her mind tore away, the sunlight fading.

It would be dark soon.

SIX

PATTY

This part happened before the forest lady, Stella, met Bernie. Bernie met his helper, Crispin. They were on a boat. Crispin was from London. That's in England.

Yes, Patty, I know. Who was Crispin?

Crispin was a grownup criminal and a really mean man. Bernie was meaner.

I don't like mean kids.

Crispin
Atlantic Ocean—London to New York
August 1894

Crispin Baker blew smoke rings as he stood on the ship's deck. He savored his smoke, enjoying the mild breeze as it carried the ghostly wisps into the dark. An excellent cigar and expensive, he thought, as he rolled it between his fingers. The deck leaned gently as the wind picked up. He prided himself on his good taste, an achievement, considering his upbringing. *Dear Aunt Meg did all right*, he allowed. *It wasn't easy; he wasn't easy.* He stood between stacks of deck chairs, secured lest they slide, toppling into the Atlantic Ocean. Fond memories . . . *Aunt's sewing basket, the hidden pearls, so beautiful he cried when he discovered them, tucked into the lining. Naughty girl. A shame, really, her death . . .*

The chairs began to rattle as the wind stirred the waves. He steadied himself. A bottle tumbled down the deck. He frowned. Someone was careless. Faint laughter drifted from the upper deck. He gritted his teeth, biting down on the precious cigar. "Buggers!" he sneered.

Examining the wounded cigar, he wrapped it in paper and tucked it away. Plenty more to be had. "Professor Theosopho at your service." He bowed to a deck chair. "Ready to contact your dear ones on the other side." The elite of New York Society beckoned.

Crispin counted on his good looks. He was the first to admit that he was no longer a lad, but he still caused many a heart to flutter and legs to open. A man of fifty was a man in his prime. His silver hair gave him an air of distinction and nobility.

The bottle rolled against his foot as the ship swayed. He picked it up. Still a bit of whiskey! Ha! He drained the remaining drops, spilling them on his tongue, and shook the bottle. How far could he throw it? Would he hear the splash?

A voice interrupted. "I seen you; can you do it? Can you reach them?"

Crispin whirled around. The ship groaned. He held the whiskey bottle by its neck, steadying himself, clutching the rail. A small figure crouched between the stacks of chairs. "Who's there? Show yourself.

The figure stands and braces against the chairs, arms wrapped around a restraining rope. Crispin moved closer. One so small would be easy to manage. It is a boy of six or so. Hard to see, the child's face in shadow. The boy steps into the light, his blond hair caught there.

"I want to reach him. I want to reach them all. There are rewards for you if you help me."

PATTY

This is what happened on the boat when Bernie met Crispin. Even though he was a mean grownup, Crispin had to do everything Bernie said because Bernie was so scary. Not to me though, because Bernie was just a big rat.

He sure was.

The Glass Man
Atlantic Ocean, London to New York
August 1894

The boy moved closer. "I want to reach him. I want to reach them all. There are rewards for you if you help me."

Rewards? Crispin snickered to himself. A brat's game, was it? He'd see who cared for the brat. If there was money, so much the better. He wondered how loud a splash a brat might make . . . "Dear lad," he whispered, "whatever are you going on about?"

The child stepped into the light.

Curious, the eyes . . . their color looked almost yellow.

Perhaps it was the lamplight. One would think them hazel, then a sort of green with flecks of gold . . . Red pools swirled in the yellow eyes as the boy began to smile, his mouth widening into an impossible grin. Crispin had seen that grin once before at Regents Park. There was a hyena at the London Zoo . . .

The boy cocked his head. "What were you thinking?"

Thinking? I'm thinking . . . his feet were caught in ice. Not possible . . . ice. His body was a block of ice. The bottle was part of him. Knock him hard, and he would smash into a million bits, slivers, and shards. The ship tilted and he began to slide . . . his feet paralyzed . . . stiff . . . a bloke in ice, a block of ice . . . tilting/listing/swinging up and down . . . rolling on the rail . . . what kind of splash . . . His heart slowed, the blood hesitating . . . still a drop left for a hungry shark.

The orphan gave a smile. "I want to go to sleep now."

Crispin blinked. Warmth ran down his leg; he had wet himself, the indignity being the first of many. Trapped, he later reflected, as surely a fly in a web, by a spider named Bernie, a very nasty spider, indeed.

Atlantic, London to New York
August 1894

The day before the ship sailed into New York's Harbor, Bernie sat on a deck chair. His tongue snaked around a mound of ice cream. "I want hokey-pokey," he'd demanded, seeing the frozen treat. The sun warmed them. Passengers lined the rails, shielding their eyes as they searched the horizon. Oblivious to their murmurs of excitement, Bernie licked the melting confection, his tongue swirling the edges.

"Precious! Precious!" A woman in her sixties pushed through the crowd. Crispin admired her elegant gray coat, made of the finest wool, its rows of ivory buttons attesting to her good taste and large fortune. Shifting from a high-pitched cry to a mournful choking moan, she sang out "Preeecc-iousss . . . Preeecchh . . . ious!" She cupped her hand to her ear and called, hoping to hear the yap of her lost Pomeranian. While he avoided any unhappy drops of the boy's treat falling on his expensive striped trousers, Crispen sat on the edge of the deck chair, observing her.

The woman drew a handkerchief from her knitted purse and began to dab her eyes. She hesitated, standing at the rail, looking through the crowd for signs of her lost dog, Precious. Arranging a look of careful concern on his face, he studied her. Had she given up hope? Not yet, he decided. The woman, a widow named Mrs. Palmer, had condescended to personally search in third class for her missing dog. Stewards had dutifully knocked on doors the night before, asking if anyone had seen the missing Precious. A reward was offered . . . Pity he hadn't considered that; he might have simply hidden the animal, playing the hero by restoring the beloved Precious to his mistress, and collecting the reward.

The pleasure of pinching the little wretch from under her Ladyship's nose was irresistible. He smiled, recalling the beast's rapid little heart as he tossed it into the Atlantic. Mustn't dwell . . . more important issues to consider. Bernie . . . how best to kill Bernie? Throw the little bastard overboard or wait until he slept and smother him with a pillow. He would leave the body hidden on the ship when he disembarked.

Bernie's sticky fingers grasped the arm of Crispin's chair. Pulling closer to Crispin's face, he whispered in his ear, "You stupid Crispin!"

An image filled Crispin's mind.

Her ladyship's purse opens, then she hands him a hundred—no two hundred—five hundred pounds! Her eyes swimming with gratitude as he hands her the shivering dog. Glad to help, he says, and by the way luv, introduce me to your posh friends . . . Of course you brave man, she sobs as she hugs the pathetic Precious . . . He really should consider the reward—go and find the dog—think of the reward . . . you'll be a hero . . .

He was almost to his feet when he began to fight the urge to find Precious. He wanted to rush to the rail and jump into the ocean, down into the cold water, calling for the lost Pomeranian as he swam about. Panicked, he looked around. Someone will stop me, he hoped. I'll be rescued, surely. He fought to stop his legs as slowly he rose to his feet.

"I can make it so that *no* one helps you. I can make it so that no one even *sees* you drop!" Bernie smiled as he licked his fingers. Crispin fell into the safety of his folding chair as the heartbroken Mrs. Palmer made her way back to first class.

SEVEN

PATTY

This happened more than a hundred years after Bernie met Crispin on the boat.

Why did we skip ahead, especially a hundred years?

Cause I felt like it. I like balloons and I saw them on the Time Ribbon, so I took a look. Don't frown. I thought you liked balloons. The Mall is a big place where people can buy a million things. It was the day it had the "Grand Opening." Bernie pretends to be somebody named Senator Arnold.

Arnold? What is his first name?

John. Why are you crying? What's wrong?

I'll explain another time. Who else do we meet?

A lady named Emma. Bernie pretends to like everyone, but he really hates them. A rat like always. Don't know who Emma is yet. I like her because she hates Bernie. How does she know he's a rat?

The Mall overwhelms me.

Maybe you'll change your mind when you see the balloons.

The Floating Mall
The Redhill Mall Opening,
Redhill, Ohio November 2004

Red balloons filled the afternoon sky. Some drifted gracefully, their upward flow slowed by their fellows, but many, caught by the mild wind, zoomed quickly towards the warm sun, rudely bumping others from their path. Gazing up at the sky filled with cherry red, the crowd clapped, cheered, and whistled its approval.

Two thousand people gathered in celebration. Lawn chairs, wheelchairs, strollers, and blankets were placed among the majority who stood patiently and waited for the main event, the Grand Opening of the Redhill Mall. They stood upon acres of fresh asphalt laid atop soil kept free of anything but the most insistent weeds. Long ago, it had been home to a profusion of rooted, tangled life.

It was shirtsleeve weather, hardly a sweater in sight, let alone a coat, unaccountably warm for the day after Thanksgiving. A host of performers delighted the crowd. Elves on stilts juggled; Victorian Ladies and Gentlemen distributed candies. The Redhill High School Band played "Beautiful Ohio" and a medley of Christmas carols. Perky cheerleaders, fetching in the red and white skirts of Redhill High, distributed coupons, good for discounts.

Looking sharp in ROTC uniforms, polite young men aided the hired security team, who dressed like the sheriffs of old Redhill a hundred years past.

The smell of the paint that created thousands of parking spaces vied with the aromas of popcorn, hot dogs, and cotton candy. In a corner of the North Pole Post Office, Rudolf, a lone reindeer, munched his feed and defecated contentedly on the sawdust floor.

Behind the raised platform, loomed the mall, its construction meant to suggest a three-floored version of Cleveland's Grand Arcade. A mammoth red ribbon was tied to the brass columns that preceded the inviting doors. Relaxing comfortably, hidden behind the platform, Senator Arnold studied his creation.

The mall shimmered with reflected heat coming from the glinting surface of the new asphalt. He imagined it floating.

Given the importance of the key speaker, the sound system had been thoroughly tested. The platform held various dignitaries. Among them was Redhill's own Mayor Randall Beckwith III, Tim West who would oversee the operation of the new mall, Cassie Ryan, Miss Cuyahoga County, and 2nd runner up for Miss Teen Ohio, and Robert (Tiny) Macgowan, owner of the Wanderin' Buckeye Truck Stop and president of the Redhill Chamber of Commerce.

Mayor Beckwith's overlong speech caused a restless stir in the crowd, which gave way to enthusiastic applause as the mayor introduced the man of the hour. Several news cameras trained on the distinguished figure as he walked to the podium. Dozens of bulbs flashed. He spread his arms out and the crowd roared its approval.

Gesturing for quiet, he began to speak, seeming to look to each of them for his or her understanding and approval. He was past seventy, his white hair expertly cut, and the lines and jowls of his face gave him an air of wisdom. Crinkles extending from the corners of his blue eyes spoke of someone quick to laugh. It was only when you looked closely, that you could see that his eyes were dead, the eyes of a predator, devoid of humor or compassion. His collar loosened, the sleeves of his white shirt rolled up and the coat of his imported suit draped in the arms of a comely assistant, John Arnold, ex con, multimillionaire and retired U.S. Senator addressed the crowd.

"It was here, in this place, where the new John Arnold was born. And from this place of sorrow so many years ago," his voice soared, full of emotion, "there will be again, new life, a new Redhill!"

He waited for the applause to peak. The man was not John Arnold, but Bernie, the servant Linda's child. Now, one hundred nineteen years old Bernie was past seventy when he murdered John Arnold. Along with taking John's life, he took his youth, physical appearance and his family. John/Bernie, the identity thief, looked out over the crowd, taking note of the number of families as well as those alone, the young, the old ones.

Although, he still thought of himself as Bernie, he was more now. John Arnold's youth and strength, his physical appearance, Bernie had stolen more than forty years earlier. Bernie possessed none of the dead man's humor, compassion, or ability to love. John's intelligence and anger gave Bernie the power to charm and influence, to persuade and rule. Bernie was past seventy again. It was time for a new identity and for much more.

A bitter woman stood behind a striped tent. Only forty-three, lines were deeply etched in her face and her dark hair was streaked with gray. Beauty lingered in her blue eyes, refusing to give way to the defeat of age and hopelessness. As she listened to her father charming the crowd, Emma Bedonne's feet ached. No change, she decided. She had promised Tiny she would be there. "He's your dad, fer pete's sake. You should at least go." Tiny was a good boss, understanding on those occasions when she might be just a little late for her shift because of a "migraine."

She had started to leave when she heard him say her name. "Families have problems," he said. One day he hoped to reconcile so that they "could come together." She fought the urge to run and instead, glanced up at him, meaning to show that she wasn't afraid. He was smiling. She wanted him dead. Scattered applause followed her as she walked out of the parking lot. She drove her ancient

Volkswagen back to the truck stop and cried as she parked the car, wishing she could go home to the trailer where she could hide.

EIGHT

PATTY

This happened before they stole Becka. This was when Stella first met Bernie. She didn't like him.

Poor Stella.

America's Heart
Redhill, Ohio
December 1900

The boy and his accomplice first appeared on a Saturday in mid-December. It was a mild December for Redhill, Ohio, a rural community, home to less than four hundred souls. Little Phil pointed to a man pulling a cart as the family reached their customary stop, the post near Arthur's barbershop.

Waving at passersby, the man made his way along the road that served the town's center. His wiry frame harnessed to a two-wheeled cart, he whistled and called out to those who paused, inviting all to "take a look-see." Several open burlap sacks spilled over when the cart's wheels encountered a dip. A variety of woodcarvings including several toys fell out, prompting oohs and ah's from a number of folk who barely noticed the shabby boy of ten trailing behind.

"I bring the world to you good people, America's Heart."

The gathering crowd grew quiet. The creased face fixed in a wide smile the salesman charmed his audience. Stella Caulkins saw his clothes could use a wash.

"Crispin Baker, at your suhvice," he said. "And this is." He paused dramatically, combing back the strings of gray hair that lay stiff on his forehead and gestured with the other hand, its palm a map of gritty trails, to the boy who sat in the cart's shadow. "My little son, Bernie." His honey-drizzled voice cracked with sentiment.

Murderer! The word entered Stella's thoughts uninvited. She dismissed it with a shudder. "Foreign," she heard Becka whisper.

Saboteur? Why such a word? Why such a thought? What did it mean?

He touched his chest as he bowed. She noted how his eyes stayed on the crowd. Young girls cupped their faces, exchanging smirks. He had been handsome once. His smile said he still was.

Something's not right! She knew what was wrong. The dread she felt was just her typical holiday gloom. "No one greets our

Lord's birthday with a long face, but you missy," her mother often said.

True, Stella hated Christmas. She whispered to Arthur that it was time to go. Then Phil began to stamp his feet and cry. Arthur and Mary Kate waited, knowing the effect of Phil's tears. When Arthur promised not to buy anything, she agreed Arthur and the children could stay. The children could watch while her sister Becka went on to the First Christian Church.

As Stella began to edge through the onlookers, a shiver ran through her. Ice chips were in her feet, sharp and cold, slicing through her legs, hips and breasts, then creeping into her arms and hands. Her hands shook as she buttoned her coat. Were clouds coming? She felt the winter sun on her face as the ice feeling faded. A breeze?

Was the weather about to change? Arthur must pay attention. If it turned, he should button the children's coats. She signaled Arthur to watch for the cold wind. Above her head, she heard a slap and a crack, like a whip. A large crow rested on a bare tree branch. The bird's red eye fixed on her. Turning away, she saw the ragged boy hunched over as he sat on the dried mud, his face a blank under the cap's shadow.

They could feel her, the protective energy she wielded as it pierced the rolling flames of the crow's demon eyes. Clawing at the milky barrier, they wailed, "Make her hurt-make her hurt-make her hurt hurt hurt hurt hurt . . ."

The Demon Rift

Get away! The coats forgotten, she hurried away. Later, after finishing her errands, Stella walked along the narrow path to the edge of town where Arthur and the children waited. The children were sitting in the back of the wagon while Arthur stared at his shoes. As she handed Arthur the few purchases on the family list, he began to blink. Beads of sweat dotted his nose. They had been married fifteen years, but she sometimes wondered if she had three children, rather than two.

Little Phil's white-blond cowlick bounced up and down. He began to squeal as he waved a toy boat in the air. Mary Kate sat quietly, hoping her mother wouldn't notice the new doll. The doll, whittled out of soft buckeye wood, had movable joints and dark buckeye knobs for eyes. Phil was inspecting his boat, his fingers exploring its details. He laughed when he saw the small wheel turned. Mary Kate, her plain face, a softer copy of Stella's, gave her mother a pleading look.

"Becka insisted," said Arthur defensively, "She came back for the peaches while you were gone." He hesitated, and then stuttered, "Sh-sh-she in-in-invited them back to the church. Sh-she said it was the l-l-l-least we could do—f-for the homeless boy."

At the mention of the boy, Stella found herself in a rage. "Since when does my sister tell you what to do, Arthur Caulkins?" Arthur flushed, his balding forehead turning red. He looked away. Little Phil clutched his sister's waist. Ashamed at her outburst, she removed the scowl from her face and smiled at Arthur.

"Next time, we'll make such decisions together. We needn't mention this to Becka."

Arthur nodded. His relieved smile reminded her of a puppy eager to please. She knew he was dreading Becka's return to the wagon and the ride home. She decided she would deal with her sister later.

She turned to her daughter. "Missy, let's wait and see what old Saint Nick brings, shall we? I know many a poor little girl who'd love such a doll." Mary Kate nodded bleakly. Phil could keep the boat until he lost interest. The doll must be given away. Stella couldn't bear the sight of it.

After her conversation with Arthur, Becka had retrieved the basket of canned peaches and walked the half-mile back to the First Christian Church, the two drifters in tow. On Saturdays, a homemade welcome sign directed travelers or those in need to the church basement where she and Mayanne West served hot sandwiches and coffee.

Stella planned to confront Becka after supper. Her younger sister was trusting, too much so and should not interfere in family matters that did not concern her.

Becka, who loved romantic novels, was a plump five feet two. With lank blonde hair that resisted the most determined curling iron to create tendrils, Becka twisted her hair tight against her nape, except for a narrow swathe several inches long that rested limply on her right shoulder. Meant to suggest a romantic nature, it instead drew attention to her short neck. Despite her best efforts, she, like Mary Kate, resembled Stella. Becka's gray-blue eyes gave her a guileless beauty, but Stella knew they rarely saw the world as it was.

NINE

PATTY

What do these people and all this love stuff have to do with Bernie? Nora was the granddaughter of some man named Bobbo who was the forest Stella's brother. This makes Nora Stella's niece or maybe a cousin. And who is John? Gram says he's important because John is part of our family, too—Russie, Gram and me. A lot of bother.

My poor John! What did I do to him?

I'm sorry you're sad, Emily. Do you want to skip this part?

No, I want to know what happened to my son.

John & Nora

Redhill, Ohio

1961

John had been working at Desimone's for six weeks when he saw Nora for the first time since they had been juniors at Redhill high school. Having finished unloading a delivery of transistor radios, he was having a cigarette with Greg, a twenty-year-old disaster-in-waiting. It was almost five in the afternoon on a Saturday. John was tired. He had stayed up reading, comfortable on his studio couch, the sound of crickets outside the window by the kitchenette vying with the loud "discussion" his neighbors engaged in on numerous occasions.

The loud door slam that announced the onset of relative quiet did not come until two, and John had wanted to finish *Profiles in Courage.* John inhaled the first drag of his Ducky Strike. Greg's irritating complaints about working two Saturdays in a row seemed less annoying now that he had found *Tales of the South Pacific.*

An elderly couple was crossing the street of the town's main intersection when he saw a young woman carrying a large paper bag and hurrying towards the entrance. Seeing the two men wearing Desimone's gray uniforms, she glanced at the hours posted on the double doors that stated Saturday's closing at five. Looking flustered, there was a touch of hope in her voice, the hope of a pretty girl that her appeal will tilt the decision in her favor.

"Is it too late?" Nora was twenty-eight. Her hair was chestnut brown and her clear blue eyes shone with intelligence and wit, but her beauty wasn't enough to buy her out of the small-town existence she had quietly accepted as the way things were. Once she had been that earnest, rather irritating girl John remembered from high school, not a good time for him.

"Depends," Greg said, clearly enjoying the power of the situation.

"Oh?" She was confused at Greg's vague answer.

"What's it for?" asked Greg, sneaking a look at John to see if he was sharing in the fun. Reaching into the paper bag, she pulled out a pair of white nurses' shoes.

"I bought these yesterday. I thought they were fine when I tried them on . . . but they slip on the carpet at the rest home and I need shoes that are comfortable."

Greg interrupted, "Ma'am as you can see Desimone's is closing for the day." His eyes glazed with delight as he watched Nora begin to plead her case.

"But you don't understand." Nora pleaded, "I'm told that white nurses' shoes are a required part of the uniform and I stalled them until after my first check and . . ."

"Greg, why don't you check the men's room; see if everything's in order." John interrupted. He disliked cruelty, especially when the target was as lovely as Nora. Greg's face reddened and he hesitated, hoping to respond with a withering reply. "Better hurry," John urged. He turned to her. "You'd like to exchange them, I take it . . ."

Her hair was in a ponytail with small barrettes restraining any unruly strands. She wore a belted cotton dress, its short sleeves revealing girlish arms that hinted at the woman she was becoming. A modest scooped neckline showed the grace of her neck and the delicate way her chin lifted. Nora's face brightened and as she smiled, her slightly crooked teeth gave her charm. John wanted to prolong this encounter. For the second time in his life, John found something to love. It was Nora.

The Suffragette and the Dentist
Redhill Convalescent Hospital
1961

"Did ya see the news? Kennedy wants to put a man on the Moon. "Mrs. Stonerock' s eager face nodded up and down. Her smile, perfect with an expensive set of dentures (choppas—Bill called them) was framed by primrose pink lipstick. Nora helped the eighty-six-year-old former suffragette put on her "face" at seven every morning before breakfast, and Bill helped with touchups. "Edmond might want to go out later and I want to be ready".

"On the Moon? How is he going to accomplish that?" Nora looked at Monday's headline as her patient waited eagerly for her reaction.

"I'm glad you took 'em back—those others just wouldn't do. These are just the thing," she said pointing her fragile finger at Nora's new white lace-ups. "Melissa, would you hand me my comb?" Mrs. Stonerock often mistook Nora for her daughter who had died in 1948.

Bill, a pleasant looking man in his forties whose skin was mocha brown, flashed a smile, revealing a set of "chappas" not quite as perfect as Mrs. Stonerock's. "If you ladies are finished, lunch is goin' on and there's gonna be a sing-along after lunch, so don't miss out."

"I'll be right there, Edmond." Mrs. Stonerock's chatter was a welcome relief from the melancholy that plagued so many in the Redhill Convalescent Center. Her stories of campaigning for the "vote" included chaining herself to the White House gates while raising three sons as the wife of a dentist and they made Nora laugh and shake her head at the older woman's audacity. Nora Tobin had dreamed of becoming a medical researcher until a white Chevy pickup took the lives of her mother and Ben, her little brother on the road to Cleveland.

"I'll be extra careful; you're such a worrier!" her mother had said. Like a horrid home movie rewinding and playing over and over, images of Ben and their mother, their dead bodies covered by a floral blanket, her mother's limp hand exposed and someone gently tucking it under the blanket, haunted Nora's dreams. Maybe if she had warned them . . . She had. There was no point in "maybes" when thinking about the past. Death could not be undone.

She had completed her second year at Oberlin when the call from her father cancelled her dreams of becoming a researcher. His broken voice rang in her ears some nights. His heart attack a few months after the accident left her with no one. The house was sold to pay for the weeks of care that failed to save him. She had left Redhill, home to five generations of Tobins and Caulkins, with hope and she had come back with her usual cautious optimism. It was what it was, and who knew, things could change. After work, she found John waiting for her.

"Thought I'd see how those shoes were working out." His voice quivered. Nora found herself wanting to put her arms around him.

"Fine, I think, but maybe we can walk for a while so that I can be sure." His shy nod was all it took for Nora to know that her search was over; she had found a man who would love her as the dentist had loved his suffragette.

TEN

PATTY

I know some people would call Stella a bully.

I don't know, maybe a little.

Not me. Number one: Stella was right about Bernie. The first time she saw him, she knew he was a bad character. Number two: I am a big sister, and sometimes, you have ta tell little sisters what to do because they don't know as much as you do.

I know, Patty. You always took care of me.

I tried.

Remembered Dreams
A Monday in Ohio
December 1900

After dinner as Arthur and Mary Kate did the dishes, the sisters relaxed in the parlor. Before Stella could begin her lecture, Becka burst into tears. "Oh, Stella, it's so sad, that poor boy." Becka's transgression forgotten, Stella listened to her sister's encounter with Crispin Baker and the boy, Bernie.

"They came to the church for sandwiches." Becka blotted her eyes. "At first, he was charming enough. He's English, the only truth he told. You'd be amazed at what some in that basement believed. I'm not as gullible as you think!" Her voice rose as Becka defended herself.

Stella decided to humor her. "So, what did he claim?"

Becka's eyes swelled with indignation. "After hinting that he was related to royalty, he talked about his life at sea, and how he came home to England to 'take care of this here angel after the drink took the misses.' He said he decided to seek their fortune in America, something to do with his stolen inheritance by the duke of something. He hinted for donations to tide him over, 'whilst Scotland Yard looked into it.' His greasy hat sat next to the coffee until I moved it. Did he mention his boy needed a mother? I found him repulsive, but you know Mayanne. She's desperate to marry."

Stella said nothing; Becka's unmarried status at twenty-seven was rarely discussed.

"He'd eaten several sandwiches and then he began to cry; we realized he was quite drunk! He must have had a flask, though no one saw. He blubbered about how hard it was to be a slave to 'him'." Becka's eyes clouded with tears. "Stella, he meant that poor little boy. The poor baby, he just sat there, spinning his little wooden top. Oh Stella, my heart nearly broke! We must do something!"

Stella felt no pity for the boy. He terrified her. "Absolutely not. It is not our place to interfere." Becka shook her head, disbelieving. Her sister couldn't be so cruel. Stella gave her a look that said there would be no further discussion.

Little Phil put up his arms. "Uh Becka, uh uh Becka . . ." Becka swooped up the boy, the happy Phil waving enthusiastically at his mother as they left the room. Stella sat with her mouth open, struggling for an explanation. Becka must understand . . . How though when she didn't understand herself? What awful thing was it about the boy? That night she knelt and prayed she'd never know.

It snowed on Monday morning. She liked the stillness, pretending that God covered the sleeping ground with a white blanket. Phil sat on the parlor's braided rug and played with a cloth turkey Becka had made him for Thanksgiving, using for the fan of feathers, scraps of different colors she brought home from Miss Edna's Millenary & Ladies Apparel where she was employed as a seamstress.

At seven in the morning, Stella was alone as she sat at her mother's oak table, a table large enough to seat twelve. Its planks were flush, and the surface kept smooth with ceaseless care. It sat in the middle of the kitchen, the largest room in the house, a two-story L-shaped structure. A one-story addition of a sewing room and extra bedroom extended the lower floor. Built by Bobbo, the addition was a wedding present for her and Arthur, but Becka claimed the new bedroom, its privacy appealing to her need for an existence separate from her sister's. Much to Stella's relief, Bobbo's bachelor days were ending. He was marrying Dora, Sheriff Gibbs's niece, a match she approved. Dora, a dark-haired girl of twenty-five, had a reserved manner, much preferable to Mayanne, Becka's choice for their brother. Mayanne's giddy laugh irritated Stella.

Allowing herself a few moments of doing nothing before she heated the iron and began the morning's chores, she sat quietly, her arms extended and her hands resting on the table's surface as if to embrace the memories that lingered in the faint grain. She remembered the arch of her mother's back as her mother stretched over the oak's planks, rolling out an expanse of dough.

When she was little, Stella's place was on a stool as she waited until it was time to carve out the rolls or biscuits using a cup, then carefully placing the circles of dough on the metal sheet. The day that she first used the rolling pin, smoothing out an even plane of dough, her mother clapped, puffs of white flour shooting from her hands like it was a magic spell. Her mother had taken the rolling pin and lightly tapped Stella on each shoulder.

"I dub you Queen Stella Bella."

Stella, who was eleven at the time, frowned. "But Mama, that's for a knight. A queen has a crown."

Her mother, whose beautiful face at thirty-one was marked by fine lines that would soon deepen into creases, laughed. "Never mind, Stella Bella, we earn that crown. God sees to it that we get it when we go to heaven."

Bobbo looked more like their mother, tall with light brown hair. Stella had her father's blond hair, broad features and stocky build, as did Becka. Becka, however, inherited her mother's optimism and good nature. The oak table and its memories of her mother were enough for Stella. Her mother's table was Stella's refuge.

Stella relaxed and admired the newest addition to her collection of thimbles, a delicate white China with blue windmills from Holland. Three raps sounded on the kitchen door. Three raps meant Mrs. Collins. Sighing, Stella placed the thimble on a small shelf with the others and lifting the latch, pulled on the door.

"Soooo you're t'home! I made some fudge last night." Mrs. Collins trilled the words as she handed Stella a bundle of crocheted blankets. Stamping the snow from her unlaced boots, the old woman tossed her frayed overcoat on a hook before placing a covered dish on the kitchen table. Inside the bundle was an ancient terrier. Pal was the neighbor's only companion since the death of her son, Davey. Mrs. Collins removed her hunter's cap, freeing strings of white hair drooping from an indifferent wad pinned high on the back of her head.

The old woman's mouth was trembling; there was something to tell. The neighbor pulled up the rocker with the side of her boot and flopping into the seat and spreading her knees, she shimmied in to get comfortable. Stella heated water for tea while the old woman rocked, her arthritic fingers stroking Pal. His paws quivering limply, Pal rested in the crook of her arm like a newborn. The chair tipped gently back and forth as the octogenarian delivered her gossip. The two drifters, she announced, were staying.

"Where are they sleeping?" Stella's heart sank; she had hoped they moved on to the next town. Pal gummed a cookie, and the crumbs fell to the floor. The dustpan was ready the moment they left.

Ignoring Pal's dribbles, Mrs. Collins continued. "Well sir, I don't know, but I heard that they turned down several invites of sheds and porches." The old woman loved a mystery. Seeing a willing audience in Stella, Mrs. Collins leaned forward, revealing gums as toothless as Pal's and mouthed each word to emphasize its value. "The story I heard . . . is that him and the boy don't want to feel obliged lest it lead to 'mis-under-stand-ings.'" Her filmy eyes glistening with expectation, she leaned forward in the rocker. Stella shook her head, unable to utter a word. Mrs. Collins frowned. Some folks were just slower than others.

"What do you think he meant?" Her trilled question went flat with impatience. The limp strings of hair vibrated as Mrs. Collins, waiting for an answer, or at the very least, a reaction to her news, was frustrated.

Hopelessness came in waves. Stella shook her head again as she gripped the edge of the table while her other handheld the kettle. Pal broke the impasse with a feeble whine. Defeated, the woman sighed, "Dear lord, baby has to go." The old white terrier emitted a low groan.

Ignoring the kettle, Mrs. Collins splayed her feet, rose from the rocker with a grunt and grabbed her cap. Pal's head covered, his black nose poked out of the blanket as the neighbor left, oblivious to the stricken look on Stella's face. She sank down on a kitchen stool, despair overwhelming her.

ELEVEN

PATTY

This part was sad because of that creep who lied about John. Another creep, not Bernie.

Oh, Patty. I left him. I should have—

You can't change it now. It's okay. Maybe we can find John and you can say . . . you wish you didn't leave. okay?

It can't be fixed.

I'll ask Gram.

A Tuesday

Redhill, Ohio

1961

John and Nora married two months later and in another six, Nora was pregnant. With their combined salaries, they were able to rent a two-bedroom bungalow with a tiny backyard. John didn't know how he felt about becoming a father. Baby Emma's arrival in the fall of 1962 overwhelmed him. Nora arranged for Dee, the landlady to care for the infant, and she went back to work at the Redhill Convalescent Home.

Though Nora's duties at the convalescent home increased, baby Emma was a happy toddler. The baby loved them all: her parents, Dee, and Nora's elderly patients who vied to hold her when Nora brought her to visit, letting the little girl give hugs and wet baby kisses to withered cheeks.

The day John's fate was sealed and that of his child and grandchildren fell on a Tuesday. John was finishing his twelve-hour shift as the supervisor in charge of deliveries when Greg showed up in the cramped office and shoved aside boxes filled with holiday dishes. John was using them as a doorjamb until it was their turn on the floor. As he shut the door, Greg's long face was devoid of his usual cockiness. His Adam's apple slid up and down his neck as he swallowed back a wad of emotion.

"Watch it; those break easy." John wasn't in the mood for Greg's problems. He had been doing damage control for weeks after Greg's last fiasco of leaving the back of a truck open while taking a long lunch.

The load's treasures included high-end women's accessories, perfumes, sets of toiletries, as well as an assortment of blue jeans. Two vagrants were helping themselves when John stepped out into the alley for a quick cigarette. Mrs. Desimone couldn't abide smoking within the store. It was then that John seriously considered firing Greg for good.

"John, I don't see what I'm gonna do if you don't help me." It was close to eight at night. Tired and wishing desperately that he had been able to escape Greg's frantic gaze, John answered him tersely.

"It'll have to wait," he said.

To John's great dismay, Greg burst into tears. "I don't know why I did it," he said. "I took something. I was so angry about h-how I never get a break . . . I guess I just lost . . .

"What?" John asked warily, "What did you take?"

Greg sighed, "A Philco."

"A new one?" John was concerned. The new Philcos were to be part of a window display and the absence of one detected immediately. "Where is it now?" If it was replaced before the scheduled display, some explanation might be grudgingly accepted. John would decide how to terminate Greg's employment when everything was back where it belonged.

The thought of Greg in prison didn't trouble John, but the distraught man in front him moved his innately decent soul. "You stupid son of a bitch. I should just let you clean up your own mess. I got enough going on in my life without your sorry shit," John told him. Greg winced.

Then John said the words that changed his life: "Let's go get it."

TWELVE

PATTY

Marlene used to be called Hildy. Hildy was a funny little kid who I knew in the orphanage.

Can we talk about the orphanage? I want to know what happened.

We will, but now I know who John was, you should know all of it.

Okay Patty, you know best.

Marlene
Redhill, Ohio
September 1960

For many years, Marlene had dreamed of owning a bookstore in a small town. She imagined the rhythm of everyday life, a slower pace than the frenetic urban classroom she had battled for thirty years. Instead, what she found in Redhill was something less tranquil, more guarded, a disquieting sense of . . . what? She had pictured front porches, fireflies, pleasant evenings talking gossip with neighbors, the children on their bikes, playing on the sidewalks ... picnics, casseroles, perhaps an older bachelor, attractive, lonely, waiting for someone to take afternoon walks while discussing Dickens and J. D. Salinger.

Instead, Marlene, the girl who prided herself on her good sense and high spirits, spent her evenings alone watching the television she swore she'd never buy, sipping glass after glass of white wine as slowly as she could manage. God it was lonely! It hurt to stare through the shop window or walk-through town seeing the serious, often listless faces that belonged to the citizens of Redhill.

What was wrong? It was as if the town itself were melancholy, not even that, more like an absence of feeling, not for the enjoyment of life's pleasures nor the endurance of its pain. No Welcome Wagon greeted her when she arrived; no friendly busybodies to talk to her about the history that mattered, gossip.

The day she hired John, Marlene was carrying a heavy box of paperbacks from her Chevy through the back door of her shop. She didn't notice the truck until it she heard the blast of a horn and a man shouting, "Jesus, lady, watch where you're goin." The load of books began to slide as she turned to see who yelled so rudely, the cardboard box splitting, sending the rest tumbling to the dirt and gravel. "Need help?" asked someone.

"Sure do," she said as she crouched on her haunches, reaching for her paperbacks, their fragile covers splayed and vulnerable.

"That Raymond Chandler, grab it would you please!" She pointed at a book that stood, its pages fanned out as it landed preventing it from falling into a mud puddle. She was on her knees, her lively brown eyes dominating her elfin face as she scanned the alley. At sixty, fine wrinkles traced the corners of her eyes, while deeper lines etched near her patrician nose. It was in her mouth the pain sat. In the press of her thin lips, grief refused to leave, forbidding any weakness.

Marlene's hair, dyed a copper red, was set in bangs and a pageboy, a look that remained unchanged since the age of twenty-four. A cotton scarf kept the bangs from falling in her eyes. If he had seen her gathering the scattered books, Hugo would have said, as he did in those first New York days when they explored Central Park, "Hildy means business." Her slender body, with just a hint of a bird's pouch and the legs still eye-catching, crouched low as she collected the few remaining mysteries. She wore pressed blue capris and a man's shirt, the legacy of a love affair ten years back.

"Can I get the box for you?" A hand reached down, tucking the Raymond Chandler securely in the center as the other hand started to lift the damaged box from her grasp, carefully holding its split edges. Marlene saw a pair of worn brown work boots standing to her right and looked up to see a young man in his twenties, his dark brown hair unevenly cut. He must do it himself she thought.

The attractive face, the nose bent from being broken, was intelligent. His blue eyes warned against asking too many questions. Rolled up torn-at-the-knee jeans and a plaid work shirt, stained with shadows of grease and specks of paint defined him as a day laborer, but Marlene knew promise when she saw it. Thirty-two years teaching for the City of New York told her in an instant.

"Sorry about the box. Greg's an asshole." He helped her stack the books on the crowded counter. Pointing to a shelf near the single door, whose thick pane glass read *Marlene's Mystery Re-Reads*, he said, "You might want to move that. It's easy for some people to forget about paying and walk out." She was annoyed with herself, thinking of what could have happened. She made a decision. She would need an extra hand after all and the budget allowed for it.

"So Greg's an asshole. Is he your boss?"

The young man's face broke into a genuine smile as he laughed. "Lady." He studied the pane glass. "Marlene? The thought of Greg being anyone's boss is a little scary. Greg is hopeless."

"And you? What hopes do you have?" She regretted the questions as she said it.

His eyes grew distant. "I get by."

Despite the minimal salary and long hours, it did not take her long to convince him to take the job. The mystery for Marlene was how such a bright young man as John could be languishing in

Redhill. He had never graduated from high school. "I left at sixteen—had to—my mother, she was . . ."

John's alcoholic mother, Emily was dead. Before the brutal murder of her older sister, Emily was adopted and spent her childhood as a servant. "She couldn't seem to free herself from all that happened. Sometimes I would hear her cry in sleep, something about being sorry."

Eight when his father disappeared, John drifted, rarely staying in a job more than a few months. Why hadn't he left town? Had he looked for his father? "No," he said; the subject closed.

The remoteness in John's eyes began to leave the day several copies of Mickey Spillane's titles had sold. Marlene was not a fan, but she knew Mike Hammer was good for business. The bell that announced a customer had been ringing most of the day. John had suggested putting up displays of the latest Mike Hammer in the shop's window. She resisted the urge to praise his ingenuity too much. He sat on a stool at the counter while Marlene went through receipts and read letters. There was a new one from her niece Gertie.

Like Marlene's brother, Hugo, Gertie was a worrier. Aunt Hildy (as Marlene was known to her loving brother and assorted nieces and nephews) should come home. Gertie insisted she come home, at least for a visit. She had promised her dad, that she would look out for her Aunt Marlene.

Marlene glanced at the counter and saw John reading *I the Jury*. A moment of sadness settled in her. *Oh Hugo we stick together you said, you swore it the day after Patty died.* "It'll be okay," her brother had whispered, and it was.

The orphanage, the Drudge and poor Patty were in the past. Except, the answer to the mystery of Bernie Baker was in Redhill. "Hildy—let it go . . . you weren't there." Hugo would plead. She did let it go until 1945 when she lost her nineteen-year-old son Henry to a sniper in Okinawa.

There was nothing left but the mystery. Her husband Parker's death from leukemia left her with a young son. Teaching supported her and Henry. Since Henry's death in Okinawa, she had spent Saturdays at libraries, searching through microfilms of old newspapers. She knew about the cabin, but nothing after the orphanage and the bakery. The accounts were vague. What happened? Who was Bernie? How did he end up with Baker?

She remembered Hugo's face that January morning in 1960. After his wife's death in '56, Hugo spent Sundays at her apartment with pastries and the newspaper. She made coffee and they shared news. Hugo insisted that she get the front page first. Then her eye caught an article on the third page. 'Arrested! Cleveland's Notorious Crusher.' She handed the paper to Hugo. "They found him."

Her brother's hands began to shake as he stared at the photograph of an old man in handcuffs. Then Hugo began to cry. "Promise me, Hildy, you'll stay away from him!" He started gasping for air; his thinning hair falling in his eyes. "H-Hildy please . . . Hildy. He's a monster, oh Hildy . . ."

She promised, but Hugo died six months later. Nothing was left but the mystery of Bernie. She tucked away Hugo's fear. He was gone, and the ache of missing him was too much. Besides, Redhill was the perfect spot for her bookstore.

She folded the letter, put it back in the envelope, and opened the desk drawer. A relic from her teaching days, the desk still held pieces of white chalk. She always used white chalk, never yellow.

She saw John eating his sandwich as he read. The angle of the overhead light in the main room cast his shadow on the books resting against the far wall. She made a mental note to bring him some better books. Another kid needed rescuing, Hugo had laughed whenever she found a gem, an undiscovered genius slouching in the back of her classroom. I'll bring them tomorrow, she promised herself.

Mysteries of Ohio

Whatever melancholy and disappointment Marlene felt lifted as the days went by. She saw John leave each evening, a book tucked under his arm. He said little other than a good night, but she knew he saw himself a little differently. Hope had entered his life. Maybe he saw it was time to leave Redhill. She knew there was little future in staying. She herself planned to leave as soon as she had found what she had come for, the truth about Baker and the shadow cast over her life and Hugo's.

Redhill's library had the requisite records of births and deaths, weddings, divorces, petty thefts, all recorded in the small newspaper, THE REDHILL BUCKEYE, but she found no stories about Bernie Baker, the child. During a trip to Cleveland, ostensibly to acquire more paperbacks by seeking out garage and estate sales, but in reality, wanting to break away from the town's pervasive darkness, she wandered into an antique shop where she happened to glance at a thin gray hardback, tossed indifferently on top of a potbellied stove. *Mysteries of Ohio written by James Beckwith* was printed in magenta across the cover. Scanning the Table of Contents, she saw that Chapter IV was entitled "Redhill, Ohio: The Murder of Becka Tobin, a Victim of Satan Worshipers."

Rather than feeling her usual excitement at digging up a valuable nugget, Marlene was apprehensive. The clerk, a tiny woman of eighty, caught Marlene's eye. "May I help you dear?" Marlene felt like she did when she was fifteen and a clerk had caught her shoplifting a lipstick. The shame stayed with her, though she escaped with a warning. In this case, the shame was realizing that she wanted desperately to pretend she had not seen the book. She decided to buy a piece of smoked glass and call it a day.

"Nope, not this lady," she said to herself. Hildegarde Marlene doesn't back down until she has an answer. "How much?" she asked casually, trembling slightly. The old woman looked at her closely, wondering what she was missing.

Peering at the book in Marlene's hand, she said, "Ten dollars."

"I don't think so." Marlene snapped, turning to walk out.

"Okay, okay—five." Marlene kept walking. "One! Low as I'm gonna go."

"Fine". Marlene's triumph at winning deflated as she realized that she was locked into learning whatever secrets the book held.

Hildy
Redhill, Ohio
1961

Two days later, Marlene sat on her patio. She lingered over her coffee, as she read the few sheets of local news that came twice a week in the Redhill Buckeye. As she folded the paper, her eye landed on a name.

"Bernard Baker, The Crusher Linked to Suicide of Guard Ron West, former Trooper credited with his capture . . ." Reluctantly she unfolded the paper. The photograph showed the same photograph she had discovered in New York, the one that reduced Hugo to tears.

A man in his seventies led out of a building in handcuffs. He looked small, frail, and he was surrounded by uniformed police. Nonetheless, there was something. Was it because of what she thought she knew? The grainy photograph couldn't hide his remoteness, the expectant smile. The eyes were pulled by sharply creased folds that wandered the length of his long thin face, their disturbing lack of color rendering them pale arcs. Wisps of white hair gave the impression of harmlessness, the fragility of age until you looked at those eyes.

He's been here all along. Why haven't I tried to confront him, ask him what happened. What did you do to my brother that followed him for the rest of his life? The paper fell to the concrete. Marlene was always up before six, and yet this morning, she felt so tired . . . It was nearly noon and starting to get warm—the sun finding its way through the oak tree that provided shade. She told herself that there wasn't any need to hurry; the prison was a mere eighteen minutes from her driveway.

"Okay," she thought, "let's go have a look."

The Prison

Marlene turned onto the long driveway that led to the prison gates. Her note pad with a list of questions sat next to her, but she had little clue of what she would ask. *The heart . . .* The thought caught her unprepared and she struggled to break free . . . *too much pain I can't . . . The heart . . . poor Becka . . . what they did . . .*

She stopped the car as it approached the chain link fence, interrupted by guard stations on either side. She could see the prison guards take note of her, waiting for why she had come. She had little to tell them. She just didn't know. Tears, that had been waiting patiently, sprang to life and began to pour out. "Nah nah nah," she sobbed, shaking her head.

She sat in her car, observed by the guards who were considering whether to ignore her or make her leave the area so that they could continue their games of solitaire and crosswords. Then, she came a decision. She could no longer bear what was hurting her so.   It was time to tell John (her one regret about leaving) he was out of a job.

THIRTEEN

PATTY

What happened in this part makes me feel bad, especially since John was once your little boy. He was my nephew. Does that make me a grownup?

I don't know if I can see this. I wish I could have come for him then. It was only one of many times I wasn't there.

We'll find him; don't worry; you can tell him. Do you want to find Gram?

No.

Time

Redhill, Ohio Correctional Facility

1963

In prison, time is everything. Doing time, killing time, making time count. From the first days of his four-year sentence for stealing a nineteen-inch Philco television set from the storeroom of Desimone's Emporium, John Arnold had decided to make it count.

He passed through the metal gates of Redhill Correctional in 1963, promising Nora he would return to her a better man. Other than an overnight stay, years before in what passed as the juvenile section of the small Redhill jail, John had no idea what life would be like when cut off from everything, having to face an existence, where backing down could mark you, and staring too long or a thoughtless insult could mean certain death.

The Redhill police had been watching as John helped Greg load the set into the back of John's car. In horror, John listened as Greg blamed it all on him, saying that John had threatened to fire him if he hadn't agreed to help. John's delinquent past made his denials fall on deaf ears and he found himself sentenced to from two to four years at Redhill Correctional. Greg received probation.

Nora's face was in John's mind each night he tried to fall asleep. Her eyes filled with tears as he tried to explain what happened. She smiled when he promised her he would come back to her a better man, promising that they would take Stella and move to California. They would move and leave all the sadness and loss that had plagued both of them in this sorry little town.

The despair that pervades prison life gripped him, causing the anger that he carried with him to well up and choke him. John had promised Nora and as the shock of prison gave way to acceptance of his new life, he saw a way to keep his promise and vent his anger by writing letters about prison conditions. The degraded cells, in some cases, designed for one inmate, but bunking two, were dismal, consisting of a sink, toilet, a desk and a thin mattress. Ray Gibbs, his bunkmate, who was serving time for fraud, advised John to just wait it out and then leave it behind by moving out west. "Don't waste your energy, my friend. Enemies in here, you don't need." Ray, a gambler, took no chances. When inside, Ray counseled, it was best to keep a low profile.

While Ray fought boredom by doing pencil and charcoal drawings, committing to cheap paper skillfully rendered images of prison life, John persisted in writing letters to pass the time. Sometimes they were to Nora; occasionally he'd drop a line to Marlene. Often, he felt unable to free himself from the rage that plagued him and he would stare out the window of his cell. A pine tree stood in the courtyard. Frequently, a crow sat on a lower branch, as if it were waiting for something. After watching it for several minutes, he asked Ray to come to the window. Was it his imagination or was the bird's behavior strange? The thing seemed frozen, unmoving, the cocked head with its reddish eye staring back at him. Ray shook his head and shuddered, advising him to ignore it.

Finally, John decided to ignore it and he continued to write strongly worded complaints addressed to the governor, the warden, state senators—to "the powers that be." He had been wronged, not just by Greg or by the society that had too easily decided his guilt, but most of all, by whatever "power" decided to make living so hard, and so he continued to write.

Beyond the cell, within the prison cell which had once been the inside of a cabin, beings gathered to nibble the despair that seeped through the pores of the rippling membrane.

John was right; there was a power that made living hard. It would soon be upon him.

FOURTEEN

PATTY

This is before the prison when they lived in New York. Bernie was just a weird little baby rat. Crispin was trying to get away from him.

It's out of order. We should have seen this before the prison.

Don't complain. We see 'em as I find "em.

Okay.

The Knife
New York
August 1894

Mr. O'Brien was singing as the baby wailed. It had been crying for an hour, when eight-year-old Charlie ran in with the bottle. "Bless ya boyo," said the relieved Mr. O'Brien. He sat at the kitchen table, holding the six-month infant, jiggling him on his knee, to no avail. After taking a swig of the cheap whiskey, the burly man funneled drops of it into the baby's mouth. Soon, blessedly, there was quiet.

Sitting near a pile of laundry, which was abandoned when the landlady left to do errands and engage in rounds of gossip, Crispin knew soon, he would go mad. Bernie was at a window, staring down at the courtyard. The boy seemed indifferent to the baby's piercing cry. Shunned by the other children, Bernie showed no desire for their company. Other than an occasional demand, the boy rarely spoke, but spent most of the two weeks they had been "guests," standing at the kitchen window. Crispin would hear him whispering at night, speaking to . . . better not to know. Sometimes there would be a giggle.

"Move on," a voice hissed. "We're waiting." Crispin always covered his ears.

The tiny closet and pile of rags that constituted the "guest room" in the O'Brien flat cost three dollars a week. Crispin was used to slums, dirty, crowded, filled with the smell of unwashed bodies, refuse and the constant cries of babes. The New York Irish slum, its floors of crowded rooms, with the small courtyard and fetid air, was no worse than the slums of London. What made it unbearable was the August heat. Sleep was impossible. He must get back. Take his chances and go back to London. Hopeless here. His best shirt clung to his body. He reeked of body odor and O'Brien's whiskey.

He'd used the same, reliable plan, not too grand to start. Work your way to the estates. Select the well-to-do, those moving up, the ambitious. "Professor Theosopho, my card," he said. "An urgent

The Demon Rift

message" for the "lady of the house." He'd done his homework, eavesdropping in the shops, chatting with the nannies, bits of useful gossip. He always dealt with women. Servants took his card and shut the door. Rude of them. Something was spinning away. His charm, his ability to persuade, where was it? There was Bernie. It would never be the same, as long as there was Bernie. Hopeless.

Last night, he had waited. The boy was sleeping. Crispin had studied him, making sure. He moved past the snoring family, opening the door, careful of the creak. Shoes in hand, he made his way down the cluttered stairs and into the street. Taking a deep breath, he began to run, stopping to put on his shoes several blocks from the tenement. He ran laughing, freedom in his lungs. *Oh, the glory! I beat the little bastard,* whispered with every stride.

He saw the pub. Perfect! Must celebrate and mark the occasion. Plans began to spring up. He'd go to Boston or Philadelphia. Money, lots of it there. He'd relieve a few citizens of their purses. Dead or alive, he didn't care. Better dead maybe. Someone had to pay, pay for what he'd been through, what was done to him by that hideous boy, that creature.

Must have new clothes, dress the part. He spent what was left, no need for rent. He wouldn't be returning to the O'Brien hell. The dark pub smelled of whiskey and cigars. Soothed by familiar surroundings, he remembered that last cigar on the ship. There will be more, he promised himself. His image in the bar's mirror, made him weep.

Thank God, he escaped. Drinking the last of his rent, he considered the patrons. Was there any money there? A couple of ancient blokes in the corner . . . Those standing, laborers, too large, too strong to risk, especially in his weakened state. He saw that the older men had not ordered in an hour, no money. Best to investigate another place, area with more prosperous drinkers, maybe a woman. He'd left the pub whistling, ready to begin his new life, when he saw the knife. It lay in the gutter near a small wagon. Not very large, from a butcher shop, he guessed.

He needed a weapon. He wondered how sharp it was. A sharp knife was always useful. He picked it up and scraped his thumb along the edge. Sharp enough to kill quickly? He should test it. The urge to cut came unexpected, and before he could help himself, the knife etched a shallow path on his throat. Not enough, he should slice his own throat, cut through the artery, and if possible, go right to the bone. Then he would know for sure.

His eyes fixed on the shadow of a cart resting under a streetlamp. Crispin studied the shadow outlines of the empty cart. Its extended poles were dark fingers pointing at him. The poles were wrapped in an indifferent tangle of leather straps, waiting for some poor beast. He'd be dead if he thought too much. Part of the shadow shifted. *Bernie!* Like a predator stalking its prey, the boy moved closer. Crispin held the knife, his thumb against the bleeding skin. He wept, the blood trickling from his wound.

"Please lad, don't make me . . ."

"Leave me and you'll finish it . . ." The demon boy's soft voice left no doubt.

So far . . . I'd gone so far . . . surely, I'd lost him. How did the monster know? More careful now . . . Mustn't ever assume . . .

He knew better than to leave Bernie behind, now. The baby was quiet. Thank God for that. *I must go back. How can I?*

An insistent voice interrupted his thoughts. "Seamus, did the housing inspector call? Did ya remember ta tell him about the rot under the window?" The lady of the house was home.

Mrs. O'Brien's bark was worse than the baby's bawling. Waking from his slumber, Seamus slapped the table. To his horror (and Crispin's), the whiskey bottle wobbled and began to fall. Four–year-old Kathleen ran across the room and caught the bottle, saving its contents. "Tank you, me lovely Kathleen!" Seamus's relief at the rescue restored his good mood.

"E'thall right Da", the little girl lisped as she skipped her rope out to play. The baby whimpered. His father dripped more whiskey into the tiny smacking lips. Between drips, the infant babbled da-da-da, flexing his plump fingers through the mat of hair on his father's arm.

"Don't make a drunk out of me child, ya villain!" Mrs. O'Brien's pregnant state made her particularly irritable. The sound of clomping feet and high-pitched yells intruded as several small boys tumbled through the open door. "Out! All o ya."

The boys laughed as they evaded her blows, dodging and arching their backs.

Crispin saw Charlie swipe the jar of pennies sitting on the counter. He suppressed the urge to inform her of the theft. He had planned to take the pennies. Perhaps he could acquire them more easily from the boys.

"Savages!" she screamed as they all ran out. She slammed the door. The baby stirred, but quickly settled down, joining his father in a drunken nap.

Muttering a litany of curses, Mrs. O'Brien continued the laundry. Crispin wondered if he could get her to wash his shirt and then thought better of it. She would ask about the rent; better not draw attention.

"I want the wood," Bernie announced. Crispin turned toward the window. The boy was looking at him, his spindly body posed in a determined stance.

Bent over a washtub, the landlady was scrubbing the stains from a shirt. She glared at her husband, who was snoring, the baby nestled in his beefy arm. Crispin felt a panic. Whatever "the wood" was, Crispin knew he'd better find it. He studied the woman. Did she feel that terrifying chill? The boy radiated threat. Slapping the scrubbing board, she continued a diatribe on her husband's faults. Odd, that she isn't afraid of the brat. Crispin knew that Bernie inspired fear in most people—adults and children alike. Mrs. O'Brien seemed immune.

"The wood, dear boy? What kind of wood?" Crispin asked timidly.

"Trees, stupid Crispin, I want trees." Bernie turned back toward the window.

"Of course, lad, whatever you say—right away then." Crispin heaved a sigh. They were leaving to find trees. What trees? He wondered. Knowing the futility of asking "why," Crispin gathered the little that remained of his possessions.

A few minutes later, he was ready. Bernie sat on the pile of rags, waiting. "We must be quiet," Crispin whispered. He peered through the curtain of their room and watched for the right moment.

"Now, stupid Crispin, we leave now!" Bernie shouted. The boy shot Crispin a look of lethal impatience.

Her head whipping around, Mrs. O'Brien saw the suitcase in Crispin's hand. "Oh, God, Bernie!" Crispin said, "We're in for it!"

Taking a deep breath, Mrs. O'Brien released a bellow, and then rushed to block their way by tossing a pair of sudsy bloomers in their path. "Thief! Help! It's thieves!"

Still napping, his head resting on the table, Seamus's drunken growl urged, "Fer God's sakes, woman, let the pair of 'em go. I want ta sleep!"

The baby began to wail. Mrs. O'Brien picked up washtub and threw it at Crispin, splashing water, but missing her target. She searched for a more accurate weapon. The whiskey bottle hurtled across the room. It barely missed Crispin, but the remaining spirits cascaded down the doorframe. "Bernie!" Crispin shouted, "The woman's mad! Run!" Flinging the door open, Crispin hurried down the stairs. Bernie followed.

The whiskey gone, Crispin heard Seamus give a distraught cry. His wife continued, "The rent! ya bastard! The rent!" Her spouse's roar silenced Mrs. O'Brien. The sounds of slaps and thumps followed them down the dark passage.

They fled through the courtyard, the simmering stench of the nearby stables greeting them. Bernie stopped and pointed to a group of ragged children playing within the enclosure. "I want that."

Crispin strained to see the object of Bernie's gaze. "Of, course, dear boy. What is it that you want?"

"Spinning," Bernie said. Seeing the boys gathered around a spinning top, Crispin grabbed the wooden top. No one followed them as they made their way to the street and began their journey out of New York City.

The Glass Man Filled
Connecticut
September 1894

There were eyes. Mrs. O'Brien perched on the kitchen table. "The rent the rent, where's the rent," she squawked. Her head was bobbing and swaying as she screamed at Bernie. Crispin wondered if she was going to eat Bernie. He hoped so. Bernie was skipping rope. The eyes floated around her head, like a halo. Then they turned into red flames.

Smoke was coming through the floor, shapes forming. Was he dead? Was this hell? "You'll go down, if you're not careful," Aunt Meg warned. Maybe she was right. He heard laughing and saw it was Bernie. Mrs. O'Brien became a black bird, and was flying . . .

"More. You must make some more." Crispin opened his eyes. Above him, the sky was between the wood planks of the bridge. How long had he napped? He sat up on his elbows and judged the bridge's shadow. Two hours. His stomach ached. It had been more than a day since their last meal, the old man's coffee, and corn bread.

Tiny insects were swarming an inch above his face, landing on him to take an occasional bite. The shade of the bridge gave relief from the hellish heat, but there was no refuge from the tiny pests. Bernie was standing, waiting for him to answer. Crispin considered suicide.

"More, Bernie?" His body ached from their weeks of travel. The "Professor" had become a vagrant traveling the roads and wooded paths of Connecticut's countryside, stealing what he could, too dispirited to do more than survive. Bernie trudged silently behind. The strain of the boy's control weighed heavily. "More what, might I ask?" Crispin was close to tears.

"Spinning" said Bernie. He gestured to a sack lying at his feet. Crispin recognized it as the old man's. They'd seen smoke the previous morning, before the heat made walking such a torment. The smell of coffee grew stronger as they traced its source. A half a mile from the road, they found it. Crouched over his breakfast, an old man in dirty overalls hummed as he stoked a fire where the coffee was ready for a battered tin cup. The cup sat by a burlap sack nestled on the ground. Sitting next to the cup, was a pan filled with fresh corn bread. The old man was alone.

Anyone else about? Crispin scanned the area and waited for a moment. Reaching for the pan of cornbread, the old man's back turned. Crispin struck him with a brick, splitting his skull but dodging the spray of blood, which splattered away from him and more importantly, away from the cornbread.

With the body hidden under branches and after sharing the cornbread with Bernie, Crispin investigated the sack. A few pieces of wood, nothing of value. He left it behind, the wood spilling out on the ground. When did Bernie pick it up? What did he mean, "more"? More what? What had the sack to do with "more"? Bernie stood waiting. Reluctantly, Crispin emptied it. Under all the wood were some excellent knives, suitable for carving, a leather strap for sharpening, and cloths meant to smooth and polish. The pieces of wood were of varying types and sizes.

Bernie pointed to the wooden top in his hand. "More."

Crispin's wariness blossomed into terror. His voice shaking, he said, "Of course, anything m'lad, but I've no experience making such things."

"More," Bernie whispered gently as one would talk to a small child. Taking a knife, Crispin selected a piece of wood and hands trembling began to work, carefully shaving it.

He worked through the rest of the day and into the night. Bernie sat on the ground and watched. By morning, it had taken the shape of a top. "Ah" cooed Bernie. With that, Crispin found that his hands were no longer his to control. He watched, amazed as they expertly worked the wood's crude surface, quickly smoothing the rough planes. Grooves appeared and what looked to be symbols.

By the afternoon, as they sat beneath the bridge, the top was finished. Bernie took it quickly. As the boy spun it, Crispin saw images of birds in flight, alighting in a tree and flying off again. "Good Crispin" the boy cooed. Then to his surprise, Crispin felt a marvelous surge of pleasure. No longer tired or hungry, he felt happy. In that moment, his stunted heart felt love for the monster who had enslaved him.

FIFTEEN

Keep Her Safe

Desimone's Emporium

Redhill, Ohio

December 1900

As Christmas drew closer, Becka became obsessed with the boy's welfare. Silent at dinner, she went to her room afterwards, saying a terse "Good night." Mary Kate took Becka's place in the parlor, working on her pillowcase, an embroidered image of a farmhouse with chickens and a small girl feeding them in the foreground.

Becka's absence wasn't discussed, but Phil would knock on Becka's door every evening. The door opened to let him in. At seven-thirty each night, Arthur waited as Becka handed the sleeping Phil to him. Drawing the quilt over Phil as the two-year old snored, Stella remembered being alone, a sixteen-year -old caring for her small sister and twelve-year old Bobbo. Becka's four-year old face, the blue eyes filled with loss . . . grieving was a luxury. Keep her safe—hadn't she always?

Finally, Stella agreed to attend a special event, hosted by Desimone's, where Mr. Baker would display items, designed especially for the coming holiday. Of course, the boy would be there too and she dreaded seeing him. At ten on the Saturday morning before Christmas, Bonnie, their patient mare pulled the wagon along the muddied road into town.

Her arms folded around a box containing a fresh baked cake. Becka sat on the padded seat next to Stella. Unlike other trips into town, Becka did not chatter in her customary guileless manner Stella found annoying but endearing.

Neither woman spoke as the wagon's wheels rolled steadily toward the town, seen as swirls of smoke from the other side of a hill where Redhill lay, its name the result of a brief but deadly property dispute between farmers a hundred years earlier. Becka fixed her gaze on the pines of the distant woods, while Stella focused on the old mare's deliberate gait. Besides the wagon, the only sound was the wind, low and mournful then wailing with intensity. The strong gusts caused both women to grip their seats. Now and then she heard the moos of cows as the animals searched the ground for what was left of autumn.

With the first glimpse of Wilson's Blacksmith & Carriages, a cluster of sheds and stables on the edge of Redhill, the wind roared in an assault so fierce Bonnie neighed and shuddered as the sisters braced against each other for balance. The frigid air pummeled the barriers of woolen scarves, coats, and mittens, seeming to warn, *turn back.* "You're making too much of this," Stella whispered to herself.

Wrapped in her gray coat and knitted scarf, Becka sat quietly. *Why do I fear him?* Stella kept turning the question in her mind as the wagon slowed.

As they came to the barbershop, she heard laughter several yards away. The door to Desimone's opened. Becka gathered her skirts, slipped her arm under the boxed cake, and left the wagon without a word, disappearing into Desimone's before Stella reached for her purse. Reluctant to follow, she hesitated before leading Bonnie into narrow shed. Stella saw a hint of sun teasing the edges of clouds that were dusting the muddied streets. Soon, a layer of new snow would hide the deep tracks.

Stella was greeted by the scent of pinecones and cinnamon, coffee and tobacco, and peppermint, a mix of pleasant fragrances was one of the few things she liked about the Christmas season. She followed two older women as they hurried in, mindful of too much heat escaping from the potbellied stove that warmed the recently enlarged store. Surprising, she thought, Desimone's allowing Baker to use their store. Desimone's discouraged competition.

Dozens of eager folk milled about inspecting the newest merchandize, including a family of ceramic ducklings following their mother to a ceramic puddle. There were beautiful red and gold tins of oolong tea and from Europe, canisters of cocoa with pink and red roses painted on their glossy lids.

There now . . . she could see the back of the boy's blond head, the hair curving over his frayed collar, the jagged strands still in need of a cut. He sat cross-legged in a corner, among sacks of white flour. The child was staring at a wooden top, cocking his head as he turned it in his hand.

"If you saw how he neglects him . . ." Becka had said.

Stella began to doubt herself. What she felt had no logic. She would combat her fear with reality. Carol the pastor's wife was serving hot apple cider, tea and holiday cookies. As the woman passed by, she saw Becka whisper to her. Wearing a smile of Christian charity, Carol made her way around the guests, who clapped sporadically as Baker displayed a variety of finely crafted toys, ladies' accessories, knickknacks and keepsakes. Drawing as close as she dared, she found herself watching the wooden top in the boy's hand as his thin fingers caressed it, turned it, then stroked it. He seemed to be listening to . . . *was he cooing like a dove?*

The top began to spin, and Stella saw images of birds perched in trees, flying off, returning, and then flying off again. The boy's head went up. She panicked and looked away as she saw Carol moving toward him. She caught the joy on Becka's face as Becka poured cups of tea. Defiance in her eyes, Becka glanced at her. Stella decided she would pretend she didn't see; it was better not to acknowledge it. Turning away, she caught a glimpse of Carol pressing a ginger cookie into the boy's hand.

"Thankee, ma'am," he said.

Carol patted his head, the crosshatch of lines in her face becoming ropes as the woman's smile spanned even wider between the knots. "You're welcome, little man. Remember, Jesus loves you." Carol returned to the counter where Becka was refilling the sugar bowl. Stella saw them exchange glances, Becka's face flushed with excitement. Approving laughs broke out as Baker demonstrated a wooden monkey climbing a ladder. He had already sold several model ships, exquisite replicas of those on the Great Lakes.

The salesman's ingratiating voice irritated her. She began to think of excuses . . . maybe a cold coming on, or a headache. She would have to find some way of distracting Becka. Make her leave. Keep her safe. Keep her safe? She searched her troubled mind. Why did she think Becka was in danger?

Shards of ice surprised her, slicing through her breast, making their way to her hands and feet. Alarmed by the pain, she steadied herself. "Melt," she said. The pain left. Familiar hopelessness gripped her, deeper than when it had announced her mother's coming death. She looked toward the corner where the boy, Bernie, sat. *Only for an instant, I'll merely glance and look away . .* .

The boy was studying the cookie, nibbling its edges. He looked up. His eyes, why hadn't she noticed? His eyes were an odd yellow, almost colorless, cold. He smiled, his face pale and soulless as he turned to meet her gaze. *I hate you*, his eyes said.

She elbowed through the crowded store and taking Becka's arm, insisted they leave. Becka began to protest that she, Becka, was needed. "I need you more right now." Stella whispered as she handed Becka her coat. A terrible headache, she later explained. While pressing a cold cloth to her head, she forbade Becka to go near the boy. Becka demanded a reason. Stella would give none. Keep her safe. I'm afraid of him, she thought. Christmas was coming. She forced the fear from her mind.

Christmas Eve morning, mixing bowls, pie pans and long metal baking sheets for cookies and rolls crowded the oak table. She planned to complete the baking and to give the kitchen a scrub before preparing the evening's meal. A ham, courtesy of the West family and two laying hens well past their prime were waiting for their turn in the oven. She and Arthur had presented the Wests with several jars of excellent peaches, a mince pie and four-dozen chewy oatmeal cookies.

At a little after six a.m., Becka finished mixing the cookie dough and wrapping herself in her old gray coat, she hummed "O Come All Ye Faithful". Her attitude had much improved, and Stella was relieved to see her sister's sweet disposition come back to her.

"I'll be just a few minutes, Stella Bella, I'm off to check on Mrs. Collins."

With no family left but Pal, Mrs. Collins became a Caulkins at Christmas. She was puzzled when she saw Becka take a covered plate of cookies and tuck them inside her coat. She rolled the dough for piecrusts, making a mental list of all there was to do. More than the usual number of chores, pies to bake, an elaborate meal to prepare, not to mention the chickens. At 8:30, Becka had not returned.

Panicking, Stella hurried to the Collins home, a half mile away. The door of the white house swung back and forth, the wind unable to close it, blocked by the old woman's blood-soaked body. *Oh Becka,* she thought, as a flood of unwelcome possibilities began to wash over her.

Family portraits torn from the walls, the broken oval frames smeared with the blood, someone had tossed Pal's body onto the settee, a lace doily wrapped tight around the little dog's neck. Figurines that Mrs. Collins' dead son Davy a merchant marine had brought from the Orient were shattered against a wall papered with tranquil images of spring bouquets. Becka's coat, streaked with blood, was discarded on the upright piano.

As she ran out the door, her mind reeling with desperation, focused on organizing the search for Becka, she saw something in

Mrs. Collins' dead hand, a small wooden top, intricately carved with strange symbols and birds.

Stella Tobin Sees Magic
A Cabin near Redhill
December 24, 1900

The buckeyes began to nod, urging her on. The arctic wind rushed down from Canada, slamming ships sailing the restless Lake Erie, pushing through frozen Ohio woods. Layers of wool protected her but slowed her pace, making it hard to keep up. Was Becka warm? *Oh God, let her be warm! Think of something else!* She banished the image of Becka's frozen body . . . *Arthur and peppermints, he's slipping peppermints into stockings, Mary Kate's new doll, blocks, the alphabet blocks for Phil . . . The ring, the pearl's gray eye, what does it truly see?* "*I'll be just a few minutes, Stella Bella, going to check on Mrs. Collins.*"

Men were breaking through the door. She rushed toward the cabin; a crack echoed. A falling branch? No, a shot. The echo fading, she heard slaps like the sound of a leather strap hitting a hard surface then a crow cawing. Thunder shook snow from the trees.

A wail came from within the cabin, and she heard someone moaning. *Arthur!* She tried to steady herself as Bobbo blocked the doorway. He gripped her shoulder, but she waved him off. She knew she must see, and removing a glove, she dropped it on the dirt floor. Her calloused fingers closed on his wrist.

"Bobbo, it's our Becka. Let me pass."

Tears clung to his sandy lashes, as he let her enter the cabin.

Stella moved under the rotting wood of the cabin's doorsill, her eyes adjusting to the candlelight. A clutter of tools and old newspapers rested on the floor next to a crude wooden table, its uneven legs causing an upward slant. Rotting food, graying chunks of meat and greenish pieces of bread lay strewn like a hideous accident, the stench of death rising from it. Fearing she might faint, she put her hand over her nose and mouth.

She steadied herself again and saw the four deputies clustered together. No one met her gaze. Arthur sat on a bench near the four men. His hands cupped the sides of his head, as small whines came from behind his gritted teeth. She thought of little Phil, he sounds like Phil when Phil tumbled off the wagon . . . Something was on the far corner of the table, a round piece of reddish meat larger than the gray chunks; this was fresh and so moist, occasional drops of.

A heart . . . was it a pig's? Her feet were waking up; the warmth was painful. Where was Becka? She looked at the sheriff, the question on her face. He avoided her glance. Then slowly, Stella looked down.

The man Crispin was sprawled at their feet, his face bloodied by a wound that had taken the top of his head. Near the dead man, in the middle of a crudely drawn star, lay Becka. Arms bound, feet tethered, her body was chalk-white against the planks, except for its center. A red cavity oozed where Becka's heart had been.

Stella sank to her knees. Becka's heart? Why not someone else's sister lying here, murdered, not able to string popcorn or rock a little one to sleep? Stella drew a deep, slow breath and began to shriek. "Nah-nah-nah" she insisted, shaking her head.

"Oh yes . . ." sighed a voice. She opened her eyes to see the boy. He sat cross-legged, his crimson hands resting on his lap. A glistening red pool had formed from Becka's blood. It had spewed, hitting the tousled hair of her murderer. Red streams followed a path from his brow to his chin, where they hesitated before falling on his narrow chest and on to the rough planks. His eyes snared her, holding her. This boy, whose wretched state drew pity from Becka's soft bosom . . .

She struggled to break free of the boy's gaze. His eyes, the red pupils swelling becoming . . . Becka! There's Becka! *Stella saw her sister's face! The boy, his thin arm raised like a warrior brought the knife within an inch of Becka's naked breast. Becka was pleading, her mouth moving in a silent prayer.* The boy's eyelids fluttered. She was pulling away until *his eyes opened wide showing the dripping heart, held in his hand like a prized baseball!*

Grief pressed its claim, as Stella fell gently into madness, where Momma, Pa, little Bobbo, and Baby Becka waited for her on a spring day. As she drifted, the thought came to her . . . there *is* magic in the world . . . and it is dreadful.

SIXTEEN

PATTY

Poor nephew John. I wish I coulda helped. The monster was too strong.

Oh John, forgive me!

Don't cry, Emily. I'm sorry.

The Passing Shade
The Death of Bernard Baker
December 24, 1965
Redhill Correctional Facility

John Arnold sat on the edge of his bunk and stared at the cell wall which showed a myriad of spidery cracks. A former occupant had connected some of the lines to form a stick man and added a crudely drawn but lovingly detailed penis. At the rectangular window that connected them to the outside world, snowflakes clung to the thick glass. The temperature inside was less than sixty degrees.

He's so still, he thought. *You'd almost think . . .* The small figure, jackknifed on the bunk, weighed little more than a hundred pounds. Wisps of white hair fanned out on the flat pillow with some standing on end, forming a sort of halo. The vertebrae in the old man's naked back were clearly defined. The skin was pale, almost white and remarkably free of the telling stains of age, hairless and translucent, like that of a small child.

Only the closest observation saw the faint rise and fall of respiration. If the old man would just stay like that and not turn . . . at least not until John could be away from those eyes.

The old man's long face had jagged lines that extended from the outer edges of his eyes and ended in draped folds. The thin mouth, sunken from the absence of teeth, and slightly feminine, always had a faint smile. His eyes . . . they seemed colorless at first until you noticed the pale yellow (hazel?) was little different from the sclera, the white yellowed with age. Tossing in his bunk at night, John could feel them on him . . . He had gotten so little sleep since the warden had arranged the transfer.

The old man's reputation was unsettling. Baker was Redhill's most notorious con, a celebrity. Until he was moved into John's cell, Baker had spent his days and nights in solitary. His presence among the general population was unthinkable after Don West, the warden's nephew, lasted less than one shift as a new guard posted outside Baker's cell. The word was, after all the fanfare that resulted from Baker's arrest and Don's part in it, the warden was planning to set Don a few steps ahead on the career ladder, intending for Don to be warden when his uncle retired. Early into his shift, Don had taken his pistol and shot his brains out. The warden wasn't too happy that his nephew proved to be such a poor example to the rest of the guards. His response was to "make an adjustment in procedure."

After the suicide, others stopped showing up for their shifts. What caused this, no one could determine, but each day a different guard placed trays with Baker's meals in the small slot of Baker's cell. No one man did more than a few, widely spaced shifts a month. Baker asked for nothing. He refused exercise. He showed no interest in books or other reading materials. How he did his time, alone with no diversions, was a mystery. At night, the guard would hear him whispering.

It was when Baker laughed that a man might want to take a break, smoke a cigarette, get the hell away from that joyless giggle. Bernie was thrilled at the chance to redeem himself! He had heard the whispers so little until just recently.

A chance for you to please Father. Take heed!

It was time for a Great Fire. The splendor of it, and at last, a reward! Bernie waited. On December 15, 1965, the crow appeared. It sat on the windowsill of the bleak little room, looking down at the frail figure sitting quietly on the small cot, the crow's eyes burning, puffing its feathers, not making a sound. When Bernie's lunch slipped through the open slot of his cell, he uncovered a dish of vanilla ice cream. Hokey pokey, he thought, remembering the frozen treat of his childhood.

Leaving, the guard laughed and said, "A reward, Baker. A reward for good behavior, old man, the warden says that you're moving, at least for a while. You're getting a roommate, or I guess . . . he's getting' you." Tickled that the Great Warden was so easy to manipulate, Wilcox laughed as he walked down the long hall. What Wilcox didn't remember were the commands hissed in his ear during the nights he slept outside Baker's cell. Inside Baker's cell, the whispers began in earnest.

"As one of their leading dogmas . . . they include this: that souls are not annihilated, but pass after death from one body to another . . ." Julius Caesar (on Druidic teachings)

John sat on the low bench, watching the clock. It was Christmas Eve and the recreation room filled with men watching the portable black and white TV and drinking the last of the fruit punch brought by the Methodist Church. He had seen Nora and the baby two days before. Nora looked tired. They were making her work doubles. Too many people were out for the holidays. He shared the homemade fudge she brought with Ray and Luke. Luke passed around the cornbread his wife Cinda made. Cinda was a damn good cook. It was almost eight o'clock and he'd have to go back soon . . . What was he afraid of? Baker was half his size and Ray said, anyhow, he'd make sure to make a lot of racket if the old man tried anything. "I'll keep an eye on 'im; don't you worry."

Before they brought the old guy in, Ray showed him the peephole, a crack in the crumbling wall between the cells. The wall divided what was once a single cell into two cramped ones. John had laughed, but when Baker arrived, John understood just how bad it was. The old man's strangeness, his eyes . . . He'd hardly slept in almost ten days.

The "Little Drummer Boy Christmas Special" was almost over now. He never thought much of the holidays. Too many sad memories, the Christmas after his dad left was only one of them. He was less than ten sitting alone in the apartment, worrying about his mother, hoping she'd be back soon, but knowing it could be days.

John finished his cigarette as the guard called an end to the evening. As John passed by, Ray sat in his cell shuffling a deck of cards. Ray glanced up and smiled, giving John the thumbs up. Luke, whose cell was one down from Ray's, was stretched out on his bunk. Luke seemed unaffected by Baker's proximity, an exception to the rest of the cellblock. They were all jittery, including the guards.

"Merry Christmas, Arnold. Be good now." Luke called.

"Merry Christmas, old man John answered as the lights on the block dimmed. Luke had turned forty, two days before. Luke invited John to share birthday cake, which Luke's wife, Cinda and Amos, his oldest son, brought to boost his spirits. Luke's father,

Lonnie had died suddenly the day after Thanksgiving and Luke blamed himself for not being there. Cinda, a devout Christian did her best to comfort her husband, assuring him that Lonnie was in a better place. "Better than that orphanage," was Luke's reply.

Cinda had reminded Luke that Lonnie had been surrounded by love from his family and his church when his dad was called home. "Okay, honey, you're right, Luke sighed. "You always know what's important." John wasn't sure he agreed.

#

"Merry Christmas, Arnold," said the guard as he unlocked the door to John's cell.

"Yeah, merry Christmas," John responded. Both looked away as John entered the darkened cell. Inside, there were whispers.

The guard turned the lock and walked quickly down the catwalk to the winding stairs.

Baker was kneeling on the floor of the cell. Though it was dark, John could see he was naked. Hoping to reach his bunk without drawing the man's attention, John moved sideways, carefully groping for the edge. The skeletal form was rocking back and forth. Baker was saying something. Was the old freak praying?

A slapping sound startled him as he reached the edge of his mattress. SLAP—SLAP . . . slapslapslap. It grew louder until it stopped abruptly, replaced by a growl which quickly became a deafening roar, causing the thick window glass to shatter. John grabbed his ears and ducked, barely managing to avoid being cut. Snowflakes speckled the cell wall as they came through the open window.

Men called out. "Whatthefuck/It's Christmas Eve for crissake/shut the hell up . . ." John shivered as the old man, who seemed unaffected by the noise, continued to rock. Pungent and sweet, an odor of soft, oozing rot rolled through the cellblock.

Luke called out, "The sewer! Something musta busted."

Within John's cell, candle-like flames appeared from nowhere, seeming to float in the air. Unnerved by the disembodied flames, John panicked when he looked down and saw Baker was kneeling in the center of a star, crudely drawn inside a circle, its edges smeared on the tiny patch of cement.

Was that blood? The old man's? Where was he cut? One urgent thought took over. He must get away. As he began to yell for the guards, he saw piles of cigarette butts and empty packs of DUCKY STRIKES. They were his; but why? His alarm mushrooming into terror, Arnold started yelling louder, screaming, as the old man kept rocking, chanting the words faster, until—OH MY GOD! Fire erupted, and John started to burn.

The shrieks of the dying man and the fire that consumed him started a confusion of screams, a jumble of noise as the prisoners began to panic, pounding the bars with whatever they could grab, clamoring for the guards to do something, get them out and away from the fast-moving fire. In the next cell, Ray shook the bars, yelling as loud as he could. It was too late for John. The fire was everywhere, and men were shrieking OPEN THE GODDAM CELL! Someone must've had heard, because there was a sudden jerk, and Ray's cell door slid a few inches. He struggled to squeeze through.

Minutes earlier, Ray had crouched low, his eye angled against the tiny opening in the crumbling wall, so that he could keep an eye on Baker. He'd had a bad feeling all day, worse than usual. His arm trembled as he tried to fit through the small opening to the catwalk, screaming along with the rest of them for help, help for himself. John was already dead, he'd seen him die and he'd seen what had happened to Baker, the smell of burning flesh and Baker changing, the bones growing longer, flesh stretching, his body changing within a prison uniform that wasn't there before, his face . . . oh God no one will believe him! As the guards ran to the burning man, whose skin melted, his hair gone and the body charred, twisted, unrecognizable, the new "John" had yelled, "Baker! The crazy old coot set himself on fire!"

Forgotten, as the guards fought the flames, "John" buttoned his shirt, zipped his trousers, tied his shoes and walked along the row of cell doors, his hands running along the bars, and what? Ray still couldn't get a handle on it.

FLAMES DROPPED FROM JOHN'S FINGERS!

Ray trembled as the imposter passed his cell, smiling, running his fingers along the bars and the flames. Focus, he thought, just get out. No one will believe you. Everyone here will be dead. *Get away!* The flames and smoke were reaching up from the lower tier when with one final tug, Ray squeezed through.

Starting to run, he saw that Luke was trying to squeeze through an even smaller opening, the only other cell door that had opened at all as fire and black smoke swirled up from the ground level. He knew it was hopeless, but Ray gestured to Luke. He would try to get to the lever, the one on the ground level that opened the cells. "Hurry!" Luke pleaded, his voice barely audible above the choking voices of the others as they were pleading, trying to bargain, splashing their toilet water, futilely trying to douse the flames, to stay alive a little longer.

As Ray went down the metal stairs, he heard Luke yell "Cindaaaa! Tell her . . . love . . ." Then, Luke was screaming.

Ray crept along the ground floor and saw that the flames shooting up through the roof, melting glass and metal beams were beginning to loosen and would soon collapse. The smoke was thick, blinding him. Crouching down, feeling his way, he tried to see if there were any guards when he saw John (Baker?) standing in an open door.

Not knowing where to run, Ray rose to his feet. With a sigh and a smile, the imposter extended his arm and pointed at Ray. A flame shot from his finger striking Ray's chest. As Ray began to scream, frantically swatting the flames, John laughed and disappeared through the open door.

Still batting at the fire, Ray followed him through the open door. Flames welled up and began to burn his face and hair as Ray reached the outside, throwing himself on to the snow-covered ground. Shivering with the cold, dazed, he listened to the screams of prisoners trapped within and the shouts of the guards trying frantically to fight the blaze.

There was a wail of sirens, and the fire trucks began to arrive. In shock, and in terrible pain, Ray raised himself up and saw the man who looked like John Arnold pick up a hose and begin to fight the fire. Ray fainted.

SEVENTEEN

PATTY

Who is this old lady named Ramona? She knows about Bernie. Is that all? How does she know him? Does she know he's a rat?

The Time Ribbon is still out of order. We will learn more when you find the rest of Ramona's Bernie memories.

Okay. I'll find them when I find them.

The Longevity of Ramona Song
Hunan Delight Gift Shop,
Redhill, Ohio December 2004

What could she do? An old woman wouldn't be a match for this one. Even when Warren was still working for the San Francisco Police, she knew it was useless; he would never have believed her. It was magic she didn't understand. She tried to forget it until Warren came to her with the news that he and Colleen were taking their young children and moving to Redhill.

Colleen had an inheritance and Desimone's was up for sale. "We can buy it for a song!" Colleen laughed at her own joke. Much of Colleen's family was in Redhill, and Ramona knew how important that was. Still, a sense of foreboding came over her. She decided then to move with them and do what she could to protect them.

The years blessed Warren's family. Ramona was thankful that she had come with them and made a new life. Her longevity was bewildering. She fully expected to be dead twenty years ago, but here she was, her picture in the paper when she turned 100. She knew the murderer, the one the world thought to be John Arnold, was aware of her and that he threatened her family.

She knew there was something evil in the mall, an evil she had known since she was a child of six. She often hid from it in her dreams. She also knew about the girl. Perhaps there was hope.

EIGHTEEN

PATTY

This part is too grownup, too scary and it makes me sad. I don't want to think about it.

We'll take a quick look. Then we'll go to the park.

> *Okay. I know they will make me sad, but I need to know what happened.*

Fine, we look, then go to the park. There are balloons and we can play hoops. Russie is there now.

> *Russie loves hoops.*

Nora

Redhill, Cleveland Ohio

Dec. 24, 1965 to Sept 6, 1969

When Dee called her about the prison fire, Nora left baby Emma with Dee and drove to the prison. As she reached the gate, her fears increased. The moans of injured and dying men overwhelmed her.

She struggled to breathe, certain that something had happened to John, that he was dead, until she heard one of the guards say "Hey, that's Arnold's wife."

The guard took her arm, "He's at the hospital, Mrs. Arnold." Dazed, she nodded and got back in her car. The community hospital was filled with grief-stricken families mixing with those who sat quietly, waiting to hear. She saw Bill who worked at the nursing home and moonlighted at the hospital.

"Nora, honey," he said, "John's just fine, they're keeping him for observation."

She managed to whisper, "Where?"

"He's in 14A."

Tears kept coming as she found the room. She berated herself for having so little faith. The door to 14A was open with people going in and out. There were four beds in it for now, their occupants unconscious or staring, one moaning in pain. John sat by the window his back to her as he looked out the window that faced the street, where muddy snow lay piled in drifts to allow traffic. She made her way around chairs filled with people, some gasping in pain, others sitting by them, dazed.

As she drew close, John became aware of her and turned around. Locking her in a tight embrace, he held her chin with his hand and kissed her. When his tongue slipped into her mouth, she wanted to vomit. She stared at him, disbelieving.

He had John's face, his hands—everything that belonged to her husband, but the person before her wasn't John; he was a monster. Her husband was dead. This man had stolen his identity. A ridiculous conclusion, but she knew it was true.

She questioned her sanity until he smiled. His soulless leer revolted her. "How's our baby girl? How's Emma?" he asked.

At the mention of Emma, her breaths came in gasps, and she sank to her knees. "Whoa . . . Honey!" his voice oozed concern. "Let's sit you down."

She quickly got up and sat on the edge of the bed. She couldn't bear to have him touch her. They were going to keep him overnight, they said. That gave her a little time. She could take Emma and run. He didn't love her. Maybe he would be satisfied with just destroying John and forget about her and their little girl.

She forced herself to smile, *he mustn't suspect* . . . "I hear they're keeping you here until tomorrow."

"They say I can go home until they figure out the transfers," he said softly, reaching out to touch her hair as she moved away.

"I'll check with the desk and pick you up tomorrow." she said. She started to leave.

"I can't wait!" he murmured and he grabbed her, putting his tongue in her mouth again.

She focused on what she would pack when she and Emma fled. She made lists as she drove back to Dee's, what she would take and whom she could trust. Dee, she would tell Dee she had to leave, and explain as best she could. She wouldn't tell Dee where she was going. If he thought Dee knew, he would hurt her to make her tell. She could not forgive herself if Dee were hurt. Dee was peering out the picture window as Nora drove up the driveway. When Dee opened the door and saw Nora's face, Dee began to cry. "Oh my poor baby, he's dead." Nora took Dee's hand and led her to the couch.

"Where's Emma?" Nora asked.

"Having peanut butter and jelly and waiting for you." Dee said, her eyes searching Nora's for clues. "I told her to stay on the bed . . . I didn't want her to be here, to see her mother's face right away, in case . . . "

Trembling, Nora took Dee's hands in her own cold ones. "Dee, you know me. You know that I'm truthful, that I never lie. There's a man in the hospital. He looks like John. He sounds like John. Dee, I'm not insane. Whoever he is . . .he's not my husband." She started to cry as she realized how crazy she sounded. "He's evil."

Dee struggled with Nora's words. She loved the girl like the daughter she'd always wanted, but it made no sense. Nora saw her confusion. She squeezed Dee's hand.

"I must take Emma and run. We'll hide where he can't find us." Nora sobbed, "I can't tell you where we're going. If I did, he'll get it out of you. He'll hurt you and I couldn't live with that."

Dee patted Nora's hand. "Honey, if you say he's not John, he's a son of a bitch who is a threat to you and the baby, then he's a son of a bitch and you get the hell away from him."

She promised Dee that she would contact her when it was safe, knowing that day would never come. Emma was in the bedroom, talking to her doll, telling her all about Santa. When she saw Nora, she ran into her arms and Nora hugged her tightly.

Nora distracted the little girl as she drove the half a mile to their bungalow. Emma sat on the couch, her legs swinging with excitement, telling her doll that her daddy was coming home soon. As Nora stumbled, trying to explain, she saw Emma's eyes grow wide as she pointed over Nora's shoulder. John Arnold was standing in the doorway. Nora shook with fear and Emma's face fell. She understood what her mother was trying to tell her. Both knew it was too late. Emma began to whimper.

Ignoring Emma, he whispered, "Do you want her to live?"

"Don't hurt her, whatever you want . . ." she whispered back.

"Excellent." he said. He led her into the bedroom. She tried to disassociate. She knew people did that when faced with traumas that were unendurable. Her eyes were closed as he tore her clothes off. When he began to pull her hair and pinch her, she let out a wail, knowing that Emma could hear and hating herself for it. The sounds of crows and shrill laughter were obscene. Then he started to scratch her, raking his nails along her torso as he raped her.

It seemed like hours before he finished. When he did, he let out a high-pitched giggle. Satisfied, he sighed and pushed her out of the bed and onto the floor. Then he rolled over and slept. Finally able to open her eyes, she crept out of the bedroom and found Emma asleep on the couch. Nora went into the bathroom and washed the blood off her body and then carrying her daughter, she put her into bed. Returning to the living room, she fell onto the couch and slept.

Human beings are adaptable and Nora, stronger than most, adapted to being married to a monster. When Dee saw her the next morning, John was there. Dee understood then what Nora had tried to explain but could not convey. She could do nothing except entertain Emma while Nora struggled to retain her sanity. "John" was praised as a hero for what people thought he did. Both women marveled at how no one saw what he was unless they got too close, something that he skillfully avoided. Within a week, John's parole was granted and Desimone's reinstated John in his supervisor's position. Within a month, a steel mill offered him a high-paying job in Cleveland. Nora had hoped that he might leave them then. Timidly, she asked if she and Emma could stay in Redhill. He smiled. "You don't understand, my dear. You're necessary, your line anyway, I'm told. For the moment, at least, that would include your brat."

She waited until he left before she allowed herself to cry. The day they moved to Cleveland, Emma and Nora were being driven by one of John's new "associates," a grim-faced man in his forties who stood by the car waiting for them. Dee and Nora, both dry-eyed, said goodbye while Emma clung to her mother's leg.

"Promise me," said Nora, "if something happens to me and Emma needs you, you'll be there."

Dee whispered softly, "Yes, baby, you know I will."

They left and Nora waved from the car. Dee tried to see them later, driving to Cleveland whenever she could, but they were as far away as if they had moved to the Moon.

Two years passed as Nora watched the name of John Arnold become familiar to those in power. She was expected to play a part and she tried, knowing that Emma's life might depend on it. Her "line" he said was important, but he made it plain that life could be most unpleasant if she did not cooperate. As his power grew, people attached themselves to him, those driven to bend others to their will, their eyes cold and determined.

More terrifying were the ones she suspected weren't quite human, as if the person she encountered were merely a costume, masking something evil. She endured his sexual assaults by closing her mind as her body was invaded and was thankful when he lost interest. When she discovered that she was pregnant, she knew that it could mean Emma's death, once he had his own offspring. She decided to have an abortion while he was out of town. If she couldn't find a doctor or someone else to do it, she would do to herself.

California Dreams

Nora sat at her desk in the study of the house on Euclid. A telephone book lay open. On a street that held the homes of the rich and powerful, the Arnold house was among the smallest, but its elegant façade and tasteful rooms claimed upward mobility. The study where Nora slept contained a couch, bookshelves, a desk and a narrow closet where she kept her clothes. Photographs of her parents and dead brother were tucked away. Nora planned to give them to Emma when she became an adult. Would her little girl survive?

Nora placed the phone book on her lap as she scanned the listings of various doctors and clinics. The radio played "Good Vibrations." She remembered how she and John had planned to move to California when he was free and closed her eyes, thinking of what might have been. A sharp pain on the side of her head caused her to fall from her chair. *What happened?* Something had hit her. As she lay on the carpet, she looked up and saw the man who pretended to be John looking down at her. He was smiling. "Honey!" he said, "Why didn't you tell me?"

He had discovered her secret. How? Frustration and anger welled up. Fury overtook her. She wasn't afraid of him. Nora rose to her feet and spit at him. "I know what you are. I won't have it. No woman would." He sneered at her as he wiped her spit from his face.

"I don't think you have a choice, my dear, but I do." Nora saw Emma standing in the hall. He closed the door. "It's your line that I need and your line I shall have and as many as I need. He grabbed her wrist twisting it. She refused to cry. Pushing her to the carpet, he put his hand on her mouth and raped her as she closed her eyes and thought of California. The next morning, she suggested sending Emma away to school. With a wave of his hand, he agreed. They both knew if he decided that Emma should die, no amount of distance would keep her safe. After he left, Nora made the calls and then told Emma that she was being sent away.

How could she protect Emma? She thought of calling Dee, but she knew that he would kill her too. No one could help her, not even Marlene. As the weeks went by and she saw her body begin to change, she knew that she had to do something. She considered trying to escape, somehow reaching Emma, telling her to hide until her mother could come and get her, but she suspected that whatever forces had murdered John, putting an imposter in his place could find them both.

Late in an afternoon, Nora became restless. The house's toxic rooms made it difficult to think; she could hardly remember what it was like before the prison fire. And she was alone. Sinister cronies and the servants whom he had assigned to watch her were gone, their help needed as he extended his power. The monster was gone for the week, giving speeches to influential businessmen across the state. For a while, she was alone. For a while, she could do what she wanted. She found herself walking down by the river. Its smell, the result of unimaginable neglect and pollution, reminded her of being trapped in that bedroom.

On the path several yards away, she saw six ducklings follow their mother into the grass. The ducklings began to quack and flap their wings, before abruptly hopping into the river, trailing their mother. Nora wept as she made her way to the shaded brush that lay off the path. She sobbed as she watched the filthy river, its burdened waters rushing past her.

While she cried, her heart yearning for what she had lost, she took care to avoid being heard by any passerby. He had her trapped and Emma was doomed. When he had enough children by her, she would die too. If he killed Emma, she would kill herself.

As twilight began to settle, she looked out at the troubled river, dreading the next few months and years. Someone was watching her. She looked up, expecting to see one of his spies, the dead eyes intent on carrying out his orders, forcing her back. Instead, a grotesque figure stood silently as if waiting for her to say hello. What skin remained on its wizened frame was soot black and mixed with burnt remnants of clothing, reminding her of strips of bark on a birch tree, peeling from the host. Sad tufts of hair on the charred skull stood on end. They were the only sign that the thing before her had once been a living creature. The figure barely stood and yet it inched closer on a trembling foot. She knew him immediately.

"Oh John," she whispered, "What can I do? He'll kill her, our baby. I'm so scared." There were no eyes in that face, no lips, but she knew that he loved her. She could protect Emma. "I love you John," she whispered. She smiled as she felt her love returned. Then she waded into the Cuyahoga River and the river carried her away.

"Hidden not foreseen!" It shrieked. Her escape was not revealed in the wall's shifts and folds. No pain, no fear, no feeding . . . Volcanoes roared, and claps of thunder collapsed the new trees it had created for the crows. The monster-world moaned. Its demons clawed at the barrier and screamed, "thewallthewall. Nothing to be done. She got away away . . ."

As he prepared to meet with willing donors to John Arnold's Senate campaign, Bernie felt the cold breath of failure on the back of his neck. *"Nora is dead,"* a voice growled. The little girl was all that was left.

NINETEEN

Marlene's Last Laugh

New York City

December 26, 1965—October 1970

Marlene, wrapped in her warm flannel robe with her feet in the warm sock slippers her niece Amber had given her, was sitting on her 59th Street balcony. Today should have been a good day. The little bit of snow, just enough to satisfy the morons who *had* to have a white Christmas, had melted. At ten in the morning, the sun had come out. She was looking forward to the end of the holidays and the return of sanity. Anxiously awaiting her next Wednesday book club meeting, she had just about finished *Catch 22*. Unfortunately, she was worried about that call from Nora.

Since leaving Redhill, much to her relief, life made sense again. Where she lived now, people yelled, cursed, loved, and fought. No more that feeling of nothing, a nothing that turned into the darkest grief she'd ever felt, more pain than the loss of her son during the war. Her tenth-floor apartment was comfortable and more important, affordable. On her living room wall, the only one that did not have a tall bookshelf filled with her beloved paperback mysteries and thrillers, were photographs of her family, Hugo's and hers, kept alive in her heart by countless stories. Photographs of several students, many still in touch, added to the display.

After reading the same headline several times, she shook her head, and went to the wall phone by the kitchen counter, lifting the receiver to make sure there was a dial tone. She scolded herself: You'll just have to wait; you don't control the world. You never did. She had vowed to work on her impatience.

Marlene had been heartbroken when she learned John had gone to prison. She felt partly responsible. Logically, she knew she wasn't, but if she hadn't sold the shop, John wouldn't have gone back to Desimone's and . . . *stop it! You're doing it again!*

Despite the tragic circumstances, she had been amazed and thrilled to read of John's heroism. She sent a telegram of congratulations and her love to Nora. Then . . . that strange call from Nora came, pleading for Marlene to hide her and Emma. She was stunned. Had prison changed John? Not the John she knew, who had one of the strongest characters that she had ever encountered.

She waited another hour, trying not to look at the phone, not to pick it up and call Ohio so that she could get rid of the feeling that something was terribly wrong. She tried to recall exactly what Nora said, but it didn't make sense. Maybe the strain of John's being in prison had caused Nora to have some sort of breakdown. No, Nora wasn't the type. The Nora's of this world kept the sorry mess together. Her type didn't break down; her type cleaned up when others went off the deep end.

But Nora had pleaded, "He's not John; you must believe what I'm telling you. The man who came out of that fire is not my husband. I don't mean that he's changed. He's not the same man!" Then Nora whispered, "He's here. I'll call back as soon as I can— please . . ." Marlene had tried to reassure her. "Of course, honey, anything, just let me know . . ." Then, Nora hung up abruptly without saying goodbye. There was no call the rest of that day. Marlene finally broke down and called, but no one answered.

Marlene didn't believe in God, but she hoped she was wrong and there was a God who cared about good people like Nora and John. She waited weeks for an answer but didn't get one. Somehow, Marlene put it out of her mind. Whatever was wrong, she knew it was beyond her to remedy, so she decided to let it go. She was able to put it out of her mind for almost five years before it came back.

A Walk in the Park

Marlene enjoyed her book club professor who was glad to walk in the park with her. There was no love, but she appreciated the walks and the company. It was on one of those walks that she saw the newspaper headline, "Politician's Wife Commits Suicide! John Arnold, a rising star in Ohio politics . . . " She grabbed the paper, stuffing a quarter into the paperboy's hand, not waiting for the change. Her hands shook as she read that Nora had drowned herself. Marlene's legs buckled and her companion (Frank) caught her, guiding her to a bench.

Not caring who saw, she began to sob, much to the concern and considerable embarrassment of Frank who waited for her to gain control and then escorted her home, relieved that his part of the drama was over. For days she stayed in her bed, barely rising to eat, inconsolable. How could she have let that poor girl down? She was Marlene, the fearless teacher who never let a kid down she could save. Nora was dead, beyond anything that Marlene could do. Finally, she decided to pull it together.

Frank had found another companion. She was welcome to him. In Marlene's opinion, Frank was a lightweight who would not be missed. She remembered Dee, the landlady who was Emma's sitter and like a second mother. Dee was a waitress and after Marlene's urgent phone call searching for Emma, Dee kept on asking until a customer said he heard that Arnold had sent the little girl to boarding school. Marlene called every teacher she knew to see if she could find her.

Finally, success, but the head mistress was reluctant, even when Marlene told her she was a teacher and friend of the family. Emma was no longer a baby, but a student at a private school, close enough for Marlene to reach in a couple of hours. She would do what she could for Nora by helping Emma. She'd seen John on television. He was running for office in Ohio and his star was rising so fast that the fat New York cats were taking notice. She could see something about him was different and very wrong. She just couldn't put her finger on it. She planned to stay out of his way as best she could. She wanted to make sure that Emma was okay, that she didn't need anything, other than a friend.

PATTY

Hildy told Bernie off! I helped, but Gram doesn't have to know.

I won't tell her. I would have done the same thing.

Of course, because we're sisters!

Mystery Solved
New York, 1970

Marlene's plans came to an abrupt end when she was murdered the following Wednesday, several hours before she was due at her book club meeting. That morning she sat, as she did every morning, drinking her coffee and reading about what was new.

As she finished the cup, she started to rise, intending to pour herself another and was startled to see John. He stood in the open door that connected her living room to the balcony. Marlene finally understood what Nora had meant. She knew in her gut that the man before her was not John. She knew he meant to kill her and wondered who he was, so she asked him. He looked surprised and then did the strangest thing; he put his hand to his mouth and giggled. Most unpleasant, she thought, poor Nora.

"The dirty coward . . . " the orphan girl, Patty whispered in Marlene's ear. Surprising, why that . . . who was . . . The fire, Patty died; someone set her on fire. And there was Miss Tandy. Before Patty's death, Miss Tandy was set on fire . . .

Then she remembered the prison fire. He's not John, Nora said . . . Marlene slapped her forehead. She had solved the mystery! "I don't know how I know this," she told him as she turned her head to the side, narrowing her eyes as she confronted him like he was a truant whom she'd caught loitering in the hall. Wagging her finger at him, she said, "You're Bernie, aren't you?" He smiled his nasty little smile and nodded.

Still rat's teeth.

"Hugo was scared of you, you know." His satisfied grin told her he did. "Patty wasn't though. Hmmm . . . What *was* it that she called you?" His face started to darken. "Oh yes, coward, that's what it was. Then of course, you traded up, didn't you?" She smiled. "I mean, it wasn't just his looks you stole. The John I knew wasn't just a little smart, he was a lot brighter than he knew, but you know now, don't you?"

She sighed, shaking her head sympathetically. "Bernie Baker was a dirty coward, and he wasn't the sharpest tool in the shed." She'd finally figured the whole thing out, this little weasel . . . poor Hugo . . . She put her hand over her mouth and snickered. She broke out into an honest laugh as he lifted her and threw her over the balcony. *Hildy means business,* she thought. Closing her eyes, Marlene laughed until her death on the pavement ten floors below.

TWENTY

Rift of Dreams
Redhill Mall Opening
November 2004

Extending his arms, his power of persuasion generating cheers of approval from the crowd, Bernie looked for resistance. The bored teenager or sniveling toddler did not concern him. There was an odd block . . . behind the tent . . . ah, there she was, Emma Bedonne, his "little girl." He had put the suggestion of possible gain in the boss' mind, the "fry cook," as he thought of him, though it had been years since Tiny had manned a grill. If Tiny could get Emma to come, John the Senator might feel beholden. Ambition was a favorite carrot. It was coming together. The renovated house, the largest and most elegant this backward region had to offer, had been prepared for his arrival. The "Elite" of Redhill were holding a dinner in his honor. He would not be attending; he saw no need. The dinner would have to be cancelled. Someone would fall ill, perhaps a stroke or a heart attack.

"Too long has this fine town been forgotten, forgotten by those who are in the public employ, forgotten by the Washington power brokers, forgotten by the those entrusted by the state to serve *all* its citizens, not just city folk, even my good friends, forgotten by Cuyahoga County." He paused, looking at the upturned eager faces and decided the athletic-looking woman in her fifties, (wondering, he realized, if he found her attractive) would have an unfortunate aneurysm in the early evening. Susan Beckwith, the Mayor's horsy wife was not in the least attractive. His taste was for more exotic fruit. He would have an "Other" arrange it.

He glanced at the two attractive young women stationed on the right side of the platform. They smiled, appearing to all as eager young volunteers, making their contribution to public service. The dark one's eyes had a faint glow and she nodded, acknowledging that the unfortunate event would soon occur. He never knew how an "Other" might appear. Sometimes it was a new custodian, the regular employee delayed because of a sick child or a hangover or a flight attendant filling in when another's car broke down, the paper trail not quite accounted for, but no matter. It was power best used selectively, to break the will of a too-strong opponent or to manifest engine failure in a plane carrying a young man, grieving for his dead father, and flying home to his beloved as she gives birth to twins.

He put his index finger on his temple, "But I did not forget. I am back to pay a debt. This place, this mall I have been fortunate enough to fund and oversee as it was built, will bring new life, infuse new blood into this area."

Thunderous applause, whistles and the stamping of feet interrupted his closing. Waiting, he marveled at how they could not feel his contempt and his eagerness for the glory of sacrificing them. He could see the news reporters struggling to remember exactly how they planned to trip him up, not just alluding to the tragedy of the prison fire, but shedding light on the numerous accidents, deaths and a string of disasters that had followed.

PATTY

This explains why the monster likes this mall place: It's because the monster thinks it would be easy to get in there and eat people. The monster couldn't find a better place, probably because the monster is almost as stupid as Bernie is.

Bernie will help the monster eat people?

Of course, Bernie wants to help the monster. Bernie is a rat. I hate the stupid monster too.

Me too.

A Rift in the Wall

> *"If space and time can change, little else is sacred. Modern cosmologists like to contemplate an extreme version of this idea: a multiverse in which the very laws of physics themselves can change from place to place and time to time. Such changes, if they do in fact exist, wouldn't be arbitrary; like spacetime in general relativity, they would obey very specific equations."* *Sean Carroll Theoretical Physicist ITT*

The mall stood where the prison burned and before, the cabin stood and the murder of Becka Tobin took place. The mall was in a place so rare that for years Bernie had searched for another like it, taking "fact finding" trips, including one to the Towning Estate in London where he had been seduced in his mother's womb. There, the barrier had been vulnerable for a time. A disappointment.

Fountains of chaos bursting from Earth's interminable wars would have nourished the demon world for centuries, but there had been no way to direct the flow. The World Wars were a wasted resource. Bernie doubted there were other places like the Redhill mall, where the barrier between universes might tolerate a permanent rift. Only the cabin in the Ohio wilderness had revealed itself. If there were more, they remained hidden. The cabin's location became the prison and now, the Redhill mall sat on it.

The barrier separating universes was an unknowable mass of stardust, unknowable even to the creature that often peered through its filmy surface, reading our shifting timeline. The creature itself was a planet. As it drifted in its dark universe, absorbing the nectar of destruction that streamed from exploding stars (rare in its bleak corner of creation) and the stray bits of matter that tumbled in their wake, it found the barrier and it became aware of us.

Drawn to cycles of life and death that shimmered, winking, and beckoning behind the gauzy barrier, the creature stayed to watch. It imitated what it observed, creating countless creatures, and then destroying them. The process gave it no nourishment.

On occasion, it lured a curious human across the barrier and the human met his death with prolonged agony. To entice more, contracts evolved., agreements that it discovered inexplicably bound it as well as its intended victims. It entered the dreams of many, whispering a promise of rewards for those who served it. Occasionally, it could manifest human forms that entered our world for a short time.

How many more assaults would it take? Bernie didn't know. Until then, Bernie would serve and collect his rewards.

For eons, universes had bubbled up in an instant. Countless moments of creation, they were joined here and there, but as far from each other as the end of Time.

Until now.

Beholden

"Questions, Senator Arnold!" A veteran journalist called to him.

"Yes?" Bernie said. The man's face reddened as he realized that he couldn't remember a single one his written list lost. "Anyone else?" Only silence as the news teams struggled.

"We hear you're planning to settle in Redhill." A young woman finally managed.

"Could be," Bernie smiled. "So, shop, my good friends and spread the word around to the Ohioans living in towns hereabouts. You don't have to go to a big city; you don't have to rely on the Internet. You have the Redhill Mall with the finest shops, the most cutting-edge toys and the best selection of clothes and appliances!"

"Rings!" shouted a girl, her embarrassed boyfriend hiding his face, while the crowd howled with laughter.

"Most especially rings!" declared Bernie. "The finest rings for the finest people I have had the honor to serve! Everyone, there's a ten-dollar gift certificate for every one of you. Let's shop till we drop!"

As the huge crowd surged forward, the security team guided them to extensive roped lines by the brass columns holding the ceremonial red ribbon. Given a large pair of scissors, Bernie snipped it with a dramatic flourish. Shouts of approval came from the two lines that wound their way in zigzag fashion.

Susan Beckwith began to rub her forehead. "A tension headache" she thought, "just what I need."

TWENTY ONE

PATTY

Now I get it. Ramona, the old lady, was a kid in 1906, which was the same time that I was a kid, which means I would be an old lady too, if I had stuck around. I wonder if I woulda liked being an old lady. The kid Ramona had a pa she really liked and a bossy ma. They were Chinese. Ramona could see into the future. She didn't like what she saw in her dreams because she saw Bernie. I wouldn't either.

I knew you'd find out!

Ramona got the allie and she didn't even like it.

Gram told me about the allie. It is truly special.

I know she was a little kid, but she should have done better. It would have saved everyone a lot of trouble. If the job had been given to me, I would have slammed the door right in Bernie's ugly face real quick.

She was only a child and very frightened.

Yeah, well look what happened.

Ramona Song
San Francisco, 1906

Daddy must not leave! Ramona was frantic. "Please Daddy, don't go. I dreamed I sat by the window waiting for you, but you never came." Her lower lip trembled. No crying, she knew how much it upset him.

Daddy assured her that her dreams were only fears. "Take care of Mommy while I'm away and wait for me." His voice was soothing. "You'll see me waving." He waved his hand to show her and gently crooked his finger under her chin. His smile made his pleasant face crease like the folds of a favorite blanket. "I'll bring a surprise back from Cleveland, *may may*," he promised.

She gave him a smile. Ramona, named for the missionary who saved Mommy from the bad people, loved his surprises, though she was rarely surprised.

Her dreams of the boy began on the day that Daddy died:

Ramona's Dream

She listened to the mournful sigh of ships resting in the Bay. Below her window, morning light would soon reveal the street's colors, the stands, and wagons ready for another day. She rested her head against the glass and watched merchants assembling their wares. Her cheek felt a vibration as the window shade began to bounce. Trying to steady it, she placed her finger on the edge. The trembling increased. She peered behind the shade; perhaps a bird or an insect was trapped. Her chair began to shake.

As if surprised, the house jumped. Her heart racing, Ramona gripped the sill of the window frame. "Mommy!" The floor rocked and kicked up and down, violently tossing the lacquered chest where her doll sat next to the cloth chicken, hurling them across the room. Ramona clung to the ledge when the window glass exploded into the street. She closed her eyes whispering and pleading for it be over; wake up! The room dipped forward. On the street, two boys chased a dog. The white of the dog's fur moved through shadows. The first rays of early morning light made the white appear then disappear as dog ran away. The earth continued to bounce and shift, and the boys stumbled when a wagon slid towards them, overturning.

The merchants shouted for others to get out of the way as objects hurdled from swaying buildings. Twirling glass sliced off the arm of an unfortunate vendor returning for his books. There was nowhere to run. An old man was pinned under his herb stand while another careened toward a small doorway. The ground heaved and started to roll.

Zigzagging around the tumbling death, the running dog doubled back to a fruit stand where some overturned baskets jumbled and shook. Then the dog began to dig, and steam hissed from under its rapid paws. Before the animal could escape, steam burst through the opening, shooting the howling creature two stories into the air. (It was always the same! Get away dog!) Steam gave way to a geyser of boiling water, holding the writhing form as it tried to escape, its legs moving back and forth.

The Demon Rift

The white fur disappeared, replaced by a rosy pink, marbled with red. As the dog let out a series of high-pitched yelps, she heard a sucking sound. The geyser reversed itself, going back into the trembling earth and the force slammed the dog into the ground where it lay on the shifting surface. Sunlight found the carcass no longer white, but a shimmering red. A split in the street gave way to a bulge that opened, swallowing the limp, dead body. Ramona always gasped when she saw the top of a boy's head burst through the opening. She knew who it was. His blond hair gave him away.

Ramona opened her eyes as Mommy placed the chicken puppet in her arms. "Quiet, Ramona, you'll wake the baby," Mommy whispered. Mommy sat on the edge of Ramona's small cot, holding a manicured finger to her lips. "Bad dream, *jan ge*, go back to sleep." Mommy couldn't help her.

Ramona longed for the comfort of Daddy's arms, as he murmured words that calmed her. "Ramona is a smart, brave girl. No dream devils will defeat her. She is too clever." She felt safe with Daddy; the dreams were only dreams.

TWENTY TWO

PATTY

The monster has a plan to eat people. But why is this girl part of it?

It is a puzzle.

I like the ICE KING where she works. I bet that stuff would taste dandy, especially with cake. Madonna uses tarot like the two sisters who lived two doors down from us. Ma used to give 'em dirty looks because she said they turned their noses up at her like she was trash. She was.

My goodness, I forgot about those old ladies. They gave us cookies one Christmas.

I remember. The cookies were oatmeal. We hid them from Ma. Her brother Gordon sells bath salts and face paints. Also, Gordon likes boys. When we lived with Ma, she was mean to the man up the stairs because she said he liked boys. The man sure didn't like Ma. Who would? He gave her dirty looks right back. I liked the man upstairs because he was nice to me. One time, he gave me some apples and told me to share with you and Russ.

*I hope the people find out about the monster while there's still time.
How awful!*

Don't you worry, I'm gonna find a way.

Parting Gifts
Madonna Bedonne
Redhill Mall Opening
November 2004

The hand on the huge clock paused at five minutes to one o'clock.
Held fast by chains suspending it from the highest rafter, the clock
face looked down on the mall's three floors where vendors
whispered to each other. What was taking so long?

The new Cineplex offered blockbusters and coming
attractions. Major department stores claimed better clothes, finer
furnishings, sturdier appliances, jewelry and hardware at cheaper
prices. Manikins posed inside the string of windows, their plastic
forms molded to impossible proportions and dressed to suggest a
look that made one sexier looking and thinner. Specialty shops and
kiosks offered sounder sleep, purely NATURAL BEAUTY aids and
the newest games.

The Cineplex occupied one end of the ground floor and on the
other end was the food court. Along the food court perimeter, logos
and bright colors topped the string of booths that included THE

CHINA BOAT, FRUITY TOOTY SMOOTHIES, BUCKEYE RIBS, and more than twenty others.

Also on the ground level, a white grand piano sat near the expensive boutiques and the upscale department store. The pianist wore a long blue gown. Silver snowflakes cascaded above her. Christmas banners, wreaths decorated the inner perimeter. Blues, white and pinks replaced traditional reds and greens on countertop trees. Three levels of subterranean parking, their concrete columns supported the framework of the mall, creating eerie enclosures that would soon echo with screeching tires and the blast of impatient horns.

The mall itself was less, not more, a design meant merely to suggest the much larger and grander Arcade of Cleveland. In its center was a large fir tree, the roots reaching deep into the ancient soil. Years ago, from his prison cell, John Arnold had seen a crow sitting on this tree. The fir tree's top pointed to the arched glass of the high ceiling, the ceiling supported by two towers and poles painted to look like rich mahogany with gold painted ridges.

Resembling those imposing structures that anchored Cleveland's Grand Arcade, the mall towers contained elevators, not offices. Above the ground level, the second and third floors had glass barriers, not the swirl of ornate brass of the Arcade. Staircases with thin banisters of polished oak, their steps covered in the marbled tile of the ground floor, competed with escalators.

Only the fountain was different. Near the fir tree, the fountain sat in the middle of colored tiles that formed a pentagram when seen from the right angle. Gargoyles, their open mouths revealing floodlights, were fixed on the lower perimeter. The brass-framed clock hung above the highest floor *was* the same as the Arcade's and in the smaller mall, it hovered, rather than presided. A crow perched on a beam and watched as the clock struck one.

New employees, most young, less than twenty-five years in age, stood at the numerous counters, doors, and kiosks. Some were confident, having work experience at other stores. A few had the advantage of extensive training, scoring high on aptitude tests and hired to manage. Others, completing applications weeks ago, were hired the day before and told when to report and what to bring for their first day.

Madonna Bedonne was focused on tarot cards spread out on a shiny blue counter. She stood behind a frosted glass barrier that shielded shallow trays, filled with a selection of sprinkled toppings. The ICE KING's "Blue Ice" was crunchy blue candy sprinkles mixed with blue coconut and it competed with colorful candy sprinkles, red hots, gumdrops, chocolates, nuts, shredded coconut in a rainbow of hues, and vats of syrups were ready to be scooped and drizzled.

Behind her were spigots, poised to swirl the vanilla or chocolate soft serve. The day before, Madonna had attended the ICE KING's required soft swirl training. When the vanilla sputtered repeatedly and the chocolate spurted chunks of ice, she decided to do a spread. The cards before her caused her great concern. Not good, she thought, very bad in fact. The Death card, followed by the Devil Card was an ominous sign. To make it even worse, the Tower was on the other side.

Madonna Bedonne, designated Ice Maiden, and key server rapped her black-lacquered fingernails on the counter as she considered the spread. Her rings, including a silver skull with three ruby chip eyes, three silver crosses, two silver ankhs and a yin yang thumb ring were tucked in the pocket of her blue and silver uniform.

Around her neck were various symbols hanging from several chains, including one bearing the gold crucifix from her great-grandmother Madonna; hanging from another were three crystals and another that had belonged to her late father, Giordano's Irish mother, Bridget, a silver four-leaf clover. Warned not to wear any black, she layered a black turtleneck (it was cold she insisted) underneath, with black knit sleeves pushed up, but peeking out from the pale blue. On the inside of her wrist was a small yin yang tattoo, beautifully done, a gift from her twin brother Gordon on their nineteenth birthday. Madonna had given Gordon a Billy Idol CD and an autographed George Michael poster for his new apartment.

Her thick brown hair, medium length and badly cut (to her brother's dismay), was dyed a dull black, making her pale skin look almost white in contrast. She wore no color on her lips, since Ted, her new boss, an ambitious young man of twenty-eight whose carefully groomed goatee gave him what he hoped was an air of authority, but in fact did nothing but serve as a trap for crumbs, drew the line at black lipstick.

"It might make people think you're sick," he said diplomatically, thinking in fact it might *make* them sick.

The black eyeliner and shadow she wore around her large brown eyes gave her a haunted look, which in fact she was, haunted as long as she could remember. Despite her taste in makeup, Madonna was strikingly pretty, with her father's short straight nose, and her late grandmother Nora's disarming smile, a fact not lost on Ted, who knew that it was good for business.

"We should be very worried. This is serious shit," said Madonna, shaking her head.

"We do *not* use the 's' word; language please!" Ted warned. He glanced at his reflection in the glass of the microwave, impressed by how smoothly professional he looked. The tie really added something. Alarmed at Ted's dismissal, she tried again. Madonna pointed to the spread.

"Ted, we might get by with just these two and not have the walls tumbling down on our heads, but, it's the God damned Tower. We could be gone in a week!"

Ted's mouth flew open in disbelief, if the other server had bothered to show . . . At that moment the pimply- faced "Ice Prince" appeared. "Sorry dude," said Kevin, "my mom's car broke down."

Ted's blistering reply was interrupted when the doors swung open, and shoppers began to pour in. Focused, a general commanding his troops, he whispered, "Man your stations."

Madonna responded with an exaggerated salute and Kevin, flashing a set of purplish braces, grinned enthusiastically. Adjusting his Ice Prince floppy cap and cupping the side of his mouth, he called, "Let's rumble!"

Perched on a corner rafter, hidden by waving paper stars, the crow flapped its wings.

Black Friday
Redhill Mall Opening
November 2004

The mass of shoppers spread out quickly. Many were thrilled at the pageantry and ceremony. Some were anxious to find the bargain that eluded them in the bigger city malls and outlets. Rows of silver snowflakes and sparkling pinks, frosty blues and shimmering white stars promised a wonderland.

Families headed for WHITE OAK DISCOUNTS searching for affordable shoes, jackets, underwear, tools for Dad, or maybe a new bike for under the tree. The well-to-do strolled into boutiques or investigated the elegant upscale department store where young women in lab coats were handing out perfume samples and suggesting the right makeup for your skin tone. Personal shoppers prepared to demonstrate how to mix and match.

In Men's Wear, older men, measuring tapes in their coat pockets, stood quietly, and chatted with slickly attired junior clerks. Adolescent boys filled PLAY IT FORWARD Sporting Goods and VIDEO GAMES GALORE. Teenaged girls filed into ON THE EDGE and FIVE MINUTES FROM NOW. Kiosks with trinkets and blinking novelties drew shoppers like sailors to enchanted isles. Children pulled their parents to the ONE thing that they wanted, at least for an hour. The pianist flexed her fingers and began to play "White Christmas."

Gordon Bedonne

NATURAL BEAUTY Shoppe

Redhill Mall Opening

November 2004

Gordon Bedonne studied the presentation of gift bags and baskets. Not bad, but he'd have Ellis check every hour to make sure they were still in order. Maybe when she gives out the free samples she should stand where the expensive bath products would catch the eye. Though Gordon considered the cosmetics line superior, NATURAL BEAUTY was known for its bath products. He wished he could persuade Madonna to try the new cosmetic line, "Strike Me Beautiful," but she was bull-headed and not happy unless she looked like a cross between Elvira and Wednesday Adams. Ellis, his waifish eighteen-year-old assistant relied a little too heavily on their new *Am I Blue* eye shadow. He'd have to gently guide her to a better choice.

Something wasn't right. A pack of *Sea-Wand Scrub* was missing. He reached behind the structure of baskets and bags, their colors arranged to suggest a large oyster shell.

> *Struggling to get a closer look, a demon raked its claw on the milky barrier, causing a spark which shot through the barrier like an invisible bullet.*

As he felt along the wall behind the stack, a sharp pain stung his finger. Letting out a yelp, "What happened? Something burned me!" He cleared a section of the display but found nothing, no fire or spark. Nothing looked remotely hot. In fact, the temperature in the shop seemed to have dropped at least ten degrees. Confusing.

He'll report the drop in temperature to mall management. No one wants to be cold when looking at bath products. Ellis found nothing to explain either the burn or the cold room. Sucking his finger where a small blister had formed, Gordon restored the display.

"Maybe it was a spider or something," offered Ellis as she glumly wondered why all the cute ones were gay. Gordon's resemblance to a young John Arnold was startling, Giordano's signature, only in his son's brown eyes.

At the sound of women laughing and talking, Gordon gave Ellis the sample basket, telling her to stand near the bath products. "Ellis," he said quietly, "I forbid you to say the word spider, agreed?" Nodding, Ellis took her position as the first customers arrived.

PATTY

Bernie got to be even meaner when he pretended to be Senator Arnold when he was really Senator Bernie. Lousy rat.

I can't disagree. I wonder—never mind.

Spill it.

I wonder who my John would have been now.

President!

I love you, Patty!

Flies, Worms, and Uncollected Debts
Demons' Glitter
Redhill Mall Opening

John Arnold strode into the mall, camera crews and aides following behind him. The Others known as Debbie and Reba were stationed in makeshift booths right inside the door, youthful idealists ready to serve their country. Debbie had a languorous charm, seeming indifferent to the frenetic pageantry of the afternoon. Her lids were half-lowered as if thinking of a holiday she'd just taken. Her sensuous mouth was set in a fixed half smile.

The girl's dark hair sleek and pulled tight against her elegant skull, made her seem foreign, Latin perhaps or Middle Eastern. Reba's hair was dark blond, and her frequent laugh made children squirm. Reba's apprising look caused men and women alike to avoid eye contact as they took the gift certificates she handed out.

Bernie moved through the parting throngs of families, the old and the young, strollers and wheelchairs gliding, people pointing and laughing, discussing what they saw, what they wanted and what they had to have.

Such endless "need," so easy to sway. Voters had "needed" more security and Bernie, a new face running for the Senate, made them *feel* safe; but reality differed. As a couple in their twenties hesitated, peering at a display of diamond rings, he felt their excitement. Lambs to slaughter, he chuckled, no challenge there at all. He remembered the wary faces of those who greeted him in Washington as he arrived with his staff of dull-eyed young men and the wan reactions of career politicians to the hollow smiles of his "handpicked" advisors. Whispered threats shattered the resolve of those who opposed him while Senator Arnold studied the various bills and bids for favor.

His goals, he told his constituents, were to protect and benefit them; he would fight to better their lot. In reality, he spread rumors of favoritism, setting one group against another. He sent deadly missions into jungles and deserts, fueling grievances in the hearts of the invaded. Disease often accompanied the state's returning soldiers if they returned at all. His favor was sought by many, though his company was avoided. His influence pressed for war and profit. Unemployment climbed as towns were crippled by the loss of factories. New industry came to his state adding poisons to rivers. Dark clouds showered them with acid rains.

Bernie wanted it all and he wanted more: his power as Senator, influence, the joy of new victims, and offerings greater than before. After the coming sacrifice, he would have more power not only to influence, but to see into the future. In the mall, demons waited, invisible to shoppers, their burning eyes perceived as the gleam of Christmas lights, the shiny reflection in a window or the glittering sparkle of enticing goods.

Flies

Senator Arnold had long been an instrument of death, pain, ruin and misery. Those who served him were the fierce ideologues, grimly passionate in the pursuit of their agendas, ruthless in their methods. Many had come to him early, helping him gain influence, destroying opposition. He stayed behind the scenes of power, persuading the funding of small armies, backing a dictator here and there, fostering distrust and enmity, coaxing wars to erupt, funding extremists who plotted murder against non-believers and encouraging destruction and fear.

Bills were introduced and pushed through Congress, legislation designed to encourage greed among the wealthy and increase poverty. He diverted funds and victims of disasters went unaided; projects were not completed. The flies of misfortune swarmed whatever he touched.

The inevitable investigations led to nothing. An air of corruption would suddenly surround the accuser; documents would disappear as rumors gained credence. The Senator had paid his youthful debt and those opposing him were cynics, using his past to bring him down. His colleagues feared him. Lobbyists courted his favors but avoided his presence. He was seldom in front of cameras, the deadness in his eyes made it necessary for no one to get too close. His campaigns were slick orchestrations of half-truths, the photographs and film of him shot at certain angles from a distance. Audiences marveled at his oratorical skill not realizing that the opinion was not theirs but suggested to them as they listened to the platitudes, catch phrases, and lies he spoke.

When he takes the girl's psychic power, he will touch millions, maybe more . . . But first, the mall must burn. It is located where the barrier is most vulnerable.

Until then, energy fueled by sacrifice generated the "Others," who watch over him and aid his cause. Gaining a new life requires more.

The restrictions are maddening. He could go no farther until the twenty-fourth. Then, the mall must burn, along with its last-minute shoppers, but only at the appointed time, when the trickle will become a steady stream of feeding resulting in incredible power. Who can stop him? Certainly not the old woman and not the girl. He is invincible.

The night the prison burned, he hadn't known what to expect, though he knew it would be grand. He had marveled as his body changed, at the power of his new mind which was at last able to grasp his purpose. That he could see what a small dull creature Bernard Baker was bothered him a little, but no matter. As his mind was far more capable, his new body had appetites denied the old Bernie. John Arnold experimented. First, the wife. The crow had cautioned him. It was foreseen from Nora would come life renewed. Confusing. Was it meant for her to have his child, one to serve as a host when the present years were gone, and it was time again for Bernie to absorb another life?

He remembered her face when she came to find her husband and realized he was gone, with Bernie in his place, no way for her to prove it, the despair and then her sudden departure, only to find him there, waiting to greet her. That night, he enjoyed her company immensely, her rigid body and tears enhancing his pleasure as he took her. He soon tired of her, only occasionally making use of her, as he discovered a variety of outlets for his needs. He would have killed the child, but the crow's warning stopped him. The daughter was of her line and might be crucial.

When he became aware of Nora's pregnancy, he was delighted. It all made sense. His child would provide his new life when needed. Her unexpected suicide threw him into a rage. He considered killing the girl. Inflicting a slow death would have given him great pleasure. The fact that she was all that remained of Nora prevented him and political capital of being a "grieving widower" with a young daughter was valuable.

It was only when the twins were born that he understood the crow's message. Emma's distraught escape into sedatives left her and the old woman unaware of his hospital visit. Gazing at the newborns, he began to plan the building of the Mall. He'd assumed that it would be the son until he saw the girl again when the twins were six, watching them as they walked to school. The girl had power, her awareness an incredible tool.

At last, he would erase his failure at the cabin, the place where the prison stood and now the mall. A pity the girl Becka suffered so little and in such a place. The feeding had barely begun when the dogs' howls forced a quick end and he cut out her beating heart.

How many more years will he gain? Sixty? Seventy? He'll use the next life to build here again and more sacrifice and more and more rewards. What would come next on this spot? Perhaps he'll build a children's hospital, a tribute to the memory of John Arnold, "a man of the people." The day the hospital burns, the rift will widen more and the feasting greater. Someday, (he smiled at the fantasy) a future sacrifice of perhaps thousands will be enough. The rift will become a permanent bridge to unimaginable destruction and pleasure. *I'll rule the world, what is left of it . . .* He suppressed a giggle.

As camera crews filmed him, he walked through the crowd. People were going in and coming out of stores, pausing to look at something new, pointing, discussing and buying. Unseen to all but him, were beings seething with hunger as they roamed an alien dimension, their restless gaze upon the stream of people who wandered through the mall. Bernie could hear the shrill buzz of their voices and smell the foulness of their breath. He felt as one with them.

PATTY

Bernie is pretending to be Madonna's grandpa, but she smells a rat. That's why she's scared of him. I wasn't scared.

I know Patty. You weren't scared of anything,

Worms
Redhill Mall Food Court
Opening Day
November 2004

The food court's tables were full when a fire flared in a wok at THE CHINA BOAT. Amazed, the startled chef froze for just a moment. A FRUITY TOOTY clerk in the next booth rushed over and poured a pitcher of smoothies on the blaze, which resulted in a lot of smoke with an unpleasant smell. This caused the long line of CHINA BOAT customers to investigate other options. Rather than being grateful, the chef became enraged. He would have pounced on the clerk if not stopped by members of the BUCKEYE RIBS staff whose business had suddenly doubled.

ICE KING manager Ted had begun to lecture Madonna on her language, and Kevin on the importance of being on time, when he was distracted by the CHINA BOAT chef who had reached over and grabbed the stripped shirt of the FRUITY server. Confident that his superior managerial skills would be useful, Ted hurried across the food court to broker a truce.

Madonna and Kevin did a high five. The vanilla and chocolate swirl spigots had worked beautifully, and the glut of customers had not stopped until shortly before the fire. Madonna was considering the possibility of the cards being wrong when she saw her grandfather across the Court, moving towards her. "Shit" she whispered. The flash of cameras and news cameras and people carrying lights flowed toward her, and there was something else. It must be the ghost of the lights. *Shapes floating, shapes with red eyes, weird.* A bright light flared up as a bulb burst.

Seeing the news cameras approaching, Ted hurried back to join his "team." Madonna shivered as her grandfather reached the ICE KING counter. His cold eyes met hers and he nodded saying to the news teams, "This is my pretty granddaughter, Madonna." He turned back to her. She could see behind his dead eyes. There were worms.

"Honey, how about making one of your delicious ICE KING treats for your old grandpa?"

"What kind? She asked him. Her hands were shaking.

"Vanilla with Blue Ice would be fine." The cone fell as she turned to hand it to him. The crowd laughed nervously. "How about one with sprinkles," he suggested. His smile made her want to scream. Someone caught her eye. A young black security guard smiled at her sympathetically.

Taking care not to meet her grandfather's gaze, she swirled the soft serve and added sprinkles. There was applause. "You be a good girl, Madonna. I have my eye on you!" He said as he left. She focused on her skull ring in her pocket as she nodded.

"Why didn't you tell me John Arnold was your grandfather?" asked Ted, relieved that he hadn't fired her. A scream came from the other side of the mall. Ted and Kevin ran to see what had happened.

Madonna's heart pounded. Her grandfather really *was* the boogeyman. Why her? Why had *he* haunted *her* all these years? As she wiped the counter, she began hyperventilating. That's all I need, to be caught blowing into a paper bag, or worse, fainting. She started to cry as she wiped the counter. Seeing mascara on her fingers, Madonna reached for a paper napkin and realized that two girls were watching her distress.

"Uh—oh, what's wrong, Madonna? Did they run out of black at the Goodwill store?" said Randy who had been one of Madonna's most enthusiastic tormenters in high school. This triggered Madonna's practiced response as she considered her opponents.

Breaking into a big smile, Madonna piled a large dollop of soft serve and then smothered it in hot fudge, whipped cream, and nuts, offering it to the two as they peered into the selection of toppings. "Don't be shy; it's on me." Madonna smiled sweetly as she displayed the oversized sundae.

Knocking over the box of napkins on the counter, they sauntered off. One of them shouted, "Bitch" as they left. She watched them go, feeling relieved that the terror she felt during the grandpa encounter had passed.

The food court started to clear as shoppers resumed their shopping, and the long line of customers turning in their coupons for a free small cone with Blue Ice had disappeared. She began to clean the counter as Kevin came bounding back.

"That was soooo intense, you have nooo idea!" Kevin said. His eyes fixed on her face; he paused to take a deep breath. "A *baby* almost bought it!" he said in a stage whisper.

As Madonna listened, her stomach hurt.

"Two ladies," he continued, satisfied at her reaction, "were talkin' and one had a baby, and it was in one of those strollers with a hood. They were talkin' and not payin' attention, lookin' at the stuff at that kiosk with the shiny hair things. Someone said that the older kid, the one on the roller blades, was actin' up and so nobody was watchin' the stroller and it musta started rollin' on its own, but I don't think that's possible," he said. "Anyway, all of a sudden, it's at the escalator and nobody sees it until it's starting to pitch over and the baby woulda fallen except for the security guard. He caught it! The kid, I mean. The dude caught the kid just as it started to fall out!" He finished his story sighing, "That was intense!"

"But you didn't see it? You just heard?" she asked him.

"Didn't see it, but I was there right after." He started to elaborate when they saw that Ted was back.

"Okay, team, we're closing soon so let's review." With that, the topic was closed.

TWENTY THREE

PATTY

Too bad he didn't kill the rat when he had the chance.

Bernie played tricks on his mind. Most people couldn't kill a child, even one like Bernie.

I guess so.

Ma wasn't most people because she killed Russie.

No, she wasn't.

Bobbo

A Cabin near Redhill, Ohio

December 24, 1900

"We don't kill children, Bobbo," Sheriff Gibbs warned him. Bobbo considered his options as he squeezed the neck of the struggling boy. He doubted that Gibbs would use force to stop him, but if he finished it, what would change? Wringing the life out of the monster wouldn't bring them back.

Stella's mind was gone. She was laughing and singing, talking to their dead mother about setting the table for Sunday supper, calling Becka, Baby Becka and reminding her little brother (Bobbo) to wash his hands. When they peeled her away from the dead girl, her head gave a swift jerk and she yelled, "In a minute, Momma." Her eyes glazed and now she sat smiling and chattering. Arthur sat with her, the pair of them on a bench.

The sheriff had sent men out to get help, women to tend to Becka's body and Stella and a wagon for transporting the bodies of Becka and the salesman. Arthur kept calling her name, begging her to tell him what to do, but Stella didn't heed him; she was someplace else.

Bobbo couldn't bear to think of Becka and what was done to her. Abomination was the only word. When he saw the boy gloating and Stella, a paralysis came over him. Arthur broke it, calling to Stella, "Stella, honey, get away from him!" Stella was already gone, but Bobbo felt his will return and without thinking, he grabbed the devil-child from behind.

So quick, a thought surprised him: Take the boy and run. The boy was an innocent victim of a depraved man. He was confused. Is that the way of it? As the thought passed through his mind, Stella began to sing to her "Baby Becka." Bastard! His mind was his own again. His fingers tightened around the child's neck. The boy appeared to lose consciousness, his face turning blue.

"We don't kill children." Sheriff Gibbs said again. Bobbo thought of the consequences. Arthur and those kids, they'll need help. If he finished it, went to prison, say, what would they do? He released the child, letting him fall to the ground. Bobbo felt grim satisfaction. The boy was breathing, but just barely, the fingerprints on his neck turning dark purple.

Good. Stella said the boy had a way of making people do things. He'll be focused on making himself swallow for the next several days. He promised himself, if he saw the monster again, he would finish the job, no witnesses. He owed it to his sisters.

The Deputy and the Pearl
The Road from Redhill to Cleveland
December 25, 1900

The faint swish of burlap shifting in the darkened interior of the wagon caused the deputy's hands to shake. His heart racing, he forced himself to breathe slowly. If it weren't for the humiliation that would surely greet him when he came to his senses, he'd jump off the wagon and put as much distance between him and "it" as he was able. *Did Randy hear that rustling sound*? He glanced at Randy Wilson. The twenty-year-old deputy was staring at the road ahead. Icicles hung from the ends of Randy's handlebar mustache. If Randy did hear, he was not letting on.

Ordinarily, Don, the deputy whose job it was to manage the "prisoner" while the other one drove the wagon, would have seen this as an occasion to have some fun. Randy was a six-footer but he had a round face, still soft with youth and with his full lips, well, the top lip distinctly bowed in the middle. Don had declared Randy's lips made him look like a girl. You're prettier though, Don laughed. The result of Randy's efforts to address the problem of his lips was a blondish growth of silky whiskers that now hung on his face like needles on a porcupine. Don had grown his own moustache, a generous bristle of brown and auburn as a solution to his receding chin, unaware the effect made it worse.

They were on their way to Cleveland as servants of the people of Redhill, the sheriff reminded them, his stare preventing Don from asking if there was some other way—couldn't . . . wouldn't someone else take the boy. . . There was no sense going over that again. The road had thankfully cleared with the help of the morning sun. Don appreciated the way Randy handled it all, driving the team through the slush and mud, maintaining a calm attitude.

A small bottle waited inside the palm of Stella's glove. Don gripped it firmly, his other handheld the rag. The doc of course was too late for Stella—no one else in that hell needed any help . . . "Take this with you; use it on the bastard if need be. Do it quickly; he tricks your mind otherwise." Bobbo gave Don the chloroform, the doc turning the other way. Doc didn't agree. That's the difference in folks.

Don had no doubt. If the demon so much as let out a fart, Don was ready for him. Randy handed him the glove, saying, "You best protect that bottle in case we hit a bump or two . . . " Always one for understatement.

The two deputies had been on the road since daybreak, making good time. Don was grateful for the holiday, the wagon's path unchallenged by other travelers. *Let's get this over with.* Danger trailed the wagon like a hungry dog and Don had decided that at twenty-four he was too young to die, denied another shot of whiskey or turn with a willing gal. There was more of life's joys due him.

The coals in the foot warmer had long given up and Don's toes were numb. He hoped the monster was freezing his weasel ass off, but not if it meant he woke up and Don had to deal with him and be quick enough . . . The wagon hit a gully causing it to dip and Don to suppress a scream. Randy kept on talking to the team. Don was ready to open the vial and pour the whole mess on the monster's face—*please don't let him wake up!* It was several minutes before the panic left them with only the familiar dread.

The afternoon sun helped calm them down. Nature could sometimes do that, changing your mood from bad to good—at least Don was able to distract himself as they reached the outskirts of Cleveland seeing scattered shacks and tents, smoke from small fires as people warmed themselves. It almost put him back in the holiday spirit.

Just as things were getting interesting, Don didn't often get a chance like this, to see so much going on, they saw the sign, Cuyahoga County Orphanage. The sun was going down anyway. Best to get it over with. Randy turned the wagon onto the narrow road, the snow hardly melted until they were close in. Don's heart started to race when Randy pulled the team up and jumped out of the wagon just as they reached the main building, a three-storied brick affair. Don saw the door open, and an older woman appeared. Someone must have seen the wagon. He knew Randy had the sheriff's letter in his pocket, the envelope that said "Mrs. Kray."

It was what came next that finally did it when he lost his nerve. Time to deliver. The duty was supposed to fall to him. He steeled himself, opening the back of the wagon and Stella's glove clutched in his hand. Sliding the monster out headfirst, not so much as a peep, maybe it won't be so bad until Don hoisted the boy up and a muffled groan caused Don's knees to buckle. He would have dropped him, but Randy caught the boy and swung him over his broad shoulder.

Without a word, Randy sprung up on the porch, taking three steps at once. Don couldn't bring himself to follow until the door shut with Randy and the boy inside. A few minutes later, the door opened a crack and a girl covered in freckles said, "Mrs. Kray says you can come in and get warm." Don shook his head, saying he wanted to have a smoke and it wouldn't be polite. After she shut the door, he decided he did want a smoke. While reaching for his tobacco, Stella's glove caught on the wool of his jacket and then it dropped to the wood planks. The bottle of chloroform spun out like a top, rolling onto a clump of snow cleared from the steps. Did it break? Don didn't want to think of not having it in case . . .He reached down in a panic and picked it up, discovering to his relief that it was still intact.

He put the vial safely in his pocket and found his tobacco pouch. Relief warmed him. The index finger of Stella's glove had dropped down onto the planks. It was pointing at him; at least it seemed so. He picked it up by its thumb. Maybe she'll come to her senses and want it back, he reasoned. As he lifted it, something fell out of the glove's opening, a white marble with a dark spot on it rolled like the bottle, but instead of hitting the snow, it kept on going, bouncing on the bare steps, and disappearing into a drift. He had decided to check it out when the door opened. Randy's face was ashen, and he looked twice as old.

They left immediately, ignoring the cries of a crow that followed them all the way to the sign that pointed back to Redhill. Don drove the team, not stopping even when Randy heaved up the sandwich Mrs. Kray had forced on him. Don wondered what had happened inside while he waited on the porch. Best leave it to another day he decided, for now it was enough to go home.

The Demon Rift

TWENTY FOUR

PATTY

Now I know why Mrs. Kray couldn't help.

This is your part of the story? Why didn't you show me before?

I'm not in this early part. I come later; you'll see.

But you didn't show me—

It's 'cause it makes me too sad, okay?

Okay, Patty.

The Teakettle and the Warrior
Cuyahoga County Orphanage
Cleveland, Ohio
December 26, 1900

"He's coming round Mrs.," the girl said. Her freckled twelve-year old face was a mixture of fear and curiosity.

"Thank you, Darcy, go eat with others now." Mrs. Kray sat in the straight-backed chair and considered her new ward, studying him for signs of trouble. Certainly not a devil, the child was too small, though experience had taught her that mischief hid behind the most innocent of faces. His blond hair was all that was visible. The boy lay covered in a bed at the end of a room of beds, a dormitory where twenty or more children slept each night.

As the boy was coming round, Mrs. Kray checked the timepiece in her apron. It was almost seven. The weak morning light coming through the windows prompted her to reach over and turn off the lamp. It wouldn't do to waste. Taking the edge of her shawl, she rubbed the frost from the narrow window. Several inches of new snow covered the grounds, and the branches of the oaks etched in sharp relief against the white of ground cover. The path leading from the gate was clear, the surface a packed smooth blue-white.

Mr. Buchner and several of the older boys must have spent most of the early morning seeing to it. She would make sure the boys received an extra biscuit for their effort.

At the end of the fenced playground, a crow hopped onto the tool shed's roof, causing snow to dust a white sparkle on the stack of firewood Mr. Buchner had cut before Christmas. They might need more soon if the snow kept up. On the playground, the swings shuddered in the mild wind. If Mr. Buckner protested the extra task, she would give it to an older boy, despite the man's protests.

Mr. Buchner kept the shed locked; he was possessive of his tools, over careful at times in Mrs. Kray's opinion. His one good leg and the other, a wooden stump, moved quickly after any errant child he caught near the shed, and he used his cane to swat those foolish enough to peer into the dusty window for a look at his precious tools.

She considered when best to allow the new boy to mix with the others, meals only for a day or so. She gave little weight to the sheriff's account. Rubbish, a small child couldn't possibly behave in such a manner. As the boy sat up, she felt cold, her fingers icy. It was winter after all. She would have Mr. Buchner check the furnace.

The boy must be alone. She hesitated . . . quiet —a room of his own—where? She began to shiver; her false teeth clacked together, and she put her hand over her mouth. But there's no . . . She thought of the storeroom. Hurry! *Why so urgent?* The boy was sitting, his feet dangling on the edge of the bed. *She must . . . she must . . .* She struggled to rise from the chair and the boy—his yellow eyes—was he staring at her?

Now! He was impatient. Her fingers curled and uncurled as she searched her deep apron pocket for the keys. There—thank God! In her haste, they slipped from her hand, falling to the floor. She bent to retrieve them and saw tears falling onto the jumbled mass of keys. Mrs. Kray blinked and frowned as she realized the tears were hers. Most inappropriate—*hurry!* Rising to her impressive height of six feet, she pulled her apron smooth against a mass of pleated gray skirt. She crossed the hall to the closet, slipped a long key into the lock, and pulled on the knob. *Open the door—be quick.* A bar of light showed through the storeroom window.

Anticipating more children after the New Year, the staff had moved the closet's piles of blankets, boxes, old books, and broken furniture to the two dormitories, but a stack of bedding still rested in a corner. *Would a cot fit? He will require a light.* She gathered the blankets and a pillow and fashioned a mat on the floor of the closet.

The boy stepped inside and examined the arrangement. She waited as he judged her effort. His small hands barely visible under the man's flannel shirt he wore, he ran his fingers over the surface of the bedding. Finally, he sat down on the blankets and looked up, his strange eyes fixed on hers. She stood frozen, caught in his gaze, her thoughts unspoken—*can't breathe—must leave—desperate . . . please—oh please— urgent—don't look at me—I'll be sick.*

"Go away now. Come back with food, I'm hungry." The childish voice carried a threat. Mrs. Kray knew she would hurry to give him whatever he wanted. Dismissed, she turned and struggled not to run, tears falling freely onto her apron.

The Potato Peel
Cuyahoga County Orphanage
Cleveland, Ohio
August 1903

"Mrs. Kray, I believe you're spoiling this child; I warn you; he'll not be ready for the world when he leaves." Mrs. Murphy was beginning to wear out her welcome. Plump, motherly and younger looking than her sixty years, the cook was causing problems, some more serious than others. Her rules, including no talking when in the kitchen and scrubbing spotless pots, were bewildering to the unfortunate orphans assigned kitchen duty. Miriam, the previous cook had given notice after fifteen years. "I've taken a position in Columbus," she said, avoiding Mrs. Kray's stricken face. Mrs. Kray didn't ask why Miriam was leaving. She already knew.

The week before they found Mr. Buchner hanging in the shed, she had seen "Bernie" standing at the open door of the classroom. The teacher's attention was on verbs. Of the fifty-three students, some sitting at the thirty or so desks, many on the floor, the little ones sitting on the lap of an older student, none seemed aware of him. "What're you doing? Go sit with the others."

She looked in horror to see seventy-year-old Mr. Buchner. The boy's face tilted up to meet his disapproving gaze. The old man paled; his sunken mouth opened, but no sound emerged. The child never moved, an owl eyeing a mouse. *Leave, run!* Inside the classroom, the children were reciting the tenses of verbs. Mr. Buchner shook his head several times as words failed to form on his moving lips. He turned, his elbows swaying wildly, his wooden leg, the result of a bullet from rebel fire in '61, clomping down the hall.

Suicide? How did such a small boy engineer the murder of a grown man? Suicide, *but they never explained the pulley. How did the old man hoist himself up?* His throat torn open, cut by his own bloodied hand, the dead fingers locked around the knife.

Poor Darcy found him. The girl still wasn't right, insisting on sleeping on the floor at the foot of Mrs. Kray's narrow bed, a liberty she had never allowed before Mr. Buchner's death. "He was looking up and his mouth . . . open . . . and . . . his tongue . . ." The girl kept sobbing.

"Darcy put it out of your mind. Think of something else. Pray." Darcy promised to try, but Mrs. Kray knew that Mr. Buchner's dead eyes looking up to heaven or the blood dripping from his stiff shirt weren't easily forgotten. The death of Mr. Buchner resulted in a series of handy men, each only staying a week or so until she found Leon. Hard of hearing and simple-minded, Leon, a large and amiable man in his early sixties, stayed. That he was less than efficient and that left many chores undone until Mrs. Kray or one of the older boys took care of them was less important than the fact that Bernie had no effect on him. Mrs. Kray thanked God for sending her Leon.

Dread now lived at the orphanage. Mrs. Murphy, newly arrived from Boston, had a crisp manner. The kitchen ran with military precision, the pots were shining on new hooks, and every scrap of food used in a stew, soup, or a pie. But the cook's complaints were more than an annoyance; they were deadly.

The trays prepared and left for the strange boy, who spent most of his time secluded in the small storeroom were an outrage to Mrs. Murphy. She had been pressing Mrs. Kray for an explanation for weeks. "He is very sickly," Mrs. Kray said again.

Mrs. Murphy narrowed her eyes in disbelief. She patted and smoothed her copper hair swept up in a knotted bun that sat like a small pot handle on top of her head. "It won't do for too much longer," she snapped, "I must be honest . . ." The cook lingered for a moment standing over Mrs. Kray who focused on a stack of papers sitting on her cluttered desk.

"Thank you, Mrs. Murphy, I'll let you know when there is a change." With a look of tight-lipped disgust, Mrs. Murphy did an abrupt turn and left.

Mrs. Kray sighed and finished the last of August's accounts. It had been a successful summer. Darcy was adopted by a family with two small boys and a set of five-year old twins orphaned by a fire, were taken by a childless couple in Cleveland.

As the afternoon light faded, Mrs. Kray decided to place an ad for another cook and give Mrs. Murphy her notice. It was too dangerous to continue. Bernie was in her care, left by the dead man, Baker. There were few facts. Crispin Baker, the suspect in the murderer of a wealthy London widow, kidnapped Bernie, the missing orphan, seen with him on a ship to New York. She'd written the orphanage in London and was shocked to discover that the person she had thought was a ten-year old child, small for his age, was in fact, almost eighteen, much too old to be at the orphanage. Many would consider him a man, yet he was scarcely the size of Darcy when she left. She wrote more letters. There were so many questions.

The London home returned them unopened. She'd have to find a way . . . perhaps if she wrote again, they might know of a relative . . .

As she began to compose the ad, she heard screaming. "Mithus Kray! Mithus Kray, help!" A small girl staggered as she came through the open office door. Mrs. Kray jumped from her chair and followed six-year old Maryanne who barely paused at the door before turning back.

"What's wrong, Mary," she asked as they hurried.

"Mmmmisss—cook! The cook lady—she—oooh—hooo." Maryanne ran toward the kitchen, her sobs echoing as Mrs. Kray followed.

At the kitchen's open double doors, a hot mist greeted her. Heavy pans lay face down on the floor. On a large table near the pantry door, she saw shattered jars of preserves, their contents spilled on several ears of new corn. Next to the table, six children huddled in its shadow, their bodies rigid with terror, eyes fixed on the huge iron stove where Mrs. Murphy was inspecting the stew for . . .

Broth, beefy and thick with vegetables was bubbling. . . What is the cook doing? Why are her hands waving? She must be waving the children away because something had fallen into the deep pot, steam rising and the hiss of boiling water splashing out onto the stove. A mouse, perhaps. No, it must be bigger to displace so much water and cause such fear in the children.

The four girls and two boys, all between eight and ten, were transfixed, watching the pot as it shuddered on the large burner. Clouds of steam rose and curled under the glare of the new overhead light. A rat must have . . . or—OH GOD OH GOD OH GOD!

Mrs. Murphy wasn't inspecting the stewpot. Her body folded, the starched white apron, no longer white, but stained with jam and grease . . . *Mrs. Murphy had wedged her face in the stewpot!* The handle of red hair moved up and down as if someone were grasping it to inspect the contents of the stewpot, then closing the lid made of Mrs. Murphy's face. Her extended arms began to make circles as if to beckon them.

"Huhhuhahhhaaaaa!" Maryanne began to wail, breaking the spell. The other children started screaming, Mrs. Kray joining them. The pot spewed broth, vegetables and pinkish lumps of tissue. Glops of stew flinging onto the stove's surface and the suction creating a loud pop, the cook pulled free of the stewpot. She stood up straight. The pot teetered for an instant, before continuing to bubble. Burgundy liquid splatted her apron as she turned. Her knob of copper hair collapsed, following her ear as it slid down the side of her neck. The eyes had melted, the sockets a shiny red.

"Miz Kray?"

She turned to see Leon and two older boys. The boys were holding baskets filled with apples. "Yes, Leon . . . " she marveled at the calm in her voice.

"Me and the boys got them apples Miz Murphy wanted" . . . Staring at the cook, whose ear now rested on her shoulder, he began to swallow and grunt, patting the wisps of grey on his bald head and feeling his own ears as if to make sure they stayed in place. He let out a high-pitched sigh. "You ladies got yer hands full, so I best let you git to it." He motioned to the boys who nodded, their mouths hanging open, the baskets poised for delivery. "Go git washed up fer supper." He backed out of the doorway and the boys dropped their baskets. As they left, Mrs Kray considered what to do.

Mrs. Murphy was trying to say something. Her lips were wide ridges supporting the drooping folds of what had been her nose. As she opened her mouth, the tissue formed an oblong opening the size of a jellybean. Steam began to leak out, a long whistle coming from it.

A teakettle thought Mrs. Kray. Still whistling, Mrs. Murphy collapsed onto the floor. Maryanne was screaming. Mrs. Kray scooped the little girl into her arms as the other children began to scream. As she comforted Maryanne and began to collect her senses, she saw Bernie standing in the kitchen doorway. He's finally grown a little she thought. It's about time, he . . . he was eating something. It was a potato peel, the lunch she discovered later, that Mrs. Murphy ordered served on his tray.

How awful! Poor Mrs. Murphy.

PATTY

Yeah, I guess. This next part is about me. Gram musta been looking at it. I see some of her thoughts on the ribbon.

That's a good thing, Patty. Gram loves you.

I know. There's something I shoulda told you a long time ago. I wish I had. I'll tell you when we're done.

It's been a long time, but I can wait until you want to.

The Fragile Warrior
Greenfield's Home for Children
Columbus, Ohio
October 1906

"If they try 'n separate us, we'll say no, huh Pattycake. You won't leave me; make a promise." Patty nodded absently, putting her hand on Emily's mouth in an effort to quiet her. It was too hard to hear what the lowered voices were saying. Mrs. Santee's breathy giggle meant they were almost finished.

Her guest was being high-toned, saying "We'll see soon if she's quality. These days it's hard to find. She best love the Lord. I want no heathen near my children."

Mrs. Santee allowed herself a touch of indignation, "Really, Mrs. Nagle all of our children here are God-fearing; we accept no other!"

Twelve-year old Patty knew different. Mrs. Santee and the rest of them feared only the lack of a profit, "placing" children for less than she had already spent on their "keep" as she often reminded them. The sisters had been there long enough, almost three months, Mrs. Santee said as she told them to put on their "Sunday" dresses, the only change allowed them.

When Mrs. Santee told them to wait in the hall, Patty was determined. "Emily and me, we go together." Mrs. Santee was a round bird of a woman with dimples that suggested humor. Patty knew her to be pitiless.

"We'll see," said Mrs. Santee.

You'd better thought Patty. *We'll run away if you try to separate us. She's all I have . . .* She heard a sigh from Mrs. Nagle as she considered Mrs. Santee's assurances. Patty knew Mrs. Nagle wanted a kid nobody cared about, so you didn't have to pay them to clean up after you and your family, do your laundry and take care of your brats. It was Christian charity until you didn't need them anymore and if they didn't work hard enough to earn their food or a place to sleep, then out they go. Throw them away and get another one, another chance to do good.

"Them holier-than-you churchgoers," Ma would say, "better watch out for them, Patty. They'll slit your throat for a nickel, praisin' Jesus all the while!" Patty hated Ma, but Ma had a point. Emily, who was almost eight, began to whimper, squeezing Patty's swollen fingers, causing Patty to yelp. Her fingers still had not healed from being slammed in the door by Ma as she walked out on them. For good this time Ma said, and good riddance Patty shouted, not feeling the pain until later.

Emily's anxious brown eyes searched Patty's face. Patty gave no comfort, not even to say it'll be okay. It had never been okay since Gram died. *I should tell Emily I forgive her. It's not her fault what happened to Russ. It was though.*

There were no chairs in the darkened hallway of Greenfield's Home for Children. Both sisters pressed against the wall, hoping to avoid the chilly drafts of air that funneled through the broken pane of a window near the stairs of the narrow, four-story house.

The door opened and Mrs. Nagle lumbered out. Other than her red nose and hugely pregnant abdomen, the woman seemed devoid of life, the eyes flat and without compassion. Mrs. Nagle's thin lips pursed in judgment as she looked at the sisters. Patty glared back. *Don't you dare take me; I won't leave her!*

Mrs. Nagle pointed at Patty. "This one's got the devil in her." The woman frowned as she considered Emily's wavy brown hair. "I tolerate no vanity, but she'll do, perhaps." Patty began to scream, flailing against the headlock Mrs. Santee employed in anticipation.

"Say goodbye, Patty, be sure to say a prayer thanking the Lord for your sister's new home," said Mrs. Santee. Through the crook of Mrs. Santee's arm, Patty could see Emily's bewildered face as the woman led her away.

"You go to hell you old witch!" Patty screamed. The curse resulted in her eviction from the care of Greenfield and transfer to the Cuyahoga County Orphanage. As she sat in the wagon on her journey to the new place, Patty promised herself she'd find Emily. She had to. *She should have told her sister that none of it was Emily's fault. It was Ma and the hammer killed Russ!*

Cuyahoga County Orphanage
Cleveland Ohio
October 1906

Patty arrived at the orphanage after a day and a half of travel. She huddled in the back of the wagon, her mind occupied with the problem of finding Emily. Although the driver had provisions, Patty had no food and only her thin coat protected her from the cold. When they arrived in the late morning of the second day, the wagon stopped a quarter mile from the house. The driver threw her small bag of belongings onto the ground and said one word, "Out."

Picking up the frayed satchel, which contained little but a change of underwear and a photograph of her, Gram, Russie and Emily only weeks before Gram died and Ma came back to claim the fifty-eight-dollar inheritance, she started towards the house.

As she neared the steps, a thought sprang up: *DIE!* She kept walking, resisting the need to give up, her hunger and fatigue urging her to lie down on the ground, close her eyes and will her heart to stop. *So simple, no more struggles . . .* something caught her eye, a face in a window, high up. A boy was smiling, leering, in smug satisfaction. She knew her death was what he wanted, but . . . Emily . . . Who would find her and rescue her from the red-nosed woman? *No one tells me what to do, especially not you!* She flashed a wide smile as she met his gaze and saw the smug look disappear.

The door opened and two women greeted her. "What's your name?" said the younger one who had dark hair and a kind face.

"Patty's my name, but I'm not stayin'." As Patty started to explain, she realized she did need to lie down after all. The world was fading.

As she awoke, she heard someone say, "Disgraceful." She opened her eyes just a crack and saw that the older woman, taller than any woman Patty had ever seen, was reading the note pinned to Patty's coat. "Some people should never be allowed near children," the woman murmured.

The younger one saw that Patty was awake. "Here Patty, take some of this." A spoon of soup was put to her lips and Patty slurped it her lips trembling. Maybe she would stay just a little while, until she could figure out what to do.

TWENTY FIVE

PATTY

I decided to skip back to the mall.

I want to learn the rest of your story.

Okay, but I need a break from it. We'll go back after this part where Greg the creep gets his. Ha! Though kinda disgusting.

To say the least. But then, we'll go back. I want to know what happened to you.

I promise.

Hunger
The Garage
Mall Opening Subterranean Parking
November 2004

Greg had been in the crowd while the balloons went up and the speeches went on. He wondered if Arnold had seen him. He wore a long coat, the sleeves frayed, and the lapels stained. His thinning gray hair hung in strings, inches past his collar. Of course, Arnold wouldn't recognize him. It had been over forty years. Greg still felt bad about what happened, but John was a supervisor and should have known better. If John had let him work it out, no one would have gotten in trouble. It turned out well for John at least. That wasn't fair. Greg knew he wasn't a saint, but that didn't justify all the bad breaks.

Greg considered how best to leave the mall. Beneath his coat was a bag filled with merchandise shoplifted within the last hour. It had been enjoyable, the gift certificate and the free coupons. He'd had a big lunch and didn't pay a dime. The best part was the whole baby stroller incident. Everyone dashed outside and during the excitement, he helped himself. He focused on what was valuable and might convert into cash quickly. After selecting a number of expensive sports watches and designer sunglasses, he saw the knives.

They were beautiful, resting in an expensive leather case and sitting behind the counter, ready to be gift-wrapped. He took a quick look around and saw the surveillance camera. Taking off the long coat, he folded it, covering what was stolen and exposing the darker liner. Then, he pulled his baseball cap low.

Moving quickly behind the counter, he grabbed the knives and stashed them under his arm. Then he was stepped out of range, near a mirrored column. The knives leaned against the mirror as Greg put his coat on. Then he slid them into an inner pocket, tucked the cap back in his pocket and walked casually out of the store where reporters were interviewing the security guard hero who was talking about how he wanted to be a cop. Greg thought that was funny. He saw an elevator labeled "Parking Garages" and decided to find a way out.

He checked out the first garage floor, knowing the cars go in and out on that level. As the elevator door opened, he heard voices. Security. Taking the elevator down one more, he would search for a stairwell near the exit to the outside one floor up. The door opened and he stepped out. Satisfied there was no one there, Greg began to walk toward the far stairwell.

As he crossed the empty lot, he heard laughter. Though not one to panic, he hid behind large supporting column, its sides advertising a coming attraction at the Cineplex. Nothing, only his imagination. As he continued towards the stairwell, he heard it again. It was louder and it echoed. There was a high-pitched buzz. Security alarm?

Slapping sounds and then a loud crack came from where? Who was following him and playing games? He would deal with them; they'll wish they left him alone. God! What was that smell? You'd think the mall would be clean at this stage. The stench was not a way to attract customers, obviously a sewer line, or someone's idea of a joke. Stink bombs maybe. He might have to crack a couple of heads. The mall should thank him for doing them a favor.

A crow circled him. How did a damned bird get in here? Diving down, it landed on a new Cherokee jeep before lifting its head and letting out an earsplitting CAW! The bird's eyes glowed like reddened coals and spreading its wings, it flew straight at him, causing him to duck. Panicking, he started to run and the bag he carried fell. Sunglasses and the watches scattered. The impact on the concrete floor had caused the knives' leather case to spring open, revealing a set of twelve steak knives.

As he bent to retrieve them, one by one, the knives pulled free of the restraining slots. To his horror, the knives rose by themselves, and hovered about five feet off the concrete. Polished steel gleamed as the heavy knives began twirling and spinning as if wielded by a phantom chef. Letting out a whimper, Greg ran towards the stairwell. When he looked back and saw the knives following him, his whimpering ceased; perhaps they could hear. If knives could float, maybe they could hear him; he must be quiet, at least until he could get through that door.

The air turned cold as he waited. Finally, he ducked behind another large column. There was only twenty feet or so to the stairwell door. His heart was racing and despite his resolve, a strangled plea escaped. "I don't know what you want," he pleaded. Several minutes went by before he decided to chance the door. As he moved, the knives were suddenly, directly in front of him. "Please," he whispered, before the screams began, echoing through the deserted lot.

TWENTY SIX

PATTY

Why do you need to see this part? I already told you what happened.

We must see it together. I want you to hold my hand. If you would let me,

You may be the grownup, Emily, but I'm the big sister. We can watch it and if you want to hold my hand, I don't care.

I will put my arms around you.

Cuyahoga County Orphanage
October 1906

Fifty-six children played in the barren yard. The yard spread across half an acre that sided the orphanage's brick building, which served as dormitory and schoolhouse. The yard had swings, seesaws, random toys, and pieces of toys, but there was little hope in the hard ground. It resisted all but the most determined sticks of those who would play hopscotch. A few girls shared a jump rope and in various locations, designated victims sought to avoid the gaze of their oppressors.

Patty decided to keep to herself. On her second day at her new home, she pretended she was in the park, with Gram, Emily, and Russ while they fed the ducks.

"Da sky, da sky, da sky is boo," Russie said.

He never could get it right. "The sky is b-l-u-e, blue," she teased.

"Ba-oo, dat's wha I SAID!" He'd shake his head. She and Emily would laugh . . .

Back and forth between the swings, around the perimeter, back and forth between the seesaws to the edge of the fenced yard and back again between the swings.

She wasn't quick enough; she should have hidden the blanket. Ma took it; it belonged to her she said, just like Gram's money and . . .

Keep moving, the way to keep warm, except when your feet slip in the snow.

"I ain't goin' ta jail!" Ma said, pointing the hammer at her for emphasis. The hammer had pieces of Russ's hair and his blood was dripping from it. Emily was crying.

"You do what I tell you or she's next! Drop him!" Patty heard the pop of Russ's head as it hit the ground five stories down. Patty closed her eyes when she dropped him, but she forgot to stop her ears. Oh Russ . . .

She walked along the side of the house, her eyes on the different reds of individual bricks as she turned the corner. *Why did I leave him there while I cleaned her up?*

There was a crack as a spear of ice fell from the house's roof. She wished for gloves so that she could hold it, waving it around like a magic wand or a sword. The sun made the ice glisten on the patch of dead grass. She wondered how long it would take to melt and disappear. As she looked closer, she saw something white sitting on the dirt, away from the slush of dirty snow. It rested near the ice spear.

She reached down and picked it up. Was it a marble? It was round and the right size, but . . . She turned it over and . . . ah pretty . . . must be an allie. Rather than a solid milky white, it had swirls of light blue that were spider web thin on the creamy surface. She held it between her thumb and index finger, turning it. She sighed when the marble captured the sun's light, its gleam holding the rays, reminding her of the park and saltwater taffy. She set it in her palm for a closer look. The blue lines curved and disappeared into a grey oval. *Looks like an eye.* The dark calm of the marble's eye was soothing . . . as if to say you're safe here . . . She held it to her cheek. *A treasure, I found a treasure . . . Maybe I can find Emily and we . . .*

Patty

I remember when I found it.

What a wondrous thing!

Gram explained what the allie is and where it came from. It was a nice story.

Yes, it is.

The Pearl

What Patty found was not an alabaster marble, an "allie." It looked like a pearl, but it wasn't. It was a piece of a wall. Not the wall the creature mired in chaos, sought to breach. Not from that dark universe.

The "allie," once the pearl in Stella's ring, was a chip from another wall. Behind this wall was a universe of light, but not the heaven many seek to reach via the arduous paths of religion. Easily found if sincerely sought, Heaven is a place beyond Creation, beyond countless universes, beyond Time. There is no wall, no gate barring the entrance to Heaven. Those who find their way can enter and exit as they please.

The orphan's new treasure came from a universe of light, a place based on the physics of order and harmony. Like pearls, these three universes, the dark, the universe of Earth and the one based on harmony and light move together along one of Time's endless strands. For an unknown reason, this piece of a cosmic wall had made its way to an Ohio farmhouse, then onto the grounds of an orphanage and into the pocket of a little girl.

Knuckle down

As Patty caressed the wondrous thing held in her palm, a fight was going on in a corner of the yard. She heard a little girl crying. "No fair no fair, I want it back! Hugo, TELL him!"

Patty tucked her treasure in her good pocket. The croak of adolescent laughter, older boys made her hesitate. Stay out of it. It's not your problem. She leaned against the side of the house to listen. There was sobbing.

"Nooo fair no fair! You didn't hit it over the line. Gimme my marble. Hugo MAKE him!"

"Winner's keepers, losers' weepers! If you wanna play, you gotta obey the rules!" A boy snickered. "Cry baby, cry for me! Waaaaa waaaa!" He laughed.

"Leave my sister alone! Give it back to her!" From his voice, unchanged, higher, and younger, Patty knew "Hugo" was no match for the bully.

"Make me, Hugo. You man enough?" the voice mocked him. A snap and a thump led to groaning as the older boys laughed.

"Hugo!" the little girl began to wail. Patty stepped away from the side of the house. She hated bullies. Setting her face in a friendly smile, she rounded the corner. Six boys were laughing and pointing at a round-faced dark-haired boy of nine who sat on the ground. The boy was holding his sister's hand and using the other hand to rub the side of his face. His sister, a red-haired skinny ragdoll of five years, with stricken brown eyes sat next to him muttering, "I'm sorry, Hugo, I'm sorry . . ."

The bully held his arms in the air, dancing around as if he had just won a fair fight. When he saw Patty, he recognized her as the new kid. It was time to learn who ran things. The bully, a lanky boy of fourteen, named Ralph, lowered his arms and winked at his friends. "Off limits, no girls. Go play on the swings, Dolly."

A large circle was lightly etched in the frozen ground. Boys ranging in age from ten to early teens were crouched or standing around its edges. Near the line were two marbles, a large red and white aggie sat on the inside near the inner portion of the edge and a smaller marble of dark blue clay rested in the middle of the dirt track. Patty kept her face friendly. "Give her back her marble and we'll go swing."

Ralph nodded in agreement. "All you gotta do is pay, and she gets it back."

"Pay what?" Patty asked. She was losing patience.

"Give us a look at what you got inside them bloomers." Ralph was pleased with the gasp that came from his audience.

The ragdoll whispered, "No girl . . . it's okay . . ."

The bully narrowed his eyes. He had her cornered. Patty's hands were jammed in her pockets. Warm, her hand was tingling with heat coming from the marble. Taking the marble from her pocket, she held it up for the bully's inspection. "Knuckle down!" She said, "Winner's keepers." She pushed away the thought of the bully possessing her treasure.

"What is that? An allie? Lemme see!" The bully started to grab. She put it back in her pocket.

"My shooter pushes yours out and she gets her shooter back and yours too." She waited as he considered her challenge.

Ralph stroked his chin in mock seriousness. "What'll I get if it don't?" he sneered, glancing back at the others. A sandy haired boy of ten was excitedly grasping the arm of a taller boy with stick-thin arms and legs, punctuated by hands and feet absurdly large in comparison. Three boys sat cross-legged, looking up in awe. All eyes fixed on Patty.

"You get a look and the allie," she said. Her smile belied the dead calm in her eyes. Her opponent considered the odds. What could go wrong? What if she beat him? He'd have to fix it. Even though the dolly looked tough, she was still two inches shorter, and he out-weighed her by twenty pounds. "Okay girlie, winners' keepers."

Patty felt a single pang of fear, what if . . . She was no coward. "Knuckle-down," she said. Her voice was confident, but . . . *what would happen if she lost?* Kneeling, she put the allie in the crook of her index finger and resting her knuckle on the dirt, she flexed her thumb down, ready to propel the white sphere towards its target, the red and white aggie.

The allie's gray eye floated in the swirl of blue threads and caught her attention, as if saying, "Are you sure? Do you want to risk so much for those you don't even know?" Cowards, her heart replied, they always lose no matter. I'm not a coward.

A tear brimmed in her eye as she shot the allie. The white marble sprang up, spinning as she held her breath. Loud hoots erupted when the allie appeared to miss its mark. Then it landed on a small pebble. The angle of impact propelled the allie straight into the red and white aggie, which rolled out of the circle, coming to rest at the feet of the ragdoll who stared at it. Patty moved quickly to retrieve the aggie and the blue.

"Somethin' ain't right," insisted Ralph. He followed her to make her set it back to what he had already decided would happen. A change of rules would fix it all. Patty whirled around and butted her head into the Ralph's abdomen. She knocked him off his feet and scrambled up, but he reached out, grabbed her coat, and pulled her back. The ragdoll and Hugo pulled Patty free.

Ralph, who now decided to teach Patty a lesson by pulling down her bloomers, grabbed her wrist. Before he could lock his fingers, the ragdoll bared her teeth, threatening to bite. Releasing Patty, he barked derisively, "Cheat! You're a cheater; those ain't the rules!" The other boys stood quietly, witnessing Ralph's disgrace.

The bell clanged and Patty and the other two children made their escape. "I'm Hugo, and this is Hildy," the round-faced boy said. "You're quality for sure, my dad would say."

Hildy nodded emphatically, "Definitely quality."

"Patty." Patty answered. "If you got a pa, why are you here?" Patty looked behind them. There was no sign of Ralph.

Hugo shrugged. "He's dead and me and my sister are charity kids. Momma went to jail because one of her gentlemen friends found his watch missing. What about you? Are you an orphan or charity kid?"

Patty decided he was too nosy, but there was something about Hugo's good-natured face that she liked, so she answered. "Don't know. I hope she's dead."

That ended the questions and they lined up with others. As they waited, pushing tight against the drab brick building, Patty stuffed her frozen hands deep into her pockets, clutching the allie.

A gust of wind made them all shiver. Teeth chattering, she stamped her feet. Icy wisps of air found the holes in her stockings, chafing the pale skin. The stockings stretched too tight; she'd been wearing them, her only pair, for two years. This year she'd grown five inches.

The two charity kids, Hugo and his sister, Hildy were new like her, but had been there a week. It seemed they already belonged. Patty wished she could be like them, always looking like you were having a good time, even when you weren't.

At least she had a scarf, Tandy's gift. Miss Tandy was the nurse who took the checkered scarf from her own head, saying, "Here, Patty, it's too cold to be without a scarf." What did Tandy want? Eventually, Patty would know. It was cold. It would be colder tonight, her second at this place. She'd try to steal an extra blanket for her and the two smaller girls with whom she shared a bed.

The door jerked open, Leon forcing his weight against the protest of rusty hinges. Clomping up the steep stairs to the second floor, there were only whispers and shoves. Talking resulted in a swift cuff from Mrs. Greer. Still shivering, the children rushed into the classroom stumbling against each other to claim a desk, the claim tacitly made by placing a token, a marble, a piece of bark declared "mine" or a pebble found and marked.

They shed their coats and scarves, hanging them on hooks near the door. Pulling off their shoes, they lined them up against a wall with four tall windows, the cracked shades rolled up. Their socks were draped on the radiator. The iron radiator with an occasional puddle forming under its ripples, stood under the windows that faced the playground. Winter sun shining through the windows brought no warmth. The radiator did though; the classroom was the warmest part of the house. It hissed as they draped their wet socks.

Mrs. Greer was writing lessons on the chalkboard. There were thirty-one desks in the room and fewer books. There had been thirty-three, but two desks were now in the new infirmary. Patty claimed a slate and a piece of yellow chalk from a stack near the chalkboard, and found a place on the floor, her back against the wall opposite the windows. Not so crowded, she decided. She liked looking at the tops of trees.

As she watched the waving branches, she noticed a large crow hop onto the crust of snow a top the shed. Was it watching her? *Look all you want stupid bird. I'm warm, are you?* As if it understood, the bird spread its wings and flying close to the window, it hurled chunks of ice against the pane. It WAS watching her, observing her with its red eyes.

> *No no no no no the bird hissed. Too strong—eliminate eliminate her—tear out her heart—no no no . . .*

She stared back as the bird hovered, then abruptly darted back to the shed's roof. Satisfied the crow was gone, Patty shrugged and crossed her legs, tucking her cold feet beneath her to warm them.

Those sitting on the floor were told to share books. Hugo scooted next to Patty. Not wanting to be left out, Hildy shimmied her tiny body between Hugo and a bigger boy. Hildy's pale face broke into a smile revealing several missing teeth. Leaning over, she gave Patty a salute. Patty gave a smile and looked up, checking for the crow. Still gone. Good, she didn't like the way it acted, as if she didn't matter.

There was little order in the classroom. A few children attempted to work. Most slept or whispered. Hugo whispered, "Think there'll really be one?" Coming loose from her two braids, Patty's straw-colored hair had become tangled and knotted, annoying.

Stuffing her scarf in her pocket, she ran her fingers through the stiff knots and unwinding the string that held them, re-did the braids. "One what," she asked.

"Party!" Hildy said too loud. Hugo rolled his eyes.

Turning quickly toward the noise, Mrs. Greer fixed a stare on those responsible. Under a tuft of dark hair, the teacher's lip curled. The lesson on long division interrupted, she moved with quiet dignity across the classroom and rapped the heads of Patty, Hugo, Hildy and the boy on the other side.

The boy, Michael, protested loudly. He hadn't done anything. Patty knew he had been sleeping, but it wouldn't do to interfere. The teacher grabbed him by the ear and deposited him in a corner, where he sat on a stool, the option of a nap gone. As Patty settled back against the wall, Hugo watched "The Drudge" as the children called their teacher, return to long division. Hugo whispered a question in Patty's ear. Had she heard the stories about the boy in the closet?

The Boy in the Closet
November 1906

"Which one?" Patty was intrigued. Several older boys passed by the open dining room door as they followed Leon outside. Snow blocked the path to the shed.

With the precision of a headwaiter, Hugo placed the dinner plates on the table. "He's not there; I seen him though. Mostly, he stays in his room," Hugo whispered. He turned a chipped dinner plate, making sure the top of the tree pattern faced the center of the table.

"He has his own room?" Patty was incredulous. Hugo was full of information. Hugo and ten-year-old Michael were setting plates on the three long tables in the dining room. Michael's carelessness prolonged the task as Hugo turned the trees on Michael's plates. Patty placed folded rag "napkins" next to each plate.

Wanting dining room duty, Patty had traded with Bertha, a shy eleven-year-old, burdened with a mouth full of protruding teeth. Preferring the kitchen (less chance of being teased Patty correctly guessed) Bertha was scrubbing vegetables. The smell of burning bread filled the dining room. "Again," said Patty. "Margaret told me she's always burning something. Get used to eating black stuff Meg says."

Hugo covered his mouth and laughed. "She takes a nap in that rocker by the big table," he said, "and forgets to check."

"She's at least a hundred something," Michael added, anxious to be included.

Patty frowned. "Why does Mrs. Kray keep her?" The ancient cook, Mrs. Gibbons, Margaret said, came after the "accident." The other cook melted because the boy was mad about the potato peel. She wanted to hear the rest about the boy and how he killed the cook.

The Stairs

Michael was taking his time as he told the story and Patty was tempted to pinch him. "Sometimes he's there and you don't know it," he cautioned. It was past eight. Lights went out at 7:30. The three children sat cross-legged on the infirmary's floor. Patty had promised to kiss him if he would tell the rest.

"What does that mean?" Patty asked. Michael was infuriating when it came to details.

Michael picked pieces of a scab on his elbow, which fell on Hugo who jabbed him in the ribs, causing Michael to yelp. "Say, don't do that, willya . . ." He turned his attention to Patty. "A sneaky kid . . . I heard Mrs. Kray call him Bernie." She shook her head. Why was he so dumb? Michael tried to elaborate. "I mean you don't see him and then you do. The Drudge knows. Mrs. Kray must have told her after the Drudge ate the chalk. It made her real sick. He was there in the doorway and Mrs. Greer looked at this kid Bernie like she does before she grabs your ear. Then she opened her mouth and put a piece of chalk in it and kept eating it until you could tell it was all coming up soon and then she ran out. You would think the kids would laugh, but everyone was scared."

"He hides?" Patty was exasperated. Michael took too long. "What did the kid do?"

"What do you mean?"

"The kid, what did he do then?"

He frowned. "I don't know, I—don't remember . . . I . . . " Michael decided he'd spilled all he knew. "That's all so pay up!"

Patty grabbed Hugo's cheeks and kissed him on the lips. "Take half a his," she said, and she sprang to her feet and opened the door.

"Not fair!" Michael called in as loud a whisper as he dared.

She had to get back before she was missed. Mrs. Kray often checked on them and Patty didn't want the attention. She hurried down the dark hall and finding the stairs, she sprinted up taking two at a time. Reaching the top, she saw the boy. It must be him. She could see his yellow eyes and felt . . . *He wanted her to jump, jump from the landing!* "You jump if you want, I'm going to bed." The boy was skinny like Michael said. She wondered if he'd try to push her. "Try and I'll push back." She was calm as she said it. The boy turned and ran. He's a dirty coward she thought, and she slipped back into the silent dormitory.

Lifting a corner of the patched blanket, she nudged one of the two small girls who turned over. Patty edged beneath the covers and took enough room on the narrow mattress to lie on her side. Carefully covering the girls, she discovered that one was Hildy who must have talked one of the others into trading.

She inched farther into bed and Hildy snuggled up, putting her head on Patty's shoulder. Patty pulled the blanket up as far as she could without uncovering either of the two younger girls. Then she put her hand in the pocket of her nightgown where she kept the allie. Turning it her palm, she said a prayer for little Russ. She missed her brother and Emily. *Don't think about it.* A tear trailed from the corner of one eye and onto the mattress where it was quickly absorbed. The other tear dropped as she fell into a sleep. The strange boy was far from her mind.

Lonnie
Cuyahoga County Orphanage
November 1906

"Patty," a voice whispered, "We need your help. Wake up."

Patty was in a dream, trying to get Russ to be quiet. He was hungry and wanted a cracker. *"The box, Pattycake, I saw some, Ma got 'em hid, want one."*

"Shh—hh Russie, you want her to hear? Wait till she goes to sleep, then I'll . . ."

"Patty wake up!" Someone was shaking her shoulder. It was Tandy.

"No more crackers, Russ, we . . ."

"Patty!" Miss Tandy's face came into focus. Patty wished that she could grow up and look like Ms. Tandy. The young nurse's brown hair was free from its usual coil and a quilted robe covered her generous bosom. It was hours until dawn and the moon shone through the window of the dormitory striking the lamp that Mrs. Kray had dimmed as she waited for Bernie to wake.

The lamp's shadow stretched, its silhouette reaching across the blanket as Patty threw it off. She started to ask why they needed her. The nurse put her finger to her lips. Handing Patty, a shawl, and some slippers, she led Patty downstairs to the infirmary.

Mrs. Kray was waiting there. Her gray hair plaited under a cap, the older woman wore a heavy lime colored robe, its folds and faded rose vine pattern wrapped tight for warmth and propriety. Perched on the examination table, was a boy of six holding a large biscuit in his hand. Although he was bundled in a wool blanket, he shivered, his thin legs peeking out of the blanket. There were bruises and fresh welts on his shins and scrapes covering his knees.

His clothes were piled on a desk. The melted ice and flecks of snow formed a puddle. "Leon found him huddled on the porch and woke me. We'll see to his needs until we make arrangements." Patty didn't ask what arrangements. The boy's skin was dark. His brown face had dimples in each cheek. Wary eyes darted from Mrs. Kray to Patty. Patty thought of Russ. She held out her hand. Grabbing the crumbs before they could fall, he stuffed a biscuit into his mouth, and shook her hand.

"What's your name?' she asked.

"Lonnie," he whispered. Despite Mrs. Kray's efforts, there was little else the boy would say other than his grannie died and the "people what took the farm" kept beating on him because he didn't work hard enough. No word of anyone missing a child came to her and Mrs. Kray knew that there was little use in trying to locate those responsible for mistreating the child.

As the days became weeks, Lonnie followed Patty, ignoring the stares of the other children. She kept him close. He sat with her at mealtimes and next to her in the classroom, where he clutched his knees as they leaned against the far wall, both sitting on the floor.

The Drudge ignored him, pretending not to see the small boy huddled close to Patty. Patty knew that would be no taunts or acts of aggression. She had a reputation.

Lonnie was determined to help at mealtime and under Hugo's approving eye, he folded the rag napkins Patty carelessly tossed on the side of the dinner plates.

Miss Tandy
November 1906

Lonnie laid the folded rag next to the plate and waited for Hugo's approval. Putting his finger and thumb together, Hugo made a circle. Patty shrugged. Why did they bother? No one noticed or cared, not the orphans nor any of the adults. Mrs. Kray, the Drudge and Leon seldom ate with the children. None showed the slightest interest. Tandy tried but was always tending to someone's cold or scrape.

Bother, it was just a lot of bother for nothing. Lonnie held out his hand for the next one. It was Thanksgiving tomorrow. In return for some of the older boys clearing dead branches and leaves from his property, a neighbor had donated a turkey, which sat in a burlap sack in the pantry. Something new, Grandma never cooked one and Ma . . . Patty closed her eyes, better not to think about Ma, Emily, or Russ . . .

Patty saw alarm on Hugo's face when Lonnie pointed toward the open door. A stream of smoke was rushing in. As it swirled through the room, hovering over the long table and its chipped plates and rags, they heard screams. Some were the high-pitched squeals of girls and others, the yells of adolescent boys as their changing voices rose to the pitch of the girls. Patty put her hand up and turned to Lonnie and Hugo. "Stay here; don't follow me." Both boys nodded. Lonnie began to shake. Hugo patted the smaller boy's arm, whispering that Patty would fix whatever had gone wrong.

The smoke trail led into the kitchen. Dark funnels rushing towards her, Patty put a rag over her mouth. Away from the smoke, under the blare of light from the hanging smoke-glass fixture, Bertha was sobbing, tears circling her mouth, her lips straining to cover the twisted teeth. She pointed at the open pantry door.

Mrs. Gibbons was clutching her chest. The old woman leaned against a wooden table; her wrinkled face clouded with fear. The cook made a feeble gesture, waving a hand towards the pantry. Her mouth trembled, the tongue pressed against the remaining teeth— t-t-t-taa—she shook her head, collapsing against the table. Patty peered into the clouds of smoke, her eyes watering. A groaning creak came from within the pantry, then a flame shot out, making her jump.

Patty wanted to run. As she turned, she saw that everyone was screaming, but no one was leaving. Why? For a moment, the funnels cleared, and she saw what made the creak.

A dead person jerked and squirmed in Mrs. Gibbons' rocker. The body shuddered as the head, encased in a sheath of flames, waved back and forth nodding. Smoke followed like the tail of a comet as the head gave an emphatic dip. A strand of unburned brown hair shot out sparks hovering in its wake.

Miss Tandy? Patty turned and glanced behind her. She wasn't sure . . . There should be a grownup; a grownup needed to . . . The children huddled together, and the Drudge stood behind them. Mrs. Kray stood frozen in the doorway. The smell was overwhelming. Was it the turkey or Miss Tandy?

"P-p-patteeeee!" Lonnie was crying. He had followed her and was clutching her waist.

"Mrs Kray?" Patty turned to ask, "what now, Mrs . . . what should I . . . " Loud popping came from the rocker.

The fire was spreading. She saw the boy, Bernie standing near the hanging pots. He leaned his elbows on a counter, his face cupped by his small hands. Smiling, his small teeth under a span of pink gums, were framed by colorless lips. The boy's yellow eyes faded into milky clots. He was telling her to mind her own business.

"Make me," she challenged. Seeing a sack of flour, she grabbed it, hoisted it up and ripped it open. As she poured flour on the burning woman, Patty sobbed. "Oh, Miss oh, Miss Tandy . . . why? Why did you . . ." Then she knew. Bernie the low-down coward did it because he knew Patty liked her. He would pay and she would be the one to make him pay. She would kill him. As she grabbed a heavy pan, he moved away from her and left the kitchen. Dirty coward, she thought, always a dirty coward.

So much sadness, and you bore it all alone. I wish. . .

PATTY

I'm okay, Emily. I'm not the only one who had it rough. You did too. I'm glad we're together now.

Me too.

Bread
Cuyahoga County Orphanage
Thanksgiving Day, 1906

Patty stood at the window in the cold classroom. No heat came from the radiator today. A gust of wind rattled the branches of trees near the driveway. Something caught her eye. The crow perched on a bare branch and watched as directly below, men were loading a wooden box into a wagon. The wind lifted the hat from one of them, pinning it against the box. Scooping his hat before the wind decided to take it again, the man gripped a corner of the box as it dropped and with a shove, the box slid into the wagon.

They were taking Miss Tandy away. *Was it cold in that box?* Leaning against the window, Patty decided she wouldn't watch as the truck and Miss Tandy left. Sliding to the floor, she rested her head on her knees. Why was it so hard to let go? She patted the checkered scarf the nurse had given her. Why hadn't she thanked her? Hugo, Hildy and Michael waited. Lonnie sat next to her on the floor.

No one believed Patty when she insisted that it was Bernie's doing, though she saw Mrs. Kray look away. The Drudge said a romance novel was to blame. Hiding in the pantry, Miss Tandy had decided to be "in-do-lent" (the Drudge said the word slowly to convey her distain). The fire resulted when a lamp overturned and caught on her skirt. It was a lie. Miss Tandy fell asleep while reading, Mrs. Kray explained. The Drudge said the nurse was remiss in her duties, a frivolous novel stealing her attention. No, not true; it was Bernie. Mrs. Kray knew, but Mrs. Kray was scared.

"I'm hungry, Hugo." Hildy tugged on Hugo.

Hugo shushed her. "Not now." The flour gone until early December, the corn meal was stretched. There would be less to eat for several days.

"The bakery, what about the bakery?" Hildy insisted.

Patty turned. "What bakery?"

"Kressin's." Hugo sighed. "Papa had a friend who worked there. We crawled through the window once." Patty's stomach growled at the thought of bread, dinner rolls and crusty loaves, broken into large chunks. She looked at Hildy. The little girl's eyes dominated her thin face. She'd never keep up, he thought. It was over a mile and back at night, too cold.

Patty began to hope. Maybe there would be cake. It had been so long . . . since before Russ. Gram baked one for her eighth birthday. She had loved every sweet golden crumb. But Gram died and then Ma came back, furious at the burden. There would be no more cake for her and Russ, no more cake for Russ ever.

TWENTY SEVEN

PATTY

Madonna isn't really Bernie's granddaughter; she's John's granddaughter. Which also means that Emma, Madonna, and Gordon are family. I am very happy about this.

This is wonderful.

Grandfather Crow
Something Very Wrong
Bedonne Trailer Home
November 2004

Her mother was right. There was something very wrong with the mall. Sitting at her desk, Madonna considered what to do. Emma was sprawled on the couch, snoring, her face buried by her arm. Half finished, a large glass of wine, her fourth of the evening sat on an end table.

Madonna loved her mother, but sometimes there was just no talking to her. Emma was upset and shaking when Madonna met her at the truck stop. When she saw her daughter's ICE KING uniform, Emma drove off without her, before turning around and opening the door without saying a word. Knowing that she would never approve, Madonna hadn't told Emma she had quit her job at the dry cleaners and was working at the mall. Emma couldn't understand that she HAD to be there.

Gordon's relationship with Emma changed the day he told Emma he was gay. Emma's wistful talk about a Giordano Bedonne IV was especially grating when she had a few drinks. Gordon loved his mother, but he lost patience with her drunken rambling one night and explained to her that there was not going to be a number four because he was gay. Things became very tense; Gordon decided to look for a place of his own a few months before the mall opened. Emma said nothing until he was leaving with the last of his possessions, including an album of family pictures with Emma, the twins, Dee and a treasured few of Giordano.

"Gordon," she said softly. Gordon turned to see his mother pulling some bills out of her purse. She handed him $100 in twenties and said. "Here, this is for your new place . . ." Gordon's calm exterior wavered, and he hugged his mother tightly. They were both in tears.

Things improved until the mall opening when Emma discovered that her son's independence included quitting the hardware store and working at the mall. Gordon was pig-headed, but Madonna refused to let her twin brother, who was the new manager at the mall's NATURAL BEAUTY, work there alone, unprotected.

Their grandfather, the person responsible for the mall, was a subject that they never discussed. She had seen him once when she and Gordon were six. They were on their way to school, and he was watching them, standing across the street. She didn't know who he was at the time, but she knew him. He'd been in her dreams from the time she could remember dreaming. When Madonna was little, she dreamed her grandfather was in the yard, and she'd hide under the bed. But he would always find her, grabbing her by an ankle and drag her out from under the bed. She would scream as Emma shook her awake, trying to soothe her. Gordon held her hand saying, "It's okay, Sis; you're okay."

In her teens, the dream changed. Madonna would be looking in a mirror as blood trailed down her forehead. Someone was behind her. Her grandfather would be there, watching her.

She didn't know who he was at first. She was eight when she saw his picture in the paper under the heading "Inquiry! Arnold denies charges of sending weapons to the Serbs." This was the man who stalked her. Senator John Arnold. Her brother was much more in tune with the "outer world", and she asked him if he knew who John Arnold was. After extracting a promise from her that she would do his share of the dishes for a week, Gordon told her.

When she insisted that their grandfather stalked her dreams, Gordon frowned and shook his head, insisting that she must have seen him before. Gordon didn't believe in psychic phenomena.

Not only did Madonna believe in precognition, she knew it was in her bloodline. Dee told her stories of her great aunt, Stella Caulkins' predictions from weather to premature deaths and her Grandmother Nora's dreams about the accident that killed her mother and brother. She knew little about Nora, but Madonna sensed that her grandmother, like great aunt Stella was precognitive. It was in her blood.

Her mother refused to talk about either woman, saying they had both come to a terrible end. After one disastrous question with Emma sobbing and retreating into a two-day bender, Nora was a subject Madonna avoided. Too painful.

Now her grandfather, the man who chased her from the time she could remember, was really here and she had to figure out what to do. She would start by researching precognition. She must be careful. Counting the crystals in her drawer, Madonna added some protection around the white candle near her bed. She would reinforce it when the lavender and herbs she ordered came.

The smudge sticks were ready. First, she would address the entrance to Gordon's shop, then the ICE KING counter and then the rest of the food court. Logging on to her computer, she clicked on *The Mystic Light Psychic Studies* in favorites and continued reading on psychic healing.

She wished she could heal her mother. Whatever ailed Emma, the wine she drank every night pushed the pain down, a pain so deep that Madonna feared for her. Since Gordon had decided to move out, at least Madonna now had a bedroom of her own. She checked her supply of red leaves. She had used them to protect the trailer since the beginning of October.

She made a note to herself to order more sage and to check for any new research on precognitive dreams. After reciting a few protective phrases, she took off her rings and chains and got into her nightgown. Tomorrow, she would go in early and recite a few prayers for guidance and protection when she arrived at the mall. *It'll be a while before I want to do a spread again,* she thought. It was too upsetting. Outside her window, the crow sat on the top of the swings set in the lot next door.

A Lucid Dream

Madonna stood in front of the mirror. I'm dreaming this. Blood trickled down her forehead and as she reached up to touch it, she saw her grandfather's reflection. "Okay, this is where it stops." She turned around to confront him.

He stood in a doorway; his eyes were closed and his hands, the fingers laced together, rested on his belt. "I'm not afraid you! Leave me alone!" she told him. No reaction. Did he represent a fear she needed to face? "Maybe I saw him when I was too young to remember and . . ."

As she reasoned away the meaning of her grandfather's intrusions, he opened his eyes. The irises were a pale yellow, SICK! Why am I coming up with this? Really gross. She noted the painting of a large rat hung framed like a family portrait on the wall to her left. Interesting, this is new.

Her grandfather changed and she knew the threat she faced was real. Red points of light glowed from the center of the yellow eyes until it seemed that his eyes were rolling flames, snapping with death.

Wake up wake up wake up, I hate this! I'm gonna wake up. He opened his mouth wide and let out a CAW! What the hell? Grandpa what ARE you? The clasped hands separated and a flurry of black wings released and swarmed through the room. Crows? That's new. I'm not going to freak. This is a dream; he can't really do anything. She would look up the meanings of birds in dreams.

He began to change, shrinking then sprouting black wings and becoming a crow except for the head, which remained a tiny version of her grandfather's head. The absurdity made her want to laugh until it flew towards her. She batted at him, demanding, "What do you want?"

Perching on top of the rat family portrait the crow/grandfather, its voice a blend of a crow's cry and the smoothness of a seasoned politician's, it squawked, "Someday we'll be together Madonna, a real family!"

Madonna woke up, her heart loud in her ears. She wanted to crawl in bed with her mother, but she knew that as scared as she was, her mother was terrified. She turned on the light by her bed. It was two a.m. She fell back sleep, with the light on.

The next morning, as she gathered her materials, including her textbook, *Etheric Energy and Paranormal Physics,* she noticed that her skull ring was gone. Emma was getting ready for work when Madonna asked her if she had seen it. Emma, who wasn't too fond of the skull ring, said no, but that it might be better if it stayed lost.

Emma left for work, leaving it to Gordon to give Madonna a ride to the mall. Putting her candles, crystals, herbs, and smudge sticks in a sack, Madonna waited for Gordon. While she waited, she recited a spell to ward off negative spirits from the trailer.

A feeling of uncertainty still plagued her, as if she were forgetting something important. She decided to grab another textbook, *Reading the Alchemical Tarot*, her favorite deck of cards. She would check for any stronger protective rituals and email her favorite professor for advice.

TWENTY EIGHT

PATTY

Can't we skip this part? It makes me sad and angry.

I promised Gram, I would watch it with you. It's what happened right before you came here. She insisted. You need to remember something. I don't know what it is, and Gram wouldn't say. Now, no arguing. I'm putting my arms around you and we're watching it together.

Okay, but I wish she told you what it is I'm supposed to remember.

A Murder of Crows

Kressin's Bakery

Cleveland, Ohio

November 1906

"How long, Patty?" Lonnie's voice shook.

"Wait; once they're at the turn, we'll go," Patty whispered. She tugged the loose strip of blanket, tucking it into her coat collar. Pieces of horse blankets wrapped around their necks; the children waited. Lonnie had seen Leon throw the strips away when clearing the shed. The rough fabric made a snug shield against the wind. They huddled behind a row of trash barrels. The delivery wagon, relieved of its sacks of flour, was ready to depart. As they waited, the biting wind found its way through the trash barrier. Was it past midnight yet? She moved closer to Lonnie, protecting him from the wind. He was too little to be out like this.

Lonnie clutched her arm. "We'll wait. S'okay Paa." Hugo and Michael looked at each other. Michael shook his head. If they came home empty-handed—she winced at the thought of Hildy's disappointment.

Patty wiggled her fingers. Tucked inside the ring finger of the right hand, she kept her lucky allie, which made the glove snug, but she didn't mind. It was best to keep it with her in case someone decided she didn't need it anymore. The gloves made her feel older than twelve. The first time she had put them on, she pretended that she was a grownup, going out for the evening. Then she shook off the fantasy. Ridiculous, where would she go? Mrs. Kray had pointed to the gloves on her desk. "Take these, Patty." The older woman was studying a small bible, her hands trembling as she gripped it.

Why was Mrs. Kray so scared? What else had he done? What *was* Bernie?

Miss Tandy's gloves felt strange on her child's hands. Despite the fur lining, her fingers were numb. She was flexing her fingers to restore feeling in her hands when the backdoor swung open and the deliverymen exited, climbing onto the wagon. Lights in the bakery went out as the two employees, pulling their collars up against the cold, locked the door and stopping to wrap their scarves tight against the wind, they began the walk home. Just a little longer, Patty assured herself, and the charity kids will be on their way back, pockets and burlap sacks full of bread and rolls and . . . She smiled, imagining the surprise when they returned. Be careful; make sure there was enough, make sure that she and hers got plenty; it was the only fair thing; they were taking the risk.

Its wheels rattling, the wagon turned the corner when the horse whinnied and reared. A tinny sounding horn gave notice as an automobile swung around the wagon, ice cracking under its tires. The wagon driver's curses faded quickly into the dark streets. In the alley, there was only Hugo's wheezing. The frigid air was harsh. It was after midnight now for sure. Hurry, only a few hours until the next shift. What if someone came in early? Despite the cold wind, she could smell baked bread. The thought of bread baking in a warm kitchen brought tears. She remembered Gram and willed the tears back. No point. Michael's eyes caught the faint light of the corner streetlamp. "Now?" he demanded. She nodded.

Hugo's wheeze grew louder as he pulled an old washtub from its place against the stoop and positioned it under the window. The sound of metal scraping against loose stones echoed. Gesturing for the others to stop, Patty dropped low. Did someone hear?

"Stupid, no one's out now. Let's go." Michael's patience was gone.

Patty cuffed him on the shoulder. "I say when."

His voice wavered. "Okay, okay. So, when?" There was a creak as Hugo coaxed the window open. Moving one inch, then another, suddenly, it slid open. They all sighed. There would be time to celebrate was later.

The latch was still broken, as it had been in the summer when Hugo shimmied through. Afraid of pity, Hugo looked down when he told the story. Mama made them leave, he explained. She had ordered them not to come back for days so her new "gentleman" wouldn't be disturbed. "Kressin's bakery, high quality, Papa always said." Hugo smiled, nodding his head for emphasis. She could see his sadness. "Hildy was only four, but she was a great look out."

Hildy had put her hand up and shaded her eyes to mimic being a lookout as Hugo finished his story.

"We ate lots and then we hid and when it got dark, we slept in a flowerbed. When we came back, Mama was cross because of the dirt."

Patty knew their "mama" slept in prison now. She wondered where hers was. Dead hopefully. Hugo poked his head out. "Clear," he hissed, "hurry!" Michael scrambled through the opening and then reached to pull Lonnie in while Patty hoisted him up. She quickly followed, giving a final look down the deserted alley. The wind was starting up again, blowing paper and debris.

Inside the dark kitchen, Michael pointed to a small lamp. He moved it to the floor behind a counter. A box of matches sat on the counter and Patty lit the lamp. Then she stood up and looked around the room. Sitting on a cart close to the window was a cake, *the most beautiful thing, oh, Russ*... The icing was swirls of caramel and vanilla, studded with walnuts. Crushed on one side, the cake was abandoned to a side table as unsellable.

"Get all the bread," she whispered. Large baskets of day-old loaves and rolls were tucked in a corner. Hugo began to wrap them up in paper and rags storing them in the burlap sack.

Opening the cupboards, Michael found pies. "Leave it to me," Hugo said.

"The cake, Hugo." She pointed at it, almost pleading. Hugo frowned as he stretched the largest sack's opening, estimating its width and the cake's. The bag was not wide enough for the cake.

"We'll need a box of some kind," his conclusion.

"I saw a wooden crate, not too big." Michael offered. He looked at Patty to see if she was pleased with his idea.

"Where," Hugo asked.

"On the side of the stoop," Michael answered as he waited for a decision. Hugo decided to see for himself. Michael wasn't always the best judge.

"Look around and see what else you can find," he ordered. Michael and Patty nodded. There were cabinets and counters running the length of the room. Long pans and metal sheets were stacked and ready to host a new supply of fresh bread, cakes, pies and . . . She heard a thud as Hugo's shoe struck the inside wall below the window. His head and upper torso were outside the window. Was he caught on something? She worried that he impaled himself on a protruding nail. Her heart pounded as she hurried to the window. Was he hurt bad?

A wave of hate rolled over the struggling Hugo and slammed into Patty. She knew in an instant that Bernie had followed them. Hunger had distracted her, and she had failed to sense him. Hugo would die if she didn't act quickly. Michael and Lonnie began to cry, "Move away, Patty, move away from the window. We'll be safe if we hide!" Michael begged. Lonnie wailed, insisting that he wasn't hungry, begging her to get Hugo and then they could all run away. *Bernie did this.* she thought bitterly. The coward meant to kill them all.

Not this time; she will fight.

Hang on Russie—I'm sorry I left you. I didn't want to wake you. Ma wanted the blanket, and it was wet. Then you were dead, and she kept hitting you. Oh God forgive me for not stopping her . . .

A rolling pin was on a breadboard. Perfect. She pulled off the gloves; she'd need a good grip. Sweeping the rolling pin from the breadboard, she rushed to the window. Hugo's struggle was slowing, his arms and legs barely moving. HURRY!

She jabbed the rolling pin through the window. She heard a cry; Bernie had fallen. Unconscious, Hugo was limp, draped on the open window frame. Pulling Hugo inside, she shouted for the others to take him. Gripping the rolling pin, she crawled through the open window, springing to her feet as soon as she hit the ground. She was ready to fight and gripped the rolling pin with both hands holding it up and wielding it like a sword.

Was he still there? *Please let him be there!* Yes, as he was scrambling to get up, she blocked his exit and tasted his fear, better than cake. He had stuffed his coat pockets, making it hard to pull himself up. A puny excuse for . . . She paused. What was in his pockets? *Who cared? He was going to die!*

"I don't know what you are, but you're a monster for sure, worse than my ma," she spat as she slapped the rolling pin on her thin coat. Miss Tandy's scarf tied under her chin, the little girl's pigtails fell free. Bernie trembled, cowering in front of her, his long face twisting in terror. Whining, he clutched his coat, pulling it up over his face as if to hide from the assault. She heard shouting. People were coming.

A stench blew in with the cold wind. The smell of a coward she decided; he shit his pants. Then she hesitated. There was snapping, like the sound of Ma's old leather strap. A loud boom, like a heavy door slamming surprised her. *Is there someone else? Does he have help?* She'll take care of them too. The coward was going to pay and anyone else who took his side. She would kill him before anyone could stop her. With a loud CAW, a crow appeared, perching on the windowsill. She looked up as it began circling and swooping. Waving the rolling pin at it, she swatted at it. With an angry CAW, it landed on the windowsill, puffing its feathers, its red eyes glowing as it bobbed its head.

The smell—something different—what? Kerosene! He has kerosene! She recognized it as he sprayed her coat and then she saw the matches. Oh no . . . no, oh no—PLEASE NO FIRE! She swung the rolling pin as he threw the lit match and the strip of blanket caught fire and she can't . . . PAIN pain pain—ooohhh—such pain . . . her lungs—*I can't breathe!* The flames . . . RUN . . . Screaming, she heard her screams, the others were . . . AGONY.

She could still see him. He smiled with those nasty little teeth. Red eyes, hundreds and hundreds, were swimming, spiraling into the flames. She heard the screams of crows feasting on her pain . . . *ohhhh. It hurts so bad . . . I can't see, oh God I can't breathe! Please let me die, oh please, please* . . . She was turning as she heard shouts. Bernie began to run, the coward . . .

Little Russ

"Patty-cake?" Russ sat on the bakery stoop. Patty sighed. No pain . . . Russ wore the same plaid jumper with the torn pockets he wore the day he died.

"I know he wet the bed; I'll wash it right now." Patty had begged. Emily screamed when Ma killed Russ and then made Patty push her little brother out the window.

Ma returned to her divan and her drink. "You're a kid." Ma had assured her as she yawned. "Who'll believe you now?"

"An accident, his sister left the winda open." Ma sobbed. Ma was right; no one believed her.

Her brother grinned. The same teeth were missing, and his head was still covered in rowdy curls cocked to the side. He crossed his arms impatiently. "C'mon, Gramma's taking us to the zoo. Don't be a slow poke." He pursed his lips and winked at her.

"Russie, I missed you! I—I'm dead?"

He shrugged. "Dunno." She still gripped the rolling pin. "Keep it," he said, grabbing her free hand. He squeezed her fingers gently as he tugged her arm. "Gramma might need it or something."

As they left, she saw Bernie flee into the empty streets. The crows were gone. The men running into the alley saw her as she burned, but they didn't see Bernie. Gram was waiting for her somewhere, a place even more peaceful than the eye of her treasure, a place of parks and saltwater taffy, a place of love.

No matter, Patty thought as she left her friends and the pain. Cowards always got theirs. She knew that for sure.

PATTY

I shoulda told you that Russie wasn't your fault.

But I peed the bed and I—

You were a little kid! Stop it! It wasn't your fault, Emily!

Russie told me and Gram told me, and now you. I'm trying to believe it.

Try harder.

I love you.

You should. We're sisters.

The Coward

It was a cold, joyless midnight in late November of 1906 when Bernie's prolonged childhood finally came to an end. The beginning of the end began as the young burglars waited for the sounds of horses, their hooves clapping on the uneven street and the crackling of tires made by the occasional automobile yielded to the cold wind sighing through deserted streets. Feeling the sting of the freezing air, he watched them pry open the bakery window.

Tucked in the deep pockets of Leon's overcoat, a garment so large that the tattered ends gathered bits of debris as Bernie crept behind the children, were rags, a small can of kerosene and precious matches he had stolen the night before.

His breath quickened when he saw Hugo shimmy through the narrow opening. He savored the thought of Hugo's death. He planned to lock Hugo in, along with his friends, especially the meddlesome girl. Then he would burn them all alive as they shrank back in fear. When Patty whispered an order to Hugo "See if the alley is clear," Bernie suppressed a laugh. Soon, they will scream for help, and no one will hear.

As Hugo poked his head out of the window, the killer lost control and his hands wrapped around Hugo's neck. Thrashing and gurgling, Hugo kicked the wall inside. Bernie focused his thoughts, suggesting to the terrified children that it was safer inside. It was best to leave things as they were. "Hide!" he urged them. Their wills began to yield.

NO! The orphan girl was pulling on his wrists! Worse was the shock of a will opposing him. She forced his hands away from Hugo's collapsing body, the others catching the boy as he fell to the floor. They began to wail, and screams echoed in dark alley. Unless he killed the girl soon, people would know. Pulling Hugo from the window, the girl jumped through the open window. He trembled as she came after him, ignoring his suggestion that she would be safer inside. "Come inside, Patty," the others pleaded, "it's not safe! Wait! We'll hide and then go back when it's safe".

"I don't know what you did; I don't know what you are," she growled. He was startled when she began to swing a large rolling pin in his direction. "You're a monster, you are," she shrieked, "worse than my ma!" He trembled, hoping Father would send his messengers to deal with this thing in her sad little red scarf, her pigtails belying her menace and rage.

Then, Father sent the crow.

The crow and Hugo's whimper saved Bernie. Flailing her weapon at the menacing bird Patty turned when she heard Hugo cry.

Distant shouting meant people were coming. He must act to save himself! Reaching into the deep pocket of Leon's coat he found the can, opened it and splashed kerosene onto the coat of the startled girl. A lit match found its target. The orphan girl in her shabby coat became a single flame. Demons wove in and out of the fire, gorging on the girl's agony. As she died screaming, the other children sobbed, huddled together inside.

Bernie knew that Father had come to his aid. Was he forgiven? He doubted it. He wanted to stay and enjoy the girl's agony, but instead, he ran. There must be a way back, to once again, bask in the light of Father's favor. He would find it. Until then, he meant to survive.

Mrs. Kray
Cuyahoga County Orphanage
November 1906

She mourned the dead girl. No family, she told them, none she knew about. The injured boy was recovering, thank God, as was his sister. The child's hysteria had resulted in a bed next to her brother's. The others were shaken, but unharmed. None of them could remember how the girl caught fire. Who had splashed her with kerosene and lit a match? Many assumed that the girl must have resisted an assault by a person or persons unknown, the boy injured when he tried to intervene.

As she sat in her office, her desk was piled with gifts of money, toys and food arrived daily. Because of the children's story, the years of violent deaths, including Mr. Buchner, the cook, Miss Tandy and now, Patty, were connected to the missing Bernie Baker, the son of a murderer. The plight of the orphans and the hunger that led them to the bakery was the subject of newspaper articles and editorials.

Despite what she had told the newspapers, she was able to locate Patty's sister, Emily. Guilt demanded that she try to let Emily know of Patty's death. The Nagles, who had adopted Emily, took the money Mrs. Kray offered and then forbade any contact. Though there were numerous large and small donations, Mrs. Kray, herself paid for the girl's burial. Guilt demanded it. Mrs. Kray knew who had killed her. It was Bernie. Now, there was no doubt that Bernie was gone. The dread lifted like an unwelcome hand. Guilt and joy overwhelmed her. She was free; they all were.

Miss Tandy's gloves, returned to her at the end of the investigation, sat folded on her desk atop a soft toy, a turkey someone had sent from Redhill. Beautifully handmade, the turkey's tail feathers were stitched from cloths of different colors. She thought of Patty's rare smile when the orphan tried on the gloves. Such a sad little girl . . .

The gloves, what should she do with them? She would have buried them with Patty, but it was too late. Picking up the right glove, she folded down the cuff. While admiring the elegant stitching, Mrs. Kray began to shake, falling from her desk to the floor, thankfully alone, her hands covering her face, her shoulders heaving with grief and the joy of freedom.

TWENTY NINE

PATTY

This is John's prison friend. He tried to help.

I know. Bless him.

The ABC's of Nightmares
Ray Gibbs
Redhill Convalescent Hospital
November 2004

"Turn it off, kid, I've heard enough. Just turn the damn thing off!" The old man and his grandson sat in the TV room of the Redhill Convalescent Home and Assisted Living Facility.

"Fair enough, Grandpa." said Alec as he turned off the console. News coverage of the mall opening hadn't finished. Alec had just been hired to work as a clerk at Video Games Galore.

Ray Gibbs shook his head. "Shouldna' been built. God help us all. Stay away from that place, Alec. It's bad news."

"Gramps, we've been over this. I need money for school and so I have to work." Alex said as he offered Ray a sip of grape soda. "No place else is hiring right now. I'll be careful, okay? Let's go for a stroll." Ray loved the fresh air and it was still warm out.

As Alex helped him into the wheelchair, Ray reflected on how much he loved the boy. Now that Molly was gone, Alec was the only one in the family who came to visit. He understood. They all had their own lives. Ray was eighty-eight and had been living at Redhill Convalescent, (he wouldn't call it a home though the staff did the best they could) since he'd taken that spill five years earlier. He had tried to protest, but they'd all insisted. None of the three kids lived close enough to keep an eye on him. He was lucky they even talked to him after what he put them through. Not there when they needed him, but then he would show up with surprises before taking off again for weeks and months.

When he came home on parole, six months after the fire, he was a changed man. Lisa had come to see him in the hospital. She'd divorced him by then, but she still loved him. Her face drained of color when she saw what was left of him, the wretched burns under his bandages and how he couldn't stop shaking.

He begged her to take him back, swearing he'd never place another bet, or even look at a deck of cards. He'd promised before, but this time, they both knew he meant it. The kids were teenagers by then and never did trust him much.

He worked when he could. Being an ex-con made it hard. How he missed Lisa. She was dead twenty years, but he still talked to her every day, and he made sure to let her know about the kids. Their two girls had done well. Both had jobs, good marriages and kids of their own. There was even one great-grandchild. Ray Jr., unfortunately, was too much like his dad. Who knew where he was now?

He had loved Ray's wife Molly like his own daughter. A good woman, dead of cancer at fifty when geezers like him just kept hanging on. Thank God, Alec took after her.

Alec unlocked the brake on Ray's wheelchair, and began to wheel him out of his room, when two news teams came through the doors near the main desk. "Ray Gibbs. We'd like to know where we can find Mr. Gibbs." The woman whose suit and hair cut identified her as a TV reporter, had the smile of a con artist—charming while looking for weakness.

"I'm Ray Gibbs." Ray said. Alec looked warily at the teams that were starting to set up right there.

"Mr. Gibbs, I'm Jennifer Tremaine of Channel 4 News, she said. She waited for a reaction from Ray as an assistant whispered something in her ear. She nodded and brushed the whisperer away with a pointed finger. "Sir, you were one of the survivors of the prison fire in '65. We've been told that you opposed the building of the new mall, saying, and I quote, 'It shouldn't be built, nothing should stand there; the place is cursed.' Now, we've also heard rumors that you don't think much of the ex-Senator. Care to elaborate on that?"

At the mention of John Arnold, Alec saw Ray start to shake. The old man opened his mouth, trying to speak, but couldn't make a sound. His jaw moved up and down and tears rolled down his cheeks where the whitened remnants of massive scars claimed most of his face. Alarmed, Alec turned Ray's chair towards the room.

"My grandfather is tired. Leave him alone!" he said firmly, entering the room as the following news teams protested. He ordered them out, shut the door and comforted Ray, lifting him onto the bed, as Ray sobbed, begging Alec to stay away, stay away from that cursed mall.

THIRTY

PATTY

Ramona got the allie and she didn't even like it. I know she was a little kid, but she should have done better. It would have saved everyone a lot of trouble. If I hadda got the job, I woulda slammed the door right in Bernie's ugly face real quick.

I know Patty. She wasn't as strong as you.

Too bad. She didn't even try.

Too bad for us all.

Ramona Song

San Francisco

1906

They found Daddy blocks away. When they carried him home, Mommy opened the package he had brought back from his trip to Cleveland and found the chicken puppet. In her letter, Sister Marsh called it a "turkey," but it looked like a chicken to her, though it had a big cloth tail with different colored feathers. There was a pair of light brown gloves made of smooth brushed leather. Daddy was gone. The gloves remained on a chair. Ramona picked one up and slipped her child's hand into the soft fur. Inside the glove, she felt something roll and when it touched her finger, she was somewhere else.

Darkness . . . The sound of a harsh wind was in her ears. There was burning and she screamed as flames consumed her flesh, but then . . . The coward-the coward . . . she swung at him again. He smiled at her . . . rat's teeth. Ramona broke free from the flames and watched the girl as she burned. Her death will come soon. Oh, please let it come; she hurts! The girl stumbled as she swung a wooden club, blindly striking out at something.

A boy with blond hair, the demon boy who had haunted her dreams stood just out of reach of the swinging weapon and watched the girl burn. The dying girl amused him. The poor girl, someone help her!

"Patty, please please come inside the bakery and hide, please, you'll be safe . . . oh Patty." Children were crying. Ramona wished she could help them. Patty was beyond help.

A slapping sound became cries as crows appeared where they had not been before. Swooping down, the birds dived into the fire where the girl screamed and twirled. As they entered the flames, the birds vanished. Then the girl fell to her knees and collapsed, her body twitching. Within the blaze, red eyes swarmed, moving rhythmically, dancing. Oh, let this be a dream, let me wake up, they're demons! Please . . . pain . . . pain . . . such pain!

She was one with the dying girl. The red-eyed demons

devoured her pain . . . no no no. Ramona broke away as she saw the girl's brother come for her. The demons swirled out of the flames and disappeared. The coward ran. They always get what they deserve.

Mommy was shaking her. The beige glove slipped off her hand and something rolled out. A pearl rested on the floor. It was looking at her. Ignoring Mommy's "Jan ge, jan ge, please, what's wrong? Tell Mommy!" Ramona reluctantly touched the pearl. The eye must not see her. She rolled it with her finger, and it spun back and settled in her palm.

She was on a mountain, so far up, only a hint of land lay under the soft gray and white clouds that moved slowly toward a distant horizon. Above her were shades of cerulean and azure blue. The sun was warm, but it did not interfere with the brace of cool, soothing air caressing her face. With every breath, Ramona sensed a purity and peace. "Oh, let me stay."

She cupped the pearl in her hand, and it began to change, the eye expanding. Ramona found herself sitting on a cliff, her child's legs dangling precariously from the edge. Streaks of dark purple mixed with violent reds dominating the sky as lightening flashed and claps of thunder caused her to shake and cry, "Daddy!"

"Send them back; they cannot come this way." It was Daddy. He looked just as he did on the day he left. She reached out her arms for him to pick her up. Compassion was in his eyes, but he shook his head. "Their servant must go too. This way must be sealed." He pointed at a door, which hung suspended in the troubled air. It lay open and Ramona could see Mommy. Mommy was screaming for

help. On the floor, Ramona saw herself as she lay motionless, her eyes open but turned back, as if she were dead.

She raised her arms again. "Daddy, I want to stay with you. Take me to the mountain. Please, don't leave me here!"

Daddy shook his head; his voice was sad. "You must . . . remember, Ramona is a brave, smart girl, no demon can defeat her . . . send them back, stop him . . . Ramona is . . ."

"Ramona! Please wake up!" She opened her eyes and saw Mommy's frantic face. She begged Mommy to throw the pearl and the gloves away. The gloves were gone immediately, but later, Ramona discovered Mommy had decided to sell the pearl. Its sale would allow them to move from the crowded room to a comfortable apartment, where Mommy could continue to forecast the future for others. Ramona insisted that Mommy keep the pearl hidden until it was gone.

In her nightmare, (Mommy insisted it was a nightmare, though Mommy knew it wasn't) Daddy said that Ramona must seal the door. The door must be kept locked, she told Mommy.

"But what door?" Mommy had asked. "Where is it?" There was no door in the parlor where Ramona had collapsed, just archways and a window. Where was it, this door? Ramona admitted that she didn't know. Not in the apartment, she decided. Not even in San Francisco, she reassured Mommy after time passed with no more similar dreams, though Mommy wasn't satisfied. Mommy finally let the matter rest. It was best forgotten. Let someone else protect it.

Although she tried, Ramona could not forget Daddy's words. For the first time in her life, she felt anger toward the human being she loved most. *I'm only six. Why must I be the one?* She decided it was a mistake. Perhaps when she was older, this was something she was supposed to do, not now . . . Still, in her dreams, evil grinned smugly back at Ramona. Somehow, it had gained entry into the world. With dismay, she knew it was her duty to fight it. She must send it howling back to the dark plane where it belonged.

THIRTY ONE

Home Fires
Cleveland, Ohio
Dec 24, 1906

"... demons reside in an infernal plane called the Abyss, where they cavort and plan the destruction and overthrow of all mankind . . . it is a place of soaring heights, huge mountains, towering pillars and balls of flame that burst spontaneously in random locations . . . The Abyss is home to demons, creatures devoted to death and destruction. A demon in the Abyss looks upon visitors as food or a source of amusement" (Scroll of Abyssal Lore)

Memories of red eyes, burning with purpose, urgent whispers and rich laughter haunted him. The volcanic plains were just beyond dull reality. Now, they only came to him in dreams. He hid near the rails where boxcars ran, transporting coal and iron ore, the yards where lumber was stacked. The smell of industry around him, he slept under bridges, taking what he needed to survive from those he killed or simply robbed.

For weeks, he stayed near the docks, listening to the sounds of ships, barely remembering Crispin and London. During the day, he wandered down to the edge and waited until workmen who were eating their lunch suddenly decided they were no longer hungry, abandoning their half-eaten sandwiches to play cards or relieve themselves before the end of their breaks. He roamed through streets of Cleveland, eyes downcast, not revealing their menace to those tossing the occasional penny into his cap. Hunger dominated his waking thoughts.

It was snowing on Christmas Eve, 1906 when Bernard Baker finally knew his purpose. He walked along Superior Street, his feet slipping in the boots removed from a woman he had murdered the night before.

Angry December winds mocked him. The evening grew colder. He was drawn to the heat of open shops and restaurants, avoiding the slush and mud that flew from horses and tinny automobiles moving along the busy street. Hearing the chatter of those out to celebrate, a wave of self-pity rolled through him. Tears trickling down his thin face burned with rage. While being jostled by hurried shoppers, he heard music. Street musicians played Christmas carols. Opportunities might present in such a gathering, with the attention of many on but a few. Pushing closer, he saw enormous doors. Above them were the words THE ARCADE.

Gleaming brass columns supported an extension, which framed the recessed entry. He gazed at the doors, marveling at the cut glass and rich wood under glowing holiday lights. People hurried in and out, packages, children, small pets in tow. He followed a family of eight, the mother distracted by one child's stream of questions. The brat's piping voice cut through the jumble of conversations. Bernie saw possibilities. The father smoked a cigar and walked ahead, oblivious to mother's frustration.

THE ARCADE

"He appeareth at first like a Crow . . ." (*The Book of the Goetia of Solomon the King*)

PATTY

The monster should have kept Bernie and eaten him. He wouldn't have tasted very good.

This is all terrifying.

As he began to plot the kill, wondering which was easier, the mother or the brat, Bernie entered a world beyond his dreams. Wreaths of fir, festooned with red ribbons, hung low, inviting him to enter a hall that sparkled like Aladdin's cave.

The murder plot abandoned, he slid the dead whore's boots on marbled floors and caressed the polished oak banisters of granite stairs leading to five narrow floors of shops, each floor open to the center of the Arcade and each confined by ornate barriers of brass swirling in patterned glass. Tall columns of African mahogany supported the arched glass ceiling. On the ground floor, toy trains whistled, and a huge brass-framed clock was suspended, its commanding presence high above the swarming masses. The clock began to strike eight.

Dolls, dollhouses, rocking horses, bicycles, bright colored balls, and toy wagons beckoned to those who strolled past shop windows where dolls were dressed in imported fashion. Majestic towers anchored the Arcade. The strings of shops shone like gems. Excited families rushed to climb the polished stairs. Breathless children pointed to toys displayed in tempting tableaus while adults urged them to hurry; we can't be late for Christmas Eve dinner. The magic of the Arcade was something new. Shops, restaurants, and services enclosed within for perfect weather.

As he began to climb to the second floor, Bernie froze. Massive gargoyles glared down at him. Their gas lamps in their gaping mouths illuminated the Arcade. "You simply can't come in here," a griffin sniffed.

"Not worthy!" agreed the lion.

Reluctantly, he abandoned the stairs. To those passing him, families strolling by the brightly lit display windows, lovers gazing at diamonds and rubies set in rings priced well beyond the means of all but a lucky few, Bernie was a young boy, transfixed by the menace of lamps whose light shone from the mouths of monsters.

Many laughed and pointed, assuming a street urchin lacked the intelligence to realize the artifice of hanging fixtures. "Oh, just let him be," a woman said as her husband grumbled about 'the street element'. "He'll wise up sooner or later and it's Christmas; good will towards all, darling," she laughed, as they swept by Bernie's rigid form on their way to supper.

He struggled to break free, panicking as something scooped him up, twirling him like a top as he zoomed toward the Arcade ceiling. The glassed arch loomed, and he screamed, closing his eyes to meet certain death. But he felt no impact, no piercing shards of breaking glass. When he opened his eyes, he was standing on the surface of a wooden top.

For most of his lifetimes, he would think of his time in the demon world as if it were a treasured homecoming instead of a nightmare. Frenzied cycles of creation vied with instant destruction. Trees grew in seconds only to explode, their hurdling branches like spears.

"I beg you," Bernie pleaded as the top's surface dipped as it slowly turned. "Tell me how to please, how to make it right!" Gathering shadows became the demon hordes. Thunder clapped and the mountains roared, as Father heard his earnest plea. Chattering crows appeared, perched on tree branches, their heads bobbing and cocking to the side. One of them spoke.

"Oh dear, you ARE a disappointment," the crow said. It spoke in Crispin's voice. "What to do?"

An indescribable force made him turn. It drew him like a flower turning its face to the sun. Father's cloud face was so terrifying, Bernie shivered with love. The gaping mouth yawned and stretched. Burning eyes glowed deep within the cloud. Bernie thought it meant to swallow him. He would have gladly died if it meant being part of such a being.

"Father, tell me how to please." He shielded his eyes from a blinding light. Then, a building appeared, floating below the shadows. The Arcade, Bernie thought; no, this one was smaller. Were there faint screams coming from within the phantom building? The delicious terror and pain in them echoed as the floating edifice burst into flames. The cloud mouth uttered a moan of satisfaction. Now, Bernie knew his task. He must find the cloud building and fill it with screams. He trembled with pleasure and relief.

As he drifted back into his body that had collapsed onto the marbled floor of the Arcade, the crow called to him, "Ducky Strike, m'boy."

"Ducky Strike!" said a dragon.

The griffin added, "You'll know, a reward, hokey pokey!"

#

"Should we call someone?" An old woman was standing over him as he opened his eyes and smiled. A group of people had gathered around him. The woman's concern froze as she collapsed, her spectacles landing on his coat.

"Take them," growled the troll.

"Joy to the world," sang the choir of the Grand Arcade. The woman's husband started to cry. Someone shouted for a doctor and Bernie was forgotten. He rose to his feet, grabbing the old woman's spectacles from the marbled floor. Putting them on, he walked through the huge doors and into the cold. He felt joy. He knew his purpose.

#

Though she resisted, Ramona finally nodded off.

Bells rang. She heard laughter and singing. "Joy to the world?" Were they at the bakery again? No, she was on a crowded street where strange people wore heavy clothes. There were no Chinese anywhere. Where is this? The blond boy stood beside her. He looked around but didn't see her. What if he knew how to find her?

A wind stirred the embers of a fire contained in a barrel as men and women bundled in rags warmed their hands and falling from the sky there was . . . snow? Once, when Mommy spoke of her childhood in China, she described the hardship of being homeless in the snow—white death Mommy called it. Ramona had never seen snow before. Hats pulled tight, scarves wrapped around their necks, people rushed past them and through huge doors. He hates all of them. Recessed, at the end of a canopied entry, protected by doormen in soldier uniforms, the doors swung open with a pop and closed with a whoosh as the warm air inside met the cold night.

Sparkling glass, brass gleaming, she heard more bells and sounds of excitement. Christmas, someone said, Merry Christmas. "Arcade Papa, the Arcade, buy me a red wagon . . . I want one." A brat, Sister Marsh would say. She watched the family go through the doors. Above the doors were brass letters,

G…R…A….N….D…A…R…C…A….D…E . . . She was grateful Sister Marsh had taught her the ABC's. Remember, she told herself; find out what they mean.

The boy followed the family. No one saw him. He was unaware of her. Wake up! I want to wake up! The boy had blood on his hands. He killed for pleasure and for the pleasure of . . .? Ramona didn't want to know.

Inside the doors a festival was going on. Shops, one on top of another—five levels—the floors open, brass railing protecting the edges and so beautiful. Black columns supported the high ceilings of the giant hall. People were climbing; excited children ran up the stairs, pointing at the displays of toys.

Toy trains, stuffed animals and wooden horses sat in the window, waiting to be taken home by some lucky child. Dolls sat on little chairs or stood next to other toys, as if they would come to life and start to play, bouncing a ball or tossing it to passersby. They resembled the doll with the blond braids and happy face that Sister Marsh had given her for her sixth birthday. Instead of a white pinafore over a blue cotton dress, these dolls dressed in rich looking wool coats and velvet dresses. They looked like tiny children with golden hair topped with ribbons or they had shiny brown curls under little sailor hats.

Stairs led to different floors where kerosene lamps made the colorful windows pockets of fantasy. Each floor of shops looked like strings of sparkling gems. Gaslight filled the massive hall. It came from the jaws of monsters holding lamps in their yawning mouths. They were like dragons. The heads hung on posts that formed a circle within the enclosure.

There was more singing. Everyone was enjoying the music. Maybe there would be a parade. So many shops, so much beauty. How Mommy would love the clothes, hats with feathers and long coats with beautiful buttons! Mommy was always complaining to Daddy, no . . . Daddy was gone. He rested in the cemetery until his bones were ready for the long trip home.

At last, the baby cried. Ramona woke to humming as baby's mother soothed him. She remembered how safe she felt in Daddy's arms when she woke from a bad dream, and he comforted her. She missed her room and her toys. Her chicken puppet sat next to her, and she reached for it in the dark. Daddy was going to build them another house, fitting for the family of such an important merchant. Daddy was gone. Now, there was no more money until Mommy sold the pearl. She stroked the cloth chicken's beak. At least I'll have my own room again. Voices. She heard Mommy in the parlor. She was telling a young man when he would marry. "She'll come soon," Mommy was positive. "Ah, good," he said happily. Ramona knew he would never marry. He'd be dead within a year, killed by a streetcar. She thought, let him be happy for a little while.

Sleep. No, I don't want to go back. Ramona drifted.

Bells kept ringing. Some rang low and steady; others rang high and sweet in celebration. People were singing "Silent night . . . holy . . ." People swept by the boy, unaware. Voices chattering about dinners and buying gifts. "We'll be late," she heard a woman say.

The Demon Rift

"Not . . . worthy," the dragon growled. *The boy was afraid because the monsters came awake. They looked down on him. They were very angry . . . He should be afraid. Were they aware of her? She must be careful, stay hidden.*

She was floating, looking down as they melted through the painted ceiling. Below, the boy's blank face was looking up. He wasn't there now. His spirit was being called. Threads of color streamed from the boy-spirit, pulling him upward as the threads wound together, forming a rope, and at the other end of the rope was a spider. Where were they going? Wake up, please let me wake up!

She struggled to open her eyes. There were no voices now to help her wake; the young man was gone. *"My pearl, you have the gift,"* Mommy had smiled at her, and pointing to the middle of Ramona's forehead, she would whisper, "Jan ge, my pearl, the Third Eye." Mommy was very proud.

"My scholar," Daddy had called her. He was determined she would be educated like the missionaries who had rescued Mommy from the bad people. Ramona sang her ABCs for him on the last day, as he lay unconscious on his bed.

So quiet now. The baby and his mother slept. Ramona fell back into her dream.

The Legions

Puffs of smoke and fire shot into the air. Mountains roared in the distance. Daddy, what spirit world holds you, she thought, where are you? Find me please, PLEASE! She saw the boy's body shudder as the spider thing landed and disappeared into what looked like a wooden platform with a stunted branchless tree growing from its center.

The rope connecting it to the boy made rapid loops around the tree as if it were a spool. As the rope wound tighter and he flew helplessly above the platform, the boy screamed. She hoped that he would disappear with the spider, but he clutched one of the tree's misshapen knots, his feet sliding back and forth on the wooden platform, to steady himself.

They were spinning, riding on a wooden top. She sat beside him, hugging herself. In her mind, she chanted Daddy's words, "Ramona is a brave, smart girl. No demon can defeat her . . . "

The boy's head moved from side to side with the motion of the spinning top. Ramona felt no motion. She sat and watched the coward struggle. Why am I here?

A foul wind pulsated, as if some giant creature were breathing in and out, its breath bringing forth decay. As the gusts increased, the top lurched, dipping down, threatening to send the boy to the ground below, where the unstable surface bubbled and cracked.

Make no sound; he can't see me, but what if he can hear me? She put her hand over her mouth. Please, wake up wake up! Baby, please cry now . . . What if . . . she didn't dare think who else might hear.

Groans rumbled from the ground. Ramona looked down to see what was making them and saw steam hissing from widening fissures. Purple-gray clouds, streaked with lightning flashes were overhead. Above, a ball of fire emerged from the menacing clouds and hovered over them.

There was a distant whine. It sounded like angry bees. Where was it? The fire separated into small flames that darted down towards them, before zooming up into the sky. Steam hissing from cracks in the surface exploded into geysers and formed columns of smoke. The boy pleaded, his thin voice drowned out by claps of thunder, "I beg you, tell me how to please, how to make it right." He covered his face.

She saw more trees. Living things are in this bad place? The darting flames began to race toward her. Instinctively, she crossed her arms in front of her face as each drew near and then abruptly sprang away. Each flame began to change, becoming the glowing wings of a black butterfly. Soon, hundreds of butterflies circled the boy, some fluttered, others landing on his face.

The columns of steam grew dense, slowly forming a wall. Dark clouds above were all she could see and as she looked up, there were red eyes. Can they see me? Daddy, help me!

A drizzle became steady rainfall, the sour drops clinging to the boy. He's here in spirit, like me, but why do they cling to him and not to me? Because he was called; I wasn't. Who sent me? Why? Spirit, send me back! I can do nothing against these devils. Please Daddy help, tell the Spirit!

As the wall undulated and shifted, a forest of tall pines rose from the ground and the hundreds of butterflies glided onto tree branches, their wings becoming flames again. CAW! The flames dwindled into points of light in the eyes of crows, chattering, perched on branches, their heads bobbing and cocking to the side.

"Oh dear, you are a disappointment, lad . . ." The voice came from a crow.

"Crispin?" the boy was uncertain.

Larger than the rest, the crow sat on a branch close to the edge of the wooden top. It flapped its wings and said, "What to do?"

The multitude of birds began to cry, "What to do!" A cacophony of shrieks welled up and the boy put his hands over his ears. Madness.

The crow preened its feathers as the shrieks continued. She shivered when a laugh came from the trees. The laugh, low and cruel, grew louder and the trees trembled, as the laugh became a roar. With a thunderous clap, the trees exploded. Pieces of wood and branches shot into the clouds. Shadows began to appear, darkening the sky and she knew it was the Legions, hordes of demons swirling in chaos, teeth bared, eyes aflame. One shadow swelled and the amorphous mist pulsated as it formed an image.

For the rest of her long life, Ramona dreamt of that face, the joyful insanity snarling from its depths. She knew it sensed her presence. It was looking for her; she prayed it couldn't find her.

Chasms formed in place of eyes and a sneering grin, the teeth sharp, the mouth misshapen, seemed to widen as the cloud shifted, drifting down towards the cringing boy. It drew closer, the mouth yawning as if to swallow him, the dark chasms faintly glowing, their depths promising despair.

The boy groveled, "Tell me." Lightening flashed and a building appeared, floating below the shadows. It was the festival hall, the G R A N D   A R CA . . . No, this building is smaller. Three levels. Screams came from the cloud building. As it burst into flames, the screams grew louder and filled with agony.

Rumbling grew louder, drowning out the screams. It was a grunt, a hideous moan of deep pleasure. The boy sighed; his face etched with pleasure. Where there had been fear, Ramona saw satisfaction. It was worse than the fear, such pleasure on his disgusting face. She knew, as he did, that the ghost building was his purpose, his task.

Abruptly, the spider crawled out of the crippled tree. It flung itself into the wind and the rope followed. The rope reminded her of the cobra that she had seen once on a festival day. The snake had nodded back and forth as it rose from a basket. Now the rope waved as it rose into the sky and then exploded into a shower of threads that disappeared into the boy's scrawny chest as he was thrown back into the Arcade. She and the boy journeyed, swirling as if caught in a tide pool.

They seeped through the ceiling of the Arcade. Looking down, she and saw his body collapsed on the marbled floor. She could hear the faint call of the crow, speaking again in the Crispin voice, "Ducky Strike, m'boy!"

An old woman was standing over the boy. He opened his eyes and smiled. Ramona wanted to warn her, but what if he heard her? There was a group of people gathering around him; someone will protect her.

The woman's sympathetic expression froze as she collapsed, her spectacles landing on boy's coat. "Joy to the World," sang the choir stationed in the center of the vast enclosure. The haze of the Monster lamps encircled the thinning crowd whose holiday spirit waned as their fatigue increased. Babies wailed; children whined and fought. A line of shoppers snaked across the open ground floor as people exited the Arcade and encountered the icy winds and heavy snowfall that would follow them home.

Waving his arthritic hands above his head, the woman's husband started to cry, "Help, my wife!" Someone shouted for a doctor. The coward stole the old woman's spectacles from where they had fallen on the marbled floor. Putting them on, he sprang up and moved quickly through the huge doors and out into the cold. She knew he felt joy. For the first time in her life, Ramona felt hate.

The baby finally cried. Ramona woke and covered her face with her blanket. "My scholar," a voice whispered in her ear. She threw the blanket off; there was no one. Then, she sobbed; she missed him so

THIRTY TWO

Cleveland, Ohio
Peeling Wallpaper

"On the causes of crime: Original sin . . . bad health . . . the violation of the law . . . silver agitation . . . lack of education . . . spots on the sun . . . crime is zymotic . . . the essential badness of the law . . . lack of fruit . . .the abomination of the English orthography." (*Death of a Legend Book Closing on Another Chapter in Ohio History* by Joe Gall)

As Bernie waited patiently for "Ducky Strike," the spectacles he took from the dead woman at the Arcade served to mask the danger of his glance, making him appear to all as harmless, one to be exploited and abused on a whim. His lack of imagination and limited intelligence discouraged him from leaving what he knew and so he stayed near the docks, lining up with the rest for work. He would survive in the poverty of the Flats.

Good with numbers, he was often hired to record ore tonnage passed to the steel mills. New Hulett Unloaders transferred massive amounts of reddish iron ore from ships and onto railcars. A boarding house became his home. He found steady employment, maintaining time sheets recording the grueling twelve-hour day, seven-days a week work of the steel workers. Workers were required to change from days to nights every two weeks. This meant one long twenty=four-hour shift. Meticulous in his work, he was indifferent to complaints about the long hours and bad working conditions.

Bernie always ate his evening meal, while sitting in a wooden chair. Then, he waited for the whispers, studying the peeling wallpaper. Red daisies would begin to dance, while bits of gold and blue formed moving images of birds landing in paisley trees. Sometimes the whispers came, singing to him of forces gathering that would soon come into this world, tantalizing him with visions of mischief and destruction, caressing and beguiling him. Bernie giggled and sighed.

The landlady was rarely able to rent the room next to his for more than a day, but she sensed the danger of evicting Bernie. She boarded up the offending space, saying that repairs were pending and raised the rent on everyone but Bernie, who sat alone in the dingy room. "When?" he asked the whispers, hearing the faint laughter, sometimes heralding a pleasant evening, but often only a teasing nod or worse, the harangues of his failures. "A heart?" he suggested hopefully, "A fresh heart?"

"Stupid Crispin? Stupid Bernie, stupid Bernie, stupid Bernie!" They would taunt him, "You let them find you— found you—you failed, stupid you! Patty Patty Patty Patty Patty beat you!"

The Demon Rift

He continued to murder, but never close to where he worked or lived. "A sacrifice," he would murmur. He took care, escaping notice by leaving his room at night to roam through dark streets. Some bodies floated in the polluted river, others rested forlornly under a bridge or in a deserted alley. Once, a steel worker placed himself in the path of the blast furnace.

"An accident," the men said, though the man was seen disagreeing with Bernie's record of his work hours right before his death. Labor riots spurred by layoffs and fears of communism covered many of his kills. Bernie watched from his window and wondered when his time would come. It would be soon. He felt worthy.

THIRTY THREE

Ramona's Choice

San Francisco

1918

As she brushed Ramona's hair, twisting it into a loose knot and securing it with hand-painted pins, Mommy made her promise. "Ramona, you are eighteen now. It's past time to marry. Soon, you'll be too old. Go to the YMCA party." Her voice was gentle, but her words were not. She tapped a finger against her lips. "You're not as pretty as I hoped, but you're pretty enough. Someone will be there; I feel it."

Compared to Ramona, Mommy's third eye was weak, but often, she was correct, a fact that kept clients paying for her advice. Mommy rarely predicted anything negative, saying that her vision was "clouded that day" if she saw something unpleasant.

Many girls at the Chinese Telephone Company, where Ramona had worked for three years, had consulted Mommy before accepting a proposal. Knowing it was too hard to lie, Ramona refused all requests and resisted Mommy's demands that she do readings, saying she could no longer see, her third eye was blind.

Mommy wouldn't accept it. "I think you don't want your gift. So ungrateful!" Mommy wanted her to feel guilty, but Ramona was determined to be normal. Mommy argued that she must quit school and tell fortunes. Ramona argued that the missionaries paid her to help in their office. "Not enough!" Mommy said.

Until her fourteenth birthday, she could not pretend, but when Ramona reached puberty, there were fewer dreams. Sometimes she could will herself to wake up. The last dream had come on her fourteenth birthday.

The Blond Slug

Ramona walked beside him as the blond slug sneaked behind a man carrying a paper sack and pushed a knife into him. The man, who was in his fifties, looked confused. What had happened? The sack fell open revealing a small apple and a hardened wedge of bread. As the man looked down, seeing blood on his hands, the slug wiped the knife's blade on the sack, tossed the bread on the ground and put the apple in his coat pocket.

It was night and the streets were full of men carrying signs. Angry people yelled and fought. They shouted "war" and "the commies are taking over." The coward willed people not to see. The man fell as his murderer walked away.

It was not the first time she had seen him kill. She had

witnessed his horrible acts many times. She wished the departing souls peace on their journeys. She was helpless to interfere, as the monster strangled or stabbed his victims.

This time, as the coward withdrew his knife from another slumping man, she shouted, "Murderer, I know who you are! Demon spawn!" The slug's face twisted, his yellow eyes narrowed and for a moment, she knew he saw her. She was amazed. He feared her! What did he think she could do? Since that night, she no longer dreamt or if she did, she did not remember.

He Must be Modern

For the one hundredth (in Ramona's estimation) time that week, Mommy considered Ramona's face. "Pretty complexion. (Ramona's smooth skin was envied by the telephone girls)." Mommy smiled and nodded, taking credit for Ramona's claim on beauty.

Then Mommy shook her head, her tongue clicking against her teeth.

"Mouth too wide, nose like a hawk (the result, Ramona suspected, of a not-too-distant Japanese ancestor on Mommy's side), but your eyes must be seen! Make sure you don't wear these." Mommy set her lovely mouth in a determined line as she took the spectacles away.

"But Mommy, I can't see!" Large and spaced evenly in her round face (so like Daddy's) Ramona's clear brown eyes held mystery and a touch of melancholy. They were her best feature.

Mommy ignored the plea. "There's no money for a dowry, so he must be modern. Now go!" Mommy tapped Ramona's head lightly with the brush. Ramona was reluctant to leave. She knew that the man she married would die prematurely. *Maybe I should marry an old one then.* There were many to choose from, dowry or no. Many men had no wives. Even so, Ramona had few suitors. There were rumors of the "evil eye."

Joey Song
San Francisco, 1918

Balloons filled the main hall of the YMCA. Banners hanging from doorframes shouted, "Welcome Home!" Long tables were laden with platters of fried chicken and sliced pork. Next came a variety of pies and towering layer cakes, some smothered in thick fudge or smooth vanilla cream; others were piled high with generous whipped frostings sprinkled with nuts and crowned with fresh fruits.

The young veterans crowded at the generous bowls of yuan xiao, deliciously spiced balls of rice as they sipped tea and congratulated each other for making it home alive.

Red, white, and blue bunting spanned three sides of the hall as the several. Missionary women, most in their seventies, directed the activities. Although she was not a Christian, Mommy kept her ties to the missionaries. One of them, Sister Ramona Turner, had rescued ten-year-old Mommy from a brothel. To spare Mommy's reputation, the story was changed to Mommy being an orphan found on the streets.

Sister Turner became Mrs. Kray, continuing her work in a Cleveland Orphanage. It was at the Cleveland mission that Daddy had found fifteen-year-old Mommy, who became his wife and a stepmother to his two sons. The sons, regrettably, never forgave Mommy's lack of family.

"Ramona, would you be a dear and help Sister Marsh with the punch?" Sister Eloise was determined that Ramona should mingle.

Ramona wanted to leave. Musicians were playing "Over There." Welcoming speeches and applause for Chinatown's "Doughboys" were over. Perhaps she could slip out the door where the deliveries came.

Ramona nodded, but she couldn't make out just which old white head belonged to Sister Marsh. As she maneuvered through the crowd, straining her eyes to see, she resisted the urge to curse Mommy's heartlessness in depriving her of her spectacles.

Young men in uniform tapped their feet to the music and sauntered around the hall, looking proud as they sipped tea or the

YMCA missionary punch. They apprised the young women who suddenly busied themselves with small tasks. Eyes downcast, the young women glanced anywhere but at the young men. It wouldn't do to boldly meet their gaze. Such behavior was unbecoming.

A red balloon drifted down and surprised Ramona, who tripped on the edge of a table bunting. As she fell, a hand reached out and caught her.

"Mam'selle, are you okay?" A uniformed young man of twenty offered his arm to help her. Ramona blushed with embarrassment as she regained her balance. She refused his offer, not wanting to look up, not wanting to see this man. "'Enchante.' That's French for 'you're beautiful kiddo'." He escorted her to a seat by the piano, which stood silent while the band played.

When she sat down, he bowed, gracefully placing his arm in front, in the European fashion. "Joseph Song, at your service." He stood up straight, a slight man of five feet seven, the smile charming and full of mischief, the eyes full of need and the heart . . . was a mystery. She thought him the most handsome man she had ever seen with his boyish face and restless energy.

Later, Mommy pronounced him a disaster, "He has no money, no family. Have you gone mad?" Mommy refused to let him into her house.

THIRTY FOUR

The Cleveland Crusher
Cleveland, Ohio
"The Flats"

In 1925, when Bernie was 39, speakeasies and jazz clubs became part of his nocturnal world. Bernie often waited in the shadows for someone to leave the clubs that proliferated in the Flats. He preyed on flappers and drunken businessmen, all unsteady on their feet, weaving their way down a dark street. He caught a couple, killing the woman while her escort lay in a stupor. When the man woke to her dying screams, Bernie shoved a knife into his throat. He often saved pieces of clothing from his victims, wearing them on another kill. It was from one of these murders that Cleveland came to fear a devil known as the "Cleveland Crusher."

At two in the morning, in early November 1927, a young man of twenty-two careened out the doors of Lonesome Al's Speakeasy and on to the deserted street.

The young man, Lorenzo, Larry to his friends, was in an alcohol-fueled rage.

Sure, that swell little blonde gave him the eye. Her boyfriend was a sap. The dame should make a choice. I know it won't be the sap. Obviously, they don't know who I am. I'll be whispering in some ears tomorrow. My car, where was it? Where did Petie go? Petie was supposed to wait.

Impatient, Larry was stumbling down a side street when the pipe crushed his skull. Bernie swung the lead pipe again and Larry's brains, along with his gray fedora, flew into a puddle of dirty water as the rest of him collapsed onto the pavement. Savoring the twitching body, Bernie wondered what would happen if he could prolong the process. As he removed Larry's shirt, pants, and jacket, he considered ways to find out. The answer came to him at Christmas.

The murder of Lorenzo Patrelli had repercussions. His father, an important man, buried his son and then ordered the deaths of those he felt were responsible, starting with the unfortunate Petie who had answered the call of nature on that night. An urgent need for privacy caused Petie to abandon the spot where he waited for the kid.

Before returning to his post, Petie decided he needed a smoke. As he continued his nightly wait, he saw a mutt carrying a hat in its mouth. He panicked; it was Lorenzo's gray fedora. The dog dropped the hat as Petie began to chase it. Then Petie found what remained of Lorenzo. It never occurred to Petie that he took risks that night that were totally out of character. His lapse cost him dearly; he was dead within a week.

Weeks later, after the revenge slayings were done, Bernie was ready to experiment. But first, he must have privacy. He found a deserted stable where he could work undisturbed. Voices told him he must learn to drive a car. It was 1928 after all. A co-worker, exhausted after his long shift, found himself spending an extra hour instructing Bernie on how to shift and steer. Others, uneasy at the sight of Bernie anywhere but behind the large desk, piled with timesheets, looked away, grateful that it did not involve them. When Bernie was satisfied that he had mastered the necessary skills, he released the man, but not before buying his car at an impressively low price. His hand shaking, the man delivered the keys to Bernie and went home to face his bewildered wife.

Exploring the decaying structure of the abandoned stable, Bernie noted the sounds of boats, gulls, and the sloshing of the river's water. Together they would mask any screams. The stalls were empty, but hanging on the walls were harnesses, riding crops, and bridles. Old newspapers cluttered the floor. In a corner, he saw blacksmith's tools including an anvil, old shoes, and parts of what he recognized as a vise. Years earlier, he had seen a child use a nutcracker and he remembered thinking that such a device might be useful to him. Here it was, he thought happily. Patiently, Bernie adapted the tool for his own purposes. He was almost ready.

The wallpaper danced and the whispers sang of the coming tide of chaos. Bernie wondered if they meant his new venture. He missed Crispin. Before Crispin died, it was easy. If he wanted something, he would simply make Crispin get it for him. He remembered the first sacrifice, the barmaid Willie, with longing. How perfect it was! The whispers' helping, counseling, telling him what to say made it wonderful. Father was pleased. Each new sacrifice was meant to bring him closer to Power. Then he failed. The cabin sacrifice was to be an important step, but it was an utter failure.

San Francisco
1928

They hid, waiting for the speakeasy door to swing open. Yesterday's newspapers swirled and floated as breezes carried them from one gutter to the next. A page of stock reports caught on his leg and as he threw it off, she saw that he was aroused. Revolting. The door was ajar; music escaped. Jazz? Someone was angry.

"Swell, swell . . . whazituh ya? Oh yeah—juss you wait . . . don't worry, I'll be in toush." The door flung open, and a young man staggered out onto the dark street. Wake up wake up! She must wake up! The young man, twenty-two, slight of build, elegantly dressed, his fedora pulled fashionably to one side of his head, reminded her of Joey. She couldn't bear it.

Ramona is a smart brave girl . . . no demon can defeat

her . . . Ramona is a smart brave girl . . . noooo. Oh, please wake up!

The monster swung a wooden club, causing the young man's brains to fly out of his head and into a puddle. The slug looked behind him. She realized he was looking for her and she resisted the urge to scream. His wariness changed to excitement as he dragged the body into an alley.

Hoping it was over, she wished the soul of the foolish young man a safe journey as the coward went back to retrieve pieces of brain. He moved through the dim streetlight. His blond hair was thinning, and his wiry youth gone, replaced by a stunted, wizened frame that belied his feral strength.

Reaching into the inside pocket of his coat, he took out a cloth and wiped the blood off the wooden club. He slipped the club into the same pocket. and withdrew a small jar, where he deposited the pieces of brain retrieved from the gutter. As she had done as a child, she put her hand over her mouth to keep from screaming . . ."

Mommy was pounding on the door. "You sleep too long; get up!" Mommy shouted. Then, Mommy paused, waiting for an answer; then she whispered, "Your children need you." Ramona found it hard to move. The thought of getting up and leaving her bed that still carried a faint scent of him made the room spin and her heart thump. Oh Joey, what do I do? Losing Joey was worse than Daddy. She had married the handsome doughboy, knowing he would die too soon. It had seemed distant; she reasoned that she was probably mistaken, though as with Daddy, she knew that was a lie.

He died because of a gambling debt and his payment made too late. "Don't worry kiddo," he assured her. "Uncle Joey has it covered." Ramona's tears made him hesitate. "Kiddo I have to do what they say, if I don't." He touched his finger to her chin and kissed her nose. "I've been in worse jams . . ." Grabbing his hat, he bowed like the Europeans and was gone. She turned and went to the window, watching him as he disappeared in the crowded street.

Two days passed before a tourist, a rancher from Montana, wandered through an alley, searching for a private place to urinate. Hearing a groan, the rancher discovered it came from under a mass of bricks and pieces of discarded plaster from a nearby building site. Although most of his bones had been broken, Joey's face was recognizable, a lesson for others.

Eight-year-old Warren, the oldest of their four sons brought the news. "They found Daddy." The boy's face was blank. Behind him stood his brothers, ages six, five and four, lined up behind him like soldiers, with Warren their commanding officer. Four-year old Joseph clutched the medal Joey won for dragging a wounded corporal to safety during the Great War. Maurice, who at six, resembled Joey, fixed his gaze on the photograph hanging on the wall behind her, where Private Song and his bride smiled on their wedding day. On the other side of Maurice, James, the five-year old, shook with emotion, his face flushed with anger and grief.

In his last moments of life, Joey lay on a cot in a hospital hall. She held his hand to her cheek. The vessels in his eyes had burst, blinding him, but his lips moved . . . She nodded and sang her ABCs as his soul departed.

Daddy, take care of him!

After Joey's death, the dreams came back.

THIRTY FIVE

Behind the Blue Sedan

Caleb Michaels

The day after mall opening

November 2004

PATTY

The security guy is named Caleb and he's related to the little kid named Lonnie who was my friend in the orphanage. I miss Lonnie and the rest of my gang.

You can have a new gang. Russie and I can be in it. Maybe we can find Lonnie.

A good start. Maybe Gertie and Hugo can join if I can find them.

We will.

It was 8:30AM when Gordon picked Madonna up in his Jetta and dropped her by the mall's food court entrance. No one was at the ICE KING counter when she arrived, and so, she lit the first sage smudge stick and went to work protecting the mall. After she applied sage to the door and windows of NATURAL BEAUTY, Gordon ordered her to stop. She ignored him until she covered the entire entrance. Then she returned to the food court and quickly lit another smudge stick, clearing the counter of the ICE KING.

After that, she lit another smudge stick, moving it around the food court booths and perimeter.

Shrinking and hissing at the girl's assault, they fled.

While she was waving the smudge stick around the ICE KING counter, Kevin arrived and gleefully promised to look out for Ted. Then, Madonna began an incantation, praying for protection. Kevin was thrilled with the process, "Hey, you really *are* a witch, right? That's soo cool!"

Completing the protection rituals, Madonna began setting up the various trays of toppings, spoons, and napkins. While she was checked the soft swirl dispensers, Kevin detailed the latest episode of *Charmed.*

When Ted arrived, he sniffed the air suspiciously. "You both know that there is no smoking in the mall, right?" Looking as clueless as they could, they nodded. Madonna told herself to light a white candle as soon as Ted took his break.

When it came time for Madonna's break, she grabbed a tray and put two cups of coffee on it from JAVA LOVE, then headed for the security office on the third level. Knocking on the door, she pushed her way in as the young security guard she'd seen at the mall opened the door. He glanced at the man behind him as they both eyed her suspiciously.

"I'm Madonna Bedonne from the ICE KING." She held up the tray. "I thought you might like some coffee. You were there when my grandfather was . . ."

Caleb laughed, "Your grandpa is John Arnold? He's a scary dude if you don't mind me saying. You looked like you wanted to hide behind the sprinkles, but you handled it." He wondered why she was working at the mall. Why wasn't rich grandpa helping the girl out? He doubted her dreams involved working in a food court.

From the time he was four years old, Caleb dreamt of being a cop like his dad. Everything else could wait. His handsome face with its wary eyes hid a fierce intelligence, but his heart had failed to heal from the loss of his dad, Amos. A motorcycle cop, Amos Michaels had stopped a car for a broken taillight and a single shot ended the life of the man Caleb loved most in the world. The newspaper picture showed the aftermath with reporters, police and the bystanders looking down at his father's body, collapsed on the edge of the highway, reminding Caleb of a broken toy. Caleb was ten when the world was drained of joy.

Apologizing for not recognizing her, "You were under some heavy-duty lights." Caleb smiled at her. "I'm Caleb Michaels, he said, and this is Wilson".

"Wilson, first or last name?" Madonna asked.

"Just Wilson'll do," said the security guard. He took the coffee and put it on a counter next to battered Herman Wouk paperback. "Thank you, young lady. It's not often that you see people make a thoughtful gesture." He sat in front of three sets of panels. Television monitors, trained on a section of the mall, included the garage levels. Wilson was a man in his mid-sixties. Forty-five years of cigarettes, too many years of whiskey in his coffee and a habit of ending workdays with nightcaps made him look ten years older.

"Wow, said Madonna, "that's quite a set-up." She pointed towards the rows of screens.

"You know it!" said Wilson, "It's state of the art. By the way, this here young man has ambitions to be a cop."

"Were you the one who saved the baby?" Madonna asked.

Wilson answered for him. "This young man's a hero."

Clearly uncomfortable, Caleb answered, "Just doing my job. I'm glad the kid didn't get hurt."

Crawling on the ceiling, scratching, pulling, and pushing against the gauzy mass that prevented it from reaching down and plucking off a head, the demon spun away.

Madonna put her hand on the back of her neck. Her skin felt cold. Resisting the temptation to take a piece of sage from her pocket and light it, she shuddered. "You okay?" asked Caleb.

"Yeah, fine.," he shrugged.

She grinned. She promised herself she would be back and find a way to make him safe. *There was danger here, too.* "I'd better get back to work. Nice meeting you both." She saluted as she left.

Caleb started to say something when Wilson interrupted him, pointing to a teenaged couple in the garage elevator. Unaware that a camera was on them they were engrossed in each other, kissing, with the boy running his hands over the girl's body. As they exited the elevator on the second level, it was clear from the garage camera they planned on continuing.

"I'd better go down there and break it up," said Caleb.

"Hey, officer, give them a few minutes. There's no hurry," urged Wilson.

"I'll walk slow, but Romeo and Juliet are going to have to take it elsewhere!" Caleb knew his job. Taking the elevator down to the second level garage, he shook his head. This wasn't what he signed up for. He needed to follow up on those applications. Redhill Police, Cleveland Police, State Trooper—surely, he'd get one of them. It was time to move on. He'd give this job six months.

There was little to hold him. His mom was dead. Diabetes. He missed her, but now he wasn't bound by her hopes and expectations. Grandma Cinda was all he had, and she was getting on. Grandma loved to spoil him, she said. He felt responsible for her. Not knowing how many years she had left, he wanted to be there for her. Lord knows she'd had enough heartache. Maybe he could talk her into moving with him if it came to that. But Redhill was where she's lived most of her life and where she had raised Wesley, Caleb's dad. Caleb knew there were bad memories here, with granddad Luke and the prison fire. As the elevator door opened, he looked around the vast enclosure. It was early and the garage floor was mostly empty, maybe a third of it filled with cars.

He saw them as they were going at it and starting to move behind a barrier when the girl let out a scream. Thinking the boy must be hurting her, Lonnie started running. The girl continued to scream. When the boy started to scream, Caleb wasn't sure what was going on. Startled, he ran even faster. The lovebirds were looking at something on the other side of the barrier. The boy vomited as the girl reached out, placing her hand on the hood of an old Camaro before sliding to the concrete and fainting. "What's happening?" Caleb shouted. The boy pointed as he began to wretch again. Then Caleb saw the body.

Its head connected to the torso by a few strips of skin. He could see a part of the spine protruding from the neck, almost completely severed. Numerous cuts oozed, some superficial and some deep. Several knives, their blades bloodied, lay near the body. One knife was sticking out of the left eye of the corpse and one embedded deep in the groin. The smell was overwhelming. Caleb was surprised he wasn't sickened. Bloodstains covered a large portion of the surrounding floor. On the column above the body written in blood, was the word "Sacrifice."

Patty

I like Cabrizzi. He gave Bernie a hard time, just like I did.

He is one of the good cops.

Cabrizzi
The day after the Redhill mall Opening

Bernie was not happy. Troy West would suffer for this. Bernie and the Redhill mall manager were on the second floor of the parking structure, as they watched the crime scene investigation completed. The floor closed, the curious saw signs saying that repairs were being made. "What could I do?" West was pathetic. "The kids had already seen it and the security guard called the cops . . ." whispered West, glancing nervously at Cabrizzi.

The detective was several feet away, busy taking a few more Polaroid's of the body, as well as what was written above it, the blood letters: "Sacrifice." It was scrawled atop an ad for *The Incredibles*, a coming Cineplex attraction. The police had just finished taking their photographs and measurements and getting samples.

"Sacrificed!" The demons hissed.

The Demon Rift

The dead man was behind a blue sedan on the concrete floor. A minor sacrifice, Bernie thought, but nonetheless a necessary precursor to the main event. What was particularly aggravating was the fact that he had no "influence" over Cabrizzi, the detective, any more than he had over the security guard. So be it. There were still ways of dealing with them. He would have a talk with the police chief Nagle, a man Bernie could make see reason. Finishing, Cabrizzi looked at Bernie, whose patronizing smile was meant to remind the detective just whom he was dealing with . . .

"I'm sure you can appreciate, Detective, what a sensitive matter we have here." Bernie said. Bernie's focused his thoughts on Cabrizzi, probing for self-doubt, telling him he was in over his head, he needed a drink; *this could all wait* . . . no use. Cabrizzi's mind was a wall.

Cabrizzi, his face a blank, looked at him, "Senator, I'm not quite sure what you mean. We have a victim here with multiple stab wounds, almost decapitated. Quite a sensitive matter for *him*, don't you agree?"

Bernie was losing patience. "Detective, this private enterprise is bringing new life into this town. Now we don't want people scared away. I want the fiend who did this caught, and I will spare no expense in making that happen."

Bernie considered whom he could get to confess to the murder. Caleb, the security guard would make sense; he did the murder to get attention. He was an ambitious young man. No, Bernie decided, he had found Caleb as resistant as Cabrizzi. Perhaps the older one—Wilson . . ."

Cabrizzi nodded. "Good, we're agreed then. So, let's take a look at the tapes." Bernie had forgotten about the tapes—tedious . . .

"I'll have them sent over immediately," he said. An Other would take care of it. The tape will be defective, he decided.

Cabrizzi shook his head. "I want to look at them now, while we're all here." Bernie looked at West.

West went on the offensive. "Detective, is this necessary? The Senator is a busy man. I'll have them sent immediately." He was starting to panic as Cabrizzi gave a tight-lipped smile and shook his head.

"I'm afraid it is, Mr. West. Let's go look and see what they show."

Cabrizzi was on his way to the security office before West could respond. Caleb decided to follow Cabrizzi. West had already yelled at him for calling the police when he found the body rather that calling him first. He wasn't about to listen to more, especially when he could watch a murder investigation up close.

When Bernie and West arrived at the security office, Cabrizzi had already put the tape in the play position. Wilson and Caleb were waiting. As Bernie started to say he had an important conference and he *must be present* when the tape was shown, Cabrizzi pushed the "play" button.

One camera showed Greg moving rapidly across the lot, then pausing, looking behind him. As he started to move again, they saw him turning and looking up, panic on his face. He dropped the bag and the knife case fell and opened. Cabrizzi zoomed in. Except for Bernie, the men in the room watched in disbelief as the knives popped out of the case and hung in mid-air. "Jesus," Caleb said.

Cabrizzi put the tape in slow motion as the knives followed the terrified man, who hid behind a column. Another camera picked up as they saw Greg hesitate. Cabrizzi sped up the tape to where Greg attempted to make a run for it and the knives zigzagged until they were directly in front of him. "Sweet Mother of God!" Wilson whispered. Then, the butchery began. Cabrizzi and Bernie watched while Wilson and Caleb turned away.

The dying man's hand reached up and wrote the word "Sacrifice" on the wall. Then knives impaled his eye and groin. While his body jerked and fell, another knife, wielded by an unseen hand, sawed his neck and spine, almost severing his head. When it was over, all but the two knives embedded in his eye and groin, fell harmlessly to the ground.

Not believing what he had just witnessed, Cabrizzi rewound and played it again. Knives that move by themselves? Forensics will love that.

Bernie decided all in the room would have to die. In the interim, he must state the obvious. "A magic trick, perhaps, or a doctored tape, Wilson?" Best to plant the seed of suspicion that would point to the flustered security guard, "Who had access to this area?" Bernie demanded.

Wilson started to stutter, not knowing what to say. Cabrizzi interrupted. "Senator, I'll ask the questions. In the meantime, Wilson, I'll take the tapes we just saw, and any others that you have will be picked up shortly. I'd appreciate your having them ready."

Wilson nodded, relieved as the men left. He waited until Caleb took his break and then grabbed his small bottle of vodka from the back of his desk drawer. It was the only way to stop the shaking.

Cabrizzi popped another lifesaver in his mouth as he sat in Chief Nagle's office, waiting for Nagle's reaction to the tape. He hadn't had a drink in over six years, but he wanted one now. Christ, this was a weird case! He had an idea that Arnold knew more than he was telling. What was it about the good Senator that made Paul Cabrizzi want to push his face into a wall? It was the smirk, the one that says, "I can get away with it." He'd seen it countless times before on the faces of career criminals. Politicians, most of them were crooks, anyway. Arnold just didn't try to hide it.

When Charles Cabrizzi decided to give small town life a go after his divorce a couple of years back, he'd figured that putting up with jerks like Nagle was just part of the trade-off for a lighter case load. Then Arnold had come into the equation, and he had seen Nagle blatantly kiss his ass. Now, he wasn't so sure that he'd made the right decision. Later, when he saw the tape, Nagle's look of disbelief was predictable. "A magic trick? That's your explanation?" Nagle demanded.

Cabrizzi shrugged. "That's as good an explanation as any . . ." A buzzer sounded. Arnold was in the outer office. Nagle glared at Cabrizzi as he rose to open the door.

Arnold came in and shook hands with Nagle, pointedly ignoring Cabrizzi. "Chief Nagle, I want to assure you that I will do everything in my power to bring to justice the monster that did this. In the meantime, I'm sure you'll agree that we don't want to start a panic. This tragedy should be kept quiet while your fine department does its investigation." Bernie found the man's pliable mind irresistible, almost too easy.

As Nagle started to reply, Cabrizzi interrupted, "Senator, there's a lunatic around who took the time to stage a very complicated trick. It resulted in the bloody death of a shoplifter who happened to be in your mall. I think a little 'panic' is called for. Maybe we should call it being aware of who or what is around you."

Bernie stared at him. "Detective, let me make it clear; Redhill needs this mall. Anything or anyone who interferes with its operation is causing damage to these good citizens and I will make it my business to stop him."

Seeing that Nagle was useless, Cabrizzi started to leave. The detective turned to Arnold, who he was now convinced, had something to do with the murder and said, "Senator, do you really give a crap about these people? 'Cause I'm starting to have my doubts . . . "

As Nagle reacted, his face flushed with anger, Cabrizzi shut the door. Why would a powerful man like Arnold do in a piece a shit like the murder victim? Why in that place and why make it a circus act? Cabrizzi knew he'd figure it out, but it was going to take a while.

Bernie was seething. It would draw suspicion if Cabrizzi were killed too soon. When the time came, he would see to it himself. He would wait until he took the form of the granddaughter. He imagined Cabrizzi's confusion when the "sweet little girl" visited slow death on the unwary detective. Perhaps he would resurrect the vise. Some things were worth waiting for.

Debbie and Reba
Redhill, Ohio
November 2004

The house stood on the lot formerly occupied by the First Christian Church. The church was razed to make way for more houses when the prison was built. Warden West and his family had lived there until shortly after the fire, after which, they moved, the Warden taking an early retirement. Bernie remembered the church was where he first saw Becka Tobin. He had given her the suggestion that he was a child in need of rescuing, a thought he suspected she might have had without his encouragement. Luring her to the old woman's house was easy. He hadn't counted on the dogs finding them before the finish . . . a miscalculation.

The three-story structure, unoccupied for over thirty years, was ready. The carpets removed, exposing the wood floors, the walls covered with scenes of mountains, forests, wild animals, and birds in flight.

He murmured words of welcome and entreaty, his thoughts making their way through the porous membrane, to the hidden realm of Chaos.

A pentagram, its lines even and proportions exact, directed his fevered prayers. It dominated the floor of what had been a large living room, now devoid of furniture. Bernie knelt in the center of the pentagram, listening to the whispers. A sour wind whirled around him. He could smell the churning ash of destruction as hordes began to gather, settling on the edges of the wallpaper trees. Flames stretched and darkened, becoming crows and their wings flapped as they flew from one tree to the next.

Whispers and chatters blended into a warning. The coming sacrifice and subsequent reward promised not only another lifetime, but power wielded and guided by clairvoyance. Bernie would be able to foresee how actions would affect his victims. Such a reward demanded perfection and the time, the place, words.

Hissing threats crawled over and into his ears. There could be no mistakes. Its eye a rolling flame, the Crispin crow cocked its head and laughed, "Remember dear boy, there is no forgiveness, remember!" Then spreading its wings and fluttering them like a macabre butterfly, it chattered, "There is no mercy, no mercy no mercy no mercy!" The chorus of demon crows continued the chant.

Fatigue and backpain distracted him. Earlier, he had dined, seated at the Moroccan table imported from England. The table had sentimental value. He had acquired from the estate of the long-dead Lord Towning. The Others had fed him the choicest bits from the elaborate meal.

Advancing years made digestion a problem at times. He looked forward to the new healthier body. As the vision faded, he decided to retire.

Naked on sheets of the finest thread he could see his reflection in the overhead mirror as the Others caressed his body, their lovely human forms naked as they stroked him. As he became aroused, he could hear the rasping sound of their breath when they revealed themselves. Burning eyes so close, he dare not look in them, teeth that could rip the flesh from his bones with a single bite, claws on misshapen fingers grasping him, able to pierce his heart. Soon, he slept.

THIRTY SIX

PATTY

This is the Ray who tried to help John in the prison. Wow is he old now! His grandson Alec looks familiar. I know! He looks like Michael Gibbs, the boy who wanted a kiss from me. Ha!

Bless Ray for trying to help. You were very pretty. I'm not surprised Michael wanted to steal a kiss.

You're just saying that because we're sisters.

No, you were.

I wonder what I would have looked like as a grownup.

Beautiful.

I'm glad Ray got to be okay.

Ray's Dream

Redhill Convalescent Hospital

November 2004

Ray Gibbs was having a dream. Lisa lay next to him, her hand in his, telling him they had to leave. He woke up and looked at the old-fashioned alarm clock Alec had given him for his birthday. It said three in the morning. No surprise, he spent many nights awake. That's what old people do, though these were spent worrying about Alec and that cursed mall. He reached over and turned on the lamp next to his bed and noticed the smell of perfume. It must be one of the nurses. Sad. Perfume was wasted in this place. It seemed familiar. It reminded him of something.

"You don't remember? I used to wear it every day." Ray's heart sped up. He turned around and there was Lisa, sitting on his bed. I could've sworn I was awake, he thought. "You are honey. You are." Lisa said. She looked like she did when he first met her. Her blonde hair was all done up; she had those naughty red lips and a flower behind her ear, like the one he gave her on their first date. She put her hand behind the flower, fanning her fingers like a pinup ala Virginia Mayo, giving him a teasing smile. She winked like an angel. God almighty what a woman! Virginia had nothin' on Lisa!

"Ray, listen to me! We have to leave now, sugar, right now."

"Why, Lisa?"

She took his hand, "They're comin' for you and I'm not going to let them get you."

"Where are we going?" he asked.

"I got us a table at the Sacked Rabbit," she said as she cocked her head and winked. Then, Lisa took a compact from her purse and checked her lipstick.

"That little club in St. Louis? Ray asked. He was concerned. "Honey, I can't even walk, much less dance."

"No, excuses, Ray Gibbs, I'm in the mood to jitterbug." She pretended to pout, bending her head towards her chest, and looking up at him.

He shook his head in a panic. "Oh, Lisa . . . I wish I could . . ." He started to cry.

Jumping off the bed like a kitten, she turned and faced him, her hands behind her back. "Which one?"

Ray shook his head at the game they used to play. He'd bring her a surprise until the surprises became a way of saying "I'm sorry, sorry for disappearing, for gambling away their savings. . ."

"Which one? He reached out to pick and saw his hand with its clubbed fingers—*oh how old I am, why does she bother?*

She gave a mock sigh and brought her hands forward. Where did that come from? Holding it by the collar, she handed him his bomber jacket, the one he wore the day they met. As he reached for it, he saw the tattoo on his arm was back, the pair of dice that he had done in London. It had burned off that night at the prison. If it's back, then . . .

The fear and the pain were gone. Ray rose from the bed and putting on his jacket, he became the young bomber pilot who fell in love with the pretty secretary. As they left, he put his arm around her and sang "Mood for love." She laughed and grabbing his arm, put her head on his shoulder. "Mood for Love" was their song. As Ray abandoned the shell that he had suffered for so many years, the Others slipped into his room. When they saw that he had escaped, they bared their teeth in rage and tore his body. The next morning the nurses found what was left and called the police.

THIRTY SEVEN

PATTY

Moving pictures have sure changed! Gram took me to the nickelodeon once. Russie was a baby, and you were too little, but I got to go with her. I remember the story was about a lady. A cowboy rescued her. This moving picture is too confusing. What's a computer? How do people get inside that box? I'll ask Gram. Maybe she'll know.

My goodness, things have changed! Movies especially.

The Redhill Mall Cineplex

December 8, 2004

Playing on the screen, one of six in the Cineplex, was *The Hacker*, a horror film where a computer stalker learns intimate and embarrassing details about his victims, then shares them with their enemies and friends alike. Ultimately, the "hacker" corners his victims, "hacking" them to death and showing their murders on a mysterious website.

Behind another "screen," the barrier between our world and the dark universe, eyes peered through, following The Hacker narrative with great interest. The wall rippled as creaks and chopping sounds vied with somber music, while on the screen, a girl, aware that someone was in the house, took a golf club and climbed the stairs.

Like the creature behind the barrier, Madonna's tormentors, Randy, and Marla, were having a great time. Earlier, they had been over to NATURAL BEAUTY and loaded up on free samples.

"As if . . . what a stupid bitch!" Marla laughed, throwing a jujube at the screen, hitting the back of a teenaged boy who was sitting with his friends three rows in front. Eyes looked down, and widening in delight, talons raked the barrier.

The theater less than half-full. The two girls sat in the middle of the middle row, directly beneath the demon, that growled, unable to reach its prey.

The girls decided to share any thoughts and/or opinions of the onscreen thriller with those in neighboring seats, who found their frequent sharing annoying.

"Hey, watch it!" a boy growled as a kernel of popcorn hit the back of his head.

"Eat me little bitch!" Marla said sweetly.

"Fuck you, cunt." The boys replied.

"All of you shut the fuck up or I'm getting the manager," warned a voice from two rows in back.

The creature ran its tongue where the barrier had thinned for a few precious seconds, hoping to taste the anger. Instead, venom dripped, seeping through a place that was briefly porous. Drops fell, barely missing the girls' *heads. Instead, it landed on the cardboard rim of their snack before falling into the container and blending with the fake butter. When Randy, whose hand was buried deep within a tub of popcorn, pulled it out and saw that half of her middle finger gone, it bared its teeth, grunting in satisfaction.*

Randy whimpered as she displayed her missing digit. The blood streamed onto her friend's new sweater. Marla clapped her hand to her mouth in horror at the sight of her friend's mangled hand and her ruined sweater.

The demon tried to follow the girls as they made their way up the darkened aisles. It howled as the women and the theater faded from view. Teeth grinding, yellow fluid coating the sharp talons, it went in search of other possibilities.

In search of medical attention and legal services, the girls decided to confront "The Manager," a portly eighteen-year-old boy with a ponytail. A pin on the lapel of his blazer said Cineplex Mgr. P. Cummings.

"What kind of shit are you serving the public?" Marla demanded as Randy carefully looked through the popcorn to locate the piece of glass or razor blade, as well as (she shuddered, feeling sick) the other half of her finger.

Mr. Cummings, who had been engrossed in the latest *Rolling Stone*, put his reading aside and watched as Randy dug in the tub of popcorn, looking for her lost finger. Frustrated but determined to establish the Cineplex as responsible before they found a lawyer, Randy pulled out her hand to display her injury.

To her surprise, the hand was uninjured, with all fingers accounted for. The girls looked at each other and then at Randy's finger. The blood on the sweater had also disappeared, leaving them shaken and confused. Mr. Cummings sighed and returned to his reading. The girls left the theater in silence, agreeing never to speak of what of what happened during *The Hacker*. Who would believe it anyway? They would have been surprised.

THIRTY EIGHT

PATTY

Poor Emma. If she was my little sister, I would have protected her. I wish Ma had been like Nora. Nora was brave like me. Dee was nice like Gram.

I wish I could have been there when she came. I'm so proud of John. Such a loving father.

He named her after you.

Do you think so?

Yes. Emma is part of your name.

I hope you're right. It means he forgave me.

Emma Bedonne

Redhill/Cleveland

December 25, 1965—March 1991

The world stopped being a friendly place when Emma was four and her daddy came home. She had made him a drawing of a house and she drew pictures of her and Momma and Daddy all together in the yard. Dee had guided her hand, spelling "Welcome Home." She had waited with Dee as Momma visited Daddy at the hospital. Emma was excited that Daddy got to sleep over and didn't have to stay at the prison anymore.

She remembered how her mother's pale hands shook when she returned. Emma wanted to know when they got to see Daddy and when he was coming home. Stroking Emma's dark brown hair, Nora tried to explain how they had to leave, how it had to be right now, as soon as they could pack. As Emma started to cry and she heard her mother gasp, Daddy in the door. Only it wasn't Daddy. It looked like Daddy, but it was someone else. Emma wanted to hide.

She remembered lying on the couch, hugging her doll, listening to her mother's cries that first night. Later, they moved when he was offered a job in Cleveland. Emma never knew what the job was, but remembered that the house was bigger, and she and her mother were alone more. At night, Emma heard voices, soft and scary coming from her father's bedroom. Whenever her mother spent the night behind her father's door, she heard lots of giggles. Emma would pull the covers over her head to block them out.

Most nights, her mother slept alone in the den. Emma often crept from her own bed to the den and joined her mother. Nora would wrap her arms around her daughter, kiss her face and hum a lullaby. They were in the house on Euclid then. John Arnold, becoming well known, was an invited speaker at political functions. One afternoon, when Emma was seven, she heard her mother screaming, "I won't have it. No woman would. I know what you are. Do you think I'd want another?" There was silence. Her father closed the door to the study and Emma's stomach churned with fear.

The next morning, Emma awoke to see her mother sitting on the edge of her bed, telling her she was being sent to a boarding school in New Jersey. Emma started to cry. "It's to keep you safe, my baby," her mother soothed, "Just know that I love you." She had been away at school for only a month when she was called in and the principal and a counselor told her that her mother was dead.

There had been an accident and her mother had drowned in the Cuyahoga River. Emma rarely came home after that. When she did, her father was usually away. The housekeeper, a hard and bitter woman in her seventies named Mrs. Ross served her meals and seldom spoke.

The school's principal concluded there was no remedy for Emma's sadness and inability to focus on her classes but the passage of time. Her father was often in the news, running for office; Emma was indifferent to news of his political progress. When she was twelve, he became a U.S. Senator. She missed her mother and cried herself to sleep most nights. She was comforted by keeping what remained of her former life, and the drawing that she had made as a four-year old to welcome home her daddy, was folded and buried in her drawer.

A listless student, Emma spent her free time in her private room, reading, watching television, or listening to the music of whatever band happened to be playing on the radio by her bed. Her classmates whispered that she was weird and pointedly avoided her until they saw that she didn't care. The girls, who offered friendship to see if they could draw her out, quickly became frustrated at her lack of interest.

On occasion, the creatures that orchestrated her father's successes would study her. Knowing that her existence was important, they followed the changing timeline, but were unable to see how or why she mattered. As the years progressed, it was sure to become clear.

At fifteen, Emma ran away from boarding school. It had been six years since she had seen her father. From time to time, she would glance at a newspaper and read about a committee he'd led, or an investigation into his controversial activities.

During Christmas break she drifted through the empty halls. "Rudolf the Red-Nosed Reindeer" was playing on someone's radio. She remembered her mother teaching her that song to sing for her daddy when he came home, and she started to sob. The she packed a duffle bag, leaving a note for the headmistress saying that her father had sent a car for her unexpectedly. Emma apologized for the late notice.

> *Her lie caused little consternation to those who watched. The wall was impenetrable, and little, other than knowledge, could be gleaned there. They waited to see where she might go.*

While waiting for a sandwich, sitting on a stool at a busy counter, Emma pulled out the drawing that she had kept and looked at the number on the back. The clang of the Salvation Army bell echoed in her ears as she put a dime in a payphone and called Dee collect. Two hours later she collected the bus ticket that Dee had called in and paid and was on her way back to Redhill.

> *Redhill! They snorted with approval.*

When the bus rolled into the crowded Redhill station, Dee was waiting. She hadn't seen Nora's little girl since Emma was four. As she stepped off the bus, Emma saw a tough-looking woman of sixty-five with salt and pepper hair, teased high and sprayed stiff. Dee was smoking a Marlboro and waiting patiently for her Baby Emma to come home. Emma fell into her arms, shaking. It was the first Christmas since her mother's death that she didn't want to die.

Her father soon discovered what she had done, but to her profound relief (and Dee's) he sent a terse note chiding her for her delinquency, but otherwise saying nothing. It was a month later as she was sitting on the comfortable green couch that barely fit in Dee's living room, looking at pictures of her and her mother in an album that Dee had lovingly labeled "Family" when Dee came in looking troubled.

She had a letter addressed to Emma with a Washington D.C. postmark. In it was a message from her father, "One day we'll be a family again, love Daddy." As Emma began to tremble, Dee looked at the note and said, "son of a bitch" before tearing it into pieces.

At sixteen, Emma became a waitress, working at the Busy Bee Coffee Shop with Dee as her mentor. It was hard, getting up at five, learning how to handle plates and to smile when dealing with the public. Many were rude and lousy tippers, where others left a dollar after just having coffee. Her favorites were the morning regulars, those customers who came in every day. She learned how dear routine is to the human heart.

Her regulars were mostly older men, and all were unfailingly patient and polite when the eggs came scrambled rather than over easy and the coffee cup wasn't filled as fast. Dee let it be known Emma was under her wing. Except for the afterschool crowd, where Emma fended off many an uninvited hand, she was left alone.

At eighteen, Emma grew restless. Dee suggested that she take a break and work in the city for a while and after finding a job, Emma moved to Cleveland. She made friends with people her own age, found roommates and what had happened to her before, the loss of her mother, the strangeness of her father and the years away at school, were disconnected. They happened to someone else.

Of course, she was followed. Disappointed by the harmony of Emma's existence and with Bernie's career yielding scattered caches of delectable misery, his interference was unnecessary. The restless creatures merely watched. They had read the portents. Her fate and the fate of her descendants were tied to Redhill. She had been destined to return.

Cleveland, Ohio
1984

Emma took classes, one at a time, laughing when she spoke to Dee who would start going on about the "value of education. In May of 1984, she met Giordano Bedonne. The café's few tables were empty except for one. It was a Thursday night. Weekends were the only time when people were crammed into café' and weather permitting, spilled out on to the sidewalk where they sat at picnic tables.

Lamps masquerading as candles of various types and colors completed what was a typical college eatery. He sat alone, his long legs stretched out as he leaned back finishing a sandwich, an open book in front of him, his beer half-finished. It was almost eleven and time to close. The soft folk music that completed the ambiance had faded.

She bussed the remaining tables, tucking her tips into an inner pocket of her shoulder bag, Then, Emma grabbed her book and sweater. As she was opening the door, she saw the same young man. He had gathered his books and was paying the cashier. Walking to her car, a 1970 Toyota and a gift from Dee for her 21st birthday, she heard him call to her. "Excuse me Miss, I wanted you to have this." It was a generous tip—too generous. Emma felt awkward.

He saw the doubt on her face and blushed as he stammered, "N-n-no, ah I didn't mean to embarrass you, it's just that I sat there for hours, and I know how that can hurt tips. You were so kind . . ."

She had never seen a man blush. His name was Giordano Alonso Bedonne, III and he was from Montana. Emma was surprised. "I never thought Italians would be from Montana."

Giordano laughed, "You thought we all just congregated in big cities, working in pizzerias?" There was something about him that made her trust him without question. He wasn't handsome but appealing with wide-set brown eyes and a short straight nose, that he told her later, was a gift from Bridget, his Irish mother. His smile was his own. It was open and without guile, shy at times, but always in his eyes. Giordano's hair was dark, like hers, with soft curls that he tried to tame by frequent haircuts.

Over the next few weeks, she saw him every day. His father had a small cattle ranch near Butte. His grandfather, Giordano, had immigrated to Montana in the early 1900's and had started as a ranch hand. Giordano was twenty-five and a graduate student, an environmentalist studying the pollution of the Cuyahoga. In Montana, the Berkely Pit had polluted huge stretches of land, including ranchlands. "It's killed the ranch and my father's sick."

"What about your mother?" she asked.

"She died when I was eight," he said. "My nona helped my dad raise me." His nona, whose name was Madonna, had recently died unexpectedly. Giordano, who had just returned from Butte, was mourning her loss.

A month passed before they made love in his dorm room. Her head resting on his chest, Emma remembered the last time she had felt such peace. On that rare Saturday when she wasn't working, her mother would fix her cereal, and they would sit on the small couch together and watch cartoons.

Stroking her hair, Giordano spoke of his home in Montana and of its desolate beauty. It all changed, he said, when poison slowly seeped into the land and things began to die. They had been together two months, when he proposed.

Emma thought of her father. "We'll be together as a family," he'd written. The prospect of Giordano being vulnerable to the menace of her father came to her as they walked along a wooded path near the Cuyahoga River. Emma blew on a dandelion, its white tufts floating in the air, some descending into the murky water as it followed its crooked path, some swirling into the dense brush that clung to the river's shore.

A family of ducks was making its way along the path, the mother duck scurrying across and her ducklings, all in a line, following as fast as they could waddle. Giordano was collecting samples from the ailing river, which was recovering from years of contamination.

As her eyes followed the river's flow, Emma blinked and shook her head. *How can I see this now? Her mother's lifeless body was streaked with mud. Nora's dark hair covered her face and strings of algae hung like sad ribbons as she lay near the river's dirty waters. It's not real! She's not here!*

The weight of her grief overwhelming her, Emma fell onto the path of dirt and leaves and wept. Giordano pulled her to him and held her, while she mourned again, for what was lost.

They married soon after, driving to New York for the weekend. Dee cried when Emma called her from the modest hotel room where they were staying, making Giordano promise to take care of her little girl. Emma told him about her father, but she knew that he didn't understand. She hoped he would never have to. Her pregnancy, only weeks after they married, was a surprise. It was not long before it became apparent that there were two babies; Emma was pregnant with twins.

The responsibility was sobering to both. With Emma unable to work, they focused on providing for the near future. Emma moved back to Redhill to the great delight of Dee and Giordano went back to Montana to settle his father in a convalescent home with hopes that steady care might help him regain some of his strength. He sold the ranch, but it brought far less than it would have years ago before the land was poisoned.

Giordano found a job with the Cuyahoga Valley National Park. Dee's house with its one bedroom was soon full of baby clothes, diapers and two cribs.

At the end of March, the babies were due in five weeks. The doctor, a young GP who delivered at the Redhill hospital, warned her to be careful as twins often came early. "A little early is probably eh-okay," he said, moving his hand like a teetering airplane. "Try to take it easy, not too much activity." Emma nodded; she wanted Giordano to be there, and he was still in Montana, his father's condition unchanged. She worried that he would lose his father and then become one, with no time to adjust.

Birth and Death
Redhill, Ohio
April 1985

On an April afternoon, Emma dozed on Dee's couch as a breeze played with the wooden blinds of an open window. The blinds, lightly hitting the windowsill, made a rhythmic click that soothed her. There were three more weeks. Her feet were propped on the coffee table and a new magazine was on her lap. As she drifted, dreaming of her babies and planning their first Christmas, a shadow blocked the window's light and snatched her from her dream.

John Arnold's appearance, after so many years, froze her. She could scarcely breathe. He smiled. "Little Emma." He laughed, "Not so little now, are we!"

She pretended to be glad to see him. "H-how are you? It's been a long time." She could barely whisper the words, her breath coming in shallow gasps. Again, he chuckled. In middle-age, the man pretending to be John Arnold was almost handsome, his body fit and muscular; his hands looked like he could easily yank an arm out of a socket.

He frowned in mock dismay. "You should have told me, you naughty girl. And twins, how very interesting!" He turned to go and then turned back, whispering, "Congratulate the proud papa for me, won't you?"

Emma's thinly veiled hysteria burst out, "What DO YOU WANT?"

"To be together as a family." He laughed. As he left, Emma heard him giggle. She panicked, remembering her mother trapped behind his bedroom door. The limousine's engine revved, and he was gone. When Dee came home from work, she found Emma moaning on the floor, well into labor. Three hours later, Giordano Alonso Bedonne, IV and Madonna Nora Bedonne were born, small but healthy. Their exhausted mother turned her face to the wall and slept, trying to forget what had happened.

It was another two days before Emma realized Giordano's absence. "Where is he?" she asked.

Dee's homely face, weary from maintaining a smile, fell. Tears streamed down her face and her eyes were full of love and compassion as she said simply, "Honey, he's not coming."

Emma looked at her, confused. "You mean his father?"

Dee took a deep breath, "No, my precious girl, Giordano's dead. It was the plane . . ." Emma shrieked. It was days before she could function without sedatives.

When she and the babies went home with Dee, neighbors volunteered to care for the babies while Dee worked. Six months went by until Emma decided to face the world. "Damn him!" She thought. "I have my babies to protect. I'm getting on with it." To Dee's great relief, she did. The twins were eight when Dee died from lung cancer, wasting away on a couch while Emma worked. After school, Gordon and Madonna would play in the living room to keep the dying woman company, bringing her water and coaxing her to eat. Dee's medical bills absorbed the inheritance she proudly thought she was leaving Emma. After her death, they moved to a small two-bedroom trailer, and Emma began to drink.

THIRTY NINE

PATTY

Maybe I woulda let Michael kiss me when we got bigger.

Alec Gibbs

Redhill Mall

December 8, 2004

The gruesome discovery of Ray's mutilated body delayed Alec's first day as a "games consultant-clerk" at VIDEO GAMES GALORE until December 8. He mourned his grandfather but was relieved to learn that an autopsy report indicated Ray had died before the bizarre mangling occurred. Must have been some psycho. He hoped they caught the pervert, because a person who would do that to a body was capable of anything.

As Alec explored the Mall on his first break, a creature that had witnessed the mutilation of his grandfather's body, glided above Alec's head.

Pushing against the wall, which undulated, shifting between transparency and cloudiness, the demon crawled and slid like a bear on an icy pond. It followed the boy, staring down at him with cold rage.

Passing the bookstore, Alec saw a girl in a Cleopatra wig and stopped, startled by how beautiful she was. The wig had transformed her into an exotic creature.

Madonna laughed at her image. The wig made her into a queen and the effect was not unlike the mysterious beauty of an "Other."

The creature hurdling itself against the barrier, knew that any harm to her was forbidden; she was vital to the destruction to come when the nectar of misery would flow freely.

Franka, who was in her sixties, reminded Madonna of a woman at the Renaissance Fair. Madonna declared herself a child of the sixties." Franka was wearing "The Princess," a wig with a swirl of bangs and flowing tresses.

"Happening Wigs" offered glamour and beauty. There were also "fright" wigs that were sure to make your friends laugh or smile at your "incredible transformation."

Franka was encouraging Madonna to try on a "Marilyn" wig. In Alec's opinion, the girl didn't need a wig. She was perfect just the way she was.

"She's hot, isn't she? She's a real witch you know, just like those babes on *Charmed*." Alec turned to see a skinny boy with red hair, freckles and a rash of pimples spread all over his good-natured face. The boy was wearing the same uniform as the girl.

"Madonna," the boy called to the girl, "Ted says your break's over and we're getting busy."

The girl glanced at him before turning back to her friend. "I'll be there in a minute and a half," she answered, taking off the wig.

Turning back to Alec and seeing his obvious interest, the boy whispered confidentially, "I hate to break it to ya, but she's really into me. As soon as I get my license back—well . . . what can I say?"

Alec smiled and shrugged his shoulders. "What's her name anyway?" he asked.

"Her name's Madonna. I'm Kevin by the way. Come by the ICE KING, dude, I'll take care of ya."

"Alec." he said by way of introduction. Like Madonna, his break was over, and he turned to go back to work.

Later, Alec took his lunch break and decided to check out the Food Court. Looking at the line-up of logos spanning the perimeter, his heart skipped beats when he saw the blue and silver icicle awning of the ICE KING. Kevin was nowhere to be found. Ted, the ICE KING supervisor, was deep in conversation with the BUCKEYE RIBS manager on the opposite side of the Court, leaving Madonna to handle the long line of customers, which she did efficiently, ignoring the occasional comments about her makeup and hair.

When his turn came, she asked him, "What'll it be?" He couldn't think; she was so pretty. Madonna looked up and saw a young man of nineteen, a little awkward in the way he stood, shifting from one foot to the other. He was tall and slender, his dark hair a little long with sideburns, an unconscious tie to his absent father who wore them in the most recent of Alec's memories of him. The boy's large eyes were a luminous brown under thick dark brows.

Good looking, but serious, she thought. He blushed. "What'll it be?" she asked again.

"Wh-whatever you decide." he stammered.

You got it," she said with a laugh. She made him a large sundae, piling on several toppings.

"How much?" He asked, fumbling at his wallet, a last Christmas gift from his mother.

"Twenty-six dollars and fifty cents." She smiled slyly.

"Okay." he said, digging into his pocket.

Madonna was alarmed. "I was teasing, really."

Ted had returned from his "conference." Trying to recover, Alec said, "Keep it as a tip." In line right behind Alec, a sharply dressed girl of thirty rolled her eyes. The girl, Francesca was the manager at the Mall's bookstore, READ ALL ABOUT IT.

"We don't allow our employees to accept tips," said Ted.

"Ted, it was just a joke." Madonna sighed. He really was a self-important little prick. Ted glared at them both and went back to BUCKEYE RIBS.

"Alec." Alec said nervously, introducing himself.

"Yes, it's on your nametag." she said. "So's mine, come to think of it." She laughed. "Nice to meet you, I'm Madonna," she answered cocking her head and pointing to her nametag that said Ice Maiden with her name under it.

He took a deep breath. "You wouldn't . . . have dinner with me . . . would you?" he asked.

"Say yes! Please! I want my cone and sprinkles sometime before next week!" urged Francesca. She poked her head around Alec and waved her hand.

"Yes, okay?" said Madonna, suddenly feeling shy herself.

"What time are you off?" he asked, trying not to appear quite as eager as he felt.

"Seven, I'll meet you here." she said. He nodded, relieved; he was off at six.

"What'll it be?" she asked Francesca.

"You owe me at least one free topping, Madonna." Francesca whispered with a fake scowl as they watched him leave, adding, "You're lucky; that guy was so nervous, it could have taken him days and a hell of a lot of soft-serve before you got a free dinner."

Alex turned and with a shy wave goodbye, he began to eat his sundae as he made his way back to VIDEO GAMES. Overhead, the piped-in Christmas music was "Jingle Bell Rock." He felt like dancing.

Above the food court, the crow looked down from atop a metal bar. Several of the Mall's silver snowflakes hung beneath it. It dipped its head and held it motionless, as if considering its next move.

Repelled by the boy's euphoria, its red eyes were faded and cold as the demon snaked through burbling alien hills. It hissed as Alec walked through it, unaware. The wall billowed and snapped like a rubber band as it clawed trying to pierce it, yearning to spear him like a fish. It wanted to bring him, struggling and glassy eyed into their world. It would suck the marrow from his bones.

Madonna frowned. For a moment, she imagined she saw shadows near the far end of the Food Court. Their hostile presence galvanized her. Telling Ted, she must take care of something, she moved quickly towards them, the herbs she carried hidden. She swung the smoking smudge stick from side to side, lit as she abruptly left her post. Indignant, Ted called to her.

Baring their teeth, the demons let out a shrill whine and escaped to the other side of the mall.

Dates and History
Redhill
December 8, 2004

Alec pulled Ray's old Datsun into the parking lot near the food court entrance. It had finally started to get cold, and he wore his gray jacket, his mother's gift to him on his twentieth birthday. Mom would like her, he thought. It still hurt. He missed his mother. It had been two years since she died. He often felt his mom's presence; he still felt loved. He pulled open the double doors and saw Madonna talking to the jerk manager Ted. Madonna waved and smiled as she saw Alec.

The fifties style vintage black coat was too large for her petite five-foot four frame. She grabbed a knitted sack and said good night to Ted, who was wrapping up his lecture on the proper way to store trays and sprinkles. Narrowing his eyes, Kevin pointed at Alec. "You! Take care of my girl," he said with mock seriousness. "Have fun Madonna!" he said, laughing, "Just not too much!"

Alec did not have a lot of experience with girls and dating. He and his mother had moved to Redhill four years earlier. Molly had worked a variety of jobs, taking care of the two of them. Alec grew up used to moving because of his dad. Alec loved his dad but didn't respect him. He didn't even know where Ray Jr. was now. It had been over eight years since he had seen him. By that last time, Alec had no illusions about his old dad. Some people just didn't get what was important. His dad always had a plan and always, the plan didn't work out and Ray Jr. would disappear, leaving Molly to deal with the people who were owed.

When things cooled down, his dad would show up and they would move. Alec was used to being the new kid at school. He'd had his heart broken once, right before they moved to Redhill. They were living in St. Louis. Alec was still in high school. Her name was Chris, a pretty girl with strawberry blonde hair and a winning smile. He was in love. They shared several classes including calculus. Chris was having a hard time understanding integrals.

He was elated the day she approached him and asked if they could do homework together. Alec patiently went through the steps and slowly. Chris seemed to catch on. He knew that she would have never talked to him if she hadn't needed help, but it didn't matter. One night as they studied for the final in her cluttered bedroom, Chris decided to share a half a bottle of wine she had stashed. Alec lost his virginity.

He was overwhelmed, but Chris told him not to sweat it, that she took the pill. He had to admit he was relieved. His mother was always friendly towards Chris, but he sensed she didn't approve. He asked her why. Molly shrugged and said it was just a mother's sixth sense, her instinct to protect her cub. As finals week approached, Alec could tell that Chris was going to pass the class.

He felt proud and close to her. Summoning his courage, he asked her to the prom.

Chris looked at him and laughed. "Hey, you and I are buds. I really like you . . . but I'm going with Allen." Allen was on the debate team and senior class president. Allen's family had money. He was a good-looking, if rather shallow boy.

The night of the prom, Alec stayed in his room. His mother kept watch but didn't intrude. Her son was a solitary soul. When Molly decided to move to Redhill after learning Ray was in the Convalescent Home with no one to check in on him, Alec was indifferent. It was only after they moved that Alec found that he enjoyed his grandfather with his stories about World War II, his jokes and insights. When Ray gave his painful account of the prison fire, Alec suspected there were things about the fire that his grandfather didn't share.

Alec began to open up again, much to Molly's relief. Ray genuinely cared about his grandson. She loved the old man because of his generous heart and for the way he related to her son, giving him that father-son relationship Alec had missed out on. When she discovered that she had terminal cancer, Molly thanked God for Ray. For a while at least, her son wouldn't be alone.

Ray decided to give Alec the house where he and Lisa lived for almost twenty years, and he had lived alone until he fell. What little money he had, he willed to his grandson. Alec enrolled at White

Oak College, hoping to continue in Cleveland at the University. Ray was enthusiastic about Alec's plans until he found out about the new job and the mall. He was scared for Alec, a fear grounded in his knowledge of what Arnold really was and what he knew his rational grandson would never believe.

As she waited for Alec, listening to Ted's "point" about how trays have to be neatly stacked, blue on white on blue, etc., Madonna laughed at herself for being so nervous. She was nineteen years old for Christ's sake, come on . . . Even Kevin had been on more dates than she had, though she wondered just how many were real dates and how many were a product of Kevin's considerable imagination. She could count on one hand the number of "real" dates she had been on in her life. When she was fifteen, she had accepted an invitation to go with her gay friend Craig to the prom, so that his parents wouldn't know that he was really meeting her brother after they had been dropped off at the hall. Gordon still owed her for that one. Another was a blind date she had accepted, trusting her friend Gayle who had assured her that her cousin Barry was cute, loved the occult and would understand Madonna's sensitivity and intuitiveness.

Unfortunately, Madonna didn't trust her instincts when it came to agreeing to go on a picnic with Barry, who assumed that her alternative look translated into a casual attitude towards having sex with a virtual stranger and an unattractive one at that. He was soon discouraged by a couple of well-placed scratches and a kick, which also ended her friendship with Gayle. She had experienced crushes, boys that she would want, knowing that her oddness made it impossible.

Madonna believed in truth. She refused to blend in. Her way of dressing was more than just wanting to be different. Her visions often exposed her to the darkness that lurked in her future. Charms, the rings, her pendants, the spells, all were tools she used, pursuing truth, and combating what she knew to be evil.

Jeremy was a handsome boy whom she had once thought she loved. His father was a lawyer, prominent in local politics and his mother hosted charity events. Jeremy rebelled, his black clothes and piercings proclaiming his independence. He was eager to understand a different way of seeing things. They spent a night camping the summer after they graduated. She let him make love to her.

It was her first time, a fact that she reluctantly shared with her lover, not knowing how he might feel. Jeremy, his caramel eyes, lined in black, looked into hers. His face was softly lit by their campfire, his blond hair dyed blacker than hers. To her relief, he reacted with tenderness. He kissed her fingertips and whispered maybe he would be her only. Maybe they would be together until they were very old. Madonna smiled at his romantic fantasy. Though less experienced with sex, she was a realist.

Weeks later, her period didn't come. She was stunned when Jeremy became hostile, throwing a chair, saying that his mother was right. Madonna wanted to trap him, a boy from a wealthy family and hop on "the gravy train." With a frozen smile on her face, Madonna left, berating herself for not seeing the truth when it mattered. He left town the following day. She didn't know why, nor did she care. Her period soon came and when Gordon found her crying with relief, he pried the reason out of her. The next week he dragged her to a clinic in Cleveland and sat and waited for her while she had an exam and a prescription for birth control.

Months later, while working at a dry cleaners, she took her lunch break at the Busy Bee Café. Jeremy was there. This time, he was wearing Dockers, his hair blond, and eyes sans makeup. He sat next to her at the counter and explained that he had been in Europe. She knew he'd been back for a while. Sheepishly, he asked if she would meet him after she finished work. He wanted forgiveness. "Sorry, we are who we are," she answered as she paid her check and left. His black clothes, the music and the chains were his way of saying that he wasn't like his parents. Ah, but it was a lie; he was. She was a phase for him.

Now there was Alec. She was afraid to hope. They decided to go to Hunan Delight for dinner. The family-owned restaurant, along with several insurance offices and a hair salon, sat inside the building that had been Desimone's for almost a century. Photographs of the Song family hung on the wall behind the register. Antique lamps, imported from San Francisco and murals, painted by Amy, the only Song to be born in Redhill, gave the room a romantic ambience. Warren Song and his wife Colleen had opened the restaurant years ago, soon after the prison fire.

The story of how they met while investigating the notorious Cleveland Crusher was known by many in Redhill. Aware of the Songs' presence in Redhill, Bernie planned to pay a visit to them after the coming sacrifice and transformation. Amazingly, the old woman, Ramona was still alive and over one hundred years old. Bernie still feared her and made sure to avoid being anywhere near her. He would wait until he possessed Madonna's power.

The old woman often sat in the gift shop, SONG'S GIFTS & KNICKKNACKS that the family owned in another part of the building. Often, Madonna would come in and look at the crystals, herbs, and charms. An old cloth toy, a turkey with a tail made from strips of faded fabric, sat next to a collection of antique fans. Like the fans, it was not for sale. There was something about the cloth toy that moved her. She did not know that it had been created from scraps and sewn by her great aunt, Becka Tobin, only that sadness would overwhelm her if she looked at it too long.

Other than the lost skull ring, Madonna rarely purchased anything; most items were too expensive compared to her Internet sources. Occasionally she would say hello to Grandma Song, who would point to her, smile, and say, "You know, don't you? You have it!" Madonna would shrug, smile and raise her hands, palms up. Grandma Song always laughed.

Strange Packages

At Hunan Delight, Saturday nights were a mix of pleasant music, currently the best of holiday favorites and heavenly aromas emanating from the white bowls and platters that rested on red tablecloths. In the banquet room, large tables hosted a reunion, a birthday celebration and a simple gathering of friends sharing the excitement and good cheer of the season.

In the softly lit main dining room, gleaming red booths were reserved for four or more, while couples filled the scattering of small tables, placed strategically in quieter, more intimate areas. Colleen Song had insisted on the tables, saying that families start with couples. Warren, who was more practical, countered that they were a waste of space. Larger tables rather than small ones would bring in more revenue. Ramona sided with Colleen and the small tables remained.

Like butterflies pinned in a scrapbook, images of Redhill lined the walls. The pictures echoed the melancholy that had so bewildered Marlene.

Alec and Madonna sat at a table, suffering the awkward silence of a first date. After waiting for Alec to start, she decided it was up to her. "So, what do you like to do for fun?" She asked. He looked startled. "I mean in terms of interests. You know . . . do you have any hobbies?"

In a panic, he considered whether he had something worthy to share, something that might deem him fascinating. His heart swelled with unspent emotion. Just out of reach, witty remarks floated in a fog. When the waitress brought the hot and sour soup, the word "Gadgets" sprang from his lips.

"Excuse me?" Madonna asked. She was puzzled by the remark and wondered what gadgets had to do with soup.

"You know . . . hobbies, that's what I like to do." He panicked at her reaction. Things weren't going well. What could he ask her? "So, Kevin says you're a witch." he said, immediately regretting it, wondering how he would recover. Madonna's "Get real" look confirmed his worst fear. "You can probably tell I'm real smooth on first dates. I'm sorry, I don't care what you are, I just . . . like you."

Seeing his stricken face, she touched his hand. "You could call it that I suppose. I don't think of myself as one, but if I were one . . ." She leaned forward intimately and whispered, "It wouldn't be for the 'dark side'."

"Oh," he whispered back, relieved that they were back on track, nodding in mock seriousness, "of course."

"Seriously, though," she said, "I study the occult because I'm developing my third eye." Realizing how strange she sounded, Madonna sighed. "If, uh you want to know the truth, I don't really know exactly what I am."

The soup was forgotten and the red booths, the holiday music and the chatter seemed far away. "It doesn't matter," Alec said, "whatever you are is fine with me."

She sighed. "Since I can remember I've been into . . . stuff that people think is weird, and now, I take online courses. I'm studying paranormal phenomena." She could see he was confused. "I mean because of my third eye, you know, my psychic abilities." She laughed. "I don't have another eye in the back of my head or anything." They both laughed as she turned for him to see the back of her head, the yin/yang barrette resembling an eye.

She paused as their dinner came, waiting until the waiter left to explain. "There's lots of things. I get impressions, warnings and premonitions, usually when something bad might happen. It's called precognition. My grandfather is part of it. From the time I was little, before I knew who he was, he played a part in my dreams and whatever it means, I know it's not good." She watched his face, hoping that he wasn't judging her, dismissing her as a flake, or worse, what she'd been called in school, a freak.

He reassured her. "My mom was like that a little. She called them hunches. You know, it's weird. My grandfather was in prison with yours."

Madonna sighed. "I'm so sorry. I forgot, he just passed away. Were you close to him?

He nodded. "We were close. He had these other sides to him that the family didn't really get. He was a professional gambler, but also a fantastic artist. He did a lot of drawings while he was in prison; they're really good." He paused, feeling self-conscious. "Uh, we were talking about gadgets; I want to explain," He needed an excuse to see her tomorrow. "If you're interested, I'll show you some of the things I've invented. They're kind of weird though."

"How about tomorrow, during a break?" Madonna suggested. Just then, the check came. They considered their fortunes. Madonna read his first. "Good things come in strange wrappings."

Madonna looked at her fortune as Alec waited. "What is it, the answer to life?"

"Maybe," she said and read, "Do your best; it will be enough." She looked at him as she considered the message on the small strip of paper. "I suppose," she said, "that remains to be seen."

Perched on the restaurant windowsill, peering through the frosted smear of a painted holiday wreath, the crow studied the young couple. The intense pleasure of "falling in love" experienced by the boy and girl repelled it. An Other had been summoned to enter the restaurant and observe the boy. His impact on the coming sacrifice was unclear. The Other's stay was brief. Waves of human bonding and the joy of dining shielded the boy from her gaze. Soon after, the crow flew away. In time there would be no shield; there would be only pain.

FORTY

Mommy

San Francisco

March 1942

"Your sons are safe." Mommy assured her. "I will watch out for them; Daddy will watch too." Mommy attempted a smile; her ravaged gums betrayed her suffering. Her beauty was gone, taken by the merciless cancer. She touched her shaking finger to Ramona's forehead. "But you know already."

Ramona's held Mommy's withered hand. Through the open window, early morning filled the room with light. She nodded and offered Mommy a spoonful of broth. Mommy shook her head and with a surprising strength, pulled Ramona closer. "The next one . . . the next one will have the pearl, but you must protect . . ." Ramona nodded as Mommy's hand relaxed and fell on the soft blanket.

Why can't I see?

Alice
San Francisco
April 1942

Ramona held the newborn and laughed as she wiggled the baby's toes. *Yes, yes . . . Mommy said it was this one. Oh Mommy, I wish you could see her.* The baby girl reached out and grabbed her nose, twisting. Sitting at the table in Ramona's kitchen, Lydia, Maurice's wife, read his letter. "He says Joseph has a cold and misses your soup." For once, Ramona was grateful for the "third eye."

The baby girl yawned. Ramona decided to keep a close watch over her granddaughter as Alice grew. Whatever threatened Alice, Ramona would be there to fight.

The Shed

> *They were in the shed again. He looks so old now, she thought, maybe he will die soon. Will the evil go with him? Screams, oh the screams were so hard to bear. She wanted to die with them. The beast twisted a lever, tormenting a helpless woman who howled and pleaded. She had seen him do it before, the light in the eyes gone . . .too many times . . .*

The baby cried, prompting the drowsy Lydia to lift her from the crib and feed her, saying "Shhhh, you'll wake Ma ma, shhh." Grateful for the baby's cries, Ramona listened to the infant's sounds as Alice gurgled and sucked, grasping the nipple while her teenaged mother rocked her and slept.

Cinderella and the Spider
San Francisco 1952

Alice extended her arm and then her foot like a ballerina. Ordinarily, the kneeling Prince Charming would have held his nose, as he had done at rehearsals, but now he took the "glass slipper" from the satin pillow. He bent his head, causing the plumed hat to tug on its bobby pin, distracting him and resulting in the "slipper" bouncing across the stage. The cast and the audience gave a collective gasp as the slipper, a pink tap-shoe, flipped, landing near the center downstage edge near the audience. The prince froze, looking at his mother, who had poked her head out from the wings. The excited mother pointed at her lips, mouthing the words "go get it." Next to the prince, the boy's sister, costumed in the padded dress of the wicked stepmother, shook her head. The wicked stepsisters rolled their eyes at the ten-year old fairy godmother standing next to them.

The wicked stepsisters sat on folded chairs as their overlarge paper maiche' feet peeked out from under long dresses. The three put their hands over their mouths and started to giggle. "Oh Prince, some magic spell is at work!" Alice said as she danced over to where the shoe lay. Turning the shoe over with her toe, she slid her foot into it.

"My princess, will you marry me?" the relieved prince inquired. Alice nodded and the "Court" burst into cheers, bringing the audience to their feet. Ramona rose with the rest, proud of Alice. Fourteen-year-old Warren Jr. shifted next to her, glancing at his watch, which had been his father's.

He's tall for fourteen, Ramona thought; his father would be pleased. The memory of her oldest' death two years earlier brought the threat of tears. She'd begged him not to work that Saturday. "Take your family out, enjoy life," she had pleaded. As she feared, death came when bullets meant for another caught Warren as he passed a pawnshop. Ramona was devastated. She had failed to protect him. What good was her gift?

Applause filled the auditorium as the cast of the fifth and sixth grade's "Cinderella" made a curtain call. Maurice sat next to Lydia, clapping loudly, nodding at his brothers and their families. There were seven grandsons. Alice was the only granddaughter, the only pearl. Beautiful in the pink taffeta dress that Lydia had spent hours making, a thousand sequins at least, Ramona estimated, Alice was the image of Joey, especially in her confident smile, as she bowed gracefully, leading the cast in a curtain call.

Ramona tapped the tall man who had rudely moved in front of her and asked him to shift to the side. At four foot eleven, Ramona would not miss a moment of her granddaughter's triumph. Alice saw her and pointed quickly at her forehead—their signal. Ramona made a quick gesture in return. Later, when Alice spent the night, she sat cross-legged on Ramona's small couch and recounted the shoe incident.

The Demon Rift

"I suspected something would go wrong. Last night I dreamt that I was on stage, and you were in the audience saying, 'watch for the magician.' But, you disappeared, and I had to decide what to do next." Alice put her arms around Ramona's neck. "I'm going to be an actress."

Ramona shook her head. "No, may may, be a teacher or a nurse."

"I'll be a psychic like you!" the little girl teased.

Ramona had supported her boys by doing readings. Mommy had finally prevailed. "Your husband's gone, you must . . ." The dreams had come back then. If she stopped, would they leave again?

"I'm retiring; you must think of something else."

"Or I'll be an actress!" Alice was emphatic. Better an actress Ramona thought, then be open to . . .

FORTY ONE

Chaos
Cleveland, 1929

He left the seamstress in tangled weeds near the river, but not before using his new device, slowly applying pressure until at last, the life left her eyes. Sorrowfully, before he discarded the body that had held the thoughts and dreams of Frannie Banks, he took a little piece of her, storing it in a small jar, the first of many memories he would keep hidden away in an old wooden cabinet that sat in the corner of the shack. The woman's body found news spread quickly about what had been done to her. With a second body (somewhat more of a success from Bernie's point of view, but very bad luck for the drunken young merchant marine named O'Reilly, the newspaper declared him a victim of the "Cleveland Crusher."

The headlines of 1929 that followed the story of the "Crusher" were dominated by the Stock Market Crash. Soon, stories of the Great Depression were all the news. Bernie admitted to himself that the "chaos" the whispers sang of was the convulsions of a stricken nation and he winced when they taunted him, laughing at his pretensions. The steel mill threatened to close during the worst days of the Depression. Many were laid off, but Bernie stayed, the vague threat of denying him freezing the will of any boss who would let him go.

#

After bringing down Al Capone, Eliot Ness, newly in charge of Cleveland's Public Safety, vowed to catch "The Cleveland Crusher" and another monster dubbed "The Torso Murderer." Though he reduced the crime rate, Ness captured neither. While the headlines heralded the New Deal and the gathering storms of war, the uneasy public read the small, frequent articles that spoke of yet another victim of the "Crusher."

By the time Pearl Harbor was bombed in December of 1941, thirty-five men and women and a teenaged boy had suffered and died in the grip of the terrible blacksmith's vise, solely for the pleasure and ambition of Bernard Baker. Some of them were found and laid to rest, mourned by their families, their names added to the list of victims. Others lay unseen, their bones mixing with the soil, their disappearance a mystery unsolved.

War brought the steel mills into full operation as production increased to meet demands. Women became part of the mill workforce. The sinister little man who kept their records caused many of them to joke among themselves. All feared him. The war ended and with the death of Mrs. Berg, the boarding house demolished. Bernie had to move, an agony catching him unprepared.

Renting a room above a furniture store, he bought a hot plate and prepared his own meals for the first time in his sixty years. After a dinner of stew or soup, he would sit in the dark and watch the glow of neon signs strike the curtains hanging in his window. The yellowing lace caught the gaudy reds, blues, and purples of EATS at MOM'S DINER and THE SATIN DOLL BAR. Bernard sat silent, grieving for his lost hopes.

He continued to kill, but it was more difficult. He needed his car to get to work. That meant he had to keep it clean because he risked exposure if he allowed bloodstains. The whispers still came. Not often, he would think sadly. The lace took on the splendid colors of the neon and sometimes, a dark landscape with distant seething mountains and tall pines would appear. He could hear the crows mocking him, but he longed to be there and see the lights play violently in the sky, feeling a kinship denied him in his earthly existence.

PATTY

Bernie was the biggest rat in the world. Somebody shoulda smashed his skull. Why didn't Ramona fight him? She wasn't a little kid anymore.

That poor girl.

Sylvia
Cleveland 1954

He's deciding which one, Ramona thought. Ramona was watching the slug as he sat at his desk in the payroll office. Very angry now—the letter—the letter—they're unhappy with my work? Ha! No name, no one signed . . . they're all afraid . . . He collected the timesheets, locking his meticulous work in a drawer . . . walking by the secretaries who pretended not to see him . . . by the loader. . . He passes the coffee shop . . . Sylvia . . . the waitress . . . yes . . . NO! Ramona couldn't bear to witness, so young a girl . . . He turns around looking. I mustn't let him see . . .

He follows the girl as she leaves. It's dark by the river, but faster this way, Sylvia decides. I'll be home in case he calls. She swings one arm assertively, the hand clinched into a fist while her purse is tucked against her with the other arm.

The hand rests limply on her chest.

The monster is close behind. He whispers, suggests she can handle any mugger. She sees the end of the path with the familiar blinking streetlight . . . they should fix it, not safe . . . she thinks. He brings the club down with a glancing blow—so much practice in not killing as well as killing. Ramona shrinks back as she follows them into the shed . . . wake up! No more . . . NO MORE! The monster hesitates, panicking . . .

Time raced by and in the shed, the girl was moaning . . . Ramona could see that she was almost dead . . . it had been two days. What good can I do now? She'll die anyway. Wake up!

Ramona woke shaking. No more readings; *it is not my responsibility!* Reluctant to sleep, she reached for her Zane Grey novel and saw a movie magazine tucked beneath the cushion of the window seat. Ramona frowned. Alice must have hidden it while she sat at the window that afternoon. Lydia came early to pick her up. There had been no chance to hide it in her pink overnight case. Ramona disapproved of Alice's fascination with film stars. The little girl was too curious about adult matters. Lydia must be more careful. She would put an end to it by speaking with Maurice. She placed the offending magazine on the dresser, closing the pages of ideal beauty, love affairs and scandals.

Then, she straightened the shade. A spider hovered on the other side of the window. Its filament legs undulated as it paused before descending abruptly into the darkness. As she saw it disappear, she clinched her fist. *I have a right!* She had pretended to be normal in the years when her sleep was mostly undisturbed, only an occasional cluster of restless nights, with her a witness to the hunt, and worse, the prolonged deaths of the tortured.

The victims screamed while her outrage urged her to grab his pale neck and smash his skull with the force of her mind. She wanted to splinter the bones of his wizened face with its deadly smile, to see surprise in the pale-yellow eyes as they turned a malignant gray, then fading. Rather than enjoy their feast, the demons would hurtle back into their own wretched world, the door shut and locked.

What frightened her was the knowledge that she might succeed. *But there was the danger of failing.* The price would be the destruction of her and those she loved. She'd seen his fear when he became aware of her. He always checked, sensing he was watched. What if she failed? He would find her and her children. She wanted to take his rat's mind, squeeze it and throw it at them. Then she would banish them as they dragged his unworthy spirit with them.

She feared the slug even more because of Alice. *Daddy, I didn't ask for this. Tell the Spirit to pick someone else. I have the right to be normal.* She looked out of her window and closed the third eye, covering the pearl with firm denial. She woke the next morning and smiled. No more dreams, no more slug. I am normal now. That morning she cancelled all of her appointments and applied for a clerk's position at a pharmacy.

Ramona watched Alice for signs, fearing that the duty rejected by Ramona might transfer to her granddaughter. To her relief, she saw that Alice's dreams were like Mommy's—marriages and births, employment, business opportunities, rarely a dark dream. "Shake it off may may, don't look at it," Ramona counseled whenever Alice seemed troubled. When Alice whispered her impression that the father of a classmate would soon die by falling down some stairs, Ramona shook her head.

"Even if it is true, you can do nothing. Put it out of your head; don't think it, think of something pleasant."

"But Ma ma," Alice pleaded, "what if I just send a message for him to be careful?"

"Even so, do you think he's going to take the concerns of a young girl seriously?" Ramona would save her granddaughter no matter the cost. Alice became distraught when she heard later that the man tripped over a small dog and broke his neck on a flight of stairs.

"Ma ma, I saw it, I saw it! Why didn't I at least try?"

Ramona was firm. "You didn't try because it wouldn't have done any good. Your responsibility is to your family. Remember always how much we love you."

Gradually, Alice's visions decreased, much to Ramona's relief. Alice would become normal.

Nothing is Forever
San Francisco
June 1960

Fifty students marched into the gymnasium to the somber music of childhood's end. Warren Jr. held Ramona's arm as he guided her to her seat in the auditorium. Parents, grandparents, restless toddlers, doting aunts and uncles, freshly scrubbed siblings, all strained to catch the eye of their graduate. The graduates maintained a dignified pace. They looked toward the stage as if they could see their future spread before them. Cameras flashed and Ramona could hear Lydia urging Maurice to be ready to snap a picture as Alice turned to take her seat with the others.

Ramona remembered Alice's performance as Cinderella. Alice was still a star, head of her class of fifty graduating seniors. Alice gave her speech, reminding the audience that it was time for her and her classmates to make the world better. Ramona nodded her head as she fought tears watching Alice accept awards with an air of grace and humility. Her sons and their families clapped enthusiastically with each honor.

Ramona often worried that her grandsons could see how she favored her granddaughter, but there was no hint of any resentment. She glanced back at the boys whose seats were in the row behind her. They would soon be young men. James's two boys were in high school. They all did their homework in Ramona's apartment.

She had refused to live with any of her children, fearing for their safety, fearing the slug. Often, she served her family the soup so missed by her sons during the war. At twelve, thirteen and fourteen, Alice's brother, George, and Joseph's two boys were younger than James' sons. All three had paper routes and were intent on making their fortunes early rather than going to college. Supporting their efforts, Ramona bought subscriptions they sold and received several magazines, including *Sports Illustrated*.

None of her grandsons seemed resentful, which soothed her conscience. Warren and his nineteen-year-old brother Raymond were less frequent guests. Warren Sr.'s widow, their mother Anne, kept the family ties with the Mission and regularly volunteered her sons' assistance when they were home from college. At his early twenties, Warren joined the San Francisco Police Department, a choice that worried Ramona though she resisted the temptation to use her psychic gift. It was safer not to know. Knowing did not save his father. The older boys sometimes came for dinner and gave her news from the Mission. Raymond, who had a gift for mimicry would imitate Sister Martha's attempts to convert him, which made Ramona laugh, something she rarely did.

The last of the diplomas given, Ramona allowed herself a rare moment of happiness as she looked at her family. Though she never stopped missing him, she told herself that Joey would be pleased at how life had gone on with their sons and their grandchildren. He would be proud. As the moment faded, images that collected, lingering behind the third eye, intruded. The faces of victims, those who died because she wanted to protect those she loved, demanded to be acknowledged.

It's my right. I never volunteered; I was only six!

Questions chewed on her resolve: What about the victims? What about those who loved them?

At the close of the ceremony, Alice was radiant, her cap and tassel bouncing as she moved quickly through the crowd. She came to her family and embraced Ramona while her parents waited. Ramona held her close, the top of her graying head barely reaching her granddaughter's ear. Alice was eighteen and a half a head taller than Ramona. The girl whispered, "I have a gift for you, Ma ma, I'll give it to you later."

In the early evening of Alice's graduation day, as the faint sound of ships' horns served as a mournful reminder that nothing is forever, Ramona sat with Alice on her bed, where boxes of stationary, expensive pen sets, a plush blanket, wallets full of currency, and tickets to a play waited for a proper thank you note.

After looking over the gifts and reading the cards, including the one with Ramona's considerable check, Alice opened her overnight bag. Reaching under a jumble of clothes, she took out a box. Ramona was confused. "May may, you are the graduate. You receive gifts, you don't give them."

Alice shook her head. "I saw this, and something told me you must have it. Please, Ma ma, don't argue."

Reluctantly, Ramona lifted the box lid. Underneath a square of white silk, was a pearl pendant. The pearl was large, and swirls of light blue mixed with a soft, almost milky white, except for a blue-black spot encircled by an oval rim of a blue-grayish-color. The pearl's eye—*NO!* The setting was plain; thin gold bars curved gently around the pearl. The chain was neither heavy, nor flimsy, but a sturdy rope of tightly closed links. Ramona gasped, dropping the box and pendant on the bed.

"Take it away; give it to someone else, I can't look at it." Alice's stricken face made Ramona struggle to explain.

"I don't know where you found this but take it and get your money back. I—I don't wear jewelry . . . and it's too . . ." Ramona turned away. She tried to change the subject. "How did you pay for it?"

Alice reached inside her small case and pulled out a flat notebook. Inside were clippings taken from local newspapers. Selling cosmetics, pointing to new appliances, wearing a summer dress as she sat on the hood of a new car, Alice's smile proclaimed her belief in the product being sold. Ramona stared, shaking her head in disbelief. "Do your parents know about this disgraceful work?"

Alice's face reddened. Her hand shaking, she took the pendant from the bed and slipped it over her head. Grabbing her case and the clippings, she stood up. "I'm going to be an actress, Ma ma. I'm not going to college; I'm going to New York. You and Mom and Dad better get used it."

Ramona hesitated, looking for the right words to say, to convince Alice that it was a mistake; it would be all right. She, Ramona, would speak to Maurice and Lydia. She would smooth it all over and they would . . . Alice turned and walked out of Ramona's bedroom and opening the door, she left. Ramona called to her trying to stop her, but Alice was already gone.

After calling Maurice to intercept Alice, Ramona gathered the wrapping from the bed and her eye fell on another folded paper, a flyer declaring: *Models Sought—Attractive, 18 to 28—Todd Herman's Hollywood Models Offices: San Francisco, Los Angeles, Chicago, Cleveland, New York.*

Those who Love

At the end of 1958, someone put an envelope on Bernie's desk. Bernie was being retired, effective immediately. No boss, from the managers to company presidents had signed it, the company seal giving it authority. Bernie considered whom he could "influence," but soon realized that his situation was futile. His car, a Buick purchased in the early days of the war when his 1921 Ford had finally stopped running, sat in a nearby garage, its owner too dispirited to continue his deadly hobby.

He was to live out the rest of his days in the little room, waiting for his destiny, waiting for Ducky Strike. During the boiling summer of 1959, a new business opened across from Bernie's window. The sign HOLLYWOOD MODELS PHOTOGRAPHY hung above the black and white door next to the bar. Bernie watched, diverted by the steady traffic of attractive young women going in and out at all hours.

Todd Herman, the proprietor, was a large man in his forties. He often ushered a girl through the door, his hand firmly placed in the small of her back. Now that Bernie spent his days as well as nights in the dark sweltering room, he took note of the air of secrecy and decided to sit by his window and observe. Peering through the lace curtains, he watched the many women, and occasionally men, who came and went. On his infrequent walks, he began to see flyers posting "Models Needed." The address on the flyer belonged to his neighbor the photographer, whose name was Todd.

When Bernie concluded that Todd produced pornographic photographs, images that held no interest for him, he was disappointed. He had hoped for more. He longed to experience, vicariously, another's murderous acts. The situation had reawakened his criminal appetite. After a long hiatus, he decided to hunt. Driving on the streets late at night, he realized how much things had changed in the years he had spent sitting in a room waiting for a reward, waiting to die a failure.

He wept tears of desperation and self-pity. There were more people out late now, and more police and ways to be discovered. He visited the stable. Lighting the kerosene lamp on the small cabinet, a cabinet Bernie had filled with jars containing relics of his past crimes, Bernie experienced a profound despair. He picked up the lead pipe that had been an instrument of destruction for so many and swung it, crashing through a stall in the wooden structure. Gulls began to squawk. Bernie thought he could hear the sound of crows.

A cold rage filled him. Walking alone, he saw the gaudy neon of The Satin Doll Bar. Then he saw Todd, the photographer emerge from a side door next to the bar. Todd turned and called to someone still inside. The laughter of a young girl floated in the night air. Distant signs flashed, creating glowing silhouettes. Bernie's heart quickened, perhaps . . .

Two days later, Bernie sat in the dark of his room sipping soup. He smiled, feeling happy for the first time in years. Never had he risked discovery as he had that night! Was it luck or was he protected? It didn't matter. There had been two bodies to manage. Bernie was over seventy now. With the skill acquired from years of practice, he dragged the girl first and then the considerable weight of Todd away from the light and into the shadows of an alley, before picking up the fragments of brain and bone.

Seeing the dead man's dentures, Bernie wondered if he could wear them and put them in his pocket. He had lost the last of his teeth soon after being retired. Then he scooped up the man's eyes and put them in a jar before returning for the Buick. Cautiously looking out for witnesses, he pulled the car to the alley and placed the girl in the backseat.

He took Todd's wallet, hoping people would see robbery as the motive for the man's murder. Todd lay sprawled, his shattered skull exposed as the local residents, a family of large rodents, discovered him. So that she could not scream and draw unwanted attention, Bernie filled the girl's mouth with a cloth he kept to clean the windshield. Her moans of terror and pain made his spirits soar.

As he worked the vise, he was careful, not putting too much pressure too quickly and as it increased, he released it after a minute or so. Tears streamed down her cheeks. The hours flew by, full of magic for Bernie and when at last, he saw her life fading, he squeezed firmly and at last, the light drained from her eyes.

He loved her in that moment. Tenderly spooning pieces of her skull into a jar, he couldn't bring himself to put it with the others. It meant too much; he put Evie's jar in a drawer. Feeling sentimental, he took Evie's body to the spot where he had deposited Frannie Banks so many years before.

Was the "Crusher" back? It had been more than ten years since the last known victim of the "Cleveland Crusher" was found. Evie's body, her face unrecognizable, lay in the morgue. People theorized it must be a copycat, that he, whoever he was, the "Crusher" was dead. The police searched through the rooms of HOLLYWOOD MODELS, looking for clues, discovering the work of Todd Duran.

The Return

Where had Alice gone? Surely, she would come back. Weeks went by with no word. Warren had made inquiries into Hollywood Models, but still no word. Though fearing what she might see, Ramona opened her third eye.

Todd's Eyes

The Satin Doll blinks neon pink and bright fuchsia. "Hollywood Models" photographer, Todd emerges from the side door. Peggy Lee's smoky voice sighs, "Is that all?" The monster hears a girl's laughter, a nervous titter as Todd calls into the darkness of the stairs behind him, "Come on Evie, let's go!" The monster trembles with delight.

Todd's shoulders strain against his gray suit. His belly drapes over his snakeskin belt. He hikes the belt to a more comfortable place but moves it back down as a girl of twenty-three emerges. The girl is young and very blonde. She steps out from the doorway. Todd grips her elbow while putting his other hand against the small of her back.

Across the street, the monster hurries home to get a better look. Soon, he sits at the window and waits. Oh yes—the coward hides behind the yellowed bedroom lace observing the couple as they walk across the narrow street. Next to the Satin Doll, Mom's Diner is closed. Ramona follows the man as he leaves his window and follows them. She watches as he slides into an alley where it meets the darkened street. He's waiting. What's keeping them? Footsteps—laughing— the girl's still laughing. He peers around the corner. Her white-blond hair glows under the streetlamp. Todd stumbles a little and leans against her. Hurry now, the monster wants time to play . . .

Please, oh let me please wake up. Oh, Alice oh Alice, forgive me!

They stop. "Not here, Todd," she whispers . . .

"Right here," Todd murmurs as his hand disappears under her pink sweater . . .

The club comes from nowhere, smashing the side of Todd's head. His dentures fly out and spin into the gutter. Evie screams. Too late.

Eyes lay in the gutter. Using three fingers and his palm he scoops Todd's eyes like in a game of dice. Eyes that caught so many young girls in a camera lens are dropped into a jar. He turns the lid tight and hides them in the car. Mustn't forget, he cautions himself.

DUCKY STRIKE
Cleveland, Ohio "The Flats"
May 1960

After the excitement died down, the police finished their investigation. A detective interviewed all who might know something, including Bernie. Bernie suggested a thought to the officer: *The old man knows nothing, waste of time...* Bernie was passed by. He was sitting by his window late on a Sunday night, wistfully reliving his time with Evie when he saw a girl approach the door of the former studio. Not like, Evie, this girl was dark, Chinese he thought.

As he watched, the door opened. *Did she pick the lock?* Deciding to investigate, he left the window and went down to the street. Finding the door shut, he tested the lock. *Unlocked! Yes!* He carefully inched the door open. The flight of stairs that led to the office unlit. Climbing the stairs, he saw the faint light of a flashlight. The girl was lifting stacks of photographs onto a table. What was she looking for? Of course, she's looking for pictures of her. What should he do? If he took the time to get the car, she might be gone.

Nothing could duplicate his love for Evie. Still, he suggested to her there was nothing to worry about. He crept closer. When she turned and saw him, *she knew exactly what he was!* With a cry, he shrank back as she threw the flashlight at him and bolted for the door. He caught her as she screamed and struggled to free herself, clawing at his face.

Stunned, he panicked. He could hear voices in the street. With ruthless efficiency, he snapped her neck. His mind frantically reached the handful of people who were deciding if they should interfere, telling them that someone had their television on too loud. The streets deserted, he carried her downstairs and into a dark alley. Whimpering at the burden, he stayed away from streetlights and moving in the shadows, he took her to the river. Then he dropped her body into the water. He wanted to forget the girl; he wanted to forget the night he killed her.

Patty

Poor Ramona. It was her fault Alice was murdered.

It was Bernie's fault.

Hollywood Models

1960

He's waiting for her to open the door. She takes a quick look.

Is she being watched? No. He puts the thought in her mind. You're safe. No one is close.

Soon, he is at the door. A small twist on the knob releases the flimsy lock. He follows her up the dark stairs—so quiet, early morning but still dark; even the Satin Doll is quiet. Why is she here? He wonders . . . naughty.

She turns the flashlight on and searches—for what? Ah yes, photographs, half-naked poses. She's worried someone will see . . . ALICE NO I CAN'T STOP HIM YOU MUST RUN! Ramona shrieks. Alice freezes for an instant then she sees him, knows what he is. Alice throws the flashlight at him. Surprise! He had willed her not to see.

No worry, you're safe, he soothed, I'm an old man . . .

She screams and runs for the door. He catches her—no time to play. He snaps her neck . . .

The telephone rang at 4:30 in the morning. Ramona waited at her window as she had waited many times to tell others the future. Warren was calling to tell her what she already knew. Alice was dead. *There is no air, how can I breathe? Get up and walk through the living room to the kitchen wall. Answer it! So loud—like the sound of the crows . . . Silence it!* She sprang up and moved quickly to the kitchen, snatching the offending instrument from its perch. The telephone's glossy blackness seemed wet, slimy with . . . an image made its way . . . Alice floating, her body swollen as it decomposed . . . Ramona held the receiver in her outstretched arm; then clasped it to her ear.

Her grandson hesitated. "She's dead." Ramona said, "They found her in the river." Silence . . . "Don't leave . . . I'm coming there." Her voice was flat.

"To Cleveland? Ma ma no, there's nothing you can do."

"Warren, listen to me! I'll be there soon. Don't leave. I must face him now . . . if I had before, my Alice, my Alice . . . my little jan ge . . ." She dropped the receiver as she sank to the floor. Reaching out, she grabbed it shouting into the mouthpiece, "Don't you dare leave!"

Very faintly she heard him say, "I won't Ma ma; I won't." With his promise, she surrendered herself to heartbreak, wailing for her dead granddaughter. Alice was gone and Ramona, truly alone.

FORTY TWO

San Francisco to Cleveland
August 1960

August's sun lay heavily on the landscape. Dry brush and parched trees cover the indifferent earth. Paralyzing heat discouraged all but the most necessary activity. It was almost ten in the morning when the train neared its destination, Cleveland's Grand Terminal. Three days of travel had passed since she had slept more than an hour. As the car swayed and passengers were in various stages of sleep, she watched the dark shapes of houses and telephone poles, billboard signs, blinking lights, anything—just . . .no sleep. The dreams were more real than the passing towns and farms.

Cleveland, Ohio
August 1960

I'm here. The train stopped with a jerk. Ramona froze in her seat, dreading the thought of leaving where she had sat for several days fighting sleep and living a nightmare. *Face him.* Passengers filed by her, rushing to meet friends, coming home, on a holiday. She waited for them all to pass then stood and lifted her suitcase from the seat beside her. The porter offered to help her, but shaking her head, she gripped the bar and took each step as if it were her last.

Looking down the length of the crowded station, she saw Warren. *Daddy, you live in Warren! He's your image and has your heart.* Someone was with him, a girl. Her dark brown hair pulled back, wisps of bangs framed the prettiness of her face with its short, dimpled chin and intelligent amber eyes. Not Chinese, Ramona thought, no surprise. Warren always was independent. Daddy defied everyone and married Mommy . . . I sensed this coming too. The passing thought gave welcome relief to her troubled heart.

Warren had met the girl, Colleen during the search for her friend Evie. Ramona's legs buckled when she heard the name. Colleen caught her before Warren realized what was happening.

"Ma ma, this is too much for you. You're going to fly back; please don't argue."

Ramona looked at her tall grandson and shook her head. Reaching up, she touched his cheek. "No, Warren, I stay; there's no choice now . . . for Alice and for all . . ." She thought of the others murdered by Bernie. It was too late to make amends, to beg forgiveness. Warren handed her a paper bag, looking away as she took it.

"I know Alice would want you to have this . . . I was with her when . . . she was so excited. " Ramona took the bag, which rattled with the sound of a chain. She glanced inside and saw the pearl. *Of course, it has found me again.*

After checking in at the White Oak Inn, Ramona sat in a booth with Warren and Colleen. They were at MOM'S DINER and the cracked leather booth was more comfortable than chairs at the scattering of tables. It was lunch hour, and the usual glut of customers was missing. Several police officers filled out papers as they ate their mounds of French fries and sandwiches. News of the murders had spread. A few regulars ordered from the lone waitress, who wrote them while looking over her shoulder.

Ramona knew this place from her dreams. Next door, THE SATIN DOLL and Hollywood Models remained closed while police investigated the murders of Alice Song, Todd Herman, and Evie Latimer. Boy scouts found Evie's mutilated corpse not far from where Alice's body was found in a tangle of weeds as it drifted near the shore. Todd Herman's body, minus the eyes lay in a ditch a few yards from where his murder took place.

"They found tire treads, Ma ma; they have a suspect," Warren said. He began to fold his straw into squares as he waited for her reaction.

"The tires marks traced . . ."

Ramona sighed. "I know Warren, I know he lives up there." She pointed to a third story window of the five-story brick building across from the diner. The ground level held a furniture store and a hardware store. Above the ground were four floors of drab apartments, few of which were occupied. She could see the curtains move. *Does he see me? Can he feel my presence?*

Astonished, Colleen covered her mouth with her hand, as she looked at Warren. He cleared his throat. "Stay out of it, Ma ma. If he's the murderer, he's dangerous. You could get hurt . . ."

Putting her hand on his wrist, Ramona whispered, "You'll bring me back tonight, promise." He opened his mouth to tell her no but nodded his head.

Dream a Little Dream
Cleveland
1960

Accustomed to the constant motion of the train, its sway, the rhythm of the engines, Ramona found the stillness of her room at the White Oak Inn unbearable. She longed for the clangs and the whistles, the chatter of passengers, anything to distract her from the thought that threatened to plunge her soul into an abyss of regret and despair. She could have prevented this. Alice . . . no use to think . . . What about Warren and the rest of her grandsons? What about the monster's future victims, if she did not act?

The pendent lay on the table by her bed, under the glare of the lamp. Wound tightly around a link in the chain was a single long black hair. The chain had been caught in Alice's hair when they found her. How many times had she sat, brushing her granddaughter's hair, justifying her desire to be "normal" using Alice's welfare as an excuse? As she picked it up, and lifted it, the pearl's eye watched her as it hung, suspended between her and the lamp. Was it accusing her or daring her to refuse it again? She slipped the chain over her head. Nothing happened. Maybe her gift was gone. *What have I done?*

A large fan wedged in the open window soothed her as she lay down on the striped bedspread. She closed her eyes, and the sound of clacking pummeled her ears. Gasping for breath, her heart threatening to jump from her chest, her eyes sprang open. Crows! Where were they?

Although the clacking stopped, her heart kept thumping. The fan's soft whir was only sound now. With shaking hands, she clutched the pearl, holding it tightly against her chest until a surge of power flowed through her. The despair lifted and a sensation of peacefulness embraced her. The feeling was so unfamiliar that at first, she could not put a name to as it.

She studied the pearl, turning it over. Despite its unusual appearance, nothing about it hinted at the effect it could produce. *He has the crows, but I have this.* The clock sitting on the chest of drawers said it was still early, only four in the afternoon. Fatigue settled in and with no more resistance, she fell asleep.

Thunder and lightning blistered the sky and black clouds turned an angry red. She sat on the wooden top as it began to lurch. Mountains hissed smoke. Flames burst intermittently from their depths. Please . . . not here, I can't . . .

As slapping sounds peppered her ears, the top turned, and the brick building came into view. It stood on the edge of a trembling cliff which caused the building to pitch back and forth. The ground shifted and it seemed that the building would soon topple, tumbling down, crushing her. Red points of light darted in and out of the dark windows. From a third story window, a single pale curtain billowed outward. He's up there waiting—oh no I can't, please, DADDY!

He doesn't see me! Purple clouds swooped down, forming funnels, stirring fragments of cracked yellow lifted from the seething ground. The scream of the angry funnels grew louder as . . .

The telephone woke her. Strange, I feel nothing . . . *pick up the phone!* "Are you all right, Ma ma?" He's hoping I'll change my mind; maybe I . . . She began to shake. "Please, Ma ma, let's reconsider . . ."

"Be here in twenty minutes," she whispered. There was silence, then, she felt him give.

"I hope you know what you're doing." He sounded resigned.

The SATIN DOLL

The full moon shone on the SATIN DOLL as she winked her invitation. Near the far end of the building that housed MOM'S, the SATIN DOLL, and the late Todd's Hollywood Models, Ramona and her grandson stood in the shadows as the DOLL's jukebox played Patty Page. Cigarette smoke followed the few patrons brave enough to dare the risk the gaze of the "Cleveland Crusher" as the murderer was known. Avoiding the neon blinks, a tall young policeman with the round face of his great grandfather stood with a small woman of sixty-three wearing a sensible cotton dress and thick, round spectacles. They stared at a lace curtained window occupying the third story of a building across the narrow street.

There he is. Ramona trembled. Then she said the words, chanting silently like a drumbeat. *There is the monster that took my Alice.* The pearl rested under her cotton dress. Across the street, the window with the lace curtain was dark.

> *He prefers the dark. Not too close . . . not tonight. How to meet him, push him down and fling him from this place and into . . . where? Through the doorway into the abyss, screaming—the red eyes swarming and feeding . . . oh please . . . wait, it's too soon.*

She became aware of her breathing. Fear, not fear for Warren or for anyone else, but fear for her own safety almost made her run. *The coward the coward—who said that? The little girl, the little girl he burned* . . . She focused her breathing. In the corner of her mind, she felt the lightest touch of anger, but it was not hers, it was . . .

"Ma ma?"

"Noon, Warren, Ramona said. "I want to be here at noon." She looked once more at the ominous window. On the short trip back to her hotel, she studied the silent streets, knowing them from her dreams. Tomorrow, she thought, tomorrow . . .

The Moon

There were no dreams until the early morning.

They were driving. Ramona could see the moon follow them as they turned to drive up a hill. A girl, a girl was driving—Alice? No not Alice, but young . . . pretty, strange . . . Ramona became aware of holding something—the pearl. My hands! What happened to my hands? Her fingers, knotted and bent, were trembling, not from fear, but from age. The skin on the back of her hands was scarred, mottled and paper-thin. She was old, so old now . . . The car stopped. He's waiting for her; they all are. Ramona stood outside the car. She reached out for balance, her brittle arm barely able to leave her side . . . so old . . . NO! Girl—don't! Stay away!

Silence . . . as if the house itself held its breath . . . the girl hesitates at the door. Above, in the windows, swarms of red eyes freeze, waiting. The girl sees the door open and she . . . GIRL! HEAR ME! DADDY SAVE HER! Oh . . . too late. . .

Too late—please don't let it be too late!

Ramona opened her eyes. Above her in the darkness, ceiling cracks and stains rolled, reminding her of the seething world of the crows. *Was she there, on that wretched top?* A sliver of light found its way across the ceiling and met the wall. Her eyes followed it back to the window where morning peeked through the tightly drawn blinds. Nausea gripped her. Staggering into the bathroom, she barely managed to hold in the bile. Ramona wished she could die, join Daddy, and Alice. A long dormant ache broke through: *Joey, oh how I miss him!* Tears fell listlessly as she sat on the bed, her shoulders bent, and her hand clutched the side of her face as she rocked herself.

Ramona . . . Ramona . . . Ramona is a smart, brave girl . . . no demon can defeat her. Someone was whispering in her ear. Daddy? Ramona found her courage. Was it . . . was that really? She didn't know. It was time to do her duty.

PATTY

Finally! Ramona has the Pearl and she's going to fight Bernie. I want to help. Don't tell Gram.

I won't.

The Pearl and the Purse
Cleveland, 1960

Warren's face was blank when he came for her. Ramona had refused his offer of lunch. There would be no more delays. "I'm going to talk to him. No laws will be broken. I'll go without you if I must."

"Ma ma this man is a murderer. He could have a weapon. Alice would not want this." At the mention of Alice, she put her hand to his mouth. *If he knew what a coward I am, how I sacrificed the lives of so many because of my selfish desire to be "normal," what would he think?* There was too much regret and shame.

Warren parked the car in the shade behind MOM'S DINER, taking care to hide it in case the old man might be watching. "Tell me again." Warren had on "his police face," as his mother called it. "What exactly are you planning?"

"One of us will die, the slug or me." A gasp escaped him. *Oh, Warren forgive me.* She was his "ma ma. She tapped her index finger on the tip of his nose teasing him, urging a smile. "I'm exaggerating, you know." They both knew she lied.

The temperature inside the Dodge rose quickly despite the shade. She opened her purse and pulled out an envelope. "If anything should happen and I don't come back, I want you to take this to your uncles. It's my will and . . ." Rather than hear the rest, he opened the car door. She pushed hers open before he could help her out. His job had been "getting the door" for her from the time he was eight. She stared at the top of the building, mostly hidden behind MOM'S and SATIN DOLL. The square envelope was abandoned on the gray leather seat.

"Wait for me here. Ten minutes, no more, if I don't come back, you leave! Don't come for me; leave!"

In her mind, she could see the window, its moving curtains. Was it the wind or was he waiting for her? What chance did a woman of sixty have against such a monster? Warren had asked what she thought she could do. There was no physical evidence, he reminded her; merely tire tracks and several disturbing coincidences that were just beginning to yield proof.

Wait and see, he had promised, begged. He, Warren, WILL take this bastard down and make him pay for Alice and all the others. If the Cleveland cops knew what he was letting her do, he might lose his job. She should just have a little faith, he argued. She was beyond his reach.

She kissed his hand. "You're such a good boy, Warren, so strong. Your father would be proud . . ." As he looked at her, his face drained of all expression the way it did when he was thirteen and she told him that his father was shot and killed. Nothing more to say . . .

Reaching through the open car window, she retrieved her heavy purse. An embroidered depiction of San Francisco Bridge covered the black leather. "It's too big a purse for you Ma ma," Alice had teased. "You need something dainty."

Why am I taking this? There was no reason other than it was something to hold, to clutch and *"to use as a shield," a child whispered* . . . Under her blouse, she wore the pearl. As she walked toward the street, she put her hand to her chest, assuring herself of the pearl's presence, tracing its outline with her finger, making sure it hadn't deserted her.

No breeze interfered with the pitiless sun. Its glare bathed the street. The part of her mind that stood and commented, scolded her for not wearing a hat. It didn't matter. Would there be a blast of heat, bursting from the crows' world, searing the flesh from her bones?

Few people were in the area. Its connection to the crimes was common knowledge. At MOM'S, a few loyal regulars were there for the lunch hour. The remaining police barely noticed the woman standing in the middle of the street that served more as a walkway than a path for automobiles.

The curtain moved. *Does he see me?* Her body began to shake. *Ramona is a smart brave girl; Ramona is a smart brave girl; no demon can defeat her no demon no demon can . . .*

A wail burst from her throat, incoherent and full of pain. Her heart raced as the wail reached its target. Her enemy's gaze found her!

She began to shriek, her eyes never leaving the window, where three stories up, the faded lace was hiding Alice's murderer. "DEMON!" I know what you are! DEVIL SPAWN, DEMON! How dare you touch her; how dare you, filthy coward. I've come for you. I know what you are—BEAST!"

She could feel him—*taste this fear better than cake . . . cowards always get what they deserve . . .*

Around her, people froze. The policemen sitting at tables in MOM'S and the two assigned to surveillance shook their heads. Thunderous booming and pounding like the sound of a hailstorm preceded an explosion, a stench so foul it caused a woman in her forties to gag and vomit her MOM'S tuna melt into the lap of her husband.

"Jesus! What IS that?" A detective muttered. He stayed rooted to his seat, while his partner of two months, a red-haired former high school quarterback of twenty-eight hiccupped, his eyes darting back and forth between the reports, spilled catsup and the window across the street.

"Shut up, will ya' just shut the hell up!" the older man whispered to the younger cop. *They must be quiet, or something awful could find them. Don't move, perhaps it won't notice . . .*

A grating sound began and ended with a bang, as if a door swung open and hit a wall, giving way to a loud buzz. Panic spread as someone shouted, "Bees!" The waitress dropped a coffee pot and screamed. No one moved. All froze, unable to flee.

Ramona stood in the middle of the street, ordering the slug to die, calling on demons to drag his spirit back to their miserable world. A breeze caressed her face and cooled the sweat on her neck. She could feel them wavering and the slug's panic. Tears of relief began to run down her face but stopped with the whisper of a child's voice—*Ramona, careful!*

Instinct caused her to raise the large purse in front of her face as volcanic heat blasted from the window. Sparks and ash fell as the embroidery caught fire and the leather smoldered. *My hands—*

oh they burn! As she struggled, fighting the urge to run, a wave of hate and a command, DIE YOU BITCH slammed into her.

It would have stopped her heart, if not for the pearl. The command's force whirled around the lustrous surface, following the curve of the blue lines. The pearl's eye gazed upon the death wish and held it long enough for Ramona to change its direction. Using what remained of her strength, she hurled the fatal assault back to the source. Groaning, she collapsed, falling to her knees. It was over; the next attack would kill her.

A howl of surprise and pain, tinged with outrage rang out shattering the pane glass image of MOM'S signature apple pie. The tuna melt woman began to sob. The red-haired detective fainted, while his partner trembled and ranted "SHUT UP DAMN YOU JUST SHUT UP!"

Ramona lay on the boiling street, waiting for the end. Like the poor dog in her dream, she thought. RAMONA RUN! HE DOESN'T KNOW HOW WEAK YOU ARE. RUN BEFORE HE KNOWS! A desire to survive took hold. GET AWAY! Her father's voice shouted in her ear. LEAVE NOW! She staggered to her feet and saw Warren was standing in front of MOM'S, a look of horror and confusion on his face.

"Warren, help me! We must leave now, RIGHT NOW!" His paralysis broken, Warren picked her up and carried her to the car. It was enough to survive. The pain in Ramona's burned hands eased eventually, but her failure to kill the monster ached within her for the rest of her life.

Bernie Meets His Destiny

After he dropped the girl in the river, weeks went by. He was sitting in the morning light, eating his muffin, deciding if it was safe to hunt, when there was a knock. He panicked. *Have they caught me? Have I failed Father again?* Two people stood before him, each with a picture in hand. The girl, a smallish brunette said she was a student at Oberlin. Like the girl in the river, the man was Chinese. Bernie willed himself not to tremble. As he decided what suggestion it was best to give them, his heart jumped when he realized she held a picture of Evie and the man, a detective from San Francisco, had a photograph of the last one, *the one who almost. . .* Trembling, he slammed the door.

The man, his name was Warren Song, talked politely through the door. "I'm sorry," he said calmly. "We didn't mean to disturb you. I just want to know if you saw anything. She's my cousin and her mother is very worried." Gasping with fear, Bernie shouted at them to go away.

"Please, Mr. Baker," the girl shaky voice pleaded, "she's my best friend. We grew up together. if you know anything . . ."

"Go away!" he said shrilly, not seeming to have any control to suggest to them that they were wrong to bother a sick old man. The man slipped a card with a phone number under Bernie's door.

Later that day, they were still there, sitting near the window in MOM'S, whispering together. He would wait. He tried to reach them, suggesting that they were wasting their time, letting the real killer get away. He saw the man look up, then say something to the girl. She shook her head. They finally left, but they were there again the next day, the girl putting up flyers as the detective asked questions. Sometimes, Bernie would see him gesture at the window where he hid behind the lace, watching. Then one day, they were both gone and after three days, Bernie knew he had won.

As people passed beneath his window, he heard a woman say, "They found another body in the river, a girl they think. It's been in there a while you know. They suspect it's the Song girl."

Bernie reasoned happily, there's no evidence, no evidence at all! The whispers taunted him; *Patty Patty Patty beat you!* Days passed without more knocks.

He considered where to hunt. Perhaps he should explore the Oberlin campus. He could find Evie's nosy friend. As he became excited about his new plan, the unthinkable happened: *In the piercing light of the noon sun, someone was in the street outside his window, and she was screaming!* With horror, he realized *she was calling to him*, shouting in a strange language. He looked through the lace to see a woman in a flowered dress, her large black purse dwarfing her small frame. *She pointed her finger at his window!* "Demon! I see what you are! Devil spawn!"

Panicked, he summoned hot volcanic ash and hurled it at her, certain that she would not survive. *But she still stood!* She confronted him, screaming her insults. He sent suggestions to all who could see, any witnesses—*the woman is dangerous, take cover, she's deranged, she's going to kill herself and anyone who approaches her.* Then he flung the force of his will to crush her, *DIE!*

With stunning force, he felt the assault returned, making him drop to his knees. Groaning, holding on to the chair, he struggled to his feet. She was gone. Outside his window, on the street, people were stopping! They were looking up at him as he clutched the lace curtains of his window, his trembling hand covering his mouth. He probed their minds. They weren't concerned about the woman and her whereabouts. *They wanted to know who lived behind the yellow lace curtain!* He had failed.

It was time to leave. That night, packing his suitcase, he fled in the Buick. He drove for hours, feeling confused but relieved. He would find a new place. As the next day began, the early morning light reminded him of the time he and Crispin had fled the barmaid's burning house. He saw a sign: Redhill—23 miles. Redhill was near the cabin, where girl had died too soon and the heart . . . he didn't want to think about that now.

As his car reached the top of a hill, Bernie finally met his destiny. A large billboard displayed a couple relaxing, enjoying their cocktails and cigarettes. There were three concentric circles and a duck in the red middle. DUCKY STRIKES! *Don't forget!* Remembering the crows and the message of the Arcade monsters, Bernie fainted. The Buick crashed into an oak tree.

State troopers who saw the accident could find no wallet in the old man's pockets. Reaching into the glove box, they found a wallet and a jar containing the eyes of the murdered Todd Herman.

The Road Outside of Redhill
1960

Parked near the billboard proclaiming DUCKY STRIKES as the cigarette delivering "the smooth flavor loved by sophisticated smokers everywhere," the Highway Patrol officers were dozing when the old Ford slammed into the oak. Hissing and smoking, the 1946 black sedan shuddered as the front end crumpled less than ten yards from the billboard.

"Hoooo—a few too many," sighed Ron West, a veteran of six years. West's receding hairline earned him the title of "old man" at the age of thirty-five. He felt the part, never missing a chance for a nap. Glancing at his watch, he saw that it was barely six am. There were three more long hours to go. The sun would soon make any kind of shuteye impossible.

Smoke poured from under the bent hood, hiding whoever was behind the wheel. The younger officer, Nagle, six feet tall, his black hair was oil slicked and weighing barely 145 pounds in his boots, opened the door of the cruiser. Nagle's hand caressed the pistol holstered snug against his hip. West shook his head as he watched Terry Nagle stroll towards the hissing wreck like Wyatt Earp in Tombstone.

Black clouds from the engine billowed into the face of the billboard model, her Ducky Strike caught by two fingers, while she locked eyes with the handsome boyfriend. The boyfriend returned her invitation, his cigarette dangling from his lips.

Why do I end up with the assholes? West thought, lighting up an ARROW SMOOTH. Assholes attract trouble. Before Nagle, West nearly always got in some extra z's. Some people were bad news, shining a light on things best left in the dark. Nagle sure liked to stir up shit, making an issue of "the rule of law."

West could see Nagle reach in on the passenger side. *I better get over there . . .* The cruiser door swung and rebounded on West's bad knee.

He hesitated; maybe it was better call it in just in case . . . He reached for the radio. What was Nagle doing? "God damn!" Nagle shrieked. Nagle sounds like a girl, West thought. Wyatt Earp yelped like nine-year-old Betty when baby Troy threw the dog turd at her.

Nagle jerked his head out of the car and stood up, placing something on the roof. Not a weapon, West wondered, why the drama? Both of Nagle's hands were gripping the top of the car's roof as he rocked his body back and forth, his head turned away from the car and West. A squat jar, the preserves kind, West remembered his grandmother using them for peaches, sat near the edge of the sedan's roof, ready to teeter over if Nagle rocked that crate too hard.

Sunlight glowed on the jar's glassy curves. Whatever was inside sparkled as it jumped like a pup. Through the rear window, West could see scrawny shoulders belonging to an old man, his baldhead barely reaching the top of the wheel. Is he dead? Doubt it, probably out cold. He hesitated. Closer in, he saw that the thing in the jar was swimming, sloshing up with Nagle's rocking . . . the morning sun in his eyes . . . can't make it out.

"Jesus, Jesus . . ." Nagle kept crying in his little girl voice. Then West saw a set of blue eyes floating and swirling in the jar. West was afraid they were looking at him . . . *blinking, winking, rolling, and laughing . . . The eyes kept saying, "Evie, right here . . . takes a while—don't it?"*

GET A GRIP FOR CHRISSAKE! Radio. He had started to radio when Nagle let out that yell and . . . West turned and fled back to safety of the cruiser. It was time to call for backup.

PATTY

This is how Bernie got in that prison and into John's cell, which happened to sit on top of the monster's favorite spot for people eating.

Awful and a nightmare.

Bernie and the monster like nightmares.

A Reward
Redhill Ohio Correctional Institute
Dec. 24, 1965

"One important thing to note is that no offspring who was a full demon of the higher classes would start with abilities. Rather they would probably grow to these abilities with time and age." "A Treatise on the Hierarchy of The Abyss" (from The World of Aslan, 2014)

The defense lawyer was greatly relieved when Bernie accepted the plea bargain, offered (unexpectedly) by the prosecution. Realizing that an acquittal was impossible and undesirable, given his notoriety, Bernie decided to put the thought in the prosecutor's mind that the appeals process and Bernie's age of seventy-four, made it unlikely that he would live long enough to be executed. It was best to spare the families details of the murders.

Sentenced to life in prison, he was soon transferred to Redhill Correctional. When they drove him through the prison gates in the fall of 1960, Bernie wept. There it was! The building, the promise, his destiny was here, the promise of DUCKY STRIKE! *It was the three-storied phantom arcade filled with screams, where a Great Fire would burn!* Overwhelmed with gratitude, he knew that it was here were he failed. The prison stood where the cabin once stood. It stood where Crispin died, and the girl's heart was offered too soon. He could make it all right now. He would watch for signs. When they came, there would be a reward!

Bernie waited.

On December 15, 1965, the crow appeared. It sat on the windowsill of the bleak little room and looked down at the pathetic figure sitting quietly on the small cot. Its eyes burned; it puffed its feathers. When Bernie's lunch slipped through the open slot of his cell, he uncovered a dish of vanilla ice cream. Hokey pokey, he thought, remembering the frozen treat of his childhood. Leaving, the guard laughed and said, "A reward, Baker, a reward for good behavior, old man. The warden says that you're moving, at least for a while. You're gettin' a roommate, or I guess, he's gettin' you!" Wilcox' laughter echoed as he walked down the long hall. The whispers began in earnest.

Ships in the Bay
San Francisco
January 1966

Ships in the Bay are calling Ramona Ramona . . .ooooonnnaaa . . . The ocean is still; there's only a faint shimmer. A strand of a spider's web hangs in front of her window. On the sill is an open copy of Alice's magazine, Photoplay. Ten-year-old Alice, dressed in her pink Cinderella dress smiles on one page, the other is an ad for a cigarette with a glossy red bull's eye. In middle of the eye is a winking duck with a cigarette hanging out of its bill. She wonders what the meaning of this part of the dream.

Then the bull's eye begins to pulsate. Faint wisps of smoke and snapping sparks jump from the red center where cracks appear in the duck and give way as a pale insect crawls out. It skitters to the edge and leaps straight to the hanging strand of web, clinging. Purrum pum pum pum. Rum pump pum. What is that sound? Ramona struggles to place it. Important IMPORTANT! Do not forget! The insect turns its head. It's not an insect . . . it's THE SLUG—DADDY OH DADDY.

It stares at her, its tiny hands holding tight to the web. Then it drops out of sight. Let it go, you don't need to see . . . she will see . . . The window is gone. She sits cross-legged on a paved road. Where is this? The slug, his scrawny carcass the size of a small child, drags himself towards the center of a huge bull's eye. Purrumpumpum rum. Music? Why? PURRUMPUMPUMPUM, I MUST KNOW!

He reaches the center; it swallows him. Despair grips her.

My fault—please Daddy—help me on my journey; I want to die . . . The ground rumbles as a burst of flame shoots from the eye's center. Something large falls to the ground, near the rupture. Purrumpumpumpum. It stands up. It's a man covered in soot. He walks in measured steps and reaches out to her. Sparks dance in his open hand as he points at her.

Let me wake oh please! Under the soot, she sees that he is young, so young . . . He stops at the edge of the target, lifts his other hand. A human heart rests in his palm. He brings it to his lips and kisses it. Blood drips on the pavement, streaming its way towards her.

"Everything you love old woman; I'll take it all."

He squeezes the heart dry and as it begins to burn, he throws it at her. The burning heart falls in her lap and she picks it up. Her hands shake as she clutches it to her breast. The heart in her hands is in flames, but it feels cold. Who is this man? His blackened hands and mouth smeared red, the young man shakes his head. A giggle bursts from his bared teeth. NO! She cries, how . . .?

"Game over, Ramona." Purrumpumpumpum.

Pumpumpumpum. She wakes with a groan. What does it mean? Pumpumpum. Someone is at her door. Still in her robe, she answers the door. It's Warren. His face is flushed and anxious. "Ma ma, he's dead, Baker's dead. There was a fire at the prison and hundreds of men died." Her stricken face makes him frown. "It's okay now, Alice's killer is dead."

She nods and forces a smile. "Yes, we can be glad he's gone . . ." His policeman's instinct knows she's hiding something.

FORTY THREE

PATTY

What happens in these parts? A dead rat, I hope. Madonna should punch her boss in the nose.

She would get fired.

I guess you're right, but the weasel deserves it.

I agree.

A Dream Come True

Redhill

December 18, 2004

Ted tapped his finger on the counter. Both Madonna and Kevin could see that it hadn't been a good day for his stocks. "Look!" he said. "Here, and here, and eeee-ven (he paused dramatically) over here." He shook his head sadly. "I can't do it all; I do have to have—a—little—BIT OF HELP!" Madonna and Kevin looked at each other. Ted was going on about finding stray sprinkles on the counter after cleanup. They could have pointed out to Ted that they had seen him giving a free cone with blue sprinkles to the pretty FRUITY manager, after, they might have also pointed out, the end of the day cleanup. "Do I make my point?" he asked. They both nodded solemnly.

Sighing, he took his paper and headed over to FRUITY TOOTY. "Dude!" Kevin whispered, "Let's hope he gets laid soon." Madonna giggled, nodding her head in agreement. She was in a cheerful mood. Alec had come by every day since their dinner, and they had spent time getting to know each other. He had brought in some of his gadgets; she was intrigued at how different she and Alec were, at least in the way they looked at the world.

Alec broke a situation down into problems and solutions. When Ray had a problem with wanting to adjust his blankets at the end of his bed, Alec had solved it by giving him a remote control that shifted the blankets, putting small sensors in the linings. Now, he was putting together something for her that measured changes in certain types of radiation and shifts in temperature that might signal psychic energy.

He had dropped her off at the trailer after their dinner and they had shared an awkward first kiss as she said goodnight. When Madonna opened the door, her mother was passed out on the couch, an empty wine bottle on the lamp table, the television providing the only illumination. Madonna waved to Alec, who waved back as he drove off. A perfect moment, she thought. Emma woke up a little disoriented. She yawned as her eyes blinked, trying to focus. "Did you have a good time? Is he nice?"

Madonna nodded. "Yes, Ma, he is, he's . . ."

Emma fell back to sleep. Taking the crocheted blanket that Dee had made years ago, Madonna covered her mother. She left the television on but kept the sound low. In case Emma woke up and wanted to move to her bed, she would have a light. Madonna slept well that night, her one dream made her laugh as she saw Ted sitting on a beam above the ICE KING counter, throwing blue sprinkles at her and Kevin. She soon realized that it too, was precognitive.

Animal Control

It was almost ten, at least another half hour before customers started lining up. Madonna was wiping the glossy counter when something plopped on the counter. Kevin looked up, "Look, a bird!" He whistled at a huge black crow, which sat on a beam directly overhead. He whistled again and it flew to another beam. Madonna felt ill. The crow seemed familiar. Where had she seen it?

Ted heard Kevin's whistle and left the FRUITY Counter, a look of exasperation on his face. "What are you doing? Ted asked. Madonna pointed to the plop of bird dropping on the counter as Kevin pointed at the bird that looked down at them as it let out a loud squawk.

"I bet it can talk." Kevin said. Madonna focused on the counter. She wanted it to go away.

Ted grimaced. "Okay, let's clean it up before any customers see it and have Security call Animal Control."

Soon after, customers began to line up for the ICE KING special, a castle-shaped cone with three towers, each soft serve-filled turret topped with a different syrup or sprinkle. A blue candy crown finished off the middle tower. Madonna hated this particular creation. For some reason, people had a harder time making up their mind when it came to deciding the toppings and inevitably, someone farther down the line would make comments about having to wait. The castle special was a recipe for trouble. Today she was grateful for it, anything to take her mind of the crow.

With a loud squawk, the crow was gone, but she was still wary, wondering when it would be back and decided that she would reinforce the protection around key areas (which now included VIDEO GAMES GALORE) when Ted went to lunch.

While Madonna was making ice cream castles, Caleb and Wilson sat in the security office and watched rows of monitors. Two policemen were engaged in conversation, one was pointing to the column where the body was found, the other shaking his head, apparently disagreeing with his partner's theory about just what happened and how.

"So, Sherlock,' Wilson asked, "who do you suppose did this?"

Calen shrugged. The older man tried too hard sometimes. Wilson persisted. "You're the one's goin' to be a cop, so how did he do it?"

Caleb considered how he could politely tell the older man to shut the fuck up and let him think. He liked Wilson but he did get on his nerves at times. Then, a shadow flashed across the second-floor garage screens. "What was that?' Wilson said.

Caleb moved closer to the screen, and it appeared again, pausing in front of the camera as if it knew they were watching. It was the crow. "I thought you called Animal Control," Wilson said, relieved that he had a legitimate topic.

"I did." said Caleb. "I just called them; it takes time. I'll call them again."

The Dream Come True

Maybe it *was* just a crow, a big ugly bird, Madonna reasoned. She stood at a sink in the ladies' room on the second floor. It was time for her to go back to the food court and she was afraid. It might still be there, hiding somewhere in the rafters. There was something about the bird that terrified her, as if it could pick her up in its beak, grab her by the neck and take her—where? Some place, a nest perhaps and in that nest were open mouths, waiting to devour her. Regardless, she had a sick feeling that the crow wasn't finished; it was waiting for her, maybe to follow her home. No, she said to herself, it was just a bird. Ghosts don't take shits on counters.

"Whatever," she sighed. It was time to get back to work and make more castles. She turned on the tap and washed her hands. There was a noise coming from a stall. She laughed nervously, feeling glad she hadn't continued talking to herself. That would have been embarrassing. As she finished, she heard a shriek, and something came at her.

"Oh God!" She turned to see the black wings of the crow! She began to scream, furiously batting at it as it continued to fly at her as if the ram its beak into her soft neck, then abruptly, it changed course and flew to the top of a stall door. As it perched, rocking back and forth, it regarded her, taking her measure.

The potent nectar of the girl's fear seeped into the porous barrier wall until like a geyser, it burst through. A swarm of demons gathered to feed.

The crow's head dipped down, daring her to leave. *Its eyes are flames!* She wasn't imagining it! No, that wasn't rational; she rejected what she thought she saw. She closed her eyes and then forced herself to look again. The bird's eyes glowed.

It zoomed down and struck her, then it began to peck at her as she tried to grab it. "Please, please . . . YOU FUCKING FREAK! LEAVE ME ALONE!"

Darting back to its perch, it spread its feathers out as if it were going to take off and come at her again. *It's toying with me! What kind of creature is this?* She stared at it, trying to show it she wasn't afraid. In its beak, it carried strands of her hair.

"I'm still bigger than you, asshole. What do you want?" she demanded. In response, the bird began to bob its head up and down, waving the strands of hair in its beak, taunting her, telling her it got what it came for.

Something was trailing down her face. Not taking her eyes of her attacker, who sat silently, puffing its feathers, she touched her cheek. Her heart sank as she saw it was blood and she turned around to look in the mirror. Blood trailed from a wound in her hairline. "Oh my God . . . oh my God—it's the dream—it's the dream—IT'S THE FRIGGIN DREAM!"

Grabbing the edge of the sink, she struggled to keep from fainting and leaning forward and she heaved deep breaths. Her head pitched back and forth as her body tried to expel the terror that had overtaken her. A convulsive sob seized her; she bent over the sink to steady herself, the drops of blood falling and blending with her tears. Her face was smeared with blood and tears mixing with black eyeliner and shadow. Her eyes wide with fright, she turned around.

The crow was gone. Shaking as she checked the stalls, she willed herself to stop crying. Rinsing the makeup off her face, she took a paper towel and applied pressure to her forehead attempting to stop the oozing blood. Uninterrupted, the girl's blood trickled down the drain.

Eager tongues licked the barrier as if it were smeared with cake batter, but the ooze of fear and pain had stopped. The demons grunted and moaned. Not a drop more, though claws and teeth tore at the wall.

The Smudge Stick

At the ICE KING counter, the customer line extended past the neighboring Smoothies counter. Kevin was working at maximum speed, but the line wasn't moving. That meant Ted had to help, which made Ted (and Kevin) very unhappy. "Hey—you guys—what's the problem? We've been in line for ten minutes," a man barked from the middle of the line that now numbered almost twenty.

"Just chill, dude." Kevin said without thinking. He saw Ted's glare and called to the man, "Sorry sir, it shouldn't be too much longer." Just then, Madonna came racing back. Kevin let out a sigh of relief and Ted was silently composing his upcoming lecture on abusing break time, when she dashed by both of them, grabbing her knitted bag. They watched in disbelief as she pulled out a stick and lit the end of it.

"Madonna, what are you doing?" Ted demanded. Madonna began to wave the stick around, its smoke trailing after the motion of her hand.

"Trust me, this is necessary." Madonna said breathlessly and she continued around the perimeter of the counter where the line of customers grew jagged and restless.

One boy called out, "You missed a spot." A few left and some laughed nervously, wondering what she was doing. Was there danger close? Where was it? Many wondered if the girl was crazy or worse, terrified. If so, what was scaring her?

A young mother with a paperback book in one hand, the other grasping the plump leg of a toddler who was saddled on her hip decided to leave. The child shrieked in indignation, reaching for the promised cone, her jingle bell shoes kicking her mother. Switching from the hip saddle, her determined arm encircling her child as if the wailing tot were a rolled up newspaper, the woman walked resolutely away. Other customers began to trail behind her.

Seeing customers depart, Ted began to give Madonna an ultimatum: either put away the stick and get back to work, or face being fired (an empty threat, because of her grandfather) when he saw blood running down Madonna's face. With alarm, he realized how upset she was. Her face was red, her eyes swollen, and her make-up gone except for faint smears. Her hair was in more disarray than usual. Having grown up with six older sisters, Ted knew that these were signs that she had been crying. "My God, Madonna, what happened?" he asked.

Madonna, finished with using the smudge stick around the counter, grabbed her bag. "I can't stop now, Ted. Uh, I'm sorry, I'll try to make up the time . . ." She hurried across the court before he could respond.

Sighing, Kevin called out "Next." He and Ted took care of the line.

PATTY

Ha! These dollies got what they deserved.

Unfortunately for them, you're right.

The Lipstick

When Madonna returned to the second-floor ladies' restroom, she lit a fresh smudge stick and quickly went around the door, the stalls, and the sink area. As she was finishing, the door swung open and two fourteen-year-old girls entered. Looking at each other, their eyes as wide as Faye Wray's when she first beheld Kong, they barely contained their laughter until Madonna left. "What—a—loser!" They mouthed the words together. Making air circles, one girl pointed to the side of her head.

"Totally." agreed the other. She took out her lipstick. "Deck the Halls" played faintly overhead. "Fa—la—la—la—la . . ." The one with the lipstick sang as she imitated Madonna with the smudge stick, using her lipstick and moving her arm around.

Hissing as it watched, the demon rolled out its searching tongue and found an opening the size of pinhead. Twirling and elongating its tongue until the point of it fit through the

The Demon Rift

tiny aperture, it moved like an invisible snake until it found a treasure in the open purse. A metal tube—interesting. It licked the ridges of it. Without warning, the rift closed, and the creature yelped in anger as its tongue snapped like a rubber band. Before it could enjoy the results of its foray, it fled.

The girl snorted and laughed as her friend mimed Madonna's frantic ritual. It was sooo funny. Uncapping her lipstick, the comedienne began to freshen her look when suddenly she shrieked.

"Oooh my God! "

"What the hell!" Gasped her friend

"It burned me!" the girl whimpered. Drawing close to the mirror, she inspected her mouth. A blister covered much of her top lip where the new lipstick had been applied. The two looked at the tube of Raspberry Blush that lay in the sink.

"That's creepy; let's get the hell out of here," urged the friend who quickly fled the room.

After tossing the lipstick in the trash and grabbing her purse, the girl left, determined to check out NATURAL BEAUTY. Didn't they have all kinds of natural healing creams for zits? Maybe they had ointments for lip sores. She wanted it totally gone before New Year's Eve.

#

PATTY

Bernie is naked? Count me out!

Make It Right

Bernie was naked as he knelt in his living room. In front of him were Madonna's strands of hair and the girl's silver skull ring. The ring's three ruby eyes glinted in the candlelit room. From trees in the scenic wallpaper, the crows' raucous calls answered his whispered chants. He could hear the sigh of steam coming from the molten ground that lay beyond the bland images pasted on the room's four walls. As he chanted, Madonna was feverishly spreading the protective smudge sticks throughout the mall. He began to complete the ritual when he was startled by angry shrieks. The crows disappeared.

Without warning, he was hurled across the room and into the hall. Stunned, he discovered that his arm was scraped and bleeding. What went wrong? There was a whine in his ears. The whispers mocked him. *"Patty Patty Patty beat you. . . stupid you!"* Whatever it was, he must find a way to make it right.

Benefit of the Doubt

Seated comfortably at the small table and chairs that was NATURAL BEAUTY's "consultation center," Gordon chatted with Grace. A forty-year-old blonde and the second "trophy" wife of one of Redhill's older physicians, her lively humor made her one of his favorite customers. He was telling her about a new product, NATURAL BEAUTY Glow & Go, a self-tanner, when Madonna came in waving a smudge stick. Gordon was showing Grace the correct way to apply the lotion, until Grace whispered, "It's your sister, Gord. I think you might want to see . . . "

He froze for just a moment as he watched Madonna wave the smudge stick through the shop. "Stop that! What are you doing?" He raced over to her and caught her arm as she moved toward the fragrances . . .

Madonna's eyes were glistening with fright. "Gordo, you don't understand. I have to do this. There is something wrong and if we don't fight it, I can feel—I know . . . " She began to cry.

Gordon put his arm around her and guided her out of the store, saying quietly, "Ellis, would you help Grace while I take a break?" Ellis' mouth hung open as she nodded. Moving to an exit, Gordon opened the door to the stairwell. He sat his sister down gently on the concrete step. Then he lifted her chin, while moving her hair and examined the wound, still moist with new blood. "Take deep breaths. You're okay now; you're okay."

Madonna began to calm down. It was important that he believe her. "Gordo—do you remember how when we were little you would sit on the bed after I woke up screaming from a bad dream?" He nodded. She struggled not to lose control. "You'd say, 'You're okay'. Gordon, I'm NOT okay. IT'S not okay. It's REALLY happening. The dream, the goddam dream JUST HAPPENED!"

Gordon's concern shifted to what HAD happened. Who hurt her and how badly? "How did this happen? Who did this?" Madonna told him about her dream and the crow's attack in the ladies' room. Gordon tried to take her story seriously. "Sis, I admit that was spooky, considering your dream, but you know it was just a coincidence. It got trapped and freaked out on you. I'm worried though. We need to get you to the hospital for a tetanus shot. Do birds get rabies? Maybe we should talk to someone about catching the damn thing so that it can be tested." He could see that he wasn't getting through.

Madonna looked at him sadly. "Just for once, I want you give me the benefit of the doubt."

Gordon thought for a moment. "I'll make a deal with you. Go with me and get this bite treated, let's talk to security and make sure someone catches the damn thing and I'll go with you after hours tomorrow. You can "cleanse" to your heart's content, only after hours. Hello?"

She nodded. Maybe she can make him see . . .

That night, MADONNA sat in her nightgown composing an email to Rhonda, her advisor. She needed help. Whatever was wrong at the mall was dangerous, not just for her and Gordon, but for how many others? After leaving Gordon, her face clean, the wound treated and feeling calm, she returned to the ICE KING. Both Ted and Kevin were careful, acting as if she was going to sprout wings at any moment and fly away. Ted helped her serve while Kevin cleaned up.

When Alec came by later, he was concerned. He'd heard that there had been an "incident" and she wasn't there when he tried to check on her. Even Kevin, usually a trove of information, was close-mouthed. "I'll explain later," she told Alex as he waited for her. She whispered, "How late are you staying tomorrow?"

"As late as you need me to be." he said.

"Okay, we'll talk tomorrow?" she asked. He nodded and reaching out, squeezed her hand. They saw that Kevin and Ted were watching. Madonna forced a smile. "See you later." Alec waved as he left.

FORTY FOUR

PATTY

Lorrie reminds me of Ma, but not as mean.

A girl like Ma? She's mean but I doubt that she would do what Ma did.

Probably not.

VIDEO GAMES GALORE

PLAY IT FORWARD Sporting Goods

After hours, December 19, 2004

Lorrie was twenty. She had looked twenty since she was fourteen and decided that she should take advantage of her looks. She had full breasts on an otherwise petite five-foot two frame and a striking if not beautiful face with tilting blue eyes and generous lips, lips she often said, her voice dripping with distain, "old bitches pay big bucks for." Old to Lorrie meant anyone over twenty-eight. By the time she was twenty-eight, Lorrie planned to be rich.

At present, things were not going well because Barry was a fuckin' loser. He'd better not expect a cut. All that was due Barry was a six-pack and a twenty, maybe, IF she was feeling generous. Kenny invited him in on their little project so let him take care of Barry.

Christ, Lorrie thought as she tossed several pair of leather gloves into a white sack; she knew Kenny would fuck it up. For one thing, Barry had a record, and she wasn't going to prison just because Kenny couldn't keep his mouth shut. She made a quick check of the cameras to see if they were covered. Good. At least he managed to do that right. She opened the cabinet under the front register, reached in the back and found Andy's new laptop. Sorry Andy. She kinda liked Andy. He let her take smoke breaks and his bowties were hilarious.

"Too bad, Lorrie," Andy had said, his voice sounding like a recording. She told him she was going to Columbus to live with her mom. "We'll sure miss you." That was a load of crap. She had been at PLAY IT FORWARD less than a week. Another Lorrie was a phone call and an application away. Andy was completely forgettable with his mousy bowties and thick glasses. She'd snuck the keys out of the drawer when Andy went to lunch and Kenny made copies. All they had to do was get by the moron security guards and they were home free. Load up the truck. Merry Christmas, Andy.

As Lorrie took Andy's laptop, Kenny began to prioritize. For this operation to be smooth and fast, you have to plan. Bringing in Barry solved a problem. How did Lorrie expect one person to carry all that crap down the stairs by himself? Uber-bitch Lorrie wasn't about to volunteer. Kenny, who took care of himself by eating right, vitamins and power lifting, was still only five feet four and weighed 145.

Sure, Barry was a little flakey at times, but he was tight. Kenny knew from personal experience that he could be trusted. Case in point was the time they broke into the warehouse. The guard had called the cops and Kenny took off, but Barry the Bear didn't make it over the fence. Much to Kenny's relief, Barry did the jail time, and he didn't rat. The man had character. The man was also six foot two, 260 and strong. Once, on a bet, Kenny saw him lift a pony. Case closed.

As Kenny did a quick inventory to make sure they got everything of real value, he saw Barry carrying a box of PLAY IT sweatpants. Kenny shook his head. "No man, leave that shit. See over there? Get those." He pointed to a stack of two-hundred-dollar athletic shoes destined for the stock room tomorrow morning if they weren't on the truck tonight. Kenny knew someone in Akron who'd take every pair and pay fifty per; that was the agreement. Barry shrugged and dropped the box, which landed with a loud thud, the sweatpants falling out and on to a display of hand weights. Lorrie's glare would have killed Barry if it had been up to her. Kenny winced. Maybe she was right.

Cleansing

While Lorrie, Kenny and Barry were robbing PLAY IT FORWARD, Gordon, true to his word, was helping Madonna scour the mall, clearing as much negative energy as her considerable supply of smudge sticks could accomplish. "I'll want to do this again and again until it feels safe," she insisted.

Gordon managed a smile. "Um, why don't you do a quick check and see how it's going." They were sitting on the ground level, near the Wig Cart. Madonna closed her eyes.

They followed her cautiously. When she continued the cleansing, they sought the protection of the wood rafters.

Madonna's mind searched. She could sense traces of disturbing energy, but it eluded her grasp. She thought she heard whispers. There was a high-pitched whine coming from the rafters. It could merely be the electric current making the various lighting fixtures hum. Either it had moved to where she could no longer get to it, or she was just feeling the after-effects of its presence.

She shook her head. "I don't know, Gordo, I just don't know . . . maybe."

Gordon laughed. "Maybe just enough to keep Gramps away."

Madonna was not surprised at Gordon's reaction to the cleansing, but she had hoped his mind would be a little more open. "You're still not taking this seriously, Bro, so what can I say, except thank you anyway. We need to do it again and again, until it's safe. That means safe for *you* and . . . that reminds me, there's someone I want you to meet."

The Wooden Floor

There was a shriek. Bernie stopped and put his hands over his ears. He had been chanting for hours and the wooden floor was spinning him as he knelt. On the walls, mountains roared in the distance and the crows filled the sky soaring back and forth, alighting in trees, and flying off again. The whispers were a steady presence, hissing the words in his ears that he repeated as he rocked back and forth, naked, on his knees. His hands trembled slightly as he waited for the shriek to stop. Minutes passed and then much to his relief, the whispers began again.

Doom

Alec was running the new game that arrived earlier in the day. When new ones came in, he volunteered to test them for bugs or flaws. So far, he was not impressed. MOTHER DOOM, also called THE MOTHER OF DOOM, had failed to respond when he pushed play. There was a red screen and the sound of a creaking rocking chair. The red dissolved to reveal a dungeon-like room and the sounds of clanging chains.

In the dungeon, an old woman sat in a rocking chair, her face and shoulders covered by a shawl. She kept rocking, but the game didn't go any further. It must be defective, he concluded. When Alec heard a soft knock on the double glass door, he paused the game and saw Madonna and a young guy he recognized from passing him in the mall. He hoped he was her brother.

Madonna saw him coming and waved. Alec opened the door, and she gave him a quick kiss on the cheek. "This is Gordon, my twin brother." The young men shook hands. Then Alec took them to the storeroom where he was testing MOTHER.

"I can't get it going; I'm glad we didn't have these on the floor yet." Madonna started to ask what the game was supposed to do when it began to play. The figure in the chair got up and walked closer into the frame until she lifted her shawl, revealing an image of a beautiful but forbidding woman in a red gown and cloak.

"Are you ready for the thrill of a lifetime? Then come with me, my pet and we'll see what Mother Doom has in her cupboard for you. Maybe, your dream-come true . . ." She stared sultrily into the camera. Her bony fingers reached up and took off her cloak, revealing animated cleavage . . . and maybe—YOUR WORST NIGHTMARE!" The skin peeled from her face until there was only a skull. Her jaws gaped and closed as she cackled. Alec explained the game involved a search through hidden rooms and obstacles where various cupboards and closets revealed points and cryptic messages.

Alec sighed. "It's a lemon, folks."

As Madonna and Gordon sat in folding chairs, a siren began to blare, coming through the game monitor speakers. The blast of sound rang throughout the mall as the three put their hands over their ears. Alec scrambled to turn the set off. Madonna frowned. "Was it supposed to do that?

Alec looked through the manual. "No, not that I can tell."

Security

In the security office, Caleb was reviewing reports filed on two incidents of shoplifting and Wilson was playing solitaire, when they heard the siren blaring. Caleb checked the monitors. "It's coming from GAMES GALORE. I'll get it. Why don't you go on home?"

Wilson protested. "I'll take care of it; you sit, then we'll both go."

"Nah", said Caleb, "I got to finish this paperwork anyhow."

Wilson smiled wearily. "Alright, son, see you in the morning." Lately, Wilson had calmed down, Caleb thought. Not a bad old guy when he took things a little easier.

Alarms
PATTY

I want to punch that monster right in its big fat kisser.

"What was that? Shit!" Lorrie quickly turned down the lights. The three of them froze at the sound of the siren. They could see the flashlight of security as it shined in some of the shops, most closed by locked gates or secured by alarm systems.

"I thought you said these guards were losers," Kenny whispered.

"The old guy is, anyway," she said.

"Smooth," Kenny muttered. He would save this for ammo the next time Lorrie went off on one of her "Kenny-can't-be-trusted-to-get-it-rights." He'd be ready.

"Okay. Let's clean the register and get out of here." Barry said. He was starting to get nervous.

Lorrie gave Barry a dirty look. "And leave all this we got piled by the door?" She wasn't about to let retardo run the show.

"Whatever you two, let's just do it." Kenny said. He saw the ice skates on the far wall. Gesturing to Barry to follow him, they went back to work.

Fatal Error

Caleb flashed the light into the GAMES shop and saw Alec standing in the doorway of the storeroom where dozens of new games waited for display. Surrounded by stacks of boxes, a vintage pinball game sat in a corner. Before he met Madonna, Alec had spent his breaks playing it. It reminded him of the few Sundays he had spent with his father before the man disappeared for good. With Alec's dad, Ray Jr., there were always games.

Opening the shop door, Caleb called, "Hello! What was that all about?"

Madonna stepped into view and waved. "Hi, Caleb."

Caleb decided to check on what they were up to. He didn't suspect anything illegal, but there might be an issue of permission. "Does your manager know you're here after hours?"

Alec gave a smile and shrugged. "Matt wanted me to test some of the new stuff that's coming in before we put it out on the floor."

Caleb looked at the monitor, pointing. "Was that what was making all that noise?"

Alec nodded, "Yeah, weird. I'm not sure what happened, but it's definitely goin' back."

Caleb frowned. "Turn it on; let's see." Alec pressed reset.

"So . . . did you catch the crow?" Madonna asked Lonnie.

Lonnie shook his head, "You know we never did. That damned bird must have a way of getting in and out. We'll get 'im though."

Madonna gave Gordon an "I told you so" look. The screen on the monitor went red as the sound of the creaking chair came through. A whine broke through the creak, getting louder. Alec frowned. "I don't remember that." The woman in the rocking chair appeared. She rose from the chair and the whine kept getting louder when the screen went black. Alec sighed. "This one goes back tomorrow."

The whine continued as letters appeared on the screen: D O O M E D . . . E R R O R. Madonna laughed nervously. "That can't be good." Abruptly, the letters disappeared. Alec started to turn the monitor off when new letters came up. S A C R I F I C E M E.

"Sacrifice me? What does that mean?" Madonna held tight to her knitted bag. In the future, she would include the interior of VIDEO GAMES GALORE in her cleansings.

"Maybe . . ." Alec suggested, "someone tampered with it. It happens."

"Definitely possible." Caleb said. He was going to track down who had access to this game. There might be a connection between the game and the murdered shoplifter. Gordon said nothing. Madonna's session with the crow and now this, he thought. The distance between his sister and reality just got farther.

There was a "whirring" sound.

"What was that?" Caleb asked. It was coming from Alec's pocket. He reached into his pocket. "Uh . . . it's just my . . . gadget." Madonna and Gordon exchanged a look.

"Your what?" Caleb snapped, becoming impatient.

Alec tried to elaborate. "I've been working on . . . well . . . It's something I'm designing, supposed to pick up—you know, electromagnetic energy, something for a security system maybe . . . eventually. Right now, it keeps starting up by itself—weird."

Madonna was impressed. There was even more to Alec than she had realized. "You made that?" Alec nodded.

Caleb reached for the gadget. "Cool, I'd like to take a look at it."

As Caleb examined Alec's invention, the pinball machine let out a series of pings. Alec felt his stomach sink as he saw the machine flippers, unassisted, propelling metal balls that zigzagged, hitting their targets, causing the machine to shake and its lights to flash.

Madonna fumbled for sage while Caleb and Alec cautiously approached the shuddering pinball unit. Behind them, on the game monitor, the MOTHER DOOM game popped back on. As MOTHER DOOM appeared, she began to change. "Guys!" Madonna yelled.

They all watched the monitor as MOTHER's eyes disappeared and the pixels defining her face became fewer, causing the image to soften. Slowly the color faded and a face, seemingly made of mist, shifted, filling the screen then shrinking to a single red dot. Again, the mist expanded, and small points of red light shone from deep within the eye sockets. The mouth yawned and grimaced into an obscene smile, the lips full, the teeth sharp and protruding above the lower lip. A cloud tongue jutted out and slowly licked the phantom lips. There was a wheezing sound as it started to speak, its voice deep, the tone amused.

The ring of an old-fashioned alarm clock came from the monitor.

Sounding like a game show host, a voice said, "It's time!" The grin grew wide.

"Whoa . . . " Alec began to reach the set to turn it off. This was too weird. He planned to find out whose sick sense of humor thought this one up. The demonic face changed again, its eyes fading into two red points. The lips became ultra-feminine, red, voluptuous, and quivering.

It smiled again. The voice was seductive as it began to speak in a breathy "Marilyn" tone contrasting with its words. "You're all going to die."

Madonna looked at Alec. His blank face told her that he had no idea how this was happening. Gordon broke the spell, by laughing and saying, "And your little dog, too!"

Caleb glared at him, "Shut up, dude; don't piss it off!"

The points of light and the lips grew larger as it uttered a sexy growl and said, "Believe it, Alec." It snapped its teeth like a dog.

Everyone gasped. Gordon began to entertain the idea that his sister may have been right all along. Her hands shaking, Madonna finally found a smudge stick. Gordon picked up the lighter that dropped from her purse and lit the end of the stick. Waving the smoking sage around the storeroom interior,

The image began to shrink then expand, over and over in a mesmerizing rhythm. Madonna, growing more panicked asked, "How do you shut this thing off?

Alec pressed down a lever on the side of the game. Nothing happened except that the lips and eyes expanded. The creature ran its tongue over its glossy lips. Madonna fought the urge to run. "Alec, turn it off!" He pressed down the lever again, but the lips smiled. It began to chuckle, exposing wolverine teeth. Gordon yanked the cord from the electric socket. The screen went blank. Alec's gadget finally stopped whirring. The pinball machine settled down.

Caleb sat in disbelief. "Uh, was it supposed to know your name?" Abruptly, the lips appeared again as a burst of cartoon flames exploded on the screen. The lips puckered and "blew" a kiss. Whatever it was, it grinned, satisfied, and soulless. Sparks started coming from the cord connected to the monitor. As they watched, the cord detached itself and slithered along the ground. They all stared at it, paralyzed.

Madonna broke the spell. "Out! Everybody get out! Everyone! Out of here! Now! Let's go!" The four moved quickly towards the storeroom exit. Just as quickly, the cord gathered speed and grew in length. As they hurried toward the exit, the snake-like cord shot forward, tripping Alec, making him fall to the floor. He struggled to get free as it quickly wound itself around his legs. Fighting to keep it from getting a stronger hold, he saw sparks coming from the cord. He panicked and began to yell for help. The cord was making its way up his legs and waist and it flung itself around his neck with a snap. Then, it began to tighten as the other three ran back.

"Alec!" Gordon panicked, "Get it off him!" Alec was struggling to keep it from choking off his air.

Caleb thought quickly, "I need a—a—a—knife—box cutters, pinching things!" The cord pulled tighter as Alec's feet flailed.

Madonna was hysterical, "No! It's not working! Hurry!" Caleb and Madonna grabbed part of the cord. Sparks swarmed, crawling over their hands as it shocked them, forcing them back. Madonna gritted her teeth and pulled as she saw Alec's face turning a pale blue. Gordon tore through the store, searching as Madonna and Lonnie yanked the cord to keep it from strangling Alec. The sparks hissed and spit, searching areas between their fingers, making them flinch and let go. Then sparks began to shoot onto Alec's neck and upper body, and he passed out. Despite the pain, Madonna and Caleb tried to get another grip on the cord. Then the lips reappeared on the screen as Caleb called to Gordon to hurry.

"Caaalleebbb—I—wannnntchahhh!"

Terror and disbelief spread across Caleb's face. Gordon's frantic search ended when he found a box cutter under a counter shelf. The sparks were stinging like angry bees, but Caleb refused let go. They both saw Gordon coming with the knife and shouted, "Hurry up! Gordon! Come on!" Grabbling the cord that looped around Alec's neck, Gordon wedged the cutter underneath and swiped through it with amazing precision and strength, causing it to go limp. Madonna and Lonnie quickly tore it off Alec.

Gordon was in shock. In a daze, he turned and wielding the sharp blade, swiveled from side to side, still ready for battle. Trembling, he said, "I can't believe . . . I can't believe I did that."

"Gordon . . . put it down man," Caleb coaxed, "Good job, it's over." Gordon let the box cutter fall to the floor and the three carried Alec out of the store as fast as they could.

Madonna sat on the edge of the fountain. Alec's head was in her lap. Gordon's eyes darted in every direction as he wondered if there would be another attack—of what? He didn't know. Something . . . Caleb went back to lock the door to the GAMES shop. Madonna examined the burn marks that encircled Alec's neck as he was beginning to regain consciousness.

Anxious to leave the mall, she looked up to see if Caleb had finished, when she saw something moving on the ceiling. It was crawling above her, seeming to be unaware of her presence. She saw its claws. The demon's body was long and sinewy. *Its face belonged to her grandfather! It had Grandpa's white hair, the jowls and a nose like Gordon's.* She looked around. Gordon was too far away.

She would make no noise. Alec groaned as he woke up. "Shhhh"—she whispered. He looked up at her. With a start, the memory of what happened came to him and he bolted upright. Madonna whipped a smudge stick out of her bag and looked around. The creature was gone.

Gordon saw the smudge stick and began to hyperventilate. "What?" he said.

Madonna shuddered. "Promise not to laugh?"

He shook his head. "Like I'm even in the mood."

Madonna's voice was hushed. "I just saw something crawling on the ceiling, a creature . . ."

"Oh, great; that'll really make me laugh," said Gordon as he looked up to see what was above him.

Madonna shook her head, "It was Grandpa."

"Oh, man." said Gordon as he finally sat down.

Make It Right

The boy lived. There must be something, some way to make it right. He closed his eyes and knelt. He felt himself lifted, and his body invaded. He was merged with a demon as he slipped into the mall and through the walls. He looked down from the rafters, his eyes burning, his claws grasping, he slides across the ceiling, searching. His lips began to move as the words were whispered to him.

"Sacrifice . . ." they sighed.

He summoned the Others. "Make sure," he said. "Leave nothing behind, nothing!" he hissed.

The Other, known as Reba, raked its claw across Bernie's graying chest. The blood dripped onto the wood floor. "Sacrifice," it growled and slipped away. Bernie knelt within the pentagram and began to chant again.

"Sacrifice," he called. The crows shrieked and swarmed through the alien sky.

Trophies

It flowed through the rift. Rituals performed on the wooden floor have softened the barrier. For a short time, there is a stippled opening, allowing its restless energy to ooze into the mall. It slides along the ceiling, undulating as it moved through the rafters. Seeping through the porous walls of PLAY IT FORWARD it finds the three young burglars as they prepare to leave. Its empty soul knows only hunger. It comes to sacrifice.

Kenny heard another thud. "What the fuck is going on? Let's load all of this shit and go!" Lorrie was cleaning out the register. A bowling ball thudded to the floor from a rack on the wall, as Barry appeared with a box of sports sunglasses.

"How 'bout these?" Barry suggested. It was obvious to Kenny now. Barry was not the source of the thuds. Lorrie looked at Kenny with alarm.

"What the hell was that?" The bowling ball began to move across the floor. Kenny moved toward it and followed it as it rolled between racks of athletic gear, right into his path causing him to trip and land on his face. "Fuck!"

"What!" she said.

"It's nothing." Kenny answered. He picked himself off the floor and looked at the pile of boxes and loose merchandise that they had accumulated by the door, estimating the number of trips it would take to get it all. Barry began to juggle tennis balls.

"Stop screwing around, Buddy. Let's go!" Kenny hated to admit it, but Lorrie was right. It was time to leave. Lorrie was punching in the security release code. Kenny picked up several boxes and waited. Nothing happened. "What's wrong?" A size twelve hockey skate lifted itself off a display. Sighing with fatigue and frustration, Kenny put down his boxes. "What's the problem, Lorrie, I thought you had this covered," he whispered.

She rolled her eyes. "I do; I have it written right here." The skate swung in the air, the blade shimmering in the security light. She turned in the direction of the light and held her palm up to see the security code scrawled on it. There was a sickening sound of flesh tearing and bone breaking. Kenny's severed head flew onto Lorrie's open hand and then bounced down onto the floor. Seeing Kenny's look of surprise as his head rolled between the college tees and racks of ladies' sweatpants, Lorrie screamed.

Barry dropped the tennis balls as Kenny's severed head rolled into his path. "Wha . . .?"

Lorrie started to squeal, "Eeewah—eewe—oooh God—oh-my-God!" She turned and desperately began to punch in the code.

Buddy shouted, "Jesus! Jesus Christ! Get us outta here!"

Lorrie was crying, "I'm trying! I'm trying; it won't work it won't work!"

Looking at the numbers, written on Lorrie's hand, Barry tried the security code again. It didn't work. "Goddamn it!" he said. As they tried punching in other combinations, tee shirts began to glide off their hangers. The shirts tied themselves together to create one long "rope" of tees. There was a gurgling sound. Something approached. As it gurgled, its tail slapped the floor.

Lorrie turned from Barry to the direction of the noise. She looked up and for the first time since she was three, wet her pants. The leering face towering above her, moved closer. As it hissed, its long gray tongue moved in and out between the crusted lips that pulled tight into a shark-like grin. The alien creature's snake-like tail swung back, sweeping the floor. At the end of what resembled human arms were claws. The talons extended and retracted like a cat's. Its milky yellow eyes, the large pupils, dark and red, were unlike any earthly creature's. Whimpering, Lorrie began to turn and run. There was a THWACK as the long tail snapped and sprang forward, spearing the girl through her chest.

Barry's face was solemn as he stared calmly watching Lorrie as she was lifted up, her eyes blinking wide in disbelief. The creature's mouth yawned and snapped down, cracking the top of Lorrie's skull. As it began to feed, the girl made kitten-like mews while she struggled, her legs moving back and forth. Making no sound, Barry grabbed the heaviest barbell he could lift.

The heavy weight shook the door as he swung it, trying to smash through. He struck it again, as a tee shirt noose swung swiftly up and over the big man's head. It tightened around his neck, and he dropped the barbell to free himself. Slowly, his clutching fingers began to relax as the noose squeezed. Choking, his sight fading, Barry squinted to see the barbell as it hovered near his eye. Like the snap of a whip, it smashed in his skull.

The rift widened. Crows swarmed into the store. They shrieked, fighting over tufts of hair, torn clothes, and bloodied garments. Tearing and feeding on what was left of the flesh, they devoured the death scene, drinking the blood. Before the rift began to close, the largest of them took the bones. All of them were trophies.

Malice

Shaking with fatigue, the deep scratch across his naked chest burning and throbbing, Bernie's strength faltered. The rasp of his breathing had become a strangled wheeze as he fought to focus. Bloodied knees, pounded by the harsh wood floor, ached as he continued to rock back and forth. His head swam from lack of food or drink. His body's aging flesh, released from the demon occupation and returned to the grueling ritual of chanting was reaching its limit. Crows flitted from tree to paper tree as they watched him. The whispers told him he must not fail. Then, with a low thump, a severed head rolled on the floor.

He looked up as an Other glided above the wooden surface. It morphed from the grotesque monster that had terrified Lorrie, back to human form. Reba smiled. "Sacrificed," she murmured.

He smiled and closed his eyes, sighing, "Sacrificed."

The Others bathed him, treated his wounds, and carried him to his bed. He slept for most of the next day. Then rising for a large meal, he began the next step.

FORTY FIVE

PATTY

I'm skipping the spooning stuff. I'm glad they're wising up.

Me, too.

"Dream a Little Dream"

Redhill

December 19—20, 2004

Madonna pulled the Datsun onto the gravel driveway of the one-story house where Ray and Lisa had lived for twenty years. She waited patiently while Alec opened the door and flipped the light switch. Still shaken by the attack, she worried about Alec. He seemed okay.

The living room was filled with photographs of Ray and Lisa's life together, their children and grandchildren. Ray's recliner, its worn leather showing the imprint of Ray's arms as he watched the PBS News Hour, sat in front of a console TV. Prominent on a wall was a picture of Alec and Molly. Molly was smiling with her arm around eight-year-old Alec. On an end table was a picture of a five-year-old Alec and both of his parents, all smiling in front of a Christmas tree. A bookshelf held Reader's Digest Anthologies, a set of encyclopedias, some historical novels and recent periodicals on engineering and physics.

Madonna frowned as she examined the welts on Alec's neck. She was worried that he was hurt worse than he wanted to admit. "Are you sure? We could get you checked out at the ER. You know you should be careful; you lost consciousness. Gordon was pretty upset that you wouldn't go."

"Nah, I'm fine. Like my grandpa, kinda hard to kill."

Madonna winced. He had almost been killed. He was meant to die, she worried as Alec made his way to the bathroom mirror. Taking a tube of first aid cream from the cabinet, he began to dab it on his neck. "I could help, you know," she offered shyly. He nodded as they walked into the bedroom, each avoiding the other's gaze.

Turning on the light, along with several *Popular Mechanics* magazines, she saw various inventions, some complete, some in the early stages. PDA sized gadgets were sitting on a long table along with old cameras and calculators, a set of screwdrivers and a box of tiny batteries. On makeshift shelves, several computers were set up, built by components Alec had salvaged from places serving as dumps for former-cutting edge machines.

Madonna turned on a lamp and flipped off the overhead light. The lamp sat on an oak chest near the orthopedic bed Ray had purchased years ago. On the chest of drawers was a picture of Ray and Lisa on their wedding day in Las Vegas. Ray was in uniform. He had a wide grin on his face. Lisa was dressed in the height of 1945 fashion, her blonde hair in a becoming pompadour and an impish smile on her pretty face. They had their whole life before them, Madonna thought. She looked at Alec and saw that he resembled the happy young pilot in the photograph. Alec unbuttoned his shirt.

"Does that hurt much?" she asked him. She began to rub the cream on the back of his neck where the welts had cut into the skin.

He nodded, saying, "It helps; the cream seems to help." She began to rub the medication on the abrasions over his ribs. He saw the burns on her fingers. "How are your hands?" he asked. She showed him her palms. He put his hand on his forehead. "I didn't imagine what happened; it really did?" She nodded. He looked at her, questioning. Madonna sighed. She rose and went to the window. Looking out, she saw the oak tree where Marlene had sat reading about Bernie over forty years ago. Almost sixty years before Marlene, Mrs. Collins had planted the tree in what had been her yard, the spring before she was murdered and Becka was kidnapped.

She turned around and faced him. "I don't know Alec; I wish I did." She moved over to the bed and sat beside him. Her eyes were troubled. "What's the point?" she said. "If I don't know what it means, if I can't figure out why, what's the point?" She began to cry. "All my life, I've been shown signs, given warnings that something bad was going to happen. I know that I can do something to stop it, but how can I fight it, if I have no idea what "it" is. I'm such a fraud." She shook her head and sobbed.

She put her head in her hands. "Oh, God . . . I thought if I could somehow learn to control, I don't know. The dreams would stop; seeing things would stop. Feeling like someone's always watching me or out to get me would stop. I've been on guard, but I don't know from what, just a sense that I'm fucked." Alec grabbed a tissue from the small table. Madonna smiled. "Thanks"

"You're too hard on yourself," he said. "You're just a student." She looked at the welts on his neck and reached up touching them gently.

She looked down, suddenly self-conscious. "So, this must be a real turn on for you, huh?"

He moved closer. "Actually . . ." He touched her hair and smiled shyly. "I'm kinda torn between terror and feeling sorry for you, and . . ." He cleared his throat self-consciously. He wiped a stray tear from her cheek, and paused, waiting for permission to move closer. Her eyes invited him and she reached up and touched the side of his face. He began to kiss her and soon, she turned out the light. After making awkward but passionate love, they fell asleep beneath the sheets and blankets left by Ray and Lisa. On the table cluttered with PDA's, cameras, and future inventions, one came to life. The gadget Alec had in his pocket began to whir. The wind blew and swaying power lines crackled.

Repelled by the pleasure of the young lovers, demon claws raked the thick membrane. They dare not get too close, even for a better view. Ignoring the frenzy, the crow sat on the other side of the barrier, its claws clutching the shuddering line, its red eye unblinking as it waited contentedly.

Dreams to Come

Madonna was in Emma's Volkswagen, driving along a deserted road. Thick gray clouds covered most of the full moon, its light barely a glimmer. The headlights of the old bug shined on a dark, tree-lined street. Turning the corner, she saw the house. It sat alone. I'm dreaming; this is new, she thought. Her grandfather was in that house. Though she didn't remember parking the bug, she found herself in front of the door, which opened silently.

The white tile of the entry way glowed. It was bare of furniture or carpet, and the oaken walls were blank. Except for the tile, the lines seeming to shift beneath her feet, everywhere she looked, there was nothing but wood. A winding oak staircase led to a hall. Doors appeared and not knowing what else to do, she opened one. Inside, an ornate mirror stood in the middle of a room bare of all else but wood. The tiles had disappeared.

The mirror was floor length, its frame composed of brass where a serpentine border curved and peaked. Small figures jutted from the swirl of metal. Gargoyles. *She stood in front of the mirror and hesitated when she saw there was no reflection except for the wooden walls. She was invisible. What now?*

A breeze crept in, bringing the odor of rotting flesh. *Not good.* She looked around. *Restless shadows moved back and forth on the high ceiling.* She found that she was naked, and hands were rubbing her with oil. *Shit! I hope this one doesn't get too weird.* As she looked down to see to whom the hands belonged, she discovered she was now wearing her ice maiden uniform and standing at the counter in the food court which extended for miles. A line with thousands of people in it waited for her to serve them.

Kevin was standing next to her. Pointing upward, he said, "I bet you can fly!"

"It's so very simple. No need to question anymore."

Her grandfather was at the head of the line. He whispered, "Feel what we shall be. You shall know strength. Your enemies will know despair." Kevin held up a castle special. As she took it, she found a crown on her head.

A deafening cheer came from the crowd, some shouting and stomping their feet. "We knew you could do it!"

"Look, Madonna!" She turned and saw Franka holding the gargoyle mirror, which was now the size of a hand mirror. Franka kept repeating, "You're simply beautiful!" Madonna saw her own reflection. *She was!* She was dressed in gray blue, which made her seem forbidding and regal. Her face was pale; she was an ice queen.

At the edge of the long counter, Ted tossed blue sprinkles as if blessing everyone in line, as he droned, "I'm making a point here." Then Ted tugged leashes attached to collars worn by Randy and Marla. Madonna extended her hand in their direction and discovered that each finger had a skull ring with black pearls instead of ruby chips serving as eyes.

The girls laughed at her and began to sing, "The hands have eyes! The hands have eyes!" Ted yanked their leash and they started to choke. Both girls began grabbing, clawing at their throats for air.

"Your enemies become our enemies," her grandfather whispered.

"A little harsh," Madonna protested. She was in front of the mirror again and saw that all the blue of her dress and crown had turned to black. Her eyes rimmed in black, her lips ebony, a trail of inky liquid ran slowly from her forehead and down her face. Her grandfather's face loomed behind her. As she turned, he was gone. She felt a tremendous surge of exhilarating power and turned back to the mirror. She could see a faint image of grandfather's face as well as hers, as if her face had become translucent mask. Her grandfather's face became her face.

The Circle

Before she could react, Madonna felt pulled as if by a vacuum, out of the house, leaving her grandfather collapsed on the floor, through the walls. Zooming backwards, she saw the house, its windows blinking, swarming with flits of light (like a beehive she thought), along the silent road, until it stopped. She was sitting at a small table under the oak tree in Alec's backyard. She wore the white nightgown that her mother had given her for her tenth birthday. A man was sitting across the table, his back to her. He stood up and began to pace around the yard. *He's walking in a circle,* she thought. *Why?* "Excuse me," she asked, "Why are you walking in a circle?"

He turned around. He was young; his hair was dark. She saw that he wore a uniform with Redhill Correctional printed on the back. He stopped and began to turn towards her.

Before the man could answer, a voice behind her said, "Madonna?" She turned to see ten-year-old Gordon behind her. He was wearing his Young Hercules pajamas, his birthday present.

"Gordon, why are you here?"

"What's going on, Madonna?" Gordon asked. His eyes were narrow slits and his lower lip trembled. Her brother's arms were crossed, each hand clinging to the opposite shoulder. It was not from the cold; Gordo was terrified.

"I'm not sure, but I think he's Grandpa, only younger, before the fire." She put her arm around Gordo as if to reassure him that nothing bad would happen; she would protect him. A loud hiss made her jump. She turned and saw John Arnold on the outside of a large circle that was now a snake. The snake hissed again before inserting its tail into its mouth.

"It's time," the man said.

"Time for what?" she asked warily.

"To know the truth. Find the door within the circle, Madonna. You must close it, or this world will fall and others, lost." He gestured toward the circle. Madonna stood at the edge. She moved to step within, but hesitated, unnerved by the snake. The snake became a chalk outline.

Awed, Madonna looked at the outline.

"Guard against your fear," he urged. Now she stood in the center. Gordon approached it, but he was not willing to step inside it.

"I died in that fire, Madonna; I never got out," John said. "You know that I'm telling you the truth."

She nodded. The man who had hunted her, the beast who had tormented her mother was not John Arnold, but someone else. Who? As questions flooded her mind he whispered, "The door is in the circle." Then he began to fade, and she fell into a dreamless sleep.

The Deck

He heard a creaking sound. "Madonna?" Alec opened his eyes and got out of bed. He looked at the clock. It was two am. The hallway was dark, and he knocked on the bathroom door and looked inside. No one. He saw light down the hallway coming through the crack in a door. Approaching it cautiously, he turned the doorknob, opening the door slowly. Seated at the table was Ray, looking much younger than the old man Alec knew as his grandfather. Playing cards were spread on the kitchen table. Alec glanced at his reflection in the oven door. He was age ten again. He felt in his mouth, his retainer securely in place.

"Grandpa?"

Ray looked up and smiled the way Alec remembered his dad used to smile. "Hey, kid. Have you ever wondered why there are no zeros in card decks?"

Alec was confused. "What?"

The Demon Rift

Ray shuffled the cards and then spread them out, forming a circle. Ray pointed up. "God deals it straighter than you'd think. The Devil on the other hand, stacks the deck."

Train Tracks

Caleb couldn't sleep. His grandmother, worried when she saw the look on his face, started to ask what was wrong. "Not now, Grandma—okay? Maybe later." He tried to eat the casserole she'd saved him, but it was hard to get food down and have it stay after what happened. He watched a little TV, the local news, but he couldn't focus. Finally, he turned off the light. It was awhile before he dropped off.

He was sitting under a Christmas tree and he saw the bike he got the Christmas before his dad was murdered. This was going to be a good dream. He was ten then. Presents, some open and some still wrapped, were everywhere. He heard a whistle and remembered the train set. He never admitted it, but it was his favorite present that year; he loved it even more than the bike. He and his dad spent hours watching it, setting up the tracks different ways.

There was a kid's old-fashioned record player, and it began to play "Little Drummer Boy." The train was going through a tunnel, around and around the tiny landscape of pipe cleaner trees and toy buildings that were set in place around the circular track.

Caleb looked down and saw he was sitting in the middle, the locomotive whistling as it made its way with Caleb in the center. A man sat in an armchair by the tree. His heart soared. Is Dad here? He felt an ache when he saw he wasn't. Who was it? He looked like Dad some, but . . .

Caleb recognized his grandfather, the one in the pictures that sat on the bureau in Grandma Cinda's room, the one killed, long before he was born. "That's right, Caleb. Remember the power of the circle," the man said. He held up one finger. "Don't forget, Caleb! We're all proud of you." Caleb looked puzzled. He was trying to think what to ask him when he woke up.

It was six in the morning. It would be dark for quite a while. He decided to report what happened. Someone had to know about the mall and that someone should do something about it.

Something Terrible

She woke up, her heart racing as she jumped out of bed. She looked at the still-sleeping Alec. The bedside clock read 4:00 am. She went into the bathroom and rinsed her face. As she looked in the mirror, she gasped as she saw red blotches, welts appear on her face, neck, chest, and arms. "Oh, God" . . . she gulped, trying not to cry.

Deciding that she was hungry, Madonna went into the kitchen and poured some Cheerios into a bowl. The kitchen still had traces of Lisa's touch twenty years after her death. Cheerful primary colors were displayed in various patterns, the place mat decorated with its intersecting-colored circles.

The clock, its rim trimmed in a sunny yellow, said 4:15. The dream, what did it mean? She scooped some Cheerios into her spoon and suddenly, she began to look at the clock and the placemat . . . and CIRCLES!

Her books spread out on the table, Madonna made notes, drawing circle after circle as she tried to make sense of her dream.

"Madonna?"

She jumped, startled. A sleepy Alec stood in the doorway. "Oh my God," she said. "You scared me."

He sat down by her and she leaned into him. "I'm sorry, " he said, yawning. "It's late, or early. What are you doing?" He saw the blotches and welts on her face and neck. "Are you okay?" She was confused. "Your face, it's covered with . . ." He said.

She realized what he meant. She took his hand. "Alec . . . something terrible is going to happen."

A Bite of Reality
Redhill Mall
December 20, 2004

It was early morning when Madonna drove with Alec to work. They rode silently, her eyes locked on the road. He looked over at her. Still visible, the blotches and welts had lessened considerably.

Caleb was waiting for them at GAMES GALORE. Troy West, the mall manager, Alec's boss, Matt, and a young police officer all stood looking at the cut-through cord and the arcade game. Caleb insisted that Alec hold up his shirt to show the burn marks. West was angry that Caleb had called in outsiders but knew that he couldn't ignore the evidence.

"Something severely malfunctioned in here, that's clear," West said, asking Alec "You all right, son?"

Caleb was alarmed. "That was more than something malfunctioning, Mr. West. I wouldn't open the mall until . . ."

West interrupted. "That's for the authorities to . . ." The knock on the glass door drew everyone's attention. Gordon stood behind the door waiting. He looked pale.

"That's my brother, he was with us last night," said Madonna. She let him in.

Gordon saw the blotches and welts were still visible. "Nightmares?" he asked in a hushed voice.

"We should talk, Gordo, all of us," she whispered.

West was laughing. "Ghosts? The Devil? Oh, good grief, Caleb, maybe you need some time off." Caleb, Gordon, and Alec looked to Madonna, who shook her head. She had no answers.

The policewoman interrupted. "Uh . . . you should have an electrician in here before this store opens again and depending on what the electrician says, send this," she pointed to the arcade game, "thing back." Matt walked the officer out.

West was furious as he berated Caleb. "NO WAY should you have called the cops without telling me first! IF you, do it again, you're fired."

Lonnie was incredulous. "Excuse what I'm about to say, sir, but are you crazy? If something's dangerous, why in the heck would you want me to put anyone at risk by not calling the police first?"

West warned him. "That's enough out of you!"

The Severed Hand

That same morning, Andy, the bewildered manager of PLAY IT FORWARD found stacks of merchandise by the locked door. The cash register drawer lay open, the money taken from it, spread out on the counter. His laptop sat where Lorrie left it. Tennis balls lay in various places throughout the store. Tee shirts were strewn throughout. A man's single ice skate was resting in a large pile of sweatpants, a faint trace of blood visible on the blade.

The police identified prints on an empty truck that sat near a ground floor exit. The prints belonged to a Barry Bodine, a nineteen-year-old with arrests and one conviction for burglary and petty theft. The truck had been rented in his name. His only family, an uncle, hadn't seen him in several weeks. Things were out of order, but nothing of value was gone, except much of it was piled near the door. There was nothing to indicate what had happened, until Andy found the severed hand tucked under the pile of Play IT sweatpants. The combination to the security pad was written on its gray, decaying palm.

Grandfathers

They met on the east staircase landing between the second and third floors. Before the four of them settled on the concrete steps, Caleb assured himself that the landing was clear of security cameras. "You cannot say a thing—ANYTHING. I'm swearing you all to secrecy." He had struggled with his decision, but he couldn't think of an alternative. They all nodded. Unable to meet their eyes, he took a deep breath. "The uniforms are stationed in the downstairs lots . . . because some dude was butchered when the mall first opened."

Madonna's eyes widened with fear. "Butchered?"

Caleb cleared his throat. It bothered him that he was giving privileged information, but it was a relief not to carry the burden of it alone. "Yeah, but that's not the real shit. We have video cameras down there."

Madonna nodded to encourage Lonnie. He was among friends. Whatever else, whatever bad news he had to share, she was ready. "And?" she said.

Caleb looked away. He hadn't thought it would be this hard. Finally, he just said it.

"There's nothing on the video tapes except for knives pulling some circus act, rising in the air by *themselves,* hurling *themselves* into this guy." All three looked with disbelief at Caleb, even Madonna. "I am not kidding—really *by themselves.*"

Gordon took his sister's hand. "Now might be a good time for us all to quit."

Madonna began to mull it over. She looked around at the walls, hoping for something to reveal itself, something to happen.

Alec sat on an upper step behind the twins. Madonna's shoulders stiffened as her brother took her hand. Whatever "it" was, the threat they all felt, Alec was determined to protect her. As long as he was breathing, nothing bad would get to her. This wasn't the cancer that took his mother, diminishing her life day by day until there was nothing but a glassy-eyed wraith clutching his hand. No, this was something he could fight. But whatever was wrong with the mall, they had better find a way to fight it and find it soon.

A stairwell door echoed with a hiss and slam on the landing below as a man made his way down to the garage. They all held their breath until he was gone. "My grandfather always said nothing should ever be built on this land," Alec told them. "When he got out after the fire, he drew these horrible pictures of . . ."

Caleb cocked his head and looked at Alec, "Wait, your grandfather was in the prison and escaped that fire? My grandfather, he was in for a year, and he died that night. Left my grandma with five kids."

Alec pointed to Madonna and Gordon. "Them, too." Finally, a clue. But where did it lead? One piece of the puzzle . . . Madonna gasped.

All three looked at her, saying "What?"

"I had this dream last night about Grandpa," she said, "about Grandpa and how he is now, which is completely freaky, and Grandpa before," she looked at Gordon, "we were even born." They listened, spellbound, as she described what happened in her dream. She finished by saying, "And then the circle burst into flames. "

Gordon let go of his sister's hand. Sitting on the cold steps, listening to the others, he felt disconnected, as if none of this was real. He must be dreaming and if he could wake up, things would make sense again. When he woke up, there would be no grandfathers crawling on ceilings. Still, he couldn't stop himself from saying, "I remember; I was there. How the hell did we have the same dream?"

Madonna looked at him and shrugged. "We're twins?" Gordon shook his head. As if that were an explanation. He wanted something rational.

Caleb was determined to get to the truth. "Okay, but then what happened after the circle caught on fire?'

Madonna shook her head, "I don't know, but I got the feeling that the circle was the answer, that no matter what happened, the circle would protect me." She saw the look of hesitation on Alec's face. "What?" she asked.

He wasn't sure it was relevant, but what harm could it do? "In my dream, my grandfather said zeroes. I didn't know what he meant," he shrugged self-consciously. It couldn't be any weirder than the others. "Maybe it was like your dream; maybe zeros mean circles. Like you said this morning, you were seeing circles everywhere."

Caleb leaned back against the wall, stunned. Madonna decided to ask. "Caleb?"

He nodded, completed amazed at what had just occurred "Yeah." He said "The same—message I guess . . ."

Madonna looked up at the ceiling as if searching for an answer. Her brother put his arm around and touched her face. Blotches and welts covered her face and neck. She burst into tears.

Her tears drained little of the power she generated, the

power clouding the barrier. The girl's light blinded them, and her psychic energy thickened the wall so effectively that all the revelations were unseen and unheard by the creatures who clamored to get close, hoping to know what plan, what defense was forming. Nothing was learned.

Had he known, Caleb would have been pleased. Rather the absence of cameras, it was the girl who protected them from the gleaming eyes of demons, their claws ready to pierce soft flesh, ready to feed.

FORTY SIX

PATTY

They can't let Bernie and the Monster win. It will even eat kids.

Oh, dear lord, what can we do?

I'll think of something.

It's Beginning to Look a Lot Like Christmas
Redhill Mall

The truth was, now that it was real, now that they knew that there *was* something "other than natural," as Gordon insisted on calling it, none of them knew what was next. Until they did, there were jobs, groceries to buy, bills to pay and errands. Life went on as it had before. As she filled cone after cone and topped the swirls with sprinkles and toppings to order, Madonna searched for the crow. She only went to the ladies' room when she saw others there, exiting quickly rather than be alone. Ted and Kevin were still careful. Both were afraid that she might unravel and leave them to manage the increasing lines of customers alone.

Much to Ellis' confusion, (and secret delight) Gordon made sure that she was always at his side. Ellis had hoped that she was wrong, that Gordon wasn't gay, just a bit reserved. Gordon knew she was getting the wrong idea and he felt bad, wishing there was a way to explain. There wasn't and he made a promise to himself: if he survived what was stalking them, he would do a makeover that would help Ellis find a boyfriend, even if it meant she found one before he did.

Considering what had happened to Alec, Matt, the GAMES GALORE manager, tested the new games himself. Alec was grateful and more than relieved. He avoided the storeroom, only entering it if someone was with him. The sight of the pinball machine made him shudder and he suggested that a tarp should cover it. A tarp would protect the game from dust he argued, and Matt agreed.

Caleb's agitation had caught Wilson by surprise. The kid, who had been so focused, had a tough time sitting still. Wilson decided this time to keep his mouth shut (always a problem for him, he was too nervous himself) and when the kid was ready, he'd talk.

On her breaks, Madonna studied a pocket-sized book entitled *Communing with the Dead*. Throughout the mall, uniformed police officers played cards and told crude jokes about Mr. and Mrs. Claus. By the mall fountain, the mall Santa sat uncomfortably on a worn red velvet chair while a line of toddlers and small children waited to sit on his lap.

A day after the meeting in the stairwell, Madonna poked her head into the security office. Caleb gave her a concerned look. "Hey, you all right?

She shrugged. "I guess. You?"

Wilson was busy with a crossword. Caleb looked at Wilson. "Hey Wilson, I need a minute."

Wilson had just found five down. "You got it," the older man said, not looking up.

Caleb shut the door to the monitor room and began to tell her, keeping his voice an urgent whisper. "Something happened at PLAY IT FORWARD, you know, the sporting goods?"

She nodded, reluctant to ask. "Okay . . . what. . .?"

"The police think that there was a burglary. The cameras were covered, stuff was broken into, there was a mess, but nothing was taken . . ." He hesitated. She could see that he was scared. "A hand." he said, staring at his own hands. "They found a hand." She frowned and shook her head, not comprehending. "Madonna, it was by itself, cut off. They found it under a pile of sweatpants. They think it might have belonged to a girl who worked there. They're gonna compare it to her prints when they locate some. There's no family here. The manager said she told him that she was moving to Columbus because of her mom, but no one has found the mom yet."

Madonna stared at him; her mouth half open. "Can you be at Alec's by nine?" she asked. "It's Beginning to Look a Lot Like Christmas" was playing softly. Caleb nodded and they both went back to work. Later that day, Madonna whispered Caleb's account of the bizarre event in the sporting goods store to Alec and then to Gordon, telling them to meet at Alec's after work.

Gordon's panic the rest of the day made Ellis reconsider her feelings for him. What if he had some kind of mental "disorder" she asked herself. Would she stand by him? She wasn't sure.

While selling video games to mothers anxious to please their teenaged sons, Alec kept doing math problems in his head. It was the only way he could forget about the storage room and get through what remained of his shift.

Before she left the mall that day, Madonna visited PLAY IT FORWARD to see what energies she could read. As she approached the free weights, the traces that lingered there made her shiver. Moving around other sections of the store, she picked up diffuse amounts of negative energy that rolled over her body like a heat lamp.

She closed her eyes periodically to heighten her perceptions. Hearing laughter, she opened her eyes. A young couple was watching her, covering their mouths. Embarrassed, she shrugged her shoulders. Maybe it was time to leave. On her way out, she passed Detective Cabrizzi who was standing by the tennis rackets, questioning Andy, the manager.

She chose a different route back to the food court and running her hand along the walls, she looked for indications of anything paranormal. There was nothing obvious, even when she checked the stairwells, feeling the steps. As she made her way down to the first garage level, the reality of what she was doing and what she faced overwhelmed her. Her heart racing, it felt as if a cold hand slapped her. The cold was not from the demons, watching her from a safe distance. It came from within, as if she were warning herself against the peril of panic, the danger of fear. Nonetheless, she ran up the stairwell and back to the first floor of the mall.

Crowds of people were milling through the mall's first floor and looking up, she saw the upper levels were full of shoppers. When she collided with the GOURMET JELLIES cart, she realized that she was running and slowed her pace. As she approached the food court, she saw the crowded doorway of ON THE EDGE, the clothing store which catered to women under twenty-five. A steady stream of young women and a few not so young who had resolutely stayed a size four argued about who was first to go through the shop's double doors.

Threads of negative energy pulled away from the shop doorway as the demons fled to a safer part of the barrier, someplace away from Madonna and her sage.

PATTY

Poor Emma. Poor Madonna. I hope they both do okay. Not just because they're family.

Yes, they are. Oh, Emma, I'm sorry.

The Burning Gift
Redhill
December 21, 2004

It was 7:30 in the evening and Emma lay on the couch. A tumbler of wine sat on the little table. The television was showing *Miracle on 34th Street*. One of her legs was hanging off the couch as she watched Madonna collecting her books on the occult. Madonna was gathering several books including *The Knowledge: An Examination of Rituals and Ancient Symbols*. She packed her box of tinctures and oils, candles, crystals, and a variety of herbs.

Her eyes bleary, Emma reached for the wine. Madonna saw how forlorn her mother was, drunk and alone. Hugging her mother, Madonna whispered, "Please just promise me you won't leave here. Please . . ." She kissed her cheek. "Mom, you were right, I shouldn't work at that mall. No one should."

Emma was already in a half stupor. She smiled, trying to focus, "Honey, you're such a good girl." Madonna hugged her mother tight. "Okay, okay." Emma said as her head fell back and she was asleep.

Grabbing her books and supplies, Madonna sighed. "Bye, mom."

PATTY

This part is swell. I wish I could say something.

My poor John! Why didn't I protect him? I was his mother. And I abandoned him.

Okay, so you did. When this is over and we knock out Bernie and the monster gets a knuckle sandwich, you can find John and say sorry. You were still a better mom then Ma. Ask Gram; I know she'll help.

Okay, Patty.

The Way of the Saboteur

At ten at night, creatures moving under the full moon spied on Ray's two-bedroom house. On the gravel driveway were three cars. The wind increasing, the little snow on the ground had turned to ice.

Swarming, the demons gathered as close as they dared. Ray's bungalow was ablaze with a power so strong only few dared gaze at it through the milky wall. Bitter and impotent, they waited. The coming sacrifice would melt all who were in the house, save one.

In the house, in the center of the dining room was a square table, one Ray had used for his endless games of solitaire. On the table was a clear glass bowl filled with water. Quartz crystals lay on two corners of the wooden table. Lit white candles sat on the other two. On the floor, a circle of white rose petals surrounded the table and chairs. Madonna's books on the paranormal sat stacked on top of Lisa's China cabinet. The three young men struggled with their skepticism.

"Usually," she warned, "the most that is supposed to happen is that we'll see a light or there will be a smell, or maybe just tapping."

"How's that supposed to help?" Caleb asked, "We're dealing with something that kills people." Caleb was trying to take it seriously, but a smell? Gordon and Alec were both trying to keep an open mind. This whole scene was out of a movie; it was hard not to see it that way.

She looked at each one of them as she spoke. "I know you're all skeptical. I don't know what I feel. Each one of us had a dream and there was a message. We have to try to communicate. Whatever is threatening us, it's chased me my whole life. I want to know how to fight it." The candle bathed her face with flickering light. Her dark eyes conveyed the depth of her fear.

"Okay, close eyes," she said. "Your hands on the table."

They placed their hands on the table, the little finger on one hand touching the little finger of another. She whispered a part of the Bible's Old Testament. "Samuel then said to Saul, 'Why do you disturb me by conjuring me up?' Saul replied, 'I am in great straits, for the Philistines are waging war against me and God has abandoned me. Since he no longer answers me through prophets or in dreams, I have called you to tell me what I should do. '"

She took a deep breath. "In the name of Good, Unity and the Oneness of Life, I call upon the spirit of John Arnold."

Several minutes went by; nothing happened but the ticking of the wall clock. She tried again; even she was beginning to doubt. "Um . . . in the name of Absolute Good, Absolute Unity, Oneness of Life, I call upon the spirit of John Arnold." There was another five minutes of sitting; nothing happened.

Gordon suppressed a laugh and muttered. "Third time's a charm."

Disappointed, she scolded, "Gordo . . ." She tried again. "In the name of Good, Unity, and the Oneness of Life, I call upon the Spirit of John Arnold. "After another ten minutes went by. Madonna finally opened her eyes. "Fine. You're right, Gordon."

Gordon frowned. "I'm right?"

She shook her head sadly. "I don't know . . . I don't know what I'm doing. I never have." Without warning, she dropped her head into her hands. Madonna gasped, as her head jerked upright. Her eyes widened.

Gordon, Caleb, and Alec panicked. "Shit! Madonna? Madonna!"

Sitting on the cabinet by the stack of books, Alec's electromagnetic gadget whirred to life. In recounting her dream, Madonna had described the face of her grandfather peering through hers, her face a translucent mask. As she sat at the table, her skin became a shimmering pool, and they could see another face just under that of the sleeping girl's. It was a young man, his hair dark, his eyes a grey blue. The pool shifted constantly, revealing, and obscuring the face that so closely resembled Gordon's. John Arnold began to speak, his voice blending with his granddaughter's always together. Words were halting, but urgent. It seemed he knew there was little time for them.

"A sacrifice is promised. It's promised for the time—the time—the time—is soon— time for chaos—to collect a life—the burning gift—feeds magic—MUST offer—at the same time—as before. In the place—the same—as it was— in the place before. The thief's reward—NEW LIFE. NEW LIFE—as mine was new to the old—so—the new life is to mine. The sacrifice—the chosen vessel—death is the way— the tool of the saboteur.

There was a pause. Madonna sighed. Gordon wondered if John was gone and then the spirit resumed his message, his hushed voice ominous in its warning.

The power—the power—the power to kill again. The promised power is MORE—the vessel's more—so the power's more. Magic comes from death. Death feeds magic.

True—makes it true—the time of burning promised—chaos seeps—through the tear— floods across the bridge to feed. The thief must reach the vessel at the time— at the place. The promise MUST BE BROKEN—it must not hold. The oath broken, the thief broken, the tear sealed. Stay within the circle—the circle must be in the place—at the time—at the place—the circle—hold the circle—the circle must hold the vessel. The circle must hold the vessel—the circle must hold the vessel within the circle—for the time at the place

Her head dropped. Losing control, Gordon reached over to make sure she was breathing. Madonna expelled a huge breath. Her face was her own again. Caleb pulled a notepad from his pocket and a small pen. He began to write.

Alec started to ask him what he was doing. Caleb put his hand up. "Hold on. I got to write all this stuff down—before we forget,"

Madonna looked at him, confused. "What stuff—what? I'm sorry! I just don't know how to do it. I'm a loser, okay! What do you want me to say?"

Gordon shook his head—he couldn't believe what he was about to say. "Okay, Sis. You were right. You were right all along."

"Just a minute—don't anyone say anything until I finish this." Caleb was determined to get it right.

When he was done, he showed Gordon and Alec what he'd written. "Did I miss anything?" Madonna moved close to Gordon. She had to know what was said.

Alec pointed to Caleb's notes. "The circle, he said," Alec closed his eyes as he remembered the words. "The circle must be at the place, at the time . . ."

Caleb nodded. "Right, at the place at the time. Gordon?"

"He said 'the saboteur;' what does he mean?" Alec asked.

"Some kind of spy who messes things up to help the enemy win." Gordon said. Gordon shook his head; the whole thing was confusing. "The burning gift. What burning gift?" he asked. It came to him. "The prison. He means the prison fire."

Alec stood up. "Hold . . . on . . . hold . . . on . . ." He went to a closet in the hall and brought out a box full of old sketchbooks. He found what he was looking for and opened it on the coffee table. "Grandpa drew these—right after he came home on parole." Alec flipped through the pages of a sketchbook in middle of the group. The pages were filled with sketches that Ray drew of an old man transforming into Arnold. "He always said that John Arnold was not John Arnold, but I just figured he just had a chip on his shoulder because of how the guy made good after prison. I wonder what happened that night of the fire."

Madonna studied the sketched faces and figures of Arnold, an old man and the man who walked out of the prison as John Arnold. The sketches revealed a startling transformation. The old man's face and body changed as Arnold burned. Blood dripped from the old man's fingertips, as he watched Arnold collapse. Fire flowed from his fingers after he transformed into John Arnold. Some drawings showed him hurling fire from his fingertips at inmates.

Caleb was starting to make sense of it all. "That must be it! The night of the fire, does anyone know how it even started?"

Madonna gasped, "God . . . anyone recognize this face?" She pointed to the image of the old man before the change. His strange eyes remote, his face was a mask of cruelty. No one knew.

Alec shuddered. "I'm not sure you'd want to."

Gordon studied Caleb's notes. "So—if the burning gift was the prison fire—then the place must be the—the prison."

Caleb said "Right, and—the place—is the prison—and?"

"Wait a minute," Alec said. "What date did the prison fire happen on?"

"One thing at a time." Caleb cautioned. "What does the part about 'true' mean?"

Alec looked at the notes. "Well, if death feeds magic and makes it happen, it's real magic; it becomes true, not fake—the hand in PLAY IT FORWARD—someone died there—that's obvious."

"Christmas Eve." Madonna sighed. "The prison fire happened on Christmas Eve, 1965." They all fell silent.

"So . . . just to be clear . . ." said Caleb, "are we agreeing that Senator Arnold isn't the real John Arnold?" They all nodded. "Then, who is the dude who built the mall?" He laughed, shaking his head. "You think they'll let me onto the force if I give 'em this story?"

Gordon started working it out. "The thief is whoever the guy is who built the mall. That guy is the thief; he stole grandpa's life and he's planning to be rewarded with a new life, the vessel, which *must* stay within the circle, *at* the same place, *at* the same time to keep him from closing the deal. Great; crystal clear." He hesitated, reluctant to say what came next. "Sis, one other thing. Grandpa said the circle must keep the vessel so that the thief can't complete the sacrifice, the burning gift. Does he mean you?" Terror spread across Madonna's face. Gordon reached across the table and took his sister's hand, "I hate to admit this more than you know; you have been right. Someone *has* been chasing you because you're the next vessel."

While Madonna was in the bathroom throwing up, they waited, each cringing at the prospect of fighting a deadly force they didn't understand, didn't believe in until now. Looking shaken, but resolute, Madonna opened the bathroom door. Motioning to them all to follow, she said, "Let's get down to business. She pulled up a chair and sat at Alec's computer. "Let's try to make sense of this. I want Rhonda to get how serious this is, that I'm not a wacko."

"Rhonda?" Caleb asked.

"Rhonda is Madonna's advisor at the Paranormal Academy," Gordon said sheepishly, half-embarrassed at what he was saying.

Alec and Caleb looked at each other. "Oh, okay," they nodded their heads and began to help her compose an e-mail requesting a consultation.

As they waited for Rhonda's answer, Madonna decided to research Redhill Correctional. Web sites ranged from accounts of the fire to the prison's construction in the late forties and the controversy associated with building site. The history of the 1900 Christmas Eve gruesome murder of a local woman, Becka Tobin, in a cabin that once stood on the prison site resulted in considerable opposition; however, the economic benefits to the area created by the prison won out.

Clicking on *Mysteries of the Heartland: The Burning of Redhill Correctional*, Madonna discovered a blueprint of the prison, including additions made after the original building was opened and the dividing of cells that was theoretically the reason the cellblock doors failed to open. The analysis featured a description of the fire's spread and its origin. A link called *On the cellblock— who was there?* got their attention.

"We're getting warm," said Gordon.

Caleb frowned. "Are you tryin' to be funny?"

"Look!" Madonna said. On the screen was a diagram of the cellblock where the fire originated, including the names of the inmates occupying individual cells. As she zoomed in, they read the names John Arnold and Bernard Baker, inmates assigned to the same cell, the cell where the fire began. Ray Gibbs was in the next cell and Luke Michaels in the one after that.

Madonna's hands began to shake. "Bernard Baker? Who's Bernard Baker?" She typed Bernard Baker into the search engine. There was a Bernard Baker listed as the author of several children's books. A Bernard Baker founded a cable network specializing in flea markets.

"Try Bernard Baker, Redhill Correctional," Alec suggested. After typing Alec's suggestion into the search, Madonna pressed enter. Immediately, sites came up that connected with Bernard Baker, The Notorious Cleveland Crusher. Silently, she scrolled down. There was *Madman, Bernard Baker . . .Chapter Four, Mysteries of Ohio, The Murder of Becka Tobin, a Victim of Satan Worshipers,* and *Serial Killers in America.*

"Okay . . . any preferences as to which site we look at first to see exactly what kind of sick fuck was Grandpa's roomie?" she asked, looking at their frightened faces. She clicked on "The Crusher" site. The newspaper photograph that had gotten Marlene's attention as she sat under the oak tree came up. They all recognized the man from Ray's drawing.

Alec laughed nervously. "So . . . your grandfather was in with a serial killer. What luck." "Let's see what else we can find out." Caleb wanted all the information about this freak he could get.

Scrolling down, she discovered a link to UsedBooks.com, offering copies of *Mysteries of Ohio,* the book Marlene reluctantly purchased. Madonna looked at the others. "Should we bother?"

Lonnie nodded slowly. "Why not?"

Opening an online copy sample, they saw the list of chapters. Chapter Four caught their interest with its mention of Redhill and the murder of Becka Tobin. Madonna and Gordon looked at each other; the name Tobin *was* on their "Family Tree" the section of an album that featured the drawing of a tree with branches labeled with the names of ancestors and relatives.

"You kids should know something about your family." Dee had told them that Christmas, her last. The tree's branches listed the names of Caulkins, Arnold and Tobin on Emma's side. Giordano's side held less, a fact that Dee regretted. "Before his grandpa come over is blank. I just couldn't find much."

"Where are you?" Madonna had asked.

"Ah, honey, I'm anyplace you want me to be," Dee had told her.

When Madonna typed in "Becka Tobin," the account of Becka's murder and the involvement of the boy Bernie came up.

"My God, he was a kid—even when he was a kid!" Gordon was horrified.

"More," said Caleb. She nodded and clicked on Bernard Baker, serial killer. *A Plain Dealer* article dated 1969 chronicled a series of murders that took place in the early nineteen hundreds. Victims included two employees of a Cleveland orphanage, a cook, a nurse and an orphan who was involved in breaking into a local bakery. "The Orphanage Murders, Bernard Baker's Suspected Role." It concluded by noting that Baker, who had lived at the orphanage since the 1900 murder of Becka Tobin, disappeared after the bakery raid and the death of "Patty" a twelve-year-old. Another link to "Ohio Serial Killers" yielded a list of the known victims of Bernard Baker, including his last, Alice Song.

"Alice Song?" Madonna clicked on the name. The details of Alice' murder, including her grandson Warren's role in the investigation came up. "Okay . . . this is unexpected." Madonna decided she would find out what she could about Baker from the Song family. They continued to read, sickened by the description of the victims' bodies and what had been done to them.

An instant message popped up. It was "spirit in the sky," Rhonda. "Madonna?"

Madonna answered. "Yes, Rhonda? Thank God!"

"What is going on, dear heart? The message that you sent is incredible, alarming to say the least."

Madonna's fingers flew. "All true and there's more." She sent the information they had found about Baker.

Several minutes went by until a message appeared. "Madonna, I have Professor Booker here. He'd like to ask you a few questions."

"Okay." she said. After waiting for several minutes, there was nothing. Madonna was wondering what to do next when the professor's first question appeared. "Tell me about the mall manifestations."

She typed a detailed account of the arcade attack, her encounter with the crow, the mall murders, and her grandfather on the ceiling. The professor asked her about prior history. Madonna wrote about her dreams and premonitions, including the most recent. An hour went by with Madonna's answering a range of questions. Alec, Gordon, and Caleb alternated between being restless, wanting an answer, a solution, and making sure that nothing was forgotten.

Finally, Professor Booker was ready to offer his opinion:

"I wish I could give you more. This magic is beyond what I know. I believe it is very old. I can't be sure . . . Druidic perhaps, they believed a criminal's life could be used to give a dying king more years. Regardless, there are planes of existence, very different from our own. I fear Mr. Baker, if he is the person we are dealing with, has tapped into a powerful force, one difficult to fight. A pact was made, an agreement. Mr. Baker is bound to execute his side of the bargain to the letter, as binding as any legal document. Perhaps that means acting as a saboteur; how and for what purpose, I don't know.

He has powers. If you should try to run, he would bring you back. Be on a plane, it will not fly, and you compelled to return and others, to aid in that return. A car will drive itself to the appointed destination, which is the mall and the time, I believe, will be on Christmas Eve, the time-of-day coinciding with the time the fire started in 1965.

My strong advice is to determine the EXACT location within the mall. Determine where the cell that held your grandfather once stood and be there at the appointed time before he has a chance to summon you.

Wait within the protected circle. Be warned. His magic is beyond my experience. I fear he has ways, traps to make you leave it. Do so and you are lost. If he fails, my guess is that he will forfeit his power at a minimum. Rhonda will review with you the elements that produce the optimum protection of a sacred circle. I hope this has been of help. Good luck."

Caleb pounded his hand on the wall. "That's it? That's what we waited on, spending all this time? Christ! Your grandpa told us most of it already." Alec and Gordon looked at each other; they were both concerned about Madonna, who had put her head down on the desk. She was crying, her shoulders shaking with it. She cried as if she had no hope, as if it had already been decided and she would be dead soon. Gordon put his arms around her, and they all watched, helpless to comfort her. Finally, she stopped.

Alec began to speak; he stuttered as he talked. "Look, you're not alone. I'm with you, Gordon's with you and . . ." He looked at Caleb.

"You damned right I am." Caleb said. "Alec's right; we're all with you, but there's other reasons. Baker murdered my grandpa. He deprived my dad of his dad. I know how that feels and look what he did to your granddad and grandma. She killed herself you said." Caleb looked at each of them in turn as he spoke. "It's personal for all of us."

Madonna's face was swollen, but she had ceased crying. She was not alone. Alec loved her and so did Gordo. Caleb was right. Baker needed to pay, whatever the cost.

"My grandpa, his face, his arms were full of scars. It was like he was haunted . . . he would get this look on his face . . ." Alec said. "One way or another, Baker should pay."

She sighed, "Okay. I'm done with my freak out" Let's see where we are . . ."

Another instant message popped up. It was Rhonda. "Be very careful! Remember the sacred circle. Study those notes from last semester, again, and again, the Alpha and the Omega. No matter the religion, sect or practice, the force is the beginning and the end. The fire that destroys is the same that gives life. If you know this truth, you have power. Best of luck, be brave, trust the circle; be not moved!"

Gordon was unimpressed. "Oh, come on! Be not moved? See now, this is why psychics get a bad name. They talk all big but notice how she's not volunteering to help you with this thing! Do you even know what she's talking about? 'Cause I sure as hell want to know that I'm not gonna lose you!"

Madonna smiled and hugged her brother tightly. "Oh, Gordo, it's okay. I need your faith in me now, okay?"

Lonnie interjected. "So . . .Madonna, do you know what Rhonda's talking about?"

She nodded. "Yeah, I think I do." She looked at the screen and read aloud. "The fire that destroys is the same that gives life. If you know this truth, you have power."

PATTY

Ramona finally tried to do her job, but it was too late. Maybe she's here in one of the places grownups like to stay. Even if she's still an old lady, we can be friends, I hope.

I think that's a wonderful idea. When this is over, we'll find her.

When it's over.

Drop Her a Line

Ramona sat in her favorite chair, San Francisco outside her window. Ah, she thought, this window was where she'd sat during her years alone, raising her sons, at the end of a day, weary from reading fortunes. I'm dreaming she thought; a good dream, I hope. She heard a knock on the door and called out, "closed!" She lowered the shades so that people would know. Too many were showing up without an appointment, expecting her to see them. Someone kept knocking. Irritating. She opened the door, intending to give them a piece of her mind for being so rude. As she swung the door open, there was Joey, indescribably handsome in his doughboy uniform.

"Hi kid, long time no see!"

No! She clutched the door's edge. Ramona saw her

skeletal fingers and her skin stained with years and scarred with the burns of failure, a reminder of her cowardice. She was so very old, too old for such a handsome young soldier. Putting her face in her hands, she sobbed. "Go away! Go away! I'm old . . .please . . . go!"

He laughed and gently pulled her hands from her face. "Stop kidding a kidder—kiddo. You know you send me to the moon and back." She looked at him, his eyes filled with his love for her. It was time to leave . . . but the girl . . . "Joey, I can't . . . I . . ."

"Honey lamb, I know you; you want to save the world, but I just want my girl . . ." He took her face in his hands. "So, honey, drop her a line." He kissed her and she knew, dropping the girl a line was exactly what she had done.

Plots and Plans
Redhill Mall
December 22, 2006

The mall's new residents were restless. They crawled along the display windows and ceilings, moving silently, hungering for the coming sacrifice.

At eight in the morning, two days before Christmas Eve, Madonna and the three boys stood in the outer parking lot as they studied the structure before them. Madonna carried the printouts of Redhill Correctional's floor plans as it stood the day it burned. On top of his old Ford Explorer, Caleb spread out a copy of the mall's layout. As she looked at the three floors of shops represented in the mall's layout, Madonna took the smaller scale drawings of the prison and spread them out alongside the floor plans.

The sun's rays barely broke through the gathering morning clouds. It looked like snow. Holding down the drawings to protect them from the wind, she motioned for the others to see what was obvious to her; the mall and the prison were nearly identical in construction.

God . . . he built the same exact place. So, if Grandpa and Baker were in cell ninety-three, that cell would be here . . . in . . ." Madonna studied the prison layout and the mall layout that Lonnie held for her. "DEVONSBERRY & PITTS? As the four were poring over the layouts, Madonna's head went up and she began to stuff the papers into her knitted bag.

"Put them away, Caleb, out of sight! Hurry," she whispered. Caleb looked at her, confused. "Okay, NOW, Caleb, please!" Opening the door to his Explorer, he quickly stashed them under the seat. As he closed the door, a large black Mercedes drew up next the Explorer. After waiting for Reba to open the door, Bernie emerged from the Mercedes. He studied the four who dared to challenge him, probing their minds to see what advantage he could take. What would allow him to interfere with whatever pathetic defenses they were concocting? Unfortunately, except for a trivial stab of fear that failed to influence the boy Alec's mind, it was useless.

It would be over soon, and they would all be gone, minor irritants. "What are you kids doing?" Bernie looked at them all suspiciously. "Why so early?"

Trying to hide her fear, Madonna gave Bernie a big smile. "Grandpa, why are *you* here so early?" CAW! The sound of the crow as it fluttered overhead before landing on the top of the Mercedes made Madonna's legs threaten to buckle and Bernie smile.

"Nasty birds," Caleb said, "Animal Control's gonna take care of this one real soon."

Alec and Gordon smiled nervously at each other.

"Careful, Grandpa," Gordon said, "it's apt to ruin the paint on that Mercedes. You know how they are, always leaving a calling card."

Caleb turned to the rest. "About that Christmas party, I'll let you know."

Bernie considered what they might be plotting. It was obvious that they had some sense of the girl's peril. He wondered if an accident might be arranged for the security guard. He'd lost his opportunity with Alec. Until the sacrifice was completed, the boy was beyond his reach. Reluctantly, he decided against it. Cabrizzi was still on the prowl, and it was too close to the promised time to risk the mall being forcibly closed due to another incident. Better to surprise all of them, more enjoyable overall, to play a little cat and mouse.

"I'm here to admire my handiwork. Anything wrong with that?" Bernie gave them all a benevolent smile. No one could answer; all were slack-jawed. Wonderful, Bernie thought, like lambs to the slaughter. "Merry Christmas, children." As he waved, Madonna saw the ring on his little finger. It was her silver skull ring with three ruby eyes.

She fought panic. *I will not let him see . . . I will not let him see, let him, WILL NOT LET HIM SEE!* He hesitated. She grinned widely. "Merry Christmas, Grandpa." He nodded and turned to the Mercedes. As Bernie entered the car and it drove it away, the crow took off from its perch on the hood and began to circle them.

"How else would you explain him having my ring? Jesus, it *is* him!" Madonna shuddered.

"What I wouldn't give for a rifle, right about now." Caleb said, his eyes never leaving the circling bird.

"Wouldn't do you any good." said Madonna, shaking her head.

Gordon sighed. "Sis, I will never doubt you again. That thing is creepier than hell."

"I think," Alec said, "hell is where it lives."

Caleb nodded. "Let's see if we can send it back home. Can we meet around 11:30? Wilson usually likes to take his lunch break right about then. He's been puttin' the moves on Franka, so he leaves and goes to the ground floor for a while. We can meet at the security office." They all agreed.

FORTY SEVEN

Redhill Mall
New Games

Caleb wondered if it was worth telling Cabrizzi what they knew on the slim chance he would help? Madonna shrugged and gave a nod. It was worth a try.

Later, as they sat sweating, waiting for his reaction, Cabrizzi began to laugh. "John Arnold is the Devil? Funny, because we suspect Troy West of being the Tooth Fairy."

Gordon tried to maintain an air of rationality. "Not the Devil, exactly, some kind of . . . demon or evil . . . I don't know what, just not quite human. Which is why you must make sure the mall is closed tomorrow."

Cabrizzi shook his head in disbelief. "Christmas Eve? Closing the mall is not gonna happen."

Caleb was frustrated. He didn't like being laughed at. "Look, you saw what I saw in the garage, Detective, and we watched the same security tapes. Can you honestly stand there with a straight face and tell us that looked normal to you?"

Cabrizzi was getting annoyed; he had more important things to do than deal with a bunch of kids who were either overly imaginative or pulling a prank. "Normal, kid? There's no such thing."

Caleb wasn't about to give up. "Well then, you at least have to consider the possibility that—"

Cabrizzi was done. "Look kid, there's no way in hell . . ."

Alec looked at Cabrizzi. "Uh, yeah," he said quietly, "I wouldn't use that word right now."

Cabrizzi grabbed his coat and opened the door. Fantasy time was over. Madonna stopped him. "Sir, please. Just, for the sake of your own conscience, investigate it anyway. If it turns out I'm nuts, it'll give you something to laugh about later. But for now . . ." She handed him the mall and prison layouts. Spreading them out over the security offices small desk, the detective compared them.

"I'll get back to you on this," Cabrizzi shrugged. "I admit, it is a bit peculiar, but it doesn't make Arnold some kind of devil, just a little eccentric." He left and the meeting was over. Madonna went back to the ICE KING and the castle special. As Alec returned to VIDEO GAMES GALORE, he happened to glance down at the fountain below. He abruptly stopped and leaning over the edge of the glass barrier, he turned his head to a forty–five-degree angle. For the first time, he saw the pentagram. His heart began to gallop as he considered what to do. Maybe if they showed Cabrizzi . . . Taking a deep breath to calm himself, he shook his head, rejecting the idea. Alec knew the detective would come up with some "rational explanation. "Cabrizzi was a dead end. Reluctantly, Alec returned to work. Several new games had just come in.

The Parting Gift

After she finished her shift, Madonna and Gordon went to Hunan Delight. She was still curious about Alice Song's death. The restaurant was crowded and as they pushed through the people who were waiting to be seated, she saw Warren Song and Alice, his daughter, named for Warren's murdered cousin. When he saw Madonna, Warren face paled and he whispered to his daughter, who nodded.

"Madonna?"

Madonna was confused. "Mr. Song, I wanted to ask . . ."

Warren Song looked uncomfortable as he gestured toward a door marked Office. "Come with me for a moment . . ."

Gordon cleared his throat. Madonna nodded. "Oh, this is my twin brother Gordon."

"Good, nice to meet you." Warren said with a tight smile. Gordon, whose confidence had deserted him, managed to mutter a reply.

Warren was now in his sixties, an attractive man whose troubled face belied the festive music that was coming from the restaurant's speakers as he led them to the unlit gift shop. "We are closed" hung on the door. He turned on the overhead light and shut the door. Opening a drawer, Warren pulled out a small box. "My grandmother died last night." Madonna wanted to cry. She hadn't really known the old lady, but her death was an unexpected blow.

"Ah, I'm sorry—I . . ." Tears welled.

Warren handed her the box, "She wanted you to have this." He looked away, uncomfortable with her tears.

Uncertain, Gordon decided to ask what they had come to find out. "I know this is a bad time, but could you tell us anything about your cousin Alice's death? We have our reasons for . . ."

"It's okay Gordon . . ." Madonna put her hand on her brother's shoulder. "I don't need to know any more. We're sorry for your loss, Mr. Song."

Warren sighed. "My grandmother was adamant about you having this. She planned to talk to you and give it to you herself. She called me yesterday and said to set up a time for her to see you and she made me promise to make sure you got it before Christmas Eve for some reason."

Madonna and Gordon looked at each other. "Did she say why?" Madonna asked.

He shook his head. "She was very old, over a hundred as you know. It's still difficult to accept somehow . . ."

Madonna glanced at Gordon. "Well . . . we should go . . . thanks again, Mr. Song." He nodded and they left. Alice Song's death would remain a mystery and like Ramona when Alice died, Madonna felt truly alone.

PATTY

Good for Ramona. She gave the Pearl to Madonna. I hope it is enough, but I don't know.

Love, Ramona

As Gordon drove her home, Madonna examined Ramona's gift. It was a small, unwrapped, flat box. Like his sister, Gordon was curious, and he was waiting for her to open it, which she did without hesitation. There was a note inside. "Wear this until you feel safe. Love, Ramona." Under a white square of silk, was a pearl pendant. The pearl was large, the size of a marble and swirls of light blue mixed with a soft, almost milky white. She noticed a dark spot on it. *It reminds me of an eye.* Madonna slipped it over her head.

Gordon was puzzled. "Why would she leave that for you and not for a member of her own family?" He stopped the car in front of the Emma's trailer.

"I don't know, Gordo. Maybe she knew about Baker. He killed her granddaughter . . . I just don't know." Before getting out of the car, she hugged her brother tightly. "Whatever happens, little brother, I love you . . . take care of Mom if it comes to that . . ."

Gordon had no words. "See you tomorrow, Sis," he whispered, "Do we have everything we need?"

Madonna ran her thumb on the white surface of the box. "I hope so." With that, she opened the door of the car. He burst into tears as he drove back to his apartment.

It's Time

She was walking along a river. It was late in the day and the light was hazy and somber. Up ahead along the path, she saw some ducks crossing. A mother duck and a line of ducklings began quacking loudly as a dark shape swooped down from the trees. It was a crow. "Oh!" she cried as the crow tried to grab a duckling away.

The mother duck began to peck furiously at the crow, which dropped the duckling. As the crow flew up and then dove back down to try again, the ducklings formed a circle around the mother, which quacked loudly at the descending crow. They waddled around the mother duck until smoke began to swirl around the little creatures and they caught fire, forming a circle of flames. With a loud caw, the crow flew off.

Afraid of the crow, she had wanted to help the ducklings but was unable to move. "Your fear is as real as you make it." A young woman, her hair and skin soaked, water dripping from her clothes, waited at the edge of the river. The sound of the river current became a roar and then abruptly ceased. The woman smiled and Madonna knew her face immediately. She remembered her from Dee's "Family" album.

"You're Grandma!"

Nora nodded. "It's time for him to pay for what he's done." Madonna began to protest, as Nora pointed to bridles hanging on a wall of rotting wood. They were in a stall of a decaying stable as they watched Bernie tightening the vise that gripped the head of a young blond woman.

Madonna groaned. "Please . . . I can't . . ." She put her hands over her face as the girl began to scream. With a rush of warm air, they were in a darkened room. Madonna saw Alice Song gripping Bernie's wrists. Bernie's eyes rolled back as he snapped her neck. He slapped the dead girl's head in rage. Whines turned into groans, then growls as he grabbed her arms and swung her over his shoulder, Alice's body dwarfed the old man's frame with his narrow bony shoulders and sunken chest. Madonna screamed. "NO! I can't do this."

"It's only as real as you make it." Nora whispered in her ear.

It was very cold. She and Nora were inside a small cabin. There was a dead girl on the floor, her chest cavity gaping open. Several men were watching as another man was strangling a naked boy. "We don't kill children, Bobbo," one of the men said. Tears running down his face as he squeezed the boy's neck, the man released the child, who dropped to the floor and curled into a fetal position.

She turned to Nora. Was the boy Bernie? Nora began to change. Her hair, now a dark blonde, fell limply around her face, which had lost its delicate prettiness and was now the plain, earnest face of Stella Tobin Caulkins.

"It's time for him to pay for what he did." Stella said, her voice hoarse from the cold and grief. Tears ran down her *broad cheeks. "It's Becka . . . what he did to my poor Becka . . . it's time."*

Madonna was crying and shaking her head. "I know, I'm so sorry, but I can't . . ." She heard shouting and turned to see from where it came. The cabin was gone, and she was standing on a street, the sun hot on her face. An older Asian woman was shaking her fist and shouting in Chinese as she glared up at an open window. The woman cried in English, "Devil! I see what you are. Demon spawn!"

"The pearl." A voice whispered.

"The pearl," said another voice. Grandma Song, her body shrunk to the size of a ten-year-old, reached up and patted Madonna's shoulder.

Another hand rested on the other shoulder. It was the murdered Alice. She smiled and sang the words, "As real as you make it." Extending her arms, Alice bowed.

PATTY

I wish I could join in.

I wish we both could.

Trust

It was seven o'clock on the morning of December 24, 2004, as her alarm woke her. Madonna shivered in the cold morning air, pulling her blankets tighter around her neck, and rolled over, looking at the photograph sitting on her lamp table. As she stared at the framed picture of her, Gordon, Emma, and Dee on the Christmas before Dee died, the thought that this might be her last day on earth came to her.

She began to cry quietly, not wanting her sleeping mother to hear. She wondered what would happen to Emma, should Baker be successful. Better not to think. If she died, was she going to be in some other person's dream, trying to coach him or her on what to do, how to defeat Bernie? She saw that she was clutching the pendant. The pearl's milky white was glowing in the light of her bedside lamp. She sighed, trying to relax and to give herself encouragement.

"I have to trust . . . it's going to be okay, I have to trust, shit shit shit SHIT! I hate this!" As if trying to escape its confines, her heart thudded against the wall of her chest. She sat up and tried to control her breathing. And what of Alec, and Gordon and Caleb? If she went down, they would die too. *"They'll die anyway, even if they don't fight him. Baker is a monster who doesn't believe in loose ends."*

After getting ready and chanting several spells, meant to ward off evil (but not eee-vill, she thought) she gathered what was needed for the circle. As Madonna waited for Gordon, Emma sat at the kitchen table, drinking coffee. Madonna sat at the tiny counter, on the edge of an old-fashioned Formica stool, the last of a set that had been Dee's pride and joy, drinking her herbal tea. She had decided that eating today was out of the question. She gazed wistfully at her mother. Emma's head bent, Madonna saw how frail she was, the determined set of her mouth, the gray in her hair blending with patches of pure white and the troubled expression that never quite left her eyes, hinting at the dark burdens of her soul.

Her mother smiled and looked up from her newspaper. Madonna saw Nora's beautiful eyes. "Mornin,'" Emma said, her voice still thick from last night's wine. "What do you two want to do for the big day tomorrow?"

"I'll let you know," Madonna said softly.

Emma smiled wearily and sighed. " 'Okay, let me know soon. Invite whatzisname —Alec if you want . . ."

"Okay Mom—I—I'll . . . let you know." She heard Gordon's horn. "Mom, do something for me. Don't leave home, call in sick today."

Emma frowned, "But it's a holiday."

Madonna interrupted. "Please, Momma, please! Okay, I know . . . just stay home this once. Don't go anywhere."

Emma looked at her daughter's face. Madonna's eyes, rimmed with black liner and shadow, were desperate. "Okay, is everything all right?"

Madonna smiled and nodded. "I love you, Mom." It occurred to Madonna that Baker owed her mother too.

Giordano Bedonne III
December 24, 2004
Redhill Mall

The motor of his Jetta running, Gordon waited for the trailer door to open. He felt like ice. Whenever something threatened to overwhelm him, he mentally reassembled the molecules that made up Giordano Bedonne III and chased every heated emotion far away. His twin sister was a magnet who attracted controversy and all that was messy. He, Gordon was the opposite; he repelled it.

Trouble was, that iceberg was threatening to crack, a chunk of it going who knows where. He'd had a panic attack this morning, the first since that day when he was fourteen and admitted to himself that he was gay. What a release! How dazzling a time, it was! They were on a spring field trip, the whole ninth grade class. A little theatre group was performing Shakespeare's *As You Like It*.

Gordon had noticed how much more attractive the actress playing Rosalind became when she masqueraded as a youth, but it was the object of her affection, the actor playing Orlando, who took his breath away. Orlando was tall, his blond hair falling boyishly on his tan forehead and his blue eyes, so incredibly like Brad Pitt's, were riveting. As the company made their curtain call, Gordon clapped, shouting "Bravo! Bravo!" Madonna looked at him, grinning and shaking her head. Gordon had been less than enthusiastic about going.

During the cast's collective bow, Gordon's heart almost stopped, overwhelmed when he saw that "Orlando," whose name was Robin, was looking directly at him. Then Robin winked at him, a golden moment, a moment that Gordon knew was *the* most perfect moment he would ever know. If it hadn't been for Madonna, he would have left Redhill as soon as he graduated from high school. But Gordon felt a responsibility for his sister and though he didn't realize it as fully, for their troubled mother.

He'd often thought about Robin, wondering what it would have been like with him. Someday, he hoped to find out. He'd had several lovers, but none had a claim on his heart. Someday, when this was all behind him, he would continue his education and so would his sister; he'd see to it. When he was satisfied that he'd done enough dating, he planned to find a partner, a love, that one person. There just might be a Giordano Bedonne IV; he would love to adopt a child if he met the right man to share his life. Right now, he was young and right now, he had no idea if he would live another day; there might be no life to share.

FORTY EIGHT

Redhill, Ohio
The Waiting Mall

As they drove to the mall, Madonna watched the sun's feeble rays bouncing off the surface of the road and roofs of houses. Gordon parked the Jetta near the outer rim of the surface lot. They sat, silent for a moment, then Gordon took Madonna's hand and kissed it.

"I love you, Sis."

"I love you little brother," she said, thinking whatever happened, she would protect him.

They held hands. He looked at her knitted bag, his mind trying to accept that in it, whatever crystals, chants, oils, and spells it contained, was their defense against someone who had been killing for pleasure since childhood, over one hundred years. Alec's car, Ray's old Datsun pulled up beside them. The snow from the night before lay on the ground. It had formed a mass of slush and puddles of water as the morning sun fell on it. Clouds were slowly starting to gather. As Alec opened his door, Caleb's Explorer drove up.

Caleb slammed the door and the four of them stood, looking at the mall. "If these clouds get going, I just may end up giving all of you a ride home tonight," he said. "When are any of you gonna break down and get a four-wheel?"

Alec looked at Madonna. "Remember, you're not alone." She nodded and the four went into the mall, where the hordes waited.

As the appointed hour drew near, demons gathered from every part of their churning world. They jostled, bit and scratched each other in an effort to be first, first to cross the bridge, first to feed.

Setting Up

When Madonna entered the mall, she saw Franka setting up. Putting on the most cheerful face she could manage, Madonna called to her. "Hey, Franka."

Franka, wearing a "Cher" wig smiled. "Whaddaya think?"

Madonna laughed. "Stunning!"

Franka nodded. "I thought so. I'll wear it tomorrow. Jeremy's taking me out for Christmas dinner."

Madonna shook her head. "Jeremy?"

"You know," Franka said in a dramatic whisper, "Wilson."

"Oh," Madonna nodded. "That Jeremy. I have a favor to ask."

"Anything for my favorite model," said Franka.

"Leave early today—say about four, okay?"

Franka frowned, "But honey, this will be my biggest day . . ."

"Please, Franka, please . . . leave early. Promise me."

Franka looked closely at Madonna. "Is there something you're not telling me?" Madonna said nothing but her eyes were pleading.

Franka had learned to trust Madonna's hunches. "Okay, darlin' I'm out of here at four."

Madonna gave her a hug. "Merry Christmas Franka."

"Merry Christmas, babe."

Gordon's Issue

Gordon was wondering about how to explain to Ellis that they would be closing early, when Ellis asked to leave at 3:30. His explanation was unnecessary.

"Oookay" he said, "may I ask why?" Regardless of the current situation, he was surprised and irritated by her request. It was Christmas Eve, after all. How did she think that was okay?

Ellis looked at Gordon with pity. "Uh, Gordon, I know that we've spent kinda alotta time together . . . okay . . . I think you are just the nicest guy, uh boss, but, you know, um . . ." She searched for the right words so that she could let him down easy and not piss him off. She liked her job, but Gordon had issues. "I've met someone and he wants to share our first Christmas holiday together and since I've worked all this overtime, I really feel I deserve . . . "

Gordon fought the urge to laugh and was only partly successful. What came out were a couple of short barks, and his eyes welled up with tears. "No problem, Ellis." He dabbed his eyes when she handed him a tissue, her eyes full of sadness for him. "I understand; it's more professional this way. Who's the lucky guy, anyone I know?"

Ellis felt a weight had been lifted. She truly hoped that Gordon would find the right woman. "Kevin."

Gordon looked at her blankly.

"You know, Kevin," Ellis said, trying not to sound too excited (she didn't want to upset Gordon any more than necessary), "the guy who works with your sister. He already got the time off . . . they're closing early; his boss is going to a singles Christmas party in Cleveland and doesn't want the ICE KING to be unsupervised. Nobody's into soft serve now anyway because of Christmas."

Gordon's mouth hung open. She dumped him, *thought*, he reminded himself, she dumped him for . . . *Kevin?* He glanced at his reflection in the makeup mirror. He should take better care of himself. He would if he survived what was coming.

The Redhill Mall
December 24, 2004

Throughout the mall, restless spirits, both human and the famished beings readying for their pitiless assault on the unsuspecting, roamed its halls, shops, and floors. As evening approached, the pianist reluctantly returned from her break. She wore the flowing blue gown of the mall's opening and flexing her graceful fingers, began to play "White Christmas." The arched glass ceiling was dotted with white flakes that steadily accumulated, blocking any view of the world outside. As she played, many in the moving crowd would pause and sing wistfully. An hour had passed since she and the others had arrived, and Madonna felt as if she were in a trance. As she made her way through the throngs of shoppers, she thought, none of this is real. *It's a dream, and I'll wake up, safe, in my own bed.*

Alec had just taken his break with her. They sat together on a bench near the pianist, but several yards away from the fountain, listening to the soft melody of "Have Yourself a Merry Little Christmas." His hand rested on hers. Neither spoke. Occasionally, his index finger delicately stroked the top of her hand, which was devoid, for once, of any rings. Madonna wore her pendants, the gold crucifix of Madonna Nucci, Giordano's Italian grandmother and his Irish mother, Bridget's silver four-leaf clover. And the pearl. It hung beneath her black turtleneck sweater and its very presence over her nervous heart was comforting.

When it was time to go back to their jobs, he silently mouthed the words "I love you." She smiled and for the briefest of instants, she was simply a young girl with her first love.

Her eyes, shiny with tears, she whispered, "Me too." Then, she said quietly, "Seven, then."

He nodded. "Seven." Both turned quickly and left.

PATTY

Funny! Greedy kids need coal in their stockings to wise them up.

Spoiled children, yes, I agree.

Santa Sid

In the Enchanted Village, Santa was very uncomfortable as he shifted on his chair. Rudy Palmer, a boy of four was on his lap. Rudy, the son of an insurance salesman and a mother who sold Amway, was counting his requests on his chubby little fingers. "An' I wannn . . . uh a new Gameboy, okay, Sanna?" Sid Kovac (Santa) had to fart but was dutifully holding it in until the little darling was through and he could politely excuse himself to go feed the reindeer. "Sanna? ARE YOU LISTENING? Make sure to bring at LEAST six games. I've been a really good boy an . . ." Just then, Sid's iron control gave out and the evidence of his kielbasa lunch made itself known, loudly and pungently.

Rudy plugged his nose with the tips of his fingers. The boy was determined to complete his order. The mouths of the nearby children formed ovals and their eyes grew bright with various degrees of delight and disbelief. The adults suppressed a laugh, but as the evidence of Santa's embarrassing breach of etiquette wafted through the waiting line, cackles began to break through.

Sighing, Sid wrapped it up with the "Little Prince" and said "Ho ho ho! Rudolf's hungry, better go feed him. We have a lot of houses to visit tonight."

The next child in line was Mindy, a girl of three. Standing patiently with her twenty-year old single mother, Rae-jean, who was on a cell phone setting up her plans for the evening, Mindy was thrilled. Barely able to contain her excitement, she called to him, "Bye Sanna . . . bye . . . say hi to Rudolf, Sanna."

Sid turned and waved. "Bye, kid. Bye, little girl. I'll be back. Be good!"

"Okay Sanna." Mindy nodded and tried to 'be still" and not to jump. Momma hated that and Mindy was apt to get the dreaded belt later. Children tugged on their parents as Santa left to feed Rudolf and the inviting store windows beckoned to them. Marla and Randy, who had been hired as photographers and dressed in elf green, put up a "FEEDING REINDEER, back in one hour" sign and left for another trip to ON THE EDGE.

PAH-rum-pum-pum-pum

Half an hour later, it was six o'clock. Sid was feeling much more comfortable and settled into his ornate chair. Ordinarily, he liked kids, parboiled as W.C. used to say, but Christ, he'd be glad when midnight rolled around, and he could leave. Back in his snug bachelors' apartment, there was a fifth of Jack Daniels with his name on it and the AMC channel was showing *Gilda*, starting at 12:30. A better way to spend the holiday did not exist.

The next kid climbed onto his lap while Mindy was sitting on the floor of FIVE MINUTES FROM NOW while her mother tried on sequined tube tops. Laura Denise's knobby six-year-old knees swung as she jumped into Sid's lap, barely missing his crotch. The mall clock began to strike. Echoing throughout, its solemn tones reverberated and caused all on the outside floor and the walks of upper levels to pause like the revelers in Poe's "Masque of the Red Death."

The huge clock, its face impassive as an executioner's after the last appeal has been denied, struck six, the sound causing the overhead music, "The Little Drummer Boy," to fade. With the sixth chime, the volume of the Bing Crosby recording increased, but the speed of the rum-pum-pum-pums slowed, the cadence seeming like a death march.

Sid looked at the clock. The face was fuzzy, and he couldn't make it out. Damn, he knew he should have worn his glasses. Laura Denise, who had been in the process of extracting a promise from the old guy to bring her a new TV for her bedroom, looked up to see if she could figure out the time, it wasn't fair; there were just letters. Where were the numbers?

FORTY NINE

The Redhill Mall
The Clock

Something about the clock, Marla knew it was wrong. What was it? Randy was busy swiping a credit card through when Marla tried to get her attention. Time to leave. She didn't know why, but it was time. "Gotta go." Marla insisted.

Randy looked at her as Caesar did when Brutus pushed in the knife. "Are you fucking kidding me? You're leaving?"

Marla gave her a pained expression and shrugged her shoulders. There were at least forty kids in line and there would soon be more. Tears of anger filled Randy's eyes as she pointed at the clock. They were supposed to stay until at least eleven thirty. Something was weird. With the green felt sleeve of her elf shirt, Randy rubbed her eyes to clear them of makeup, and looked again. On the face of the clock, the numbers were all the same—VI. What was going on? Was it a trick to get people to stay an extra hour while they fixed it? What?

The HACKER popped into her mind. Her eyes blank, her mouth slack, Randy looked at the impatient parent, waiting for her 'package of memories.' "Sorry," she said to the woman, and grabbing her designer purse from under the counter, Randy hurried through the nearest door, to snow and the bitter cold. Fuck all of this, she thought, maybe I'll go for that degree in Psych after all. This is nuts.

The Fountain

Troy West looked forward to January. "Just get through the rest of tonight," he said to himself. It had become a mantra. Arnold's constant bullying had caused West's blood pressure to soar. The money though, who could resist that kind of dough? It made it almost worth it. Almost. Whatever, soon it would be over and maybe the old coot would back off some. Troy hoped so. If not, he planned to give notice. What was a lot of bank if you weren't around to spend it?

The mall closed tomorrow, and he planned to catch up on his sleep, then, a few hours of internet porn. There was a new site called Hungry Nymphets. Totally legal. Troy was careful. The girls were over eighteen but looked as young as twelve. He owed it to himself to try and relax. It was Christmas.

The pianist had gone home. Troy looked up at the clock striking six. "Sixes?" He said to himself. "It's all sixes . . . what the fu . . ." A gush of red spurted from the nearby fountain, sprinkling Troy's new Brook's Brothers suit. He put his fingers on the wet wool as some droplets sunk into the fabric and others were bouncing off, making their way down to his shoes and the fake granite floor. It looked like blood. He panicked. Was he bleeding from somewhere and didn't feel it? Where, oh, God . . .

Then he heard yelps and screams and a loud teenaged girl voice saying "Eeeewww—yuck, nasty!"

Like an opened fire hydrant, the fountain was spewing wildly. Around him, people were hit with varying amounts of the fountain's geyser. What the hell was it? Someone was going to lose his job. Merry-Christmas and bah-humbug. Goodbye nymphets. Damn! Troy stormed away from the fountain as all around him, with cries of alarm and disgust, people fled the area. Those security guards, especially that wise-ass black kid better deal with this NOW.

The Blue Sweater

Kelly waited until she saw the FIVE MINUTES FROM NOW manager head down to the food court on her break. Kelly knew that the manager, a barracuda named Brianna, liked an extended lunch. Some people had no ethics. She, Kelly, always brought her lunch and ate in the break room of ON THE EDGE. *Some* managers took their jobs more seriously. She felt bad about firing Marissa, her niece, but honestly, telling customers to go "fuck themselves" was an anger–management problem and Marissa needed to work on it. When Kelly saw the big "SALE" in the "FIVE" window, she decided it was time to make a move before things got out of hand.

In the ladies 'room, Kelly put on a red wig and glasses and strolled over to the rival store. Things were jumpin,' she admitted to herself. People were naive, looking at the price and not considering the quality or value of what they put on their bodies. Young women lined up to try on dressy tube tops with sheer over-blouses. Kelly knew after New Year's Eve, the demand for the tops, as well as the tacky dressy dresses FIVE was famous for, would drop like a rock, so she decided to see what was new and what she could undercut with the right price on the right garment.

A rack of newly arrived turtlenecks in soft wool and spring colors was positioned on the back wall, away from the sale items where dozens of twenty-somethings were pronouncing judgment on the tops and dresses with calls of "cute", "when you lose another five pounds cute" and "makes you look kinda chunky." The word "fat" was verboten.

Selecting a powder blue sweater, Kelly hurried into the communal dressing room where the frenzy of trying-on was under way. With a fake smile and a "I hope you don't mind sharing" which the current occupant, a seventeen-year-old, did mind but reluctantly agreed to, Kelly took advantage of one of the few partially enclosed dressing areas. She took off the wig and slipped the sweater over her head. "No" . . . she said as she looked at herself in the mirror, "This thing would make Ally McBeal look chunky. The neck's uncomfortable to boot, way too tight."

She decided to see what else they were saving for sales. She started to pull the sweater off, but it was stuck. Frowning, realizing that she would encounter Brianna soon if she wasn't careful, she tried to loosen the neck by slipping her fingers into the folds around her face. Somehow, she couldn't get a grip and . . . wha! She felt the sweater around her neck quickly tighten. Frantically, she began to pull it over her head, trying to force it off as it strangled her.

Eyes watched in amusement as the girl struggled. The tip of a lengthy talon had made its way through a tiny break in the thinning wall separating the madness of destruction from the ordinary frenzy of holiday shopping and the talon hooked the neck of the powder blue sweater, twisting and tightening. The being sighed with pleasure at the girl's twisting like prey on a hook.

Kelly stretched her arm and hand out grasping the air, pleading for help. The seventeen-year-old rolled her eyes. "What the fuck does this woman think?" she thought, "That she, Christy, works here? No way." Grabbing her six bags of purchases, Christy left Kelly, whose face, obscured by the sweater, was beginning to turn purple. Kelly's squeals were drowned out by the shrill laughter of thirty tightly packed young women.

For the delighted demon, they were merely squawking geese, soon to be plucked one by one.

Kelly's arms flailed, and she was blinded by the powder blue wool, which pulled itself tightly over her eyes as it squeezed. Within a few minutes of fighting the pitiless sweater, Kelly collapsed and died, falling against the wall mirror.

Looking down at the girl's limp body, the eyes of many who had gathered to partake in the death, gleamed with satisfaction. No one else noticed for quite a while.

The Demon Rift

Nagle's Christmas Elvis

The soothing vibration of the chair felt good to Chief Nagle after all that damn shopping. What he wouldn't give for a rum and coke right about now. He needed to relax. Cabrizzi was a fool, and he would see to it that Cabrizzi took his retirement a little early, like five years early. Christ, Arnold was still on his back about the investigation. What did he expect? Killings like that spooked people. While Jill Nagle shopped for last minute stocking stuffers for the multitude that was her family, Terrence Nagle decided he would take a little nap. He noticed the radio headphones. Perfect, something early sixties maybe or some Christmas Elvis.

Putting the earphones on, Nagle fiddled with the controls, trying to find a station to his liking when a sound came through the earpieces. The frequency was not Christmas Elvis; it was a deadly assault, so strong and piercing that it quickly traveled through the Chief's ear and into his brain. His back arched slightly, his feet extended out from the chair and then collapsed on the raised footrest. The soft folds of the Chief of the Redhill Police Force's brain filled with liquid, mixing with the blood of burst vessels.

To all that passed by, his head lolling, tilting to the side of the recliner's cushy headrest, mouth open and eyes closed, the headphones clutching his skull, he looked like just another middle-aged man, taking a break while his wife shopped. He was quite dead though. Seeing the chair and the sleeping man who looked a little like her grandpa, three-year old Mindy crawled up into his lap and dozed while her mother made another call.

PATTY

Rae-jean is just like Ma. Poor little kid, Mindy deserves better.

I agree, Mindy deserves better.

Rae-jean

"Too bad, Rae-jean, are ya sure there's no place where you can park the kid, just for a while?" Dustin's voice was low and sexy. "Ah wannnchoo babe," he groaned.

Rae-jean was torn. Her mom told her if she took Mindy to see Santa, she would watch Mindy on New Year's Eve, but her mom, Trudy, was firm. "That child needs her momma on Christmas; for Christsake, Rae-jean, what's the matter with you?"

Trudy still held out hope that Rae would turn out okay. So far, she was too much like her dad's sister Brenda.

Rae-jean was beginning to fume. God damn that kid. "But, Dustin, she wouldn't be any trouble, we could put her on the floor with a blanket, and . . ." She heard him sigh, never a good sign with Dustin. Tears came into her eyes. She thought about all she'd had to give up. What was she thinking, having a kid at her age? Serve the little brat right if she just left her sleeping on top of that ole' fart conked out in the recliner. Rae-jean could just walk away and make up a story about how Mindy got separated from her frantic mom on Christmas Eve . . . oh man . . . this was good . . . Rae-jean's ear started to ache.

"Rae? Raaeeee, what's wrong? Bitch! Answer me!" Disgusted, Dustin hung up.

Rae was in pain; she couldn't get the cell phone off her left ear. Somehow, it was stuck, and it hurt! "Ooo—oowwah! She started to scream. "It's burning, it's burning! Its . . . " Rae-jean's shrieks startled Francesca who had just left the READ All ABOUT IT! Bookstore and was following a teenaged girl she had seen slip a copy of the *Kama Sutra, the Sequel* under her sweater.

Francesca blinked in disbelief as she saw the cell phone seemingly welded to Rae-jean's ear. As a crowd gathered, people were transfixed. Forgetting the shoplifter, Francesca decided to help the frantic girl since no one else was and she began to pull on the phone. Suddenly, the phone came off and spun across the floor in front of an oncoming stroller. Attached to the cell phone was Rae-jean's left ear. Quite naturally, Rae-jean fainted. Mindy, who had awakened when her mother began to scream, climbed off the dead Chief Nagel and crept between the legs of the gathering crowd. She looked down at Rae-jean who lay unconscious with blood starting to spread from under her head. She was confused.

"Momma? What 'bout Sanna?" Before anyone could react, a man shouted FIRE.

FIFTY

The Time, The Place
Redhill Mall
December 24, 2004

"It is there that spirits live, and demons---it is there that are the ashes of the great burning." Stephen Vincent Benet, *By the Waters of Babylon.*

"Around and around the circle is bound." Spells of Magic.com

People were pounding on the door. DEVONSBERRY & PITTS, *the* trendiest store in the mall, in the opinion of many, was closed and locked. Caleb had told the bewildered and outraged staff, safety violations made it necessary and immediate. When the manager demanded to see the order, Caleb said it was at the security office and he should talk to Wilson, (who had left with Franka at 4:00).

After chasing out everyone, including a customer who was determined to buy a tight tee that said "Christmas Ornaments" across the chest, Caleb locked the door and set the alarm in case a determined employee should try to use a key.

"Now what?" Caleb said. He felt a fear worse than when he heard about his dad, even more than when the "lips" said "Caaallebbb—I waannntchahhh," but he was here.

"The *Bible*, did you bring Grandma Cinda's *Bible*?" Madonna asked Caleb as she checked to see if it all was in place.

"Yeah, I brought it . . . she wanted to know what for, but I told her I couldn't say. Here it is though." Caleb kept trying to get hold of himself. He was feeling a little light-headed.

Compass in hand, Alec determined the east, west, north, and south directions of the area in DEVONSBERRY & PITTS where the cell once stood. Gordon brought the rope, a gift from Beau, a pro-rodeo cowboy who had been a summer romance two years ago. After poring over the prison blueprints and the mall's floor plans, they all agreed that the area where the cell that held Baker and John Arnold, the place where the 1965 sacrifice occurred, now held POLOS and BUTTON-DOWN SHIRTS.

They moved the racks and portable shelving piled with hundreds of shirts sporting the three berries logo atop the letters D&P. A space, nine feet in diameter, was cleared and the rope, various parts of it sprinkled with oil and rubbed with sage and lavender, was laid down and fashioned into a circle that encompassed what had been the prison cell.

In the center of the circle was a makeshift altar on the card table used in contacting the spirit of John Arnold. Stones, painted green, light blue, white, and gold, were placed to mark the directions determined by the compass. A small oil painting of a pentacle, the benign five-pointed star, its middle point upward, lay on the card table, along with white candles, Cinda's *Bible*, a collection of white crystals, a clear bowl of cool water and sea salt. Sage and lavender incense burning on the small altar soothed the troubled air.

It Begins . . .

The clock struck seven. Bernie had waited as they dressed him. When he was ready, he descended the oak staircase as a prince, his expensive suit immaculate, with jewels in his cuffs and his shoes gleaming and the Others, their eyes downcast, deferring to his power.

As the Mercedes pulled up to the main entrance where the double doors swung open and closed without ceasing, shoppers passing in and out, Bernie remembered The Grand Arcade. Rather than a ragged failure, begging for redemption, this time he entered as a conqueror, commanding, important and soon to be rewarded!

The power of his magic was much stronger than it had been in the prison and confident of his success, he began to call up the flames. The legions made ready. Soon, the tear would widen, and multitudes would be filling the mall. Soon, they would feed.

The Circle
Redhill Mall
December 24, 2004

"What time is it?" Gordon asked. His voice was barely audible; he hoped he wouldn't puke.

"Almost seven-thirty," Alec answered. Somehow it didn't seem real, and he half suspected that they would wait for an hour or so and nothing would happen—nothing . . .

"Oh my God, he's coming!" Madonna's eyes wide, she looked ready to faint. They could hear shouting from the lower levels and the sound of alarms.

"*Now* they work." Alec said. At six, they had attempted to set them off, hoping to clear the mall of shoppers, but there was only silence.

"We all need to get inside the circle, immediately!" Madonna's face was white with terror.

Gordon grabbed her hand. "Remember . . . everyone he's hurt. We stop him here, Sis." They stood together within the circle created by a rodeo rope. Spells of protection and their love for each other pronounced it sacred.

"Okay," she said, looking at the three young men who stood waiting for her to tell them what to do next. "Hold hands and pray." They held hands and she began, "Dear God . . ."

With a loud bang, the shop doors to the catwalk flew off their hinges, shooting across the store. One landed in "Spring Fever," a display destined for February and the other door did a twirl before landing upright between men's briefs and socks. Smoke drifted through the doorway and the four could hear screams as people panicked.

An odor filled the room. Overlaid with a sweet candy scent, the decay reminded Madonna of the septic tank that had leaked into the area near their trailer the summer she and Gordon were nine. Emma had tried to keep it out of the trailer by using air freshener. It only made it worse. This smell was awful, bad enough to make her queasy and thankful she had restricted herself to drinking tea.

"Jesus, God what a smell!" Gordon strained to see where it was coming from. Caleb said nothing but began to breathe through his mouth while Alec recalled the sad odors of sickness he associated with his mother's last days and the convalescent home where Ray had struggled to keep his dignity.

People shouted, "THE DOORS—THE DOORS—SOMEONE GET AN AXE—OH MY GOD—OH MY GOD!"

"Remember, no matter what I say, no matter what things look like, no matter how we feel, if we leave this circle, we're dead—

please . . ." she whispered "don't anyone leave . . ." She opened Cinda's Bible and began to read. "And the glory of the true kingdom is forever, deep in the belly of the righteous flames where the only truth is the fire of the first and only Lord, the One that all fear and all come home to in the end . . ."

Dear Children

"My dear children, whatever are you doing? I'm so glad I found you." Bernie's voice oozed concern. "We have to get out! Some mad man has set fire to the mall. We only have a little time, so please, whatever you're doing, we must go NOW!" Bernie stood in the doorway staring at them, a look of paternal goodwill on his face.

The four looked at each other, unsure . . . then . . . Gordon addressed his "grandfather's" concern. "Nah, I don't think so Gramps. You go ahead. Caleb here knows a shortcut, so just take care of you." Gripping his sister's hand, Gordon grinned at Bernie.

Bernie's face clouded and with a controlled fury he boomed, "I ORDER YOU ALL TO LEAVE NOW! I will have to take steps . . ."

The four looked at each other and Gordon started to giggle. They were all terrified, but 'take steps?' Oooo aaaaah, 'steps!' A series of shrieks and groans came from the mall outside. They could see the flicker of flames. Bernie's face, the aging mask of John Arnold, broke into a sneer.

"Alright, Arnold, it's over," a voice said, "you're under arrest for the murder of Greg Tucker." Cabrizzi appeared in the doorway, brandishing a gun.

Arnold smiled at him. "Detective, I'm sure this can be cleared up; it's a misunderstanding . . . "

Cabrizzi was unimpressed, "I'll read you your rights soon asshole, but in the meantime,"—he glanced at Caleb. "I'm gonna need some help until backup comes."

Caleb heaved a sigh of relief, while the other three looked confused. "You got it!" He said as he gathered Cinda's Bible and started to leave the circle.

The gathering hordes rippled with excitement as they prepared for the rift to open. There would be feasting until the it closed. If it remained open long enough, they would spread the flames beyond the mall, raining pain, suffering and death on surrounding communities.

The flames might reach Cleveland and destroy parts of the city. With future sacrifices and stronger vessels, the rift will grow wider and stay open longer until all inhabitants of this world, and there are so many, so much to destroy, all will be wed to pain. Some will live, like jars of preserves, granting them a reprieve from death while inflicting endless suffering. After this world was spent, they would use the victims who remained alive, inflicting maximum pain to maintain the breach. Then, they would search this universe for other worlds to destroy and consume.

Bernie was mildly disappointed; success came with so little effort.

Still, he was wild with triumph, the color in his aging face a rosy red.

"DEMON! I see what you are! DEVIL SPAWN!" It was Madonna, yet it wasn't. She stood at the edge of the circle pointing at Bernie, her face and body radiating a righteous fury. Startled, Caleb froze, the *Bible* in his hand. Cabrizzi started to change. His face shifted, the body elongated, and a long serpentine tail emerged and started to slap the floor as the detective's face grew, the features twisting and forming a grotesque grin and flat yellow eyes, their pupils dark red, full of hate. Caleb's hand shook and it seemed that he might faint. "Easy, take it easy, we know what's going on now." Alec put a hand on Caleb's arm to steady him.

"You think you're immune? Rich! That's rich!" A circle of flames surrounded them.

"Alec, your face!" Madonna let out a gasp. Alec felt his face, discovering the thickened masses and ridges that had been a part of Ray's face. He saw that his hands were covered with masses of tissue, red and oozing. He let out a little cry, fell to his knees and dropped to the ground. As he struggled to stand, paralysis made it impossible.

"Alec, honey, he won't let me go; please help me!" Molly appeared like a holographic image that shifted in an out. His mother pleaded, "Honey, please!" She reached out her hand extending it just far enough. Painfully dragging himself to the edge of the circle, he reached out to her. He wanted to leave the circle to touch her. He began to whimper.

"That's not your mom, dude, don't look." Caleb grasped Alec's outstretched hand.

Alec turned away, and began to cry as he heard "Alec, my baby, help me!" The image shifted into an undulating mass of black flapping wings and points of red light, before expanding and becoming Debbie. Beautiful, the image of the young intern who handed out twenty dollar bills the day the mall opened, she was holding Molly's severed head. Debbie's jaw stretched, and as her mouth yawned open, a gray tongue licked a set of shark's teeth.

"Oh my God . . . oh no!" cried Madonna.

"Don't look!" Caleb shielded Alec, blocking his view.

Bernie shook his head sadly. "You care so little for that good woman—abandoning her to . . ."

"You're a real asshole." Gordon said. He'd had enough.

The Flames

Before the battle within DEVONSBERRY & PITTS began, the fire had already been started. Like the prison fire, flames dripped from Bernie's hand as he grasped the escalator rail and they continued to spread throughout the mall. Frightened young women pushed to escape the confines of FIVE MINUTES FROM

NOW, as they saw tube tops begin to explode, popping like firecrackers on the Fourth.

Gathered at the trembling rift, which continued to lose opacity and thickness, the legions waited for the coming sacrifice.

In the food court, the only open remaining booths were FRUITY TOOTIE SMOOTHIES and BUCKEYE RIBS. The staff abandoned their stations as soon as they saw the vacant smoothie blenders twirling and shuddering on their stands. Fruit resting in the decorative hanging baskets was beginning to smoke as the red-hot wire frames cooked them. The griddles and fryers of the Buckeye Ribs poured clouds of smoke that billowed into the common area. FRUITY and BUCKEYE staffs joined the screaming crowds of shoppers and salespeople as a way out was sought and not found, all exits seemingly barred.

Mall exits would not open; sealed tight by forces unknown. Overhead, silver snowflakes that had created the illusion of an enchanting winter wonderland, now created hell, the twisting sheets of burning metal rained flames and sparks down on the terrified mob as it struggled to escape.

Demons who failed to push their way close to the soon-to-be rift, contented themselves by selecting which group of shoppers they would devour first.

Scars and Tricks

Alec was groaning in pain, reaching out, and moving towards the edge of the circle. Madonna began to chant, "In the name of Absolute Good, Absolute Unity, the Oneness of Life. . ."

Gordon and Caleb pulled Alec away. "That wasn't real, that wasn't your mom, just one of his slimy tricks." whispered Gordon. He turned to Bernie, "Fuck you."

Alec closed his eyes. "That wasn't her, that wasn't her," he repeated and as he opened his eyes, scars covered his hands and grew on his face.

"Son!" Caleb saw his father, Amos in uniform . . . Smiling, Bernie had a gun to the man's head. "Son . . . help me!" his dad begged. Bernie pulled the trigger, spilling the policeman's brains onto the nearby displays of humorous tees. Caleb screamed and lunged forward, Gordon catching him just before he left the protection of the circle . . .

"I call upon the one Spirit, the alpha and the omega, the One with no beginning and no end," Madonna chanted. Flames sprang up around the circle, the intense heat and smoke threatening the four within.

A stream of crawling insects appeared within the circle, a blanket of ants and spiders moving swiftly, covered Caleb within seconds. As Gordon worked to free Caleb from the swarming biting army, Madonna, Cinda's *Bible* before her, continued to chant. "Oh God, please hear me! Fear not, for I have called you by my name, you are mine. When you walk through the fire, you shall not be burned."

The Other, Reba, appeared as the young intern with the unsettling gaze before becoming the creature that had feasted on the young burglars after hours in PLAY IT FORWARD. The demon's yellow eyes narrowed and opening its jaws, it emitted a chilling wail full of rage. Bernie, his face distorting and shifting, bared his teeth in a grotesque smile. Caleb was frantic as he put his hands over his eyes as the insects skittered over his hands crawling through the small openings between his fingers. The crawling army ignored Gordon, who brushed and scooped them off Caleb, flinging them out of the circle where they ceased to exist.

Alec lay crumpled on the ground, covered with scar tissue and oozing sores. Madonna's faith in her ability to fight the wills of Bernie and his inhuman aides faltered. "Close your eyes! They aren't real! It is only the alpha and the omega in our sight! In our hearts! In our minds!" she pleaded.

By now, Caleb, biting, stinging insects crawling over his face, was screaming in pain. As fast as Gordon took them off Caleb, they appeared two-fold. Tears of frustration and fear rolled down her cheeks as she continued "Nor shall the flame scorch you, for I am the Lord your God, your savior." There was a shriek of pain and as she turned to see, Gordon began to burn.

Mindy

The flames were spreading; many people had already succumbed to the smoke and were lying inert, slumped on benches, the mall's floor littered with bodies. Using fire extinguishers that had failed to function, as battering rams, men were trying to break the door of the main entrance. The food court was engulfed in flames, the smoke making exits unreachable.

As Mindy narrowly escaped being trampled by a determined Troy West, she saw Sid as he struggled to keep his footing. "Sanna?" she called to him as she crouched near a deserted cart to avoid being crushed. Sid's attention turned towards her. Parents, their children scooped up in their arms were being pushed aside by those unburdened and determined to survive.

Troy barked at Sid, "Get out of my way." Above them, rafters began to smoke. Then, wood beams came crashing down on the hapless manager. Troy West lay under it, calling out for help.

Sid quickly lifted it, yelping as the smoldering wood burned his hands. Leaving the injured man, he found the child who was hiding under the cart. "Let's go find Rudolf." He whispered to the little girl.

"Okay Sanna," she said as she put her arms up.

PATTY

I'm butting in and nobody can stop me!

Please, Patty, help them!

The Pearl

Gordon was screaming. Flames had begun to melt his hands as Madonna searched for a way to help him. Stripping off the turtleneck that covered her uniform, she tried to smother the flames. Caleb's face was half eaten by insects, his body writhing, the white bones of his wrists exposed by the creatures as they fed. Alec started to choke, his breathing obstructed by the increasing scars that covered his face.

"You can stop this immediately." Bernie's voice was full of concern and compassion. "Just step outside the circle and you have my word, these fine young men will be as good as new!" he urged. "I swear to you, they will suffer no harm from me."

Gordon's pain was beyond anything he could have conceived, but he tried to say, "Don't, he's lying," before his mind began to shut down completely.

Madonna, sobbing, began to move towards the edge of the circle. The pearl hung exposed, around her neck. As she clutched it for comfort, it glowed faintly. She was weakening. Bernie was elated. Then it changed.

The thinning rift stalled; streaks of opacity had begun to grow back. Wild with frustration, the hordes began to howl. Hurling themselves against the streaks, they scratched and gnawed, but the streaks grew back as soon as they were eliminated.

"Just in time," Bernie thought happily. Eagerly, he waited for the coming transformation. Stretching the elastic membrane, one demon's claws reached for the circle, ready to scoop her up as she burned.

When the girl was almost beyond the protection of the circle, she was thrown back inside. Bernie was outraged. The other two boys began to burn, their screams inflaming the hordes of demons waiting for the girl's burning death and Bernie's transformation.

Instead, the girl stood up and her face had changed. It was the face of Stella Tobin Caulkins. "*Becka . . .* " *she said.* "*You need to pay for what you did . . . to my Becka.*"

Bernie panicked. There wasn't much time left to complete the contract. Only seconds remained. He fell to his knees and began to chant. Surely there was a way to shift the girl's focus.

The girl's face shifted again. *"I see what you are."* It was Nora's; then it was the face of Alice Song.

When Alice pointed at Bernie, Alice became Ramona on the day she confronted Bernie. *"Demon! Devil spawn!"*

When Ramona's face faded, her middle-aged body began to shimmer and then dissolved into the raw-boned frame of a young girl in an ill-fitting coat. On her head, she wore a checkered scarf. Patty, the orphan, confronted her murderer. *"I know what you are . . . worse than my ma; and now, you're going to pay!"*

A rolling pin appeared clutched in the orphan's hand, and she threw it at Bernie. The rolling pin shuddered and then began to rotate, up and down, and it spun like one of the lethal knives during the first sacrifice.

Bernie shook his head, chuckling at the girl's 'weapon.' "Ridiculous," he thought, until Patty's weapon struck him on the side of the head, and stunned, he fell.

There was silence. Bernie and the fearsome demons were gone.

PATTY

Ha! At last, the rat is gone for good. Bernie got what's coming to him. And that goes double for monsters sticking their noses where they're not welcome. Stella and Nora helped. And then Alice got Ramona to come, and Ramona reminded me about the rolling pin. Ha! Bernie forgot I still had it!

I'm proud of you! Are they gone forever?

They better be if they know what's good for them.

Ha! They'd better!

Wails echoed through the hordes like a series of cannons. The waiting line of demons, gathered in anticipation for the coming feast writhed and then exploded into millions of smaller, duller creatures—crows, black butterflies, bees and hungry lizards. Volcanoes erupted and fire raged. Before the rift closed completely, a monster snatched the spirit who was Bernie Baker.

The Others, Reba and Debbie were trapped within the mall, unable to maintain, their human forms. They became scorpions, creatures whose nature was comfortable in both worlds. They skittered away and hid, hoping for an opportunity to escape, back to their own dimension. If there was a chance that another lingering rift could be created, it was here, where the cabin once stood and after that, the prison cell. Surely there must be another, hopefully soon.

Joy to the World

The three young men, their bodies unmarked, lay unconscious within the circle. Madonna stood impassively, her hand clutching the pearl. Outside, the fire and smoke disappeared, leaving the shaken crowd stunned. Doors swung open and firemen, whose axes and equipment were unable to gain them entrance, rushed in. Moans and cries mixed with the sound system as it played "Joy to the World." Moving through the crowd, the rescuers discovered the injured and dead. Those who died succumbed to heart attacks and strokes brought on by stress and terror, except for a few, who died of injuries caused by being trampled by their fellow shoppers.

Sid delivered Mindy to her frantic grandmother, Trudy. He left the confusion and arriving news cameras, going home to the comfort of *Gilda* and Jack Daniels.

No evidence of fire was found. The silver snowflakes hung untouched by any flames, the rafters fresh with new paint, were all intact. Francesca, who fainted when a determined group of women in dressy dresses and tube tops had knocked her down to reach the main entrance, awoke to find herself being carried through the double glass doors.

The FRUITY blenders sat on their stands, waiting to swirl the next smoothies. Sequined tube tops were strewn on the floor of

FIVE MINUTES FROM NOW where they had been abandoned. Troy West was dead, the pressure of his job finally causing the stroke he had feared. Kelly lay dead, having choked on her tongue, as was Chief Nagle, whose autopsy showed a brain embolism. Rae-Jean's ear was still attached to her head, though her phone was crushed and beyond repair. Mindy remained in the custody of her grandmother.

Emma's Saturday Dream

Emma was dreaming. She was four years old and sitting on the green couch with her mother. They were watching Deputy Dawg and Top Cat had just done something funny. Emma and Momma were laughing. Emma loved Saturdays. Momma let her eat her cereal in a cup so that she could watch TV. There was a knock on the door and Momma said come in. It was Daddy, her real daddy. He smiled like he did when she and Momma came to visit him at the prison. As he crossed the room he said, "Any room for me?"

Momma said to Emma, "Whaddayou think, can Daddy watch too?"

Emma nodded and Daddy sat down on the other side of Emma, saying, "I love you, Baby; you and Mom are my girls." He put his arm around Emma.

Emma woke up and smiled at the dream. It was still Christmas Eve She looked at the alarm clock. She was beginning to drift off again when a voice whispered in her ear, "I love you, Baby." She sat up, stunned. It was her father's voice, and it was real, not a dream at all.

Little Brother

In DEVONSBERRY & PITTS, Madonna sat on the floor, trying to rouse her brother. Caleb and Alec had regained consciousness. Both were shaken and disoriented, but physically unharmed as they struggled to account to the skeptical Cabrizzi what had taken place. Cabrizzi put an end to Reba and Debbie's hopes of rescue. When he saw two scorpions making a dash for the open door, the detective smashed both with the heel of his shoe.

Gordon seemed to be in a light coma, the paramedics, unable to restore his consciousness. As Madonna stood anxiously watching them work, she heard him moan. "Gordo," she said, it's over; he's gone, all of it is gone."

His eyes opened. His hand was trembling as he reached out to her. "How bad is it?" He asked. "How badly am I burned?"

"Oh, little brother, not at all," she said, "you're fine."

He looked at his unmarked hand and cried. "I can see it, my hand, it's all black and it hurts so . . ."

"No, honey, no it's fine I swear it's fine . . ." He closed his eyes. Madonna put her face in her hands and sobbed.

Alec put his arms around her. "He's okay, you know; it will just take him a little longer . . . none of us knew . . .

PATTY

So old Bernie the rat got a taste of his own medicine. Cowards always get what they deserve. And that goes double for monsters who shoulda stayed in their own stupid universe! I heard the demons crying when I slammed the door in their fat faces. I can go to the park now.

Yes, you can.

Let's go on the carousel next. I'll find Russie and Gram and we can all go.

I must find John.

I'll help you find him, but after the carousel. Be my little sister for a little while.

Okay.

Evie

The Shed

Eternity

Bernie drifted. What remained of his former reward, the appearance, intelligence, and life force of John Arnold was gone, part of the price he paid for failure. He wondered where he was. He could see little. There was a river . . . yes . . . it looked familiar. He was floating above it. How interesting, he thought. Perhaps it wouldn't be so bad . . . no power, but he could watch as others . . . after all he had served, so many sacrifices, so many lives taken for the pleasure . . . how could he have known?

The old woman's gift, the pearl, was an unfair advantage; they should understand. He had begun to descend when he saw the stable. Oh, the memories! With a rush of cold air, he was pushed through the door. It was dark . . . he wanted to see. Someone lit the oil lamp, the old one that sat on the chest that held the jars, where parts of his victims were kept . . . it had been a long time, he wondered if they were still preserved, waiting for him to claim them. He felt a jolt. Who was spinning him around and around, like the top? He thought perhaps there might be yet another opportunity, way to redeem himself, oh, if only . . .

The spinning stopped and instead of standing with his feet on the wood of a spinning top, he was lying down. Puzzled he tried to lift his head to see what was around him and discovered that his head was restrained; he couldn't move it. He became aware of being watched.

The stable was much larger. He scanned the area within his sight lines and saw rows of beings, all looking at him. With a start, he recognized the faces. They were the faces of his victims, Becka Tobin, Willie, the first sacrifice, the orphanage nurse . . . more . . .

from his days at the steel mill, the young man from the Speak Easy
. . . all looking at him, waiting. Their eyes . . . not human . . . the
legions, it was the legions. Fear shot through Bernie.

He heard metal against metal; he knew that sound . . . it was
the vise as he began to twist it ever so slowly. Ohoooh, EVIE!

it was Evie as he had last seen her. Her face was a ruin of
ruptured skin, the nose split, the mouth twisted in an oblong
grimace, vestiges of her missing eyes oozing down her bloodied
cheeks. She twisted the vise. Ooohh . . . it hurt so.

He saw what looked like a smile on the misshapen face and
though there were no eyes, points of red light gleamed from the
ruined sockets. Nonononononononono! He whimpered. It's not fair
that I should die this way; I've served . . . There was another twist
and the pain shot through his head. It was blinding, indescribable.
He whimpered again. Then it came to him. He wasn't going to die,
HE WAS DEAD! How long, he wondered frantically, how long
must he suffer? Evie gave another twist of the vise and Bernie
squealed with pain, crying and begging as had so many of his
victims. To Bernie's eternal regret, the answer never came.

God Bless Us Everyone
December 24, 2005
San Francisco

They sat together, Emma, Madonna, and Alec, as Warren toasted. "To our guests," he said. Colleen, now an attractive woman in her early sixties, raised her glass as well. "Welcome!" Almost seventy-five gathered in the large private dining room of a San Francisco restaurant for Christmas Eve dinner. The Songs were a prominent family and Warren and Colleen's moving back to the Bay Area was cause to celebrate. Applause broke out.

People had heard of what happened and of Madonna and Ramona's pearl. Madonna had received numerous invitations to study and develop her gifts. Caleb had called with apologies; his schedule was tight, and he just couldn't make it. Although Cabrizzi, the new Redhill Chief of Police, never acknowledged the truth of what had happened, he decided to act as a mentor for Caleb who was now on the Cleveland Police force.

Not wanting to await the formalities of probate, Bernie had transferred most of his assets to Madonna. Madonna discovered to her astonishment that she was quite wealthy, almost two hundred million in fact. The only burned body found inside the mall was that of the Senator's. His remains were under a pile of sweatpants at PLAY IT FORWARD. He was identified by his granddaughter, who shuddered as she saw the corpse, her skull ring still on his finger. No other evidence of fire found; the mall incident was explained as mass hysteria.

The charred condition of the Senator's body remained a mystery that was under investigation, the autopsy proving inconclusive. None mourned him. After his death, Senator Arnold's record of fraud and betrayal was exposed and many suspected that his death was murder. The case was open and unsolved, no one, including Cabrizzi, cared to investigate.

Emma lifted her glass and toasted. While most of the guests drank champagne, Emma's glass contained ginger ale, her days of abusing alcohol ended with the closing of the mall and Gordon's illness. Her son needed her, and she wanted a clear head. A year had passed. Gordon was finally beginning to heal. Months had passed before he could sleep, undisturbed through the night. Too many images of demons and burning haunted him. He was unable to look in a mirror, convinced, that he was burned, disfigured.

"Can't you see it? I'm in such pain, Mom, it hurts so."

Emma would sit by his bed at night while he tried to sleep. The wealth that Madonna inherited paid for the expensive therapy; Gordon was improving, getting better every day. Soon, Madonna hoped, Gordon could join her at the University in Cleveland. She and Alec lived in dorms, tentative in their relationship, hoping that it would endure the inevitable pressures that change, and time would bring.

Emma lived with Gordon close to the campus, often taking him to places where she and Giordano spent their short time together. This trip was a major step and as they sat listening to Warren, Madonna and Alec smiled at each other. Gordon's face was again full of life and irreverence. As Warren finished his speech, much to the delight of his sister and mother, Gordon called out, "God bless us everyone!

PATTY

I'm real happy. Gram isn't mad at me. The best part is that you showed up here. It took you a long time to find me and now you're a grownup

Do you want to be a grownup?

Okay, if you remember that I'm still your big sister. Being a grownup might be fun though I like being twelve. Maybe I'll find Michael.

The Death of Redhill

There was a fire after all. No one knew how it started. Some said it was supernatural, others, arson. Whatever the cause, the mall was gone. The fire meant to claim hundreds that night, delayed by Bernie's failure, finally burst through the tear, razing the building within an hour. The damage to Redhill's economy was devastating, and at last, the town began to die, as people decided to leave. They sought a life free of the darkness that had haunted Redhill since the death of Becka Tobin.

Though much of it had burned, the large pine in the middle of the mall, its roots reaching deep into the ancient soil, still stood. Its roots were alive and beginning to regenerate. Shoots of growth sprang from the blackened trunk. As Madonna and her family sat with the Song family toasting the holiday, a large crow sat on a delicate green branch, its eyes, gleaming red.

END

About the Author

M. Noble's other work includes *The Floating Mall, The Demon Rift* is in the process of republishing under a new title) a horror novel. Her short stories are *The Seventh Folding of Willow Sprite* and *The Why of Denise,* were published and are available on Strange Fictionzine. She has published articles regarding the nature of dreams in *HuffPost*. He blogs include reviews of books and movies. marjoriekayesbabylondreams and marjoriekayesbookblog are through Wordpress. She has an author's page on Amazon and on Book Bub.

A native of California, she fell in love with science fiction as a teenager. She is currently writing a sequel to *Babylon Dreams*, *Shemathra's Realm,* about a spy in a VR Animal Farm.

Made in the USA
Middletown, DE
15 September 2022

10513619R00325